DANGEROUS TRAITOR

DRAGONERA: THE DARK ONE CHRONICLES BOOK 4

CHARLIE ROSE

PROLOGUE

$\mathcal{R}$ichmond, the capital of Virginia, isn't exactly what Detective David Striker would call the most exciting place in America. It might have been a large city, but past efforts from the local police department had kept crime in check. Gangs hardly existed on the streets and all the local known drug dealers had either been arrested or fled the state. By all accounts Richmond was a safe place to live, work, and play.

Not exactly the most exciting time to be a police officer. Striker had joined the police force to protect innocents. But the young twenty eight year old, with blonde hair and brown eyes, had found out that life as a police officer wasn't the most exciting or rewarding. Months of physical training and studying felt like they had just gone down the drain as he sat in his office, going over the mounds of paperwork laid before him.

Striker rubbed his eyebrows with a hand shaky from endless hours of paperwork. He laughed, remembering the first words of his instructor at the police academy. 'Being a policeman means that we give our lives to protect the innocent. Always remember, we serve the greater good.'

"Serve the greater good huh?" Striker asked himself. "What greater good is there when everything that could have been exciting has dried up over the last few months?"

Striker sighed as he reached for his cup of coffee. The sweet aroma of the drink reached his nostrils. The sweet heavenly sent power of the beverage filled his lungs with a strange kind of euphoria. It was the only thing he looked forward to at this job since all the problems of the city had supposedly been solved.

As he was about to enjoy his coffee in peace and quiet, it was shattered.

"Striker!" A gruff, tough voice called out behind him. Striker flinched a bit. His time working for the police department had left him familiar with the sound of a pissed off captain. "My office, pronto!"

With a heavy sigh Striker placed his coffee down on his table. Guess peace of mind would have to come later. Looked like was about to get his backside chewed for something. He knew that not all police captains were like those he saw in the action movies that he grew up watching. Lucky him, his captain was straight from central casting - gruff, shrill, balding, and impatient. Sometimes he could swear that steam would actually rise from his captain's ears during one of his rants.

"Not that he has anything to be ranting about to me." Striker thought to himself. "The damn city has been peaceful for the last three months, nothing for him to get on my ass about."

"Hurry up, Striker!" His captain shouted again. "My great grand-mother could get her ass over here faster than you, and she's dead!"

"Coming, Captain!" Striker cried back before forcing himself up from his chair. The last thing he needed right now was a ranting boss pissed off about how "slow to respond" he allegedly was. As he walked towards the office, a few of his fellow officers chuckled.

"Try not to piss him off, Dave." One of them said. "The last time someone pissed the cap off, he could have popped a blood vessel. Though given how you don't listen to him at times it's not surprising."

The officer running his moth, Tony McGinnis was a PITA. He was a young brown haired and green-eyed smug looking idiot. Tony was a kiss ass. The captain played favorites, and Tony was definitely one of his pets. Striker didn't have time to get into a debate with him, but he did have enough time for a quick parting shot.

"Up yours, McGinnis." Striker responded as he passed by his fellow officer. "If I need your mouth running, If I need help from a kiss ass I'll let you know."

"Have fun." McGinnis responded in a mocking tone.

Striker rolled his eyes as he entered the captain's office. He closed the door tightly before glaring at McGinnis, who went back to his own paperwork.

"Asshole." He said with a bitter taste in his mouth.

"Stow it, Striker." The Captain said. "Take a seat, we got something to talk about."

Striker frowned as he took a seat in front of the Captain. Whenever he was called into the office his Captain would often have him stand the entire time while he chewed him out. He only had people sit down when it was a serious matter.

The Captain sighed as he adjusted his glasses before staring right into Striker's eyes. In his left hand he spun a pen around with seemingly no end in sight. Striker felt a bit of an unease rise up through his body as he cleared his throat.

"You wanted to see me, sir?" He asked.

"Yes. I did." The Captain said. "Son, I've gone over your records from when you were at the Academy. You're one of the best to ever graduate from that institution. You were good at the physical exams and the weapons practices, but the one area you excelled at was being able to find evidence faster than anyone else could."

"There a reason why you're reminding me of this, sir?" Striker asked. "I don't think I need to be reminded of my grades at the Academy."

"Watch your mouth, boy." The Captain said. "I'm getting to my point and I don't need you running your mouth."

The Captain reached into his desk grabbing a document. Striker blinked as this commanding officer placed the file down in front of him. He noticed that the tab of the file had the title 'The Occult' Striker quirked an eyebrow up as he turned his attention back to the captain.

"Something happening that we don't know about, sir?" He asked.

"You're damn right something is going on." The Captain replied as he took out a cigarette. "A few days ago, we got some reports of some kids dressed up in these long dark purple robes walking the streets at night." He opened the file up, revealing a shoddy picture of the robe-wearing individuals fleeing the scene. Striker's eyes glanced over the photo carefully as he analyzed it precisely.

"We don't know what it is that these kids are up to, but Intel seems to think that they're some kind of new gang trying to take over the streets."

"What kind of gang goes around wearing robes like this?" Striker asked. "Last I checked gang members don't wear something so out of place."

"Good question, Striker." His captain said. "The thing is, we're not even sure what this is ourselves. If they were gang members they would have been more of them. But eyewitness reports state that these kids travel in groups of two, and the odd thing about this whole thing is that whenever they're spotted, they supposedly vanish before anyone can ask them any questions."

The Captain frowned as he pointed to the picture before them.

"We got damn lucky with this one. The policeman that took this photo gave chase trying to apprehend these kids, but the moment they turned a corner, they just apparently, vanished."

"Vanished?" Striker asked. "Sir, with all due respect, people just don't up and disappear into thin air like that."

"You think I don't know that, Striker?" The Captain retorted. "I've been on the force longer than you've been alive. There's no way that this is ordinary."

"What do you want me to do?" Striker asked.

"I want you to open an investigation into this mess." The Captain said. "Everyone in this precinct knows that you're the best at finding evidence. And I sure as hell don't want any of the newbies walking around trying to solve this."

"Sir, with respect, that's what you are asking me to do." Striker responded. "If I'm gonna be investigating this mess, I'll need more information."

"Don't be a smart ass Striker." The Captain's eyes narrowed in anger. "We both know that your eyes have already found something about that photo to start investigating."

Striker couldn't deny that. His eyes had spotted something else on the photo. While it wasn't the largest image on the photo, one of the robbed beings had exposed their wrist, revealing a tattoo.

The tattoo was of a large eyeball, with the iris of the eye a pale yellow color, where the whites that an eye would normally have been were replaced by a dark grey color.

It was a start. Striker sighed as he leaned back in his chair for a moment.

"Do you have any idea where I should begin, sir?"

"Check downtown." The Captain said. "The last time we heard of any activity was down there. Apparently the locals are worried that these kids are doing something that they sure as hell shouldn't be."

Striker nodded as he stood up and began to move towards the door.

"And Striker?" The Captain said moments just before he left. "For the love of God, don't go shooting any kids. The country's already upset enough about the recent police shootings going on all over the place."

"Duly noted, sir." Striker said. "I can't promise that it won't come down to that, but I'll try my damn hardest to avoid it."

At that moment, as left his captain's office, Striker had no idea that he was getting himself into something that was way more excitement than he could have ever asked for.

* * *

DOWNTOWN RICHMOND. A place where the people who lived there either had it good or had it rough. Most of the crime in the city lately had been the result of a turf war between gang members and drug lords trying to establish a source of easy income.

Just because the police department had driven those problems out of the city didn't mean that downtown was transformed. There was still poverty crippling some housing, and thanks to the gangs and drug lords several of the houses had been ruined by their war.

Striker felt bad for the people who still lived in the poor part of downtown. He truly did, their living situation was deplorable. The governor swore they would be getting relief funds soon and that they would be take care of, but so far those were empty promises. Striker would believe it when he saw it. Politics were always a waste of time and politicians never got anything done other making sure they were reelected.

The detective walked down the sidewalk of one of the local shopping districts. Mom and pop stores owned by the local residents had fallen on hard times. Most were either closed completely or rarely open. Those that were open did have their fair share of regular costumers. Striker's heart swelled to see these people, who have been through some incredibly hard times, face each new day with a strong will to continue onwards.

He kept his hands in his jean pockets as he walked down the sidewalk. His ever-observant eyes glanced around the area for any clues, or even a group of teenagers that he could question. Summer was ending, and the streets were full of kids spending what few hours of summer vacation they had left before being sent back to the grind that was school.

Striker's eyes moved in all directions looking for a group of teenagers that would give him useful information. Based on what the captain had told him about the case, he had ruled out the possibility of large groups of people being associated with this, for lack of a better word, cult. It would be too easy to spot members of the cult if they stayed together in giant groups. Striker stroked his chin as his searched for any teens that were traveling in groups of two.

"Shouldn't be too hard." Striker told himself.

Time crawled. It came with the territory of his job. Patience was something that he had to sharpen over time, proving to be one of the toughest hurdles he had to overcome. When he started Striker wanted to chase after criminals, bringing them down, arresting them on the spot. To hell with the rules and regulations, back then he wanted to take action the moment an opportunity presented itself.

The memory of when he was impatient made him laugh at himself.

"Damn, I was such a foolish kid back then." He thought to himself.

Striker blinked for a brief moment, spotting what he assumed to be his targets. Two young teenage boys, walking very close together, made their way across the sidewalk as fast as they could.

Striker took note of their body language. His objective now was to pinpoint if these boys were a part of the cult in the picture. Both of them kept their heads down, barely looking where they were going. Their hands stayed in their pockets, only their thumbs peaking out. Another key fact that Striker noticed was they both were wearing dark purple hoodies over. Which was peculiar since it was the end of summer, and it had not gotten cold yet.

"Well then." He said with a slight smile. "Looks like I just hit jackpot."

The detective followed the two boys. The last thing he wanted now was to lose this lead.

Unfortunately for Striker, teenagers are a lot smarter than people give them credit for. While everyone knows that hormones often control teenaged minds, they did have moments when they could outsmart adults. Striker learned that the hard way. Never underestimate them.

Striker tried to look inconspicuous. If he were spotted now, his chances of finding where this cult was meeting would be lost. He felt his hands slowly start to sweat as the kids kept checking to see if they were being followed.

"At least those years of training didn't go to waste." He thought to himself as he hugged the wall for the fifth time.

After tailing after the duo of teenagers for at least an hour, maybe more, Striker took notice of the setting sun. Just as he had thought. No cult would dare to meet during broad daylight. Well, at least not the ones with something to hide from the world. He kept his eyes on the two teenagers.

One of them finally spoke the moment they reached a dark alleyway.

"Are you certain this is the place?" The shorter of the two teens asked. "It's just a dark alleyway back there, why would we meet there?"

"You know that we never meet in the same spot." The taller teen responded. "We have to keep the rest of the world from knowing exactly where we meet."

"But some of us already got caught." The smaller teen argued back. "They could reveal our locations!"

"Not a chance in Hell. When they joined, they swore an oath to keep every secret hidden from the society that has rejected them."

"And just how do you know that they won't though?"

"You know why." The taller teen's voice turned a bit harsher at this point. "Those who break our covenant rules will be located, and exterminated."

Striker felt his heart grow cold at that statement. This cult was willing to kill any of their members that dared speak out. While he was use to hearing adults say such a thing in similar situations, he never once thought he would ever hear those words uttered by a young teenager. The smaller teen must have had the same reaction as he did, as he began to back away slowly.

"You know I hate it when you say that." He said as dread filled his voice. "No one wants to talk about the punishments one would have to endure for daring to go against our vows."

"And that is why they will never betray us." The larger teen said as he grabbed the smaller one's shoulder. "Now come on. We got to move."

The conversation was not brought up again as the two of them made their way down the alley. Striker glanced out from where he was hiding, looking down the alleyway. His palms clenched into fists as he realized that the situation at hand was now far worse than he first thought.

But what he'd heard wouldn't be enough. He had to find out more before bringing his findings to the captain. He needed to confirm who these occult members were and record anything they might be doing. Lives were on the line - God he loved his job!

Decision made, Striker took a deep breath, steeling himself. No one else was going to tail these teens, and he was too close to let his only lead go now. He summoned his courage and began to move after the two teens. Making certain to walk as quietly as possible.

Striker hid beside a large garbage can as he watched the two teens when they stopped waling once again. The larger one grabbed something out of his pocket before opening his palm. Striker couldn't tell what it was from his location, but he could make out that the item was some kind of parchment paper, much like a scroll, with a seal wrapped around it.

"With the removing of this seal..." The tall teen said slowly as he pulled the seal off. "We attend."

What happened next could only be what Strike later described as a dream. The moment the seal was taken off the parchment a flash of purple light erupted. Striker was forced to cover his eyes for a second as the light surrounded the teens, not realizing the light had expanded to where he was hiding as well.

When the brightness died down Striker's eyes readjusted so he could see properly. Now flat on his back, his body feeling like it was filled with lead, he groaned in pain before realizing where he was. What he saw bewildered him, he was no longer in the alley. Instead, all around him, were a multitude of trees. Above him a starry sky of night with the ever present glow of the moonshining down.

Several thoughts raced through Striker's head as he tried to reason what was going on. That parchment the teen opened had done something. Maybe they had spotted him and they had used a flashlight to blind him before they injected him with some kind of drug. There were reports he'd read up on about these kinds of twists happening to other cops. Not once did he think that he would have fallen for the same trap that other officers of the law fell for.

"How the hell did you let yourself fall for something like that, Striker?" He asked himself as he did his best to push himself up.

The feeling of his limbs being weighted didn't exactly help. Each step he took felt like his body was about to shatter from the pressure he was applying. It took every bit of his willpower to not shout out in pain.

Overtime he felt his body began to recover from the numbing feeling that had overtaken his muscles. While he still felt groggy he could at least take steps without his leg muscles screaming in protest.

"Calm down." He told himself. "You have to take this slow. Let your body recover from whatever the hell happened to you."

Easier said than done of course. Striker had a job to do and he couldn't afford to let the two teenagers he was tailing get away now.

It then occurred to Striker that he didn't even know where in the world he was. He grabbed his smart phone from his pocket and began to open its map app. As the app opened a small ray of hope came to his lips and then swiftly turned into a shocked expression what he saw where his phone had taken him.

Dragon Run State Forest. Located right in King and Queen County. Which was hundreds of miles from the city of Richmond.

"How the hell did I end up here?" He asked himself. He took notice of the time and date. Eight o Clock PM, August 22nd. "The date's still the same as it was before. But it takes hours to get here from Richmond..."

Confusion was plastered all over his face. If his phone was correct the teenagers had somehow knocked him out and made it to Dragon Run all in a mere couple of hours.

The answer to his questions would elude him for awhile longer as a noise caught his attention. Striker turned to the source of the noise, which came from his left, noticing a bright light.

He knew that Dragon Run State Forest was a recreation park, and no one was allowed to create a fire in it. Must be the teenagers from before. Something about them felt really off when that bright flash of light covered them and him. He couldn't be a hundred percent sure, but his gut feeling told him to head towards the the fire.

Perhaps he could find his answers there as well.

Striker took a deep breath before he trudged towards the fire. In the back of his mind he could only picture what his Captain would be saying to him for being too slow on the initiative. He gave a short dry laugh at the image of how red his boss' face would be right now. It wouldn't be the first time that would happen either.

"I can just hear his voice now." Striker grumbled as he placed a hand over his head. "It's giving me a headache already."

A new sound came from where the light shone. Strike reached for his gun as he crept close to the ground. He couldn't exactly make out what it was, but it sounded a lot like chanting. If he was right, then there were people here.

Striker moved as quietly as he could towards his target. His brow covered in sweat as he approached. If he truly was alone in this wilderness, then he should have nothing to fear. Right? It's not like there was anything out here that could be too dangerous.

Oh how he wished that he was wrong.

Before him was a large gathering of teenagers and young adults. Each of them varying in shape, size, gender, and color. All of them looked anxious, on edge. Every single person wore a dark purple robe with a demonic looking eye on the back of the robe. Strike gritted his teeth.

"Dammit. Too many here for this to be a 'small' cult." He muttered to himself. "It's like a small army!"

As the insistent chatter in the group continued to go on, a loud 'clang' was heard from the makeshift stage they all stood before. The sound deafened any sort of chatter as Striker swallowed a lump in his throat. If he had to guess, the head honchos of this cult would be gathering together there.

Sure enough, there they were. A middle aged man with a goatee, a teenaged boy with black hair hanging over one of his eyes, and a young girl with black hair just like the boy before her, but with some of the saddest eyes Striker had ever seen. The last one caught Striker completely off guard as she crawled onto the stage.

Words escaped him, there was no way to accurately describe the large monster on the stage besides the three humans. She had pale green skin, sickly yellow eyes, and the palest blue short cut hair. While she had the body of a young woman, the rest of her body was anything but human. Somehow, this creature had a massive dark grey spider body for legs and her abdomen was covered in what looked to be bits and pieces of bones from life forms that Striker couldn't identify.

The middle aged man grinned as the crowd gathered before him. As silence took ahold of them, he held his hands above his head.

"Welcome, to you all. On this glorious night." He spoke out. Striker could practically taste the venom dripping from every word the man spoke. "Many of you are new to our family. To you, I say, welcome. Welcome to a place where you will finally be accepted, where you can finally open your eyes to the truth of this world: it's corruption, it's wickedness, it's perversion."

The man began to stroll back and forth across stage. Some of the gathered youth nodded their heads in agreement."

"You are here, because society has rejected you." He continued. "They have rejected each and every one of you...for a multitude of reasons. Reasons we shall not discuss here; reasons that are no longer relevant. But, it is the truth, that this world has led you into isolation. They have forced you into hiding, fearing their retribution, their bile, their hatred..."

The crowd became more rowdy at this as they all shouted out in agreement about how they were treated. Striker clenched his fists. The bastard was using mind games on them, and it was working. The man spoke again.

"They have rejected each and every one of you...for a multitude of reasons. Reasons we shall not discuss here; reasons that are no longer relevant. But, it is the truth, that this world has led you into isolation. They have forced you into hiding, fearing their retribution, their bile, their hatred..."

The crowd screamed about how poorly they were treated. A sly grin slipped over the leader's lips as he watched them pledge to do as he asked.

"On this night, you join our family." A glint grew in his eyes. "Nay, our ARMY. Which grows each day! On this night, we rise! On this night, we will begin destroying the fools for our master, who will make all things equal under his rule! No more will you be judged, no more will you be mocked, tonight, you are now blessed with the powers you need to take your revenge! So say I, Grandmaster Dimitri! Do you swear loyalty to the Dark Eye?!"

"We swear!" Was the unanimous chant of the crowd.

A chill ran down Striker's back as he watched the crowd chant Dimitri's name over and over again. The spider lady on the stage looked barely impressed while the two teenagers gave different reactions. The girl hid her eyes and face. The boy though? He grinned as he began to laugh loudly.

Things were much graver than Striker, or any of the police force, could ever imagine. Without wasting a second, and using the loud shouting of the crowd to his advantage, Striker ran as fast as he could from the cult. God help him, no one saw him.

God help them all, they were going to need it!

THE FLEA MARKET

*A*iden sighed as he leaned back in the seat of his parent's car. It was one of the last few days of summer vacation, the new school year was starting soon. The old Aiden would be dreading returning to school. He would be a sophomore this year, busier than his first year in high school, but he didn't feel any dread about the upcoming school year. The long days of lectures, answering questions without trying to look awkward, the seemingly endless homework that the teachers would give out were all starting to look more welcome to him as the days went on.

What had happened only a few months ago felt like an eternity to him. Since the events that took place in the Mage Academy, but Aiden couldn't get any of the images out of his mind. The collapsing walls, the drying blood, the endless horde of Shadow Demons leaping from every dark corner, and, worst of all, the haunted image of the Grand Mage's son, curled up in a ball after being freed from the darkness.

It had gotten so bad that he was beginning to have nightmares of the events that took place in the academy. Some nights he would wake up, drenched in a cold sweat. During the day time he would be constantly glancing over his shoulder for attacks from a hidden enemy. Even during training with the dragons he felt on edge. That Raven, his master, or some demon that was hiding in plain sight would jump out and attack him. He almost hit Garrett straight in the chest with

Warfang one time because he was so overly concerned about surprise attacks.

Theresa would often call training sessions short when Aiden freaked out in the heat of the moment. She did her best to help him try and remain calm whenever he had these attacks. She never yelled at him when it happened. Instead she would simply take him in her arms and help him with breathing exercises so that he could get through the moment. Sometimes she would even use her wings to cover them both up so that he felt safe and protected from any danger. Her support meant more than it ever had before.

The more he thought about it, the more he began to realize how different his life was now compared to when he was in middle school. He barely remembered just how sheltered of a life he had before he started learning how to wield a sword and magic. And it always kept coming back to what Ivan had done to Lewis.

Aiden often took for granted how his parents raised him. They could have easily been harsh with him growing up, restricted what he could and could not have interests in, or even go as so far as to tell him what kind of friends he was allowed to have. He was no fool about how the world worked in some circles. He knew there were children who were neglected, used, or even hurt by their parents. But hearing and seeing it happen was a completely different experience.

No matter what he tried to do he had a hard time pushing away the image of Lewis curled up before him. He doubted he would ever be able to get forget it. The very sight of the young mage begging to be killed, his body looked like it had been drained of its life energy, was enough to break even the most stone cold of warriors.

Part of him felt like he was focusing too much on what happened to Lewis. Ivan had been stripped from being the Grand Mage of the Academy so he would never be in a position to harm Lewis again. It also helped to know that the school was now following the lead of a person that Aiden knew would be able to take care of not only the remaining students, but also Lewis - Ryan. They may have only met him for a day when they arrived, but the ordeal they went through forged a bond that Aiden knew would never be easily broken. At least, that's how he felt about the new Grand Mage.

As the car drove on Aiden found himself mindlessly watching the passing trees. Back when he was little he always imagined that he was the car. That he was the one moving so fast that it made every tree look like a blur. It was a childhood memory that Aiden affectionately held in his heart. Of course back then Aiden never imagined that he would be trained by beings that could move even faster than that. Nor did he ever imagine that his seemingly normal life would end up becoming one where fantasy was actually real.

"Aiden?" His mother, Helena, spoke out from the passenger seat of the car. Aiden almost jumped at the sound of her voice, before turning his head back to her. "Did you hear what I just said or are you daydreaming again?"

"*Crap.*" Aiden thought. He was so lost in thought about Lewis, the Academy, and old childhood memories that he had, unintentionally, put his mother on 'mute.' It didn't happen as much anymore, but when it did happen Aiden found himself in trouble.

However, Helena didn't groan in annoyance. Nor did she get upset with her son. Instead she just offered him a smile before sighing.

"You don't have to say a word." She said. "Your face clearly tells me you were daydreaming, again."

"S-Sorry, mom." Aiden quickly spoke up. He didn't want to cause an argument with his parents. It's not like he could have told them that he was thinking back to an ordeal that he had endured last summer. How would they even begin to understand?

"It's fine dear. I was just telling you that when we get to the Flea Market that you're more than welcome to look at things that interest you."

"But you need to be careful." Aiden's father, Connor, spoke up. "Flea Markets tend to be filled with people that are vague about their products. A lot of them have items that are counterfeit. They will try to pass them off as authentic to any person who doesn't have a good eye."

Aiden had to force himself not to let out a large groan. His father would often give him this lecture whenever they went to any kind of Flea Market. And it all stemmed down to Connor being a highly respected salesmen for his company. Though Aiden didn't know why his father could tell fake items apart from the real ones, especially when his company sold fancy furniture to people with a lot of money.

Whenever Aiden did ask Connor about how he was able to tell

the difference between a real and fake item, his father would either dodge the question completely or go into a lengthy description about the process. Both of which were answers that drove Aiden up the wall.

"And this should go without saying, young man, but no weapons. You can look, but you are not allowed to have one." Connor continued. Aiden almost let out a small snicker at his father's order. If only he knew that the figurine he had given Aiden was a mystical sword itself. Not that he would want any other sword now though. Strange as it may have sounded Warfang had become part of him. Like an extension of his own body. No, even more than that. Like an extension of his very soul. He would never use a different blade. Not after everything he had been through with the fabled sword.

"I promise, I won't be reckless at the Flea Market" Aiden said. "I'll keep my eyes open for anything fishy and I swear I won't go picking up anything sharp." As much he didn't want to admit it, Aiden was looking forward to this trip to the Flea Market. When he was little his family would often go to Flea Markets to see what the vendors had on display. He could vividly recall several sellers that had always caught his interest, even when he was just a little kid. From stands selling vintage toys, old cartoons, rare issues of comics, classic video games, and his favorite thing, fantasy novels.

In a weird way, going to a Flea Market was like going on a treasure hunt. He never knew what kind of items he would find in the many vendors. Some of them fake, some of them genuine. But that's what made it exciting for Aiden.

"With the training from the dragons I should be able to tell fakes easily now." He thought to himself.

"It's been awhile since the three of us have gone out like this." Helena interjected, a kind smile on her lips. "It might help the three of us forget all the stressful things going on in the world today."

"What makes you think that, my love?" Connor asked.

"Connor, you know what I'm talking about." Helena responded. Aiden noticed that her smile had turned into a concerned frown. "The news has been talking about this.... cult lately. They've been growing in numbers recently and I worry that they might make their way to our little neighborhood."

Aiden knew what his mother was talking about. Recently news

about a new cult had begun to spread throughout their state. Their actions at first were seen as teenage youth rebelling against the establishment that society expected of them. Those in power weren't concerned about their actions as they saw them as 'fickle youth' who were just doing what teenagers do.

The stories about this cult continued to grow more frequent on the news as the summer passed on. They talked about how the cult members would attack people in the middle of the day, sometimes severely injuring them. Their criminal activity was catching the eye of local law enforcement. Aiden often saw police cars driving by the local shops, towns, and even the mall now.

Aiden didn't blame his mother for being concerned about the rising cult activity. No one even knew their name. Witnesses could only claim that when they spotted members, that they would simply vanish when approached. Every single witness claimed they disappeared like magic. He had a suspicion that there was some kind of actual magic at work. When he brought this issue up with Theresa she agreed. People don't suddenly vanish into thin air. Not unless they have a teleportation spell of some kind letting them move from one place to another. The very thought of that sent shivers down Aiden's spine. If the cult could use magic like that, how many young teenagers had they recruited to create such power?

Aiden wasn't the most knowledgeable about cults, or how they recruited, but he learned quickly that, when feeling isolated in high school, teenagers looked for any clique where they could feel like they belonged. But what would happen to those teens that couldn't find a group to connect with?

The thought got under his skin all too easily. The rejected youth of society forming under one banner to strike out at those who pushed them away. If they had access to magic, Aiden could only imagine what might happen if they proved to be a serious threat.

"Dammit." He thought. *"What am I doing? Freaking out over something that hasn't even happened yet. You shouldn't be worried about such a thing, Aiden."*

He glanced to his parents, both of whom were busy in a conversation about how his father's job was going. If he had to be honest, he really couldn't care less about his father's work. It was so insignificant compared to what he'd been through ever since learning the truth.

"Great." Aiden rubbed his eyebrows. *"I'm starting to sound like Garrett with how different my life is from my parents."* The thought of the great dragon rolling his eyes for even saying that came to his mind. Aiden didn't know if he should chuckle at that or feel dread that he was finding himself more comfortable with the large dragon's personality.

A frown crossed Aiden's lips as he thought back to a couple of months ago concerning the events at the Academy. So much happened there that Aiden found it particularly hard to move past it. What made it even harder to believe was how Garrett acted. Aiden had grown use to the largest of the three dragons ridiculing him or barely tolerating him. But he noticed that the muscle of the dragons went out of his way to help him at the academy.

Once saving him from being crushed, and most likely eaten, by the Teleranta. And the other time stopping him from killing Ivan with his own hands. It was almost surreal, to see Garrett not treat him like he was the lowest scum. It almost made Aiden believe that the large dragon was starting to warm up to him.

"Not in a million years."

Aiden had lost track of the time so much that he suddenly realized the car had come to a complete halt. He blinked before realizing they had arrived at their destination. A smile came to his lips as he looked upon the sign of the Flea Market he had not been to since his childhood.

It read 'The Fleet Foot Flea Market!' with the subtitle under it reading 'Kindest Flea Market in America for 50 Years!' Aiden felt himself suppressing the urge to chuckle at the sign. In terms of colors, it wasn't the most vibrant of flea market signs. What was once was a combination of bright blue for the outline, vigorous red for the letters, and pale white for the background of the letters, had begun to fade. The blue and red had begun to slowly turn into a grayer version of their former glory, and the white paint had dirt marks scattered in the spacing between the letters. Everyone knew this sign had seen better days, and there was some calls to replace or repaint it, but the general public loved it. Many of them claiming that it gave the sign, and the flea market in general, character.

"All these years later and it still hasn't changed a bit." Connor said with a hint of nostalgia in his voice. "Remember when we used to come here all the time, Helena?"

Helena laughed fondly. "Oh do I ever. We used to come here when money was tight finding stuff for Aiden when he was just a young child."

"I am right here you know." Aiden reminded his parents. A slight feeling of embarrassment filled his body whenever his parents talked about him being a child.

Helena turned to him and smiled. "Yes, why do you think we bring it up so often?"

In some ways he was still that small boy. Though he would never admit it to them, he did like it whenever his parents talked about his youth. It made him feel like he was still a normal human being and that those memories mattered to them as much as it did for him.

Not wasting any more time Aiden's family left their car, to which Aiden noticed that they had parked in the grass, and turned their gaze towards the flea market. Aiden smiled at the sight. Fleet Foot was an outdoor flea market, but there were some booths that had been placed within buildings with a curved top. Certain sections of the market had been designated as food courts with stone tables and wooden chairs.. They were usually filled with a team of five to six people that would cook good food for people that were hungry.

While there was more vendors this year than there usually were, the true heart and soul of the market had not changed. People were walking about, many of them at louder volumes than most, vendors were promoting their booths, and there was haggling between customers and sellers.

It was business as usual.

"This place hasn't changed that much." Connor said with a wistful smile. "It should be good to see what kind of antiques they have."

"Oh I can help but think that something we haven't seen is here within these booths!" Helena exclaimed with a giddy grin.

"And you wonder where I get my excitable nature from, mom."

Helena smacked his arm. Even Connor found himself laughing at his family's antics. It was moments like these that made Aiden feel really glad about that his own father was nothing like Ivan.

"*Dammit. Stop thinking about what he did!*" He told himself. "*Today's suppose to be a fun day, not a day to think about what that bastard did.*"

Though he told himself this, he knew he was going to have a hard time letting it go. The incident at the Academy felt like it had placed a hamper on not only his love for fantasy but on his life as well. He rubbed his eyebrows for a moment while his parents weren't looking. Aiden couldn't let them know how troubled he was. They wouldn't be able to understand at all.

Not that they could even begin to understand. His life had changed so much that he doubted that anything his parents could tell him would make him feel any better.

"Now then. I do believe we have a flea market to explore." Connor spoke out. "And Aiden, don't blow your entire money on one purchase again."

Aiden felt his cheeks flush, remembering the first time he was given spending money for the flea market. He went and spent all of it on a very rare figurine from one of his favorite fantasy series at a vendor. The lecture his father gave him for spending all his money in one place lingered in his memory.

"T-That happened one time!" Aiden responded, his voice going a bit higher than he intended.

"And that's why you haven't done it since." Connor replied. "But please do be smart with your choice of purchases."

Aiden gave his father a quick nod before turning to the right. His eyes had already found the spot he wanted to look at first. The 'Other World' section of the flea market. Out of all the places in Fleet Foot Flea Market, it was his favorite. The section was known for selling the kind of merchandise he enjoyed. Figure collectables, books, movies, and even old video games were a plenty in 'Other World.' In many ways, it was like The Griffon in the mall.

Once Aiden was certain he was away from his parents he headed towards 'Other World.' A part of him hoped that seeing some of the booths and their wares would make him feel like his old self again. To help him forget what Ivan had done.

"Damn it all." He muttered under his breath. "Why does it still bother me so much? It happened months ago and that bastard is locked up. So why do I still feel terrible?" Aiden rubbed his eyebrows very roughly for a moment as he stopped just short to the first booth. He shook his head once more before taking a deep breath and letting out a sigh. "Okay. Just, enjoy the Flea Market. Look around, find what you like and get your mind off of Ivan already." He told himself. "Just, try to enjoy yourself."

He smiled slightly as he glanced up at the booths before him. They were stocked with all the things he enjoyed as a small kid. There were booths where old fantasy statues were being sold, booths where books ran rampant, booths where video games were aplenty, and many booths that had a mismatch of the other booths. For a nerd, it was basically a paradise. As vendors and customers all talked over one another. Many of them trying to make a bargain for a rare item, but most of them were talking with one another about their love for their hobbies. Outside of a convention, or specialized stores, you wouldn't find this many people with the same interests together.

Well, the interest of things that would be considered 'nerdy' from the rest of society. *"It still looks as good as it did before."* Aiden thought, *"Just enjoy yourself by looking around. Just be a normal kid for a moment."*

The booths proved to be a good form of stress relief for him. The sight of all the things he loved as a kid was so nostalgic. He knew it must have looked silly to an outsider but not a lot of things could bring him joy like this. Even if he couldn't afford what he wanted, which was often, he still enjoyed window shopping and imagining being able to purchase it.

Aiden felt like a burden had been lifted off his shoulders as he glanced around the shops. While it was still amazing to know that all the things he loved were real, it was nice to look back at these kind of items and feel at ease. However, as he had learned, the joy and peacefulness would come to an end. As he glanced from one vendor to another booth if he was holding something valuable, he would have dropped it at the sight of a person he never thought he would see again.

It was the girl who saved him and Liza from dying in the forest the summer of last year. And she was checking out another booth.

REUNION

*S*he looked a bit different from before, her outfit had definitely changed! She wore a knee length black sleeveless dress and black ballet flats. Her short hair still reached the back of her neck, though Aiden noticed it was a bit spikier than before. Her orange eyes still stuck out like a sore thumb.

Aiden tried could feel the blood rushing to his cheeks and it was all he could do to keep from shouting out loud. The memory of last summer lingered in his mind as he beheld the beautiful girl who had saved his life. After it happened he thought she was nothing but a dream, or at least she looked like she came from one, but that could not be true, she was standing right in front of him!

The girl carried a large bag on her right arm. From a distance Aiden couldn't tell if it was full or empty. But it was clear to him that the girl was just as excited as he was to be looking at the fantastic fantasy items in the flea market. He could tell from the way her eyes shown that she was having the time of her life.

He smiled as he watched her. He didn't know if it was because she was beautiful or if it was because she was so captivated by what she was looking at, but something about her happiness made his heart beat faster. She looked like she was seeing it all for the first time in her life. Hard to believe since she looked to be around his age. Her audible 'oohs' and 'aahs' could be heard even from where he was standing when she picked up a large orange orb with four red stars in it.

"At least she has some taste." Aiden thought as he folded his arms. *"Not a lot of people give the series that orb is from the respect it deserves."*

The girl couldn't help but chortle as she placed the orb back down after staring at it for a good few seconds. Right away Aiden noticed that she was quick to jump to another item to examine it. In a lot of ways, Aiden couldn't help but think she and him were alike. At least, when he was younger.

"Better look around myself before I get accused of being a creeper." He thought at first, right before shaking his head. "What *the hell am I thinking? This is your chance to figure out who she is! She saved your life and Liza's and she never gave you a proper answer!"*

He narrowed his eyes. All he had to do was approach her and tap her shoulder to get her attention. That's it. It shouldn't be that hard to do. Right?

Aiden groaned as he rubbed his eyebrows. Maybe he was overthinking this more than he should. The girl he was looking at could just be someone who looked like the one he saw in the forest. But then again no one could have the same vibrant orange eyes that girl had. In fact no one had those kind of eyes, like at all.

Just another mystery to add to this mysterious girl.

Another audible 'squeak' brought his attention back to her. Right as he noticed her looking down at a table, he spotted someone he didn't want to spot.

Eric's lackey, Harold Shiftly. Unlike Eric, Harold wasn't a big kid. He was a lanky, greasy kid who always looked like he was up to trouble. He had oily blonde hair and slick green eyes. Aiden had personally seen Harold bother students who he and his boss saw as perfect 'prey' for their taunts, their jeers, and rumors. Many of them freshmen from last year of course, they dared not mess with the upper class men.

Harold also had a reputation for harassing female students. It was amazing that he hadn't been kicked out of school, particularly given how often he inappropriately approached girls. The first time he tried it with Theresa though, she nearly broke his wrist when he attempted to grab her rear. Aiden swore she would have done it had he not grabbed her shoulder in time.

Theresa wasn't here this time though. And right now, Harold had his sights set on this new girl.

Aiden did wonder why he was here in "Other World" though. Harold didn't like the kind of merchandise that was being sold. Which could mean only one thing. He was 'hunting.' A term that Aiden hated when he first he heard him run his mouth about it with Eric during gym.

"Hey, baby cakes." He said to the girl. "What's a fine looking thing like you doing here in a sad pathetic place like this hmm? Girl like you should be away from this loser crap."

The girl didn't raise her head at his question. Instead she continued to glance over the items in front of her. The same awe and wonder still filling her eyes and face. Aiden couldn't help but snicker at the reaction Harold had when she ignored him.

"Hey. Did you hear me or not?" He asked. "In case you didn't, why is a fine thing here in nerdland?"

Again. No answer from the girl. This time, Harold's face began to turn red as he clenched his fists.

"Are you deaf or something you stupid broad? I'm talking to you!"

This time, he caught the girl's attention. Her eyes blinked as she turned her head towards Harold. She tilted her head slightly as she stared up at the lanky teenager.

"Oh...hello there." She said with a toothy grin. "Sorry, I was too busy enjoying these wonderful wares. Aren't they fantastic?"

Harold scoffed.

"These things? This is nothing but a bunch of crap for losers that will never have a girlfriend in their lives." He grinned. "I'm more interested in what's in front of me." Aiden gritted his teeth and clenched his fists tightly. Even outside of school, Harold was just as lecherous when it came to members of the opposite sex. However, the girl just grinned as she nodded her head at him.

"I know right? This sword right here is a finely crafted blade that looks like an honorable decoration for a room!" She grinned. "Though I think it would be a bit too heavy to use though. Your arms don't look like they could handle heavy blades like this." Aiden had to fight back the urge to suddenly break out in laughter at her retort. It was like she didn't even understand what Harold was talking about.

The color in Harold's face soon reached the top of his ears. If there was one thing he hated, it was the notion that he wasn't strong at all.

While it's true he didn't have the bulk Eric had, Harold was known for starting fights and winning them because of his lanky build. Of course, the girl was right about one thing. Aiden could tell that even if he tried to use both hands Harold would have a hard time picking up the replica sword on the table and actually doing anything with it.

"Do you even know who you're talking to?" He asked, spittle forming on his lips. "Do you want to cause trouble right here, right now?"

"Oh, I'm sorry. I didn't even ask for your name." The girl frowned. "Why don't you introduce yourself? Then we can continue our conversation about what's for sale."

"I don't give a damn about the crap on this stupid table." Harold responded, his eyes narrowed. "You're starting to piss me off, girl."

"Piss...you off?" The girl tilted her head. "What do you mean?"

If they weren't in a crowded area, Harold would have been shouting in anger. Instead he made a move to grab her wrist. Aiden's eyes narrowed.

"Right. That's it." He said as he took quick steps towards the two. "Hey! Harold!"

Harold lifted his head up and noticed Aiden striding towards him and the girl. A look of great disdain for Aiden filled his sick green eyes. Aiden brushed his shoulder past the girl's own as he stepped in front of her. There was a slight gasp from her at this action, but his attention was directly on Harold right now.

"Don't you get enough grief at school, jerk?" He asked. "How many times does any girl have to tell you they're not interested before you learn some actual manners?"

"What the hell does it matter to you, Russell?" Harold responded. "Not that you'll ever get any with how much of a wuss you are." Aiden clenched his fist as he took a threatening step towards the lanky bully.

"Is that really all that's on your mind? That you'll 'get lucky' by acting like some kind of creep? News flash, she's not interested in you. Now back off."

"Or else, WHAT?" Harold asked as he stepped forward as well. Aiden felt himself controlling his body from lashing out and punching the bully in the face. It wouldn't be good for him here, or at school when it started back up.

"Or else I go and find the local security. How would it look on your record if I told them that you were trying to harass a girl with unwanted advances? Wouldn't look good when school starts back up now, does it?"

A sly grin crossed Aiden's lips as he pulled out his next trump card.

"Or would you rather I tell Theresa about your attempts and have her almost break your wrist again?

Harold scoffed as he began to back away. The memory of what happened during freshman year still burned. The lanky bully placed his hands into his pockets before turning away from the two.

"Screw it. She wasn't even that hot to begin with." He said before shooting Aiden a glade. "You watch your back, Russell. You hear me?"

"Try it, you'll end up regretting it."

The lanky teen walked away, spitting out a string of curses that Aiden dared not repeat to his parents or in front of the girl. Once he was out of 'Other World', Aiden turned his attention to the new girl.

"Hey are you...okay?"

A look of confusion plastered his face as he noticed what the girl was doing. She had her entire face covered by both of her front hands. Aiden couldn't tell if she was crying at first, but then he saw a hint of red sneak out on her cheeks.

"Oh my gosh!" She squeaked out.

"Er...I'm...sorry?"

The girl grabbed his left arm and hung on it tightly. Aiden nearly fell over from the strength of her sudden embrace. Then his own face suddenly began to warm as he felt her nuzzle her face into his arm.

"Y-you ca-caught me off guard!" The girl leaned in close, lowering her voice, speaking in a knowing tone, "I had no clue you felt that way...Ragnakin."

Aiden's ear perked up again. He'd heard her call him that word before, and while it sounded like a draconic word, he couldn't find any translation for it in Seamus' teachings.

"Wait, what did you call me?" He asked. The girl giggled as she hid her eyes from him, pressing her nose into his bicep muscle like a child would a giant teddy bear.

"It's nothing." She sang in a tiny sing song whisper. Her face still pressed into his arm, hiding a playful grin.

"A-And what were you talking about?" Aiden asked, looking around to make certain no one was staring at them. "I just bumped your shoulder by accident."

The girl looked up at him, her orange eyes now filled with confusion.

"By...accident?" She asked before tilting her head. "You...don't want to be together then?"

"U-Um..." Aiden shook his head. The girl's cute charms being intentional or not, it was starting to work on him. "T-That's not exactly what I said but-"

The girl grinned as she hid her face in his arm again. The blush on both of them growing even larger now. The girl more so than Aiden though as she lifted her left leg up slowly.

"Oh then you do want to be with me then? That's terrific!"

Aiden almost let a groan out in response. Sure she was cute, but landing her as a girlfriend wasn't exactly the goal he had for today. The back of his neck began to tingle as he could feel the many eyes of the vendors, and customers, watching them with confused expressions.

"Hey, come on knock it off." He told her. "We're drawing a lot of attention to ourselves here!"

"Ah they're just happy for us, Ragnakin." The girl grinned at saying the word. "Let them bask in our happiness!"

Aiden facepalmed at the girl's oblivious nature to what the other customers were doing. It felt like she didn't even know human customs when it came to these kind of things. He was also really perplexed by her decision to just continue to latch onto him.

"Would you like...let go for a bit? You're gonna knock me over the more you hold onto me like that you know."

"It'll be fine. You'll soften the fall for me."

If his face wasn't as red as a tomato before, it was now. Aiden couldn't tell if this girl was truly into him or if she was putting on an act. Regardless of her intentions, he had to take her to a place where the two of them could talk. He had a lot of questions for her that he didn't get to ask the last time they met. And this time, with no fatigue holding him back, he was determined to get answers from her.

"Okay, look, you and I need to talk." He said in a firm voice. "But not around here. Have you eaten yet? We'll talk at a lunch table."

"Oh my, you're treating me already? How kind of you!"

Aiden let another groan as he took the girl's wrist and gently pulled her away from the Other World vendors. The faster he could get out of there without being embarrassed by the others, the better. He could only imagine the reactions he would have gotten from Theresa, Seamus, Garrett, and all their friends if they saw this scene play out.

The girl just grinned as she happily allowed Aiden to take her by the wrist. A part of Aiden felt bad for literally dragging her like this. Most girls would be against being pulled by the wrist by some guy. This one though made him wonder if she even knew what this would look like to the other people around them.

"Theresa would be chewing my ass off right now." He thought before spotting a table at a local food court in the Flea Market.

"Here." He said. "You sit here while I go get us some food to eat. Anything in particular you want?"

"Oh, we're already taking things that far. I didn't realize..."

"Ugh, never mind. I'll pick something for you."

The girl grinned as she took a seat at the table. As Aiden walked away he scoured his wallet for enough money to pay for the food. He grabbed himself two hotdogs with just plain ketchup. For the girl he bought a cheeseburger with lettuce and ketchup. She looked like she would only have a hamburger if there was some kind of green vegetable accompanying it.

Of course he was just assuming this based on the shape her body was in. Curvy, smooth looking skin, and beautiful eyes. In a way, she was just as pretty as Theresa but it was a different kind of pretty. Theresa looked regal and other worldly with her long white hair that flowed in the wind. This girl though looked more down to earth and humble.

Wait, did he think Theresa was actually beautiful? His best friend of all people? He shook his head violently, trying to push away the blush crossing his face.

"Get a hold of yourself, Aiden! You sound like some kind of old lech!"

It didn't help that the girl acted really cute too. Aiden didn't know if she was pretending to be an airhead or if it was intentional, but it seemed to work on him. The red tint of his upper cheeks was proof to that.

"Here." He said as he sat down with the food. "I didn't know what you wanted to have, so I got you what looked like the best menu on the item."

The girl's orange eyes seemed to glow with curiosity at the hamburger before her. Aiden gave her a look at she picked up the burger before her with one hand. She licked her lips as she took a sniff of the burger before taking a bite of it. If her hair could stand up from the taste of the burger, it would have by now. Aiden noticed her eyes glimmer with fascination before she took another bite of the burger.

"This tastes so good!" She proclaimed, "I've never knew that such a delicious dish could be found at a place such as this!"

"You...don't get out much, do you?" Aiden asked. "It's just a cheeseburger with lettuce on it. It's nothing that special."

The girl grinned as she leaned her head onto his shoulder again.

"Are you kidding? It tastes fantastic." She took another bite of the burger. "It's the best meat I've had in a good long while. Thank you, Ragnakin!"

Aiden opened his mouth again to speak, or rather to ask her why she kept calling him that title, but she placed a finger on his lips.

"Ap ap, I know what you want to ask. You want to know how I saved you and your friend's lives, right?" She gave a knowing grin. "It's all over your face."

Aiden gave her a short nod.

"Where have you been? It's been like nearly two years since I last saw you. For awhile I was convinced you were some kind of hallucination I was seeing based on the pain I was going through."

"If I was a hallucination, I wouldn't have been able to heal your wounds though." She pointed out to him. "You and your friend were quite injured too, if I hadn't found you there you might have died from blood loss."

Aiden quirked an eyebrow at her as he folded his arms across his chest.

"And you somehow were able to drag both me and Liza out of a raging river with little to no effort? You're skinnier than she is."

The girl gave him a short grin and wink.

"I know I may not look the part, but I'm stronger than my body portrays me to be." She said in a sing song tone. "Pulling the two of you out wasn't that hard to do. The river made it slightly difficult, but I adjusted to it."

"*That answers that question.*" Aiden thought before clearing his throat. "You still haven't told me where you've been though. Or how you even knew that me and my friend were even in that river."

"I saw you two fall for one thing." The girl said before taking another bite of her burger, she swallowed before speaking out again. "And as for where I've been, I can't...exactly tell you that, Ragnakin."

"And why the hell not?" Aiden frowned. "For an entire year I thought you were nothing but some kind of dream. And you just suddenly reappear here at this flea market?"

The girl dragged her left foot in the ground at his question before placing her burger down. Aiden noticed a morbid smile come to her lips as she moved a strand of hair behind her ear.

"It's...complicated." She told him. Aiden's eyes narrowed as he gently took her hand and gave it a squeeze. Her gleaming orange eyes glanced towards his ocean blue eyes.

"Try me."

It felt like an eternity passed between the two of them. Her orange glistening eyes seemed to sparkle like a star would in a clear evening sky. For a split second, Aiden could feel her grasp his hand. The same melancholy smile remained on her lips though as she leaned forward and pressed her forehead against his own. Her eyelids closed, hiding her eyes before she shook her head.

"Sorry, Ragnakin." She said as she pulled her hand away from his. "I'm afraid that I still can't tell you. Maybe one day, I'll be able to tell you."

Aiden sighed in defeat. So close. He was so close to getting a complete answer out from her that he could have tasted it on the tip of his tongue. This girl was either really good at keeping her secrets, or she enjoyed teasing people about the truth.

"*She probably does both.*" He thought before shaking his head.

The girl got up from her chair and stretched her arms above her head. Aiden noticed that she almost hesitated before releasing his hand to do it. Once she was done stretching she returned her gaze back to him.

"Why don't you come with me?" She said. "I wanna look around here for a bit longer before I go back."

"Go back?" Aiden quirked an eyebrow. "Go back to where?"

All he got for an answer was a giggle from this girl. She always seemed to give a short giggle to questions she didn't want to answer. Before he could speak out, she took his hand and pulled him back up.

"Just enjoy the market with me for now." She said. "I'd like to have some more time with you before I leave."

"Um...s-sure?" Aiden stuttered out before she began to drag him back to Other World.

The girl's grip on his hand was stronger than it was before. It felt like she was holding onto him for dear life. Or that she felt like she was afraid of something. He frowned as he watched her movements ever so carefully.

Throughout their time together Aiden noticed several mixed signals from the girl. At one moment she would make hints towards who she truly was, but then she would immediately pull away from revealing any more information.

The way she held his hand as she dragged him back to Other World felt odd as well. He could feel her rub her thumb over his fingers ever so softly. Almost as if she was afraid to let go of him. In a weird way he began to feel that he was her lifeline.

Aiden sighed as he pushed such thoughts away. Maybe it was his imagination overreacting again. This girl was so mysterious that he couldn't help but try to figure out what she was hiding.

He wondered if Theresa would have been able to pull answers out from her. She was always better at pulling information out of someone by just simply talking to them.

The more he thought about Theresa though, the more he began to realized how different she was compared to this girl before him. Not just in looks, but in personality. Theresa was more open and warm with everyone. She didn't hide anything from them either, unless they had no right to know, and showed great care for her friends.

This girl though? She was almost the exact opposite of her. In every sense of the word she was different. She didn't open up easily, hid everything that she knew, and was reluctant to even talk about herself.

Aiden took notice that she happened to be very mischievous.

Compared to Theresa's no nonsense attitude, this girl seemed to enjoy the little things in life. She wasn't tense most of the time, commanding, and she didn't look like she was smart enough to have all the answers. Whatever answers she did hide though she seemed to keep secret behind her playful attitude.

Maybe that was something Aiden liked about this girl though. Theresa would often give him an answer, but this girl? Her determination to keep her secrets made her more alluring than most girls her age.

"Why is this girl getting to me like this?" Aiden thought to himself. *"I should be keeping my cool around her, but she's not even meeting me halfway. What the hell am I gonna do if she ups and vanishes again?"*

Aiden didn't have long to contemplate that thought as he and the girl arrived back in Other World. A smile came to his lips as he saw her eyes light up at the vendors and all the materials that they were selling. The girl gracefully hopped over to one section as she examined a vendor with mini statues of fantasy creatures.

Among the mini statues were different kind of imagined dragons. Aiden had to suppress a laugh. Before he found out about real dragons, Aiden would have thought they would look like these. And despite all the horrors he saw in the Academy, it wasn't enough to take away the amazement he had whenever his three dragon friends took on their true dragon forms.

If only the artist of these little statues could see what dragons really looked like. They probably would have been blown away.

"Wow!" The girl proclaimed. "Look at how pretty these are! The details on this one are incredible!"

Her eyes glanced over to another dragon statue. The joy in her eye turned to annoyance the moment she saw its wings.

"Ugh, the wyvern style?" She groaned out loud. A clear distaste for the dragon's forelimbs being wings. "I hate this design."

"What's wrong with it?" Aiden asked.

"It's just, wrong!" She proclaimed. "It looks so stupid and ridiculous for something like a dragon to walk on its wings instead of four legs! Plus, wyverns are totally different from dragons anyway!"

"That sounds a lil be like prejudice against wyverns." Aiden thought to himself. He could only imagine if Theresa, Garrett, and Seamus all shared the same thoughts this girl did.

As the girl went on about why the wyvern design was a terrible design for a being like a dragon, Aiden's eyes caught a glint in the corner of his eyes. Something shiny and bright that seemed to only affect his eyes. Try as hard as he might though, the glint wouldn't stop hitting him in his eyes. Aiden finally relented and turned towards the source of where the light was coming from. What he saw made his mouth drop.

At the bottom of a table in the booth that he and the girl were staring at was a pair of greaves. But these greaves weren't like the decorative ones on the fake suits of armor that the vendors were trying to sell. They were bright crimson red with a golden outline, with the sides of the greaves with detail from the golden outlines resembled fire.

Aiden knew immediately what these greaves were. Just like the two shoulder pauldrons that he gained before, they shown brightly. But they also seemed to only be noticed by him as well, a pattern previously established when it came to these pieces of armor. He turned to speak to the vendor, who had his back turned to Aiden, but he wasn't able to utter a word as a familiar voice boomed in his mind.

"Say nothing." The voice commanded. "Remember, they cannot know. Now, take them. Just like the other two before, claim them as your own."

Aiden tried to argue back to the voice in his mind, but decided against it. Not just because he would look crazy in front of a lot of people, but because he felt a sort of...pressure from the voice. One that he couldn't really describe, but whenever it spoke out to him he felt weak.

"Take them. Take them now."

Aiden knelt down to the greaves. After making certain that no one was looking at him, he reached out towards the greaves. At the very touch of his fingertips, the greaves flashed once before disappearing. Aiden gasped as his feet suddenly felt heavier.

His eyes glanced down and sure enough, the greaves had been equipped to his body. Aiden glanced to his shoulders, noticing the pauldrons had also appeared alongside the new pair of greaves. And though the armor pieces made his body feel heavier, a part of him felt stronger. Much stronger than he did before.

"Good lad." The voice boomed. "Keep your eyes open. We'll speak again..."

"Who...who are you?" Aiden asked.

"Aiden!"

His head popped up as he looked towards the source of the voice that had just called his name. There at the end of the hall was his mother, with a bag of antique papier mache houses.

"Are you almost done? Your father and I want to go home soon!"

Aiden blinked before realizing that they had been at the Flea Market for quite some time. He turned to say goodbye to the girl, but....

She had just vanished.

"...What in the hell is going on?"

KEEPING AN EYE OPEN

*I*t had been a few days since the trip to the flea market and Aiden was still bothered by what had happened. Not just because of the sudden greaves that formed around his legs, but the way the girl just vanished. It reminded him way too much of their previous encounter at the river, where she vanished as well. The strange disappearing acts gave him an uneasy feeling.

He wasn't the only one who was concerned, or feeling uneasy, lately. The dragons had officially ordered his group meet so that they might speak about an important matter. They also ordered everyone to meet at the apartment the harpies and Kali had been sharing ever since the incident at the Academy. What that was all about only added to Aiden's uneasy feeling.

Despite being worried about what had just happened between him and the mysterious girl, Aiden was brought back to reality at the sound of Liza's voice.

"Agh, this game is so confusing!" Liza cried out as she glanced at the cards in her hand. "I don't understand how you can figure this out, Aelly."

"Oh it's not that bad, Liza." Aello offered her friend a sympathetic smile. "It's actually easy once you figure out all the rules of the cards…"

"There's too many rules on these cards to begin with! How in the world have you not lost your mind?!"

Aiden chuckled under his breath at Liza's frustration. He didn't blame her though. It was one of the many reasons why he never got into card games. The rules often overlapped with one another and confused anyone that was looking for a simple game. Still, it was fun to watch Liza attempt to learn the game for Aello.

A new voice cut through the frustrated venting Liza was spewing.

"You two are taking that game way too seriously."

Aiden turned his head towards the bathroom door. There, in her human disguise, was Kali. The lamina demon that Garrett somehow convinced to join them. He had to fight the urge to not look up and down the outfit she had chosen to wear. Kali had chosen a short black skirt paired with a white midriff exposing tank top, along with a pair of dark blue flats.

"Honestly, what value is there to gain from looking at pieces of cardboard and acting like they're real beings? Honey, you're a harpy yourself. Don't you find this all ridiculous?"

"Well...n-no." Aello meekly said. Her fear of snakes seeming to get more intense whenever she spoke to Kali. "I-It's just a lot of fun to p-play!"

Liza glared at the lamina before speaking.

"Lay off, Kali. No one asked you for your opinion."

"Maybe. But that doesn't mean that I'm not going to give it anyway." The demon retorted before folding her arms across her chest. "And I don't remember inviting you to our apartment."

"Orders from the dragons." Liza replied as she picked up the cards Aello had let her borrow. "Not like you care or pay attention to that though. What with your 'perfect being' stick you have going on for yourself." Just as Kali was about to respond with a venomous insult, Aiden cleared his throat to get their attention.

"Could you two knock it off? We're here for only a little bit, and once we're done we won't have to talk to each other for the rest of the day."

A twinge of regret stirred in his chest after saying that. Aiden's tone was a bit harsher than he intended it. Aello's eyes looked down at the ground, like she had just been screamed at.

"D...Do you not want to hang out with us, Aiden?"

"T-That's not what I meant!" Aiden shook his head violently. "I just don't want everyone to start fighting with one another. T-That's all!"

"Aiden." Liza spoke next. Aiden saw in her eyes that she was not amused with his tone. "I hope you don't take this the wrong way, and I'm only saying this as your friend, but the truth is this. You've kinda been acting like an ass ever since the Academy."

"Blondie's right, boy." Kali took a turn to speak. "When I met you and the other mortals in that stupid school, you were far friendlier than you have been for the past few weeks." She gave a shrug of her shoulders before putting her hands behind her head. Never once though did her cold gaze leave sight of him.

"Not that I care. You mortals aren't exactly what I would call worthy enough to be called my friends."

Aiden let out a sigh as he looked down at his feet. It wasn't Kali not seeing any of them as friends that made him feel bad. It was how the two of them noticed that he had not been the same. And they were right. The events at the Academy had changed how Aiden viewed the world.

It was all for the worse too. While Seamus had shown him the good things a person could do with magic, Ivan had shown him just how far people could fall into darkness. Whether it was intentional or not, it had deeply shaken Aiden's faith in the wonders of magic. Where he once saw amazing power, he now saw a means for cruel people to abuse for their own personal gain.

He had tried to keep his temper hidden from his friends. After all they weren't responsible for what happened. They didn't deserve to be chewed out at for something they had no part in. Even Kali, who was dragged here by Ivan's summoning, wasn't really at fault for what happened.

"Aiden..." Liza frowned. "Come on, talk to me. You've been on edge for the entire summer."

"I..." Aiden stammered, his hands clenched into fists. "I..."

"Oh humans." Kali sighed as she folds her arms. "It's no wonder that your race is so easily controlled by us demons. You let your darker instincts control you far too often."

Aiden's eyes darkened as he turned to yell at Kali. But the moment he opened his mouth one of Kali's long slender fingers landed on his lips. A dangerous glint formed in her eyes as she licked her lips.

"I wouldn't argue with me, cutie. It's best to not anger a Prime

Demon like myself. Unless you want to see just how much the difference is between beings of your caliber and a perfect creature as myself."

"Enough, serpent."

There, standing in the entrance to the apartment were the dragons. Garrett's voice cut through the tension like a hot knife through a slab of butter as they entered. Kali grinned as she removed her finger from Aiden's lips as she looked over to Garrett.

"Aw, you think you can order me around, big guy? That's adorable." She said in a sing song tone. "You must have some kind of delusion that we're equals, it's just so sweet. You act all tough but you really have the imagination of a child, don't you?"

"You're on thin ice as it is." Garrett warned her as he completely ignored her attempts at what Aiden had to guess was flirting. "You survive only because we allow it, demon."

"Knock it off, Garrett." Seamus interrupted with a sigh. "We have more important things to talk about today."

The largest dragon gave him a short nod before turning back to Theresa. Her long white hair seemed to glow in the bright apartment room as she stepped forward. Aiden's face warmed for the briefest moment before he shook his head. Now was not the time to get caught up in how pretty his best friend's hair looked.

Theresa glared at Kali before pointing to a chair. The lustful Prime Demon could have argued with her, or even made some smart remark, but instead she grinned and took her seat. Aiden felt a wave of relief this. Over the summer Theresa and Kali had gotten into many arguments. Some of which could have turned incredibly violent if one did not maintain control over her emotions.

"Aello, Liza." Theresa spoke out. "Put the cards away. There is a matter that we all must speak on."

"Um...do you want us to get her guardians?" Liza asked.

"Don't bother, Liza." Aello answered. "They're at work for the moment, calling them back here would waste time."

"Precisely." Theresa agreed. "And time is not what we have right now."

The white dragoness nodded her head at Garrett and Seamus. Without arguing, the two of them sat down as well. Liza and Aello moved as fast as they could to pick up the trading cards off the table as they sat down as well. Once everyone was seated, Theresa took charge.

"As you all know, what happened at the Academy was a terrible event. Like all of you, I too do not like to think about what could have happened if we had not stopped the Overmind...or rather Lewis, from breaking out." Her emerald green eyes seemed to dim at the mere thought. "The world is not ready to remember not only magic, but other sentient races."

"On that much, I agree." Kali added. "No offense meant to the humans, but they tend to be prejudiced against each other all the time. What makes it worse is that they are the most numerous race of the old kingdoms on the planet."

She put her hands behind her head as she leaned back in the chair. Aiden had come to learn that Kali took pride in showing off her curvy form to anyone who would look at her, anytime they would look.

"Why waste their time tearing each other down? They have to know they're all garbage anyway."

Liza shot the prime demon a dark glare.

"That. Was unnecessary." She said behind gritted teeth.

"She's right about one thing though. Humans do tend to hate things that are different from what they know. It's just how they've always have been." Garrett replied. Theresa nodded her head.

"Remember Samael? Before him, Humans were renowned for their acceptance and wonder at the world around them. They fearless went into the unknown for the betterment of everyone. But...after Samael killed the queen...they lost that wonder, that acceptance. They never trusted the rest of us again, and when the rest of the races vanished, that built up xenophobia and prejudice, turning it inward, at themselves..."

Aello shifted uncomfortably in her chair at the mention of her uncle's name. Aiden couldn't blame her. The mere thought of that crazed harpy man was enough to send shivers down his back.

"But we're not here to talk about Samael." Theresa continued. "We're here to talk about...well, a new threat. A threat that we should all take seriously."

"A new threat?" Aello asked. "Are those...are those Shadow Demons threatening things again?"

"No." Theresa frowned. "I was watching the news the other night with my parents. At first I thought it wouldn't be anything special or attention grabbing, but then I saw this."

Theresa snapped her fingers once. At her command a spark of white fire flew from her fingertips and began to swirl around. The room watched in amazement as the white fire took shape. The flames at first took the shape of an open eye that seemed to be staring into infinity.

But, as she snapped her fingers again, it began to change. The pupil became thinner, transforming into a malevolent slit. As it changed, so too did the color of the flames change, becoming a sinister shade of violet. It continued to change, the iris becoming a deeper and deeper shade of violet while what should have been the white of the eye turned pitch black. The longer he looked into that gazing eye, the more Aiden felt as though he was falling into its murky depths. He could almost hear the screams of the suffering this symbol had caused, echoing ceaselessly in his head, threatening to split in half.

The room went deathly silent. The only sound that could be heard was a low growl from Garrett's throat at the image. Everyone, with the possible exception of Kali, looked terrified at this mark.

"This is the symbol I saw on the news." Theresa spoke, her voice shifting into its leadership tone. "The symbol of the Dark Eye."

Aiden could barely hear the words Theresa was speaking. The longer he stared into the pupil of the giant eye, the more he felt draw to it. The massive headache he was feeling, the non stop screams of torment, and the ever increasing sense of dread began to grow within his soul. He couldn't explain why, but he felt it. A twinge something, or someone, watching him intently. That in that one moment this intruder knew every single bit of information about Aiden Russell right down to his very core.

His palms turned sweaty, his vision started to blur, and his mouth felt like the driest desert on the planet in the span of a few seconds. Yet for some reason, he could not pull his vision away from the eye. Try as hard as he might, something...primal, was holding him against his will. He felt trapped!

"AIDEN!"

Theresa's shout, accompanied by the snapping of her fingers

dismissing the symbol of the cult, brought Aiden back to reality. He took a deep breath. It felt like it was the first time his lungs had actually worked in a while, as he panted in his seat.

"W-Wh-What was that?" He asked. Theresa ran over to him and quickly put a hand over his forehead. Whispering under her breath 'Amalla' to help his body recover.

"Are you alright? What happened?!"

"I...I don't know." Aiden told her as his body began to tremble. "It...it felt like I was having my soul pierced."

"Rexkin." Garrett's voice cut off their moment. "Perhaps we should not form that symbol in front of the whelp for the time being. It's clear that it has a negative effect on his body."

"And that's because he's weak." Kali added. "Clearly he's like most other humans, the first sign of intense magic like that and they start to feel weak."

"It wasn't like that!" Aiden snapped at them. "I've seen magic before! Hell, I've been using it for awhile too! This was just...I don't know how to explain it but it felt so..."

Theresa put one hand over his mouth. Before he could protest further she gave him a quick 'shush' before her attention to Garrett and Kali.

"I don't know why he had such a violent reaction to seeing the eye, especially when it was just a recreation of it from my magic, but from now on, we will not make that symbol. Not until we find out what is going on." Her eyes turned steely. "Is that clear?"

Garrett gave a short nod, dropping the argument. Kali grinned.

"You're awfully protective, dragon girl. It's almost kind of sweet to see it, if only he wasn't a mere human right~?"

Theresa glared at the Prime Demon as steam came out of her nostrils. For a moment Aiden thought she was about to spit a large fireball at Kali. Before the two could get into each other's faces Garrett grabbed Kali's shoulder with a very tight grip.

"Can it, snake." He told her. "You can mock any other mortal you want, but do not dare insult my Rexkin."

Kali smiled as her tongue, still forked even in her human form, rolled out her mouth before it rolled back in.

"Oh my. It seems I forgot how loyal you dragons are to your

precious leaders." She laughed before walking back to her seat. "But you have to accept that he and the other mortal girl can't always be around us, little dragoness. They cannot rely on your protection forever."

As she sat down, Theresa sighed before taking charge of the room once more.

"Despite our differences, Kali. You are right about one thing." She turned to Aiden and Liza. "We cannot always be around to defend the two of you. Which is partly why we've decided to call this meeting today."

"And the other part?" Liza asked.

"That, is to discuss the cult." Seamus spoke out. "The three of us held an emergency meeting about this Dark Eye before we brought this up to all of you."

At Theresa's nod of approval, the dragon of magic stood. He began to pace back and forth between Aiden, Liza, and Aello. The normally teasing dragon had a more serious expression on his face as he spoke.

"We looked into this cult, based on the findings of the local news and rumors discussed amongst the humans." He said. "All the findings confirm the same thing. The cult is made up of teenagers to young adults. Sex and race aren't discriminated against in this cult. All that matters is that the members share one thing in common."

Seamus stopped pacing as he stood in the center of the apartment's living room.

And that, is that they all hate society."

"It's no surprise that humans tend to isolate those who are different from what they consider 'normal' in their communities. You've probably have seen and heard of it from those schools you are forced to attend." Garrett added. "Most cults are formed in response to society's cold rejection. It just makes sense that they all gathered together as a result of this."

"Wait." Aello interrupted. "How come they hate society? Humans are social beings like harpies are, aren't they? They need to be around each other because they can't survive without interaction."

"Like I said before," Theresa spoke out, "The ending of The Great War greatly effected the human race. All the prejudice they hold against each other right now, it all stems from the aftermath of that war."

"And after thousands of years of human history, they can't seem to understand that rejection of others causes these cults to come forth." Seamus continued. "This new cult, The Dark Eye, is formed by those that society does not deem 'normal.' That's not to say that every single member is evil, but for them there is no where else to go."

The dragon of magic folded his arms across his chest as his expression turned sour. "Normally we would just ignore this as it doesn't matter to us. However as reports across the country continue to grow about their antics and numbers. Public attacks on innocent bystanders, instigating riots at schools, destroying public property, and threatening those who dare challenge them. That's usually the standard for most cults." Seamus snarled. But something caught my attention from one person who said he was tailing a sketchy teenager. For one moment the teen was in his line of sight, but after a turn into an alley, the purser said that it was like the teen 'vanished' into thin air."

An eerie feeling spread across the apartment. Aiden knew right away that there was only one way for a person to just 'vanish' like that. The answer did not need to be said out loud. Magic was at work. That made it their business.

"By the looks on your faces, I can tell that you three have already figured out that there's only one man that could gather these young members and teach them the ways of magic. The very same man that influence Ivan to the point of using his own flesh and blood in a sick experiment."

"Dimitri." Aiden's tone turned somber.

"Exactly." Seamus confirmed. "He's the only master of the dark arts that could gather so many youths, and corrupt them into believing that they have to commit violent acts as a way of 'revenge' against society."

"Damn that bastard." Liza scowled. "It's bad enough that he was trying to take the harpies and his influence got to the Grand Mage of the mage school, but now he's corrupting the youth of the country?"

"I don't think he's just started it." Theresa said. "To gather a cult like this in a short amount of time like this is impossible, even WITH magic. He's been doing this for some time. Years even."

The reality of the situation began to dawn on Aiden. His face turned to a sickly pale grey as the next question escaped his lips.

"Are...are you saying he has an army?"

"It is...most likely that he has more than enough members in his cult to form an army of sorts."

A chill ran down Aiden's spine. An entire army of cult members, all of them possibly learning magic from Dimitri. It was already bad enough that Dimitri and Raven were capable of summoning demons to their side. To make matters worse, members of the Dark Eye could be everywhere.

"Needless to say, whelps, but we are outnumbered. Even with the power that dragons possess, it would prove to be difficult to fight every single member of this cult in a full on battle." Garrett grimaced. "They might be children, but the reports we found about the Dark Eye members convinced us that each one should not be taken lightly."

"Does...does that mean that we're in a losing situation here?" Aello asked. "We don't even have the numbers to fight an army, even with my mother's flock backing us!"

"Calm down, birdie." Kali snapped. "You're freaking out before they can even finish. It'd be cute if it wasn't so pathetic."

"Watch your mouth, viper." Liza said with daggers in her eyes.

"Enough." Theresa ordered. "Yes, we could very well be outnumbered. I won't lie, we have way more work to do. But that's why we called this meeting today." The white dragoness took control of the situation again as she paced back and forth in the living room. "The Dark Eye has the numbers advantage. As such, that puts us at a disadvantage. If any of you come across its members, do not take them lightly."

Aiden flinched as her normally calm emerald green eyes glinted. In that moment Theresa Goldwin became Theresa of the White Flame once more.

"Everyone in this room that goes to high school with me must keep their eyes open from now on. We don't know who is among their numbers. Mind what you say around anyone you don't know. Even more so to people that you DO know." She gave Aiden a dark look. "That means no trying to start any trouble with Eric and his sleezeball lackey."

"Got it." Aiden accepted. "But I think those two idiots could ever be part of a cult like this one."

"No risk taking, whelp." Garrett reiterated. "With this cult growing in numbers, you could convince either one of those fools to join their ranks."

"I said I got it." Aiden mumbled.

"That being said," Seamus spoke next. "You and Liza have both become quite adept with your weapons. Aiden, you handle Warfang as well as our late King. And Liza? The way you handle Gitanel is a dream come true."

"T...Thanks, Seamus." Liza blushed. "I wouldn't call my skills with the dagger amazing yet..."

"Young one, considering how we kind of forced you into our little click back when you were in middle school, it is quite amazing that you've mastered it." Seamus responded. "That being said, the three of us discussed what to do about you two."

Theresa nodded as she took another turn to speak.

"Kali is correct about one thing. The three of us and her can not be around you or the harpies at all times. As such, we conversed about our options. And we've all agreed that it's time for you two to take the next step in your training." She looked over at Seamus. "Do it."

The dragon of magic snapped his fingers. In a flash of blue white light, two new radiant weapons materialized out of thin air. Aiden and Liza both had to squint to adjust their eyes to the bright light, but when their eyes adjusted they both gasped at their new weapons. For Aiden, at least, the joy he felt was like he had just gotten an upgrade in one of his old RPGs.

Magically floating in the air was a radiant looking shield and a straight, sharp dagger. The shield had the more complex design of the two. The front resembled a dragon's outstretched wing. From top to bottom it was a white golden color, with the silhouette of a dragon head in what Aiden guessed was Theresa's dragon form.

The shield was one of the most beautiful things Aiden had ever seen.

The new dagger, compared to Gitanel, was not as impressive. But there was no denying it had its own unique beauty. Unlike the curved blade of Gitanel, this dagger had a straight blade with a silver white color. The hand guard took the shape of a dragon wing, with the fingers of the wings, or as Aiden had learned from Theresa their accurate name was the phalanx, pointing upward in the same direction as the blade. The dagger's hilt was covered in a brilliant bronze color that shown in a lit room. To top off the design, the pommel was decorated with several small sapphires.

"These, will be extra weapons in your arsenal." Seamus said. "After what happened at the Academy, we took it upon ourselves to craft you these fine pieces. For you kiddo, we grant you this shield to protect you from harm should we not be around to keep your ass out of trouble."

Aiden stared silently in awe of the shield that floated before him. He couldn't believe Seamus' had words. This wonderful looking shield in all its brilliance, was his?

"Its name is PeaceGuard." Seamus continued. "Forged from one of Theresa's scales. With it as your shield you'll have her protection even if you're not in the same area."

Aiden caught only a small glimpse, but he could have sworn he saw Theresa blushing.

"I..." Aiden stammered. "I don't know if I'm worthy to even-"

"Welp." Garrett cut him off. "It's not a matter of being worthy or not. The truth is this. You need to learn to defend yourself. Our King's great weapon alone won't always be the best way for you to survive in battle. Remember that."

"Take it, Aiden." Theresa told him. "Yes you will have to learn how to use a shield properly, but just like with your training with Warfang, handling PeaceGuard will come to you. I promise."

With Theresa's encouragement, and Garrett being as blunt about things as he usually was, Aiden reached out towards PeaceGuard with one hand. At the touch of his fingertips, the shield flashed a brilliant light before turning its back to him. Aiden didn't hesitate as he slipped his left arm into the straps before grasping its handle. Once the brilliant glow around the shield dissipated, the reality of the shield's weight came crashing down on his arm.

"Agh!" Aiden cried out as he struggled to keep the shield from hitting the ground. "Okay, I didn't think it'd be THIS heavy."

"What did you think it would feel like it was the same weight as Warfang?" Seamus asked. "That may have been forged from Theresa's scale, but it is not a light weight. It's designed to do its primary job, protect you from attacks."

"Don't focus on the weight of the shield, welp." Garrett added. "In a fight any distraction could be the one mistake that takes your life."

"Kinda hard to do that, considering how heavy this shield feels!" Aiden retorted. A sigh came from Theresa's lips.

"You'll get used to the weight of PeaceGuard soon, Aiden." She said. "Listen carefully now, just like Warfang your new shield also can be summoned by speaking out the draconic word for shield. *Hisdel.*"

Aiden nodded in acknowledgement before looking down at Peace-Guard. If it truly was like Warfang, it must have a different form outside of combat to fool the ordinary person. Once he had a better grip on his new shield, he cleared his throat before speaking.

"*Hisdel.*"

At his command PeaceGuard floated off his arm. The radiant shield began to shrink in size right before his very eyes. What was once a large and radiant shield had now shrink into a puny 2.5 inch sized version of it. It was now the size of an average belt buckle, a perfect disguise for the shield. PeaceGuard floated back over to Aiden, gently falling into his open palms with a soft thud.

"That...that was incredible." Aello says in amazement. Liza nodded in agreement.

"You got that right…"

Right now, Kiddo, we made sure that it took the form of this belt buckle so that you will never be unprotected." Seamus explained. "Unlike Warfang, you can't summon PeaceGuard to your side just yet. Until then keep that buckle with you at all times."

Aiden gave a short nod to Seamus before placing the buckle into his left pocket. He never really wore belts, he had no reason for it, but now he had an excuse to do so. At least until he could summon PeaceGuard like he could with Warfang.

"As for you, Liza." Seamus continued. "This second dagger is special. Like PeaceGuard, it was forged just for you. Its name is Oceanus. We forged it from one of Garrett's fangs."

Liza just stared at her new dagger in amazement as it floated over to her. Oceanus' sapphire flashed a brilliant light as it turned upward for her grab its hilt. After a few seconds of hesitation Liza reached towards the hilt of Oceanus ever so carefully with her left hand. Any uncertainty and fear disappeared as a coy grin spread across her lips. At the mere touch of her hand, the dagger's otherworldly glow stopped as the blade accepted her as its master.

"Oh HELL YES!" Liza said, grinning as she held Oceanus above her head. "This thing is an absolute beauty! Just imagine the badass moves I could do with both this AND Gitanel at the same time!"

"This isn't a game, welp." Garrett said with a growl. "That dagger came from one of MY fangs. Do not treat it as if was some kind of simple toy."

"Aw, big lizard, that truly came from your teeth? It looks so small in comparison to your true form's teeth." Kali taunted. A short amount of smoke erupted from the former's nostrils as he glared at her. Theresa stopped the larger dragon from snapping as she slammed her hand down on a table.

"Don't even start, Garrett." Theresa ordered. Both Garrett and Kali scoffed before turning their gazes away from one another. Theresa rolled her eyes before she turned back to Aiden and Liza.

"But he is right about one thing. These are not toys, as I'm sure you are aware. Both of you will train even harder now to master your new weapons, as the art of using a shield and two daggers is entirely different from what you already know."

"Um, not to question you or anything, Thes…" Liza interrupted for a moment. "But where the hell are we going to train? We can't go back to that forest anymore, especially if the cult is lead by Dimitri and his asshole student."

"I am well aware of this, Liza. In truth, we have been trying to find a place where training can be held not just in private, but without interruption."

"We'll keep looking for the right place." Seamus spoke out. "Garrett and I have been looking all over, we have a few ideas where you two can resume your training without worrying about the Dark Eye."

"Until then, do not attempt to use these weapons on your own without proper training." Garrett ordered. "You do, and I'll burn you both myself."

Both Aiden and Liza turned a bit pale in the face at that threat from

Garrett. The color in their skin came back as Theresa grabbed ahold of the larger dragon's ear and squeezed it really hard.

"You will do NO such thing." She ordered. "As leader of this group, I will not tolerate any more threats or insults to our trainees. You will do well to remember who is Rexkin, Garrett." Her eyes glinted. "Unless you would like to challenge me for that title."

Garrett grunted in pain at Theresa's grip on his ear before nodding his head. No matter how many times he had seen it, Aiden could never get over the fact that Theresa always managed to pull Garrett back in line when he started to push buttons.

"At any rate, he is right about one thing. If you run into any cultist, or demon for that matter, neither of you are to use PeaceGuard or Oceanus in combat. Not until you have had the proper training to do so." Aiden and Liza didn't argue with her order. It was not wise to do that after she had brought Garrett back under control.

The realization began to seep into Aiden's mind as he looked down at the belt buckle version of his new shield. Two new weapons. And a brand new threat to deal with. He clenched his hand around Peace-Guard as he thought about the possible battles inevitably coming.

All he could hope was that he would be ready for them when the time came.

STARTING THE NEW SCHOOL YEAR

A week had passed since the Dragons gave Aiden and Liza their new weapons. A week where Aiden felt on edge from start to finish. Not just because of the Dark Eye Cult, which had begun to grow in numbers based on reports from the news, but because summer was coming to an end soon.

Aiden groaned as he sat alone in his room, trying to lose himself in an old fantasy book he had read a thousand times before. He thought reading would help him get his mind off the situation at hand, and possibly make the inevitable end of summer feel like it was a lifetime away. Sadly that alone was not enough to make him feel any better. About both school approaching AND the situation the team now found themselves in.

No one was looking forward to the start of the school year. The four members of the team that did go to school would be entering their sophomore year. Of the four, Theresa was the one who was most frustrated by this. While Garrett, Seamus, and Kali had the freedom to explore for their foes, she was trapped in an education system that she called 'a mockery' of learning. That alone was enough for Aiden to be taken aback, as she had always lectured him about the importance of school.

With Dark Eye members possibly running amok, Aiden would dare not blame her for feeling annoyed about being forced to return to school. People's lives could possibly be in danger if the cult was allowed to get away with what they wanted. As powerful as their friends were, Aiden worried that even with their strength the cult members would outnumber them and prevail from sheer numbers.

He hadn't seen numbers be too much a problem for the dragons before, but if the Dark Eye truly had members across the country even the dragons would have a problem with an army of angry misunderstood teenagers and young adults. Especially if they were given access to incredibly powerful magic. The damage that an army of that size could do if they were pushed too far? Aiden abhorred the very thought of such an event happening.

As much as he hated it, almost as much as Theresa, school sadly had to come first. It wouldn't have been such an annoyance if there wasn't a cult running around that endangered possibly everyone in the country. It was enough to make him slam his book closed as he placed a bookmark in it.

"Goddammit." He groaned. "Why the hell is nothing making me feel better?"

Aiden rubbed his eyebrows before placing the book back on its spot in his bookshelf. He would attempt to get back into it another time. Hopefully when things finally calmed down enough for him to relax. His eyes glanced up and down the collection of fantasy novels before him. All lined up in chronological order per series. A collection of stories he was quite proud of reading.

"You know," He said to his collection, gently running his fingers across the spines of some of them. "If any of you had an answer to the crap that my friends and I have found ourselves in, that would be great. Any that may provide a solution to this can speak now."

He had to laugh a bit at himself for saying that. Aiden was pretty sure that he had at least read each of the books multiple times. Enough to know that they didn't provide him the answers he would need.

"God, Theresa would be lecturing me right now for looking towards my fantasy novels for guidance about the situation we're in." He brushed his bangs back as he looked over the books before him. "She would probably say something like 'Aiden these fictional stories aren't going to provide the answers! Take this seriously!'"

"Funny." A new voice said behind him. "I was actually about to say that to you."

"Gah!" Aiden almost jumped out of his skin as he turned around to spot Theresa. "T-Thes?! What the hell?!'

"Your mom let me in." She said with an eye roll. "At least you're able to tell what I was going to say to you before I even got in here."

Theresa strolled over to one of his comfy chairs, plopping herself down on it before she crossed one of her legs over the other. Aiden sighed as he took a seat in his own chair as he awaited the full lecture from her. However it didn't come.

"I know that the situation we are in looks dire now, Aiden." She said with a frown. "Believe me no one else wanted it to happen like this. Hell, it shouldn't have happened in the first place."

"And yet it did." Aiden finished for her with a sigh. "Mom and dad talked about it the one time we went to the Flea Market, barely. Mom's worried that the cult will somehow make its way to our small town. The worst part is? I believe it will happen, soon."

"It more than likely will happen, Aiden." Theresa apprehensively said. "Dimitri has to have been at work with this cult for some time now. Reports are spreading all over the country about how they continue to grow in power and numbers. More teenagers and young adults are being pulled into their fold. If they're not stopped, the entire country could become a nightmare for anyone who is not in Dimitri's cult."

"What are we gonna do Theresa?" He asked before leaning back in his chair. "If they truly have an army of Dark Eye members how can we ever except to fight them all?"

"I'm afraid I don't have the answer to that one." Theresa folded her arms across her chest. "Dammit all. If we weren't constrained by school I'd lead the charge to find out where their base of operations is!"

Aiden frowned as he watched Theresa's frustration mount. He never really thought about it before, but the burden of her past life must weigh heavily on her mind. It wasn't just whenever he asked to talk about her previous life, but even when they weren't together. Her usually pretty green eyes that were filled with vibrant life, now dimmed with a dark hue of frustration and all the weight of the world on her shoulders.

It was in that moment that Aiden noticed the simple truth about his best friend. Strong as Theresa could be, hailed as the greatest warrior who ever lived in her time, she was still his best friend. His own heart ached in sadness for her as her long white hair, which usually shown, looked dull and lifeless.

"H-Hey, take it easy." He said finally, grabbing her wrist with a gentle touch. "You don't have to feel like everything falls on you."

"But..." Theresa started, he stopped her as he pulled her hand up gently.

"No buts." Aiden firmly told her. "You're always acting like you have to know what to do and how to do it at all times. And I get it, you're the leader of the group. I wouldn't dare challenge you for that spot. But whenever I see you upset like this, I feel pain my heart for your burden."

Theresa blinked at Aiden's words as he squeezed her hand in his own. For a brief moment Aiden saw her eyes shimmer before he continued.

"You're always taking everything on yourself. Ever since the day Patrick tried to kill me you've put so much weight on your shoulders. You took on the task of training me in the ways of combat, taught me magic spells, and showed me just how marvelous the world you guys once lived in was. Sure we got through some bad times, especially with what happened at the harpy's den with Samael and what Ivan did to his own school. Despite all of it you never once flinched."

He offered her a kind smile before placing his second hand, unconsciously, on her left shoulder.

"But just because this Dark Eye cult is running around doesn't mean you have to be doing everything yourself, Thes. Even if we have to rely on Garrett and Seamus to keep an eye out for us during class, we'll get through this. I know that we can."

Time seemed to halt as Aiden held onto Theresa's hand. He hadn't noticed it before, as he stared into her emerald green eyes, just how...well, pretty she looked today. Everyone in their high school, at least in their class, had always talked about how in their eyes Theresa was the epitome of beauty. And while Aiden had been her best friend since they were children, he never once stopped to think about it.

He could feel his heart beat a mile per second as he and Theresa locked eyes with one another. The back of his mouth felt dry. What was happening? Why did he suddenly feel so incredibly nervous to just be around her in this second?

Just when it seemed like time would completely stop forever in that spot, Theresa closed her eyes and gave a small giggle.

"Aiden?" She spoke out. "I'm gonna need my hand back now."

"G-Gah!" Aiden blurted before letting her hand and shoulder go. "S-S-Sorry! I didn't mean for that to get awkward! I swear I was just trying to cheer you up and-"

A lone finger on his lip silenced him as Theresa gave him a playful smile.

"You know you don't have to go explaining everything when it happens, right?" She asked with a wink. "It's endearing, but you don't have to worry. You made your point to me. And...well, it really means a lot that you want me to not carry such a burden."

Aiden glanced away from her gaze for a moment to hide the rise of pink on his cheeks. He already felt awkward enough that he had held onto her hand like that for such a moment of time, he'd rather not feel even more foolish by letting Theresa see his pink cheeks.

"Y-Yeah, well at least you're not looking so frustrated anymore." He abruptly spat out. "The last thing we need from you right now is to feel so burdened that your guiding light leaves the group."

Theresa giggled for a second before putting her hands on her hips. Aiden quirked an eyebrow at her as a smile came to his best friend's face.

"You know, you may not act like it at times but you can certainly sound like a leader when the need arises for it, Aiden."

"Ha. ME? A leader?" Aiden laughed. "Nooo, trust me. Bad things happen when I lead. A lot of people end up getting lost."

"Oh please tell me you're not talking about when we were in First Grade." Theresa laughed. "Aiden, that happened years ago."

"And yet the memory still stings." Aiden dramatically covered his forehead with his left hand as he leaned back. "Oh the long single hour of me leading us around a toy store for an hour without finding our parents! The horror!"

Theresa laughed at the over to top delivery he had just given. Aiden couldn't help but laugh too at how silly he ended up sounding. It was moments like these that he had begun to miss the most after his life had changed. Just hanging out with Theresa, laughing at things in life, enjoying each other's company without having to worry about the problems of the world. Days that had gone by all too quickly, Aiden had realized.

That was all part of growing up though.

"Okay, let's be serious here for a moment." Theresa managed to get out after a few seconds of laughter. "It's sweet that you're concerned for me, Aiden. Believe me, it really is. But you don't have to be so worried about any burden I'm carrying on my shoulders."

She folded her arms across her chest once more as the two friends leaned back in their respective chairs.

"I've been leading soldiers for a long, long time Aiden. Even before I became my King's right hand, I was renowned for being a natural leader on the field. I can handle it."

"I know you can, Thes. But you gotta understand something. You might have been the greatest warrior of all time, hell, you may have been the greatest leader the world's ever seen too. But when you're with me, and just me, you're not any of those things." Aiden smiled. "To me, you're always Theresa Goldwin. My best friend in the world."

It was a few seconds of somewhat awkward silence between the two of them. Aiden swallowed a lump in his throat. Had he pushed too far with his kind words? All he wanted was to make her feel comfortable around him. His heart felt like it skipped a beat the moment he saw the genuine happy smile from Theresa.

"Thank you, Aiden." She said, "It's nice to hear those words from you. With everything going on lately, I just want the world to feel like it's normal once more. So to have you say that to me puts my mind at ease. At least for awhile."

Aiden scratched the back of his head in embarrassment. Theresa cleared her throat before taking a more somber tone with him.

"But let's not get too much off topic. While I know that we have to rely on Garrett, Seamus, and Kali to look out for the Dark Eye members I don't want me, you, or Liza get soft. When we have a new place to practice, we'll spend every free hour we have there."

Aiden's face paled at that. Every free hour they had?

"A-Are you certain that you want that?" Aiden asked. "We're getting into our sophomore year of high school. We'll be swamped with more school work than we were in ninth grade. Not to mention our parents will get super suspicious if we're out of our houses every day just to train."

"I am well aware that school will conflict with our schedules. And before you ask, no we will not use the clones that Seamus can make to take our place during classes. Those only last a few days and if the Dark Eye is truly lead by Dimitri, I have a feeling they'll know a fake from the real thing."

"Dammit."

"Like it or not Aiden, and I certainly do not like it, we are stuck with the life of high school students."

"Thes, there's something that you're forgetting though. We can't go back to the forest to train anymore." Aiden frowned. "How am I expected to learn how to use PeaceGuard when we can't even go back to where we trained?"

Theresa sighed. A feeling of dread crept up Aiden's spine when she did. Over the years he had learned that it never was a good sign to hear a sigh from Theresa Goldwin. Whenever she did, it was about something that Aiden never wanted to hear. And the forewarning that Aiden felt in his spine felt like it wouldn't be enough to brace him for it.

"There is one place, but you are not going to like it." She said with a glance away.

"Oh HELL no." Aiden loudly protested.

"Aiden-"

"Absolutely NOT. If you think for a moment that we are going back to the Academy-"

"Shut up and let me finish." Theresa snapped. Her pupils had turned into slits, reflecting that of her dragon form. "I know. Going back to that place after what happened is going to be painful. We all have bad memories of what happened there, and Ivan's revelation of what he forced upon his youngest son was one of the worst things I have ever seen from a human. But Ivan is no longer in power of the Academy. Ryan is. And I know for a fact that he has heard about the Dark Eye right now. Don't you think he would want us to be prepared for something like them?"

"I..." Aiden sighed as he rubbed he eyebrows. "I guess you're right, Thes. It's just...are we really gonna go back to that place? I feel terrible that we'll be using their school to practice when they are still recovering from the Shadow Demon outbreak."

"As bad as the Shadow Demon crisis was, the Dark Eye could potentially become even worse, Aiden." Theresa sighed. "Ryan will understand. He has to know about the reports."

"You really think he will?"

"If it will prevent something like what happened to his little brother from happening again? Absolutely." Theresa sat in deep thought for a few seconds. "But my question is how long has Dimitri, if he even is the one behind the formation of the cult, been recruiting members? Months? Maybe even years? Time is not on our side here."

"Hey, calm down." Aiden spoke up, noticing she was starting to stress herself out again. "What'd I say earlier about not worrying so much? We'll figure this out. I promise."

Theresa gave a short smile at his kind words before she leaned forward in her chair. "You sure you don't consider yourself at least a natural wordsmith?" She asked with an eyebrow wiggle. He scoffed at the question.

"Please, do you not remember how I get tongue twisted?"

"Heheh, come on it's not that bad." She teased before pushing his shoulder. "You gotta start believing more in yourself."

"Yeah....right." Aiden nodded as he took in the sight of a happy Theresa.

In many ways, he was reminded of the black haired girl. So more open about things with him, willing to answer any question that he may have for her. It really was one of her more endearing traits.

Wait. The black haired girl! How could he have forgotten about her? Her and the word that she would constantly call him! Aiden's eyes narrowed as he sat up in his chair.

"Thes, I need to ask you something." The tone in his voice far more serious than before. Theresa blinked in surprise at the sudden change. "When I was out, there was some kind of...girl."

"...A girl?"

"Not like that." He quickly spoke out. "She kept calling me something, a word that I don't know if you'll be able to translate for me or not...Theresa, what does Ra-"

Before he could even get the word out of his mouth, the door knob on his door suddenly twisted. Both Aiden and Theresa about had a panic attack as they turned to the door. As it opened, the face of his mother. In that short moment of time, Aiden felt like a car battery had just shocked his heart into exploding out of his chest. Not even the most tense and fierce battles he had in the past came close to the near fright his mother nearly gave him.

"Are you two okay in here?" She asked with a kind smile.

"Perfectly fine, mom!" Aiden blurted out. The color in his lips felt like they had just faded away. "No problems here!"

"You two sure? You've been in here just talking for sometime, usually the two of you go out somewhere." Helena pointed out. "Are both of you certain you're fine?"

"Yes, mom. We're okay." Aiden prayed that she would eventually leave. "We're just talking about..."

"About your upcoming year in high school?"

Yup! That's it!" Aiden once again blurted, "Totally about next week's start of the new year!"

The awkward silence that passed through the three of them went on for a couple of seconds. To Aiden it felt like it had lasted an hour as his mother just looked at them. He could almost feel Theresa glaring in a a way that was screaming "SHUT UP." Luckily for him, Helena broke the silence.

"I um...wasn't interrupting anything was I?"

"N-Not at all, Mrs. Russell." Theresa replied. "We were just talking about what we should expect from the new year at school now that we're Sophomores."

"I...I see." Helena frowned. "The news has been reporting so much about this cult I was beginning to worry if they had already tried to get to both of you as well. I guess I am just hoping the two of you aren't going to get caught up in that mess. R-right?"

Aiden felt a twinge of guilt as he saw the concerned look on his mother's face. He knew she meant well, he could never blame her for that. Any good mother intended the best when it came to her kids. It bothered him that he had to keep secrets from her, but he knew it was for the best to keep her and his father safe.

"Mom," He gave her a short nod. "I promise, we're not going to get involved with any of that mess. Thes and I know better than to cause trouble."

Helena smiled before letting out a sigh of relief. "Okay. Just, if something happens please, don't be afraid to come to me Aiden. Okay?"

"I promise."

With that, Aiden's mother closed the door as soft as she could. Aiden and Theresa waited for a moment before hearing her footsteps walk away. Once she was far enough away, they let out a huge sigh together.

"THAT. Was too close." Aiden said.

"No need to tell me that." Theresa agreed. "Aiden, things are going to get more complicated as this goes on. We cannot allow your parents, or mine, to know what is going on. If they get dragged into this mess..."

"I know." Aiden frowned. "I hate it, but I know what you mean, Thes. I just wish we could tell them a bit of what is going on."

"Do that, and they'll think you're crazy." Theresa laughed before standing up. "I hate to do it as well, but for the sake of keeping them safe we have to lie. Hopefully not for long."

"On that, I agree." Aiden said as he stood up as well. "Should we get out of here? Go to the mall or something? I need to get my mind off this whole mess."

"Sure." Theresa smiled, but before she took a step out she asked. "Aiden, what was the question you were going to ask me again?"

"It's...not important." Aiden lied. There was already enough on their plate as is. The last thing he needed was to make her feel more stressed. "Come on, let's just go to the mall and enjoy what summer we have left."

Theresa nodded before opened the door. Aiden knew that eventually he would have to tell her what he heard from the girl, but for now? It was best to enjoy what was left of their summer vacation.

Sadly, in a short amount of time the last week of summer passed. The start to the school year began its slow trek of insanity. The bus ride to school proved to be uneventful, for once, as slowly the students headed to their classes. Aiden could only hope that the teachers would have mercy today and spare the students from a a massive load of homework.

His first class? Algebra. Not exactly his strong suit. To make matters worse, Theresa, Liza, and Aello were not in the class with him. That was always the worst thing about high school classes, put in classes with people you don't exactly know that well.

As he waited for the teacher to come into the room, he opened up his text book to glance over the problems that lay ahead. Aiden almost laughed as the confusing equations seemed to be more complicated than learning the draconic language. At least the language of the dragons was a bit more fair and far easier to learn than these confusing mathematical problems.

"All right, all right. Settle down folks!" The math teacher said as he entered the room. "We got a lot to go over what to expect from this class today. But before that, we got a new student today. All of you look up from what you're doing and pay attention."

Aiden looked up from his text book for a split second at the teacher's order. His mouth dropped to the ground as he spotted the girl standing before the class, wearing the same outfit she wore before at the flea market. In that moment, he could have sworn he saw her give him a warm smile as she introduced herself.

"My name is Erienne Ivy. It's a pleasure to meet you all!"

THE NEW GIRL

*A*iden almost shot out of his chair in shock at seeing her. Erienne Ivy. The girl who had been a mystery to him since summer camp, finally he knew her name. A mixed bag of emotions rose up in his chest as he saw her amber eyes make contact with him. Confusion, happiness, and a longing to ask why she was in his school.

It was a very brief moment, but to Aiden it felt like everything had slowed down at Erienne's smile. Her amber eyes shown in the dim lighting of the classroom, a shining example compared to the dark boring days of school that laid ahead of Aiden and his friends. He felt a joy rise up in his heart from her smile. Such a different, but almost similar, beauty compared to Theresa's own.

"Take your seat, Erienne." The teacher instructed. "I'll call role soon, I want everyone to be quiet and pay attention."

Erienne nodded her head as she made her way to the only empty seat in the classroom. Right by Aiden. Someone was either playing a cruel joke on him, that had to be it. Aiden could not even begin to believe that after so long, he would get more answers out of her. He would get her to talk, even if he had to constantly bug her for them!

But then he remembered that they were stuck in school. And randomly asking private questions about who she truly was would make him look like a slimeball. Not to mention if they were in earshot for other students that were besides them or behind them. He cursed the fact that out of all the times to run into her again, it would be at friggin school. Damn his bad luck!

"Dammit all!" He thought. *"Why does it have to be at school?!"*

Erienne took her seat beside Aiden, the latter still seething in frustration. Once he saw her beside him, Aiden cleared his throat in an attempt to get her attention. She didn't react at first, her eyes staring right at the teacher as he opened up his text book.

"Everyone, turn to the first chapter. We're going over what to expect in this class and the the first bit of chapter one today."

Almost all of the students reluctantly groaned as they opened their text books. The only one who didn't groan was Erienne, who just grinned as she opened her own. Aiden quirked an eyebrow at her as she glanced over to him for the briefest of moments. Her orange eyes glistened for a second, then she winked at him before leaning her head onto his shoulder.

"Good to see you here, Ragnakin." She whispered to him before removing her head from his shoulder.

Everything felt as though it had exploded in a rush of heat. Starting in his heart, rushing through his chest and even to his reddening cheeks, just a tiny touch from Erienne was enough to cause him to space out for a moment. Part of him desperately wanted to ask her to lean on him again, to recapture that moment in time for just a small moment.

"Get it together, Aiden!" He shouted in his mind. *"You're letting her get to you when you shouldn't!"*

It felt painfully obvious that Erienne was playfully toying with Aiden. At least, that's what it would have looked like to anyone else who didn't truly know him growing up. A girl interested in him? The only time any girl, with the exception of Theresa, would talk to him during elementary and middle school was when they thought he could do their homework for them.

But this was different. Just by their simple interactions with each other alone he could tell that Erienne didn't give off the air of a popular girl who only wanted someone to do her homework. A wave of confusing feelings swelled up in his head the more he thought about it. He wanted to know more about her.

No, it was more than want. He had to know more about her and who she truly is.

That would have to wait until after class though. As the algebra teacher had no intent of letting them talk in class, aside from asking questions or providing answers. This was what Aiden despised the most when it came to his math classes. The restrictions of what was allowed and what wasn't allowed. The only kind of lessons Aiden could think of that were more restrictive were Garrett's physical training exercises.

"Listen up." The teacher spoke out, breaking Aiden's train of thoughts. "I forgot to mention this at the beginning of the class, but all the teachers have been instructed by the local law enforcement that all of you are to be wary of this cult going around. Personally I think it's a load of hogwash, but I trust that each of you isn't stupid enough to join this "Dark Eye" fad going around."

The room was dead silent at the mere mention of the cult. The mere silence in the room was so intense that he could have dropped a needle and it would have been the only sound. Aiden glanced over to his classmates and saw that each had the same shared expression. He became quite familiar with that look ever since the events at the Academy.

Absolute terror.

Aiden began to slowly realize something about the growing fear of the Dark Eye Cult. Despite working from the shadows, they were beginning to accomplish a goal. To strike fear into the hearts of the human populace. Several students turned to one another as they began to talk loudly over one another.

"The Dark Eye?" One cried out. "Aren't they really scary?"

"I hear that they have branches all over the continent..." Another spoke out.

"My friend says that they're getting recruits every single day!"

"I heard that they actually have killed people, in broad daylight!"

"For real?! Are they going to take down society itself?!"

"Settle down!" The teacher ordered. "I didn't give you all permission to speak out so loudly!"

Aiden felt a shiver run down his spine as the students continue to share their fears about the cult. They talked back and forth about what the cult members did, where the leaders were recruiting them from, where they meet, and the most outlandish thing Aiden's heard, live sacrifices to some 'god' for power. Some of the students started to tremble as the conversation about the cult continued. Unease filled the room as the teacher tried to regain order.

Somebody had to do something.

"ENOUGH!"

Everyone stopped at the loud shout. Everyone of them, the teacher included, turned their heads to the person.

That person, was Aiden, who stood up from his seat.

"Mr. Russell, do you mind explaining why you decided to shout so?" The teacher asked.

"I'm sorry sir," Aiden quickly apologized. "But the only way to get everyone's attention was to do that. You can chew me out later, but this has to be said right now." He turned back to his classmates, all of them had their eyes glued on him. "Everyone, listen. I know that you're all terrified about what Dark Eye Cult. Hell, I'm scared of them too. But what all of you are doing right now is exactly what they want you to do. To be afraid, to panic, and inadvertently cause mayhem throughout the school. If you let yourself be consumed by fear, then they will have achieved what they wanted."

The students all looked surprised at Aiden. How he had brought the entire panic induced room to a halt by a simple speech. Even Aiden had to admit, he never thought he would speak out like that. One of the students quirked his eyebrow at Aiden.

"And why should we believe a word you say?" He asked. "You're not exactly popular you know."

"Does that really even matter?" Aiden retorted. "In the end of the day they don't care whose popular or not, right? The best thing we can do is just try to remain calm and find some hope in the police that they'll stop them from getting into our school."

Just when the student was about to argue back at him, the teacher cleared his throat to get their attention.

"Yes. Thank you for that rousing speech, Mr. Russell. But I do believe that it is time to return to class so I can finish my point?"

Aiden gave a short nod as he slid back into his chair. The rest of the students also began to calm down as they each turned their attention back to the teacher. A wave of relief filled Aiden's body as he sat down. Never before in his life did he have to do what Theresa would have done if she was in the room with him. At least her response would have gotten a more positive reception.

"Now then, class." The teacher continued, "I'm certain you all know that if you see anything suspicious from any student in this school, you are to tell the administration immediately."

Aiden thought to himself as he listened to the teacher ramble on about what his class was suppose to do and not suppose to do. It was almost comical to him that they were told to 'report' any activity from suspected cult members. What the hell could they even do to cult members that had access to magic? The entire thing sounded like some kind of PR stunt from the school board.

The bad mood he was feeling began to lift off his mind though as her felt Erienne lay her head on his shoulder. Aiden wanted to pull his shoulder away from her but she gave him a kind smile as their eyes met with one another. She then leaned her lips up to his ear and whispered.

"I thought that was very inspiring. You sounded like a very cool leader right there, Ragnakin."

Again there was that strange word. As much as he wanted to ask her what she meant by that word, he couldn't. His heart began to race within his chest and his face turned dark red, distracting him from flat out asking her what that word meant. Aiden shook his head though as he tried to pull himself away from Erienne.

"Knock it off." He told her in a hushed whisper. "We're in class."

"Knock what off?" She asked before tilting her head. "I'm just showing you my gratitude."

Aiden sighed as he rubbed his eyebrows. It was like Erienne was deliberately trying to get the two of them into trouble. He wanted to tell her why, but his keen eyes caught the glimpse of the teacher turning back to the board.

"We'll talk after class." He whispered to her before facing back to his textbook.

Erienne had a big grin on her lips at his promise as she paid attention to her own textbook. In all honesty, Aiden was looking forward to the end of the class more than she was. If he could find out any more information about her, it would make things a lot easier for him to explain to Theresa and the others.

After an hour of lecturing from the teacher, first period finally came to an end. Aiden was more than happy to join his fellow students as they all rushed towards the door. As they all piled out of the classroom, Aiden felt Erienne grab onto his arm from behind and lean into him. Determined not to have a shade of red come across his cheeks, he cleared his throat at her.

"Do you mind?" He asked, trying to sound intimidating. "People are gonna get the wrong idea if they see you hanging onto my arm like that."

"Why's that a bad thing?" Erienne retorted with a happy smile. "I think everyone should know that I adore you, Ragnakin."

"*Adore?*" Aiden's eyes shrunk at that. "We barely have even talked to one another that much, how can you adore me if you barely even know me?"

"Spoilers~" She replied in a song tone. Aiden groaned in frustration as she nuzzled her face into his bicep. "Besides, who would get upset about you and I, Ragnakin?"

"*I can think of at least one person.*" Aiden thought as he tried to imagine Theresa's reaction to this situation.

Oh God. That realization had suddenly hit him like a ton of bricks landing on top of his head. Theresa! If she saw Erienne hanging onto his arm like this, if she took things the wrong way...oh the trouble he would get himself into with her about this! This was bad. Oh this was really really bad.

"Hey, Erienne." He spoke out, his voice sounding a bit worried. "What...what do you view me as?"

Erienne blinked as she pulled herself away from his arm. She scratched her chin for awhile before eventually giving him a kind smile.

"I view as a very important person to me, Ragnakin. Why do you ask?"

"Just...how important am I to you?"

Erienne frowned as he asked her that question. The confusion in her eyes felt like a sharp knife had just ran through Aiden's heart as she tilted her head at him.

"You're...you're very important to me...but.." Her eyes looked like they were about to swell up with tears. "Am I not important to you, Ragnakin?"

"I-I didn't say that." Aiden quickly answered. "I was just wondering why...well, why I am so important to you. Especially since we've barely even spoken that much before."

Erienne sighed before a small smile came back to her lips. The black haired girl gently flicked his forehead before giggling.

"Dummy." She said. "It's because you're the first person who wasn't mean to me."

Aiden let a frown come across his lips when he heard that information. Mean to her? What did she mean by that? By all accounts Erienne was, despite her odd tendencies, a nice young woman. Why would anyone treat her poorly? Just another tidbit of information that just added to the already deepening mystery.

"You really are going to make this hard for me to figure out anything about you, aren't you?"

"Heh, sorry. I'm just that kind of girl."

Erienne winked at him before simply leaning into his shoulder once more with a tranquil smile. Several of the students walking by the two of them gave Aiden confused looks at the interaction. It wasn't enough that things felt awkward before, but now there were prying eyes all around them. Aiden cleared his throat loudly as he moved his arm away from Erienne's head.

"You don't have to do that all the time you know." Erienne tilted her head in bewilderment at that.

"But your arm is soft to lean on. And it feels safe."

"Y-Yeah? Wait, no. It's just that you can't."

"Why not?"

"Um..."

"Aiden Jerome Russell!" A new voice called out in shock from behind them.

Aiden felt ever hair on the back of his neck rise up at the cry. He slowly turned his head back to look over his shoulder. It wasn't Theresa. But it was Liza. And based on her expression, he could tell right away that she was taken aback by the sight of him with someone other than Theresa.

Did she HAVE to use his middle name though to get his attention though?

Liza stormed over to the duo, looking back and forth between Aiden and Erienne. Befuddlement was all over her face as she tried to take in that Aiden was with a completely different girl. Or for that matter, a girl that was with him that **wasn't** Theresa! Every single part of Aiden's body felt like it had frozen as his friend glared daggers right into his very soul.

"Who, is this?" She asked.

"N-Now hang on!" Aiden started, flailing his arms in front of him like she was about to launch right at him. "Before you go assuming anything, you need to know Liz, you have the wrong idea!"

"WRONG IDEA?" Liza repeated as she leaned up to him. "You're telling me that seeing you with a different girl other than Theresa isn't the wrong idea?!"

"Liz, keep your voice down!"

"And why should I?! For the entire time I've known you there I've never seen you with any other girl besides Thes! I never thought you would-"

"LIZ!" Aiden interrupted her. "For the love of God, you're overreacting! I swear it's not what it looks like!"

"Um…" Erienne's voice cut in between the two of them. "I hate to interrupt but…what are you yelling at him for?"

Liza turned her gaze to Erinne. Her short blonde hair could have been standing up from the anger she was feeling.

"You. Hussy." Liza spat. "I don't know who you think you are, but if you think for a moment that you are just going to come and take Aiden as your own, you got another thing coming."

"Take him as my own?" Erienne blushed. "I don't think…"

"Okay. That's enough." Aiden quickly pulled the two of them apart. "Liza, there's a lot that you don't know about with this girl."

"I'll say." Liza remarked. "I never took you as this kind of guy at all Aiden."

"Would you stop screaming that for a moment and listen?" Aiden spat as he leaned into Liza's ear and whispered. "This girl, I saw her in the forest before! She's the one that saved us when we fell into the river!"

Liza blinked at this as her entire body language began to change.

"What are you talking about?" She whispered back.

"Don't you remember when we fell? Like, two summers ago at that camp?"

"Oh right. That." Liza grumbled. "No one likes remembering that."

"Shut up and listen." Aiden said. "I know this sounds crazy, but she was there to pull us both out of the river we fell into. It was her that healed our wounds, which need I remind you could have been life threatening."

"And you trust her?" Liza asked.

"It's not that I trust her, it's just I barely even know anything about her." He frowned. "She's the one who seems to think there's something there."

"Aiden. She's hanging off your arm like you just confessed your feelings to her."

"Y-Yeah. I know." Aiden grumbled. "All I did was tell Harold to back off when he was trying to hit on her."

Liza's eyes went flat with a displeased look at that confession. Aiden felt a chill run down his spine as she tapped her foot at him.

"Are you telling me that you were trying to 'white knight' for her when that slimeball was attempting to hit on her?"

"In my defense, he was about to make a scene!"

Liza face palmed at that confession and a audible groan escaped her lips.

"Dammit, Aiden."

"Oh please, you and I both know that you would have done the same thing if you were there too."

"Um." Erienne interjected. "Are you two still whispering over there?"

Both of them turned back to her in that moment. While Aiden had told Liza that there was nothing going on between the two of them, the suspecting look in Liza's eyes never changed once as she tapped her foot at the new girl. Erienne tilted her head at the action in confusion.

"Is something wrong with your foot? It's not hurting is it?"

"No it's...hey don't try to change the subject here!" Liza replied as she folded her arms. "I don't know what you're trying to pull, but if you think that you can just come in and take Aiden-"

"Would you PLEASE stop saying it like that?" Aiden snapped back. "You really got the wrong idea here."

"Aiden, I saw her hanging off your arm like a lost puppy."

"That doesn't automatically make her my girlfriend though!"

"Then what do YOU call it?"

As the two of them bickered with one another for a moment, the rest of the students that were walking past them quirked eyebrows at the arguing duo. Each reaction was different from the other but all of them each were perplexed by their spat. Aiden and Liza barely noticed their looks though. Not like any of them could have started any kind of rumors about the two of them without Liza shutting them down immediately. That was just one of the many perks Aiden gained with having a popular friend like her.

Granted right now he wanted nothing more from her other than for her to shut her mouth about a simple misunderstanding.

"You two are going to make a scene." Erienne mumbled loud enough for the two of them to hear.

"Not my fault that she read the scene the wrong way." Aiden replied as he folded his arms across his chest. Liza pursed her lips up.

"Oh yeah? What do you think Theresa would say if she saw some random girl hanging off your arm?"

"What girl?" Theresa's voice cut through them. Aiden felt himself shudder at that question.

Both of them turned to face Theresa and swallowed nervous lumps in their throats.

"You do realize you both look like idiots arguing in the hallway, right? Anyway, Aiden...who is she talking about?"

"T-Thes, I can explain!" Aiden said as he put his hands up. "It's a grave misunderstanding on Liza's part-"

"She was literally hanging off your arm!"

"Shut it Liz! Seriously, though, this girl was just-"

Theresa put a hand up in front of him before pointing behind him. Aiden swallowed a lump in his throat as he glanced over his shoulder.

Erienne was gone.

THE SYMBOL

"*B*ut..." Aiden stammered. "She...she was right here!"

Once again, at a critical moment, Erienne had left without explanation. This time though, Aiden wasn't the only one who knew she was right there. Liza, forgetting what she had accused Aiden of, couldn't believe it either. Both of them looked at one another before they faced Theresa. The white dragoness had a very displeased look on her face as she tapped her foot.

"If you two are just trying to get out of going to classes..." She started.

"That's not it at all!" Liza interrupted. "Theresa, I swear to you, she was right here!"

"It's not an excuse to not go to classes, Thes." Aiden added in. "There really was a girl here!"

Theresa sighed as she reached up to Aiden's ear and grabbed it. A sharp pain erupted through his ear as Aiden let out a small yelp. She may not have been as muscular as Garrett, but Aiden had forgotten until that moment how she was still really strong like Garrett. Her grip was ironclad, Aiden could not pull himself out of of it.

"Listen very well." She said slowly. "If you are making an excuse, I swear I will make certain that Garrett's training next time is ten times tougher than it already."

"I swear! I'm not getting involved with anyone!" Aiden managed to sputter out as he tried to pull away.

"He's not lying, Thes." Liza spoke out as the white haired teen looked over to her now. "There was a girl here before. She was latching herself onto his arm like they were going out with one another."

Theresa quirked an eyebrow as she looked right back at Aiden. He could have sworn that her eyes had started to burn with her signature white fire at that.

"Aiden Russell, is there someone that you haven't told ME about?"

"Hell no!" Aiden said as she finally let his ear go. "Come on, do I look like the type of guy who would hide a girlfriend from anyone?"

"I dunno. You never even talk about wanting a girlfriend." Theresa responded.

"Theresa, have you met me? What girl would want to date ME of all people?"

A small giggle escaped Liza's lips at their little spat with one another.

"You know what? Maybe I'm mistaken. There's no way that Aiden would go out with someone else with the way you two act around each other."

"AND JUST WHAT IS THAT SUPPOSE TO MEAN?!" Aiden and Theresa both shouted with dark red cheeks.

"Now whose making a scene?" Liza jested before looking at her phone real fast. "Oh crap, we gotta get going to our next class guys!"

"This discussion is not over." Theresa warned them as she took Aiden by the wrist. "Let's go."

As the trio separated to head to their next class, Aiden couldn't help but keep his eyes on the spot where Erienne last was. She couldn't have vanished so quickly. Not naturally at least. A frown crept to his lips as confusion spread through his mind. She was right there. He could even feel her standing close to him while he and Liza argued.

He should have guessed that something like this would have happened though. After all this wasn't the first time that she had suddenly vanished.

Aiden felt a tingly sensation run up the back of his spine as a thought ran through his mind. What if she was hiding something from him? And, even worse thought plagued his mind now at the mere thought of her hiding something. She could even be a member of the Dark Eye Cult running around the country.

How could she be a member of that group? She was such a kind, sweet girl, if a little weird. There was no way someone like her could be a member of the Dark Eye. She was just an ordinary...well, maybe not ordinary girl.

Perhaps it was better, for now, that he kept her out of his mind and focus on the rest of the first day. Thankfully his hardest class was already over with. The rest would prove to be nowhere near as challenging. Even the dreaded gym class that once made him cower at the very thought of it was cakewalk. Hell, he didn't fear Eric anymore after everything he had gone through.

The one person that he did fear though, was Theresa. She was not known to be the kind of person to lose her temper, but when something upset her there would be a price to pay. Aiden knew her well enough to know that the one thing she hated more than evil was being tricked, or lied to. And the latter was something he began to wonder if she thought that he had lied to him about Erienne.

"Note to self. Try to explain who Erienne is to her, or attempt to keep her in the same room so Theresa knows I'm not lying." He thought. *"And make certain Liza never makes another scene like that again."*

The rest of the school day passed by slowly without much of a problem. Something that Aiden felt didn't happen often when it came to the mundane tasks that school life gave students. But at the same time, he never thought he would end up missing it after what happened at the mage academy. Now that was something he never thought he would secretly admit to himself.

As the last class of the first day began to wind down, Aiden felt an uneasy tension start to rise up both around and within him. He couldn't put his finger on it but it seemed like there was something foul at work. Like there was something, or someone, waiting for the right moment to attack. Aiden laughed to himself as he shook his head. It was probably just his imagination at work again. First day of school was always so dull that he always imagined something dreadful was about to happen.

Regardless of how dull the school day was though, it was still hard for Aiden to not picture the destroyed hallways and classrooms of the mage academy. The claw marks on the walls, the sense of dread, the foul odor, and last but not least, the demons. Aiden felt a shiver run down his spine the more he thought about it. Every single species of the Shadow Demons were ones that could haunt the nightmares of any regular human for the rest of their days.

"Dammit, get out of my head already!" He thought. *"I refuse to let you ruin my life!"*

Was this what it was like to have post traumatic stress disorder? Was Aiden going to have to accept that he would never be rid of the horrible images he saw? There were too many questions that came to his mind, and the answers just didn't come to him.

He found himself looking up to the clock on the wall, watching at the clock hands slowly ticked away. Aiden groaned at the sight of the big hand. It read one twenty-five PM. 25 more minutes of waiting for the first day to end.

Despite it being a very slow day, the start of it wasn't so bad at least. He finally knew the name of the mystery girl. Aiden felt a small smile come to his lips as he thought about her. Erienne. Such a beautiful and unique name. It matched the odd beauty that she had herself perfectly. As the teacher rambled on about the class and what to expect, Aiden began to think about where she was now. If she was in a room that wasn't that far off, or if she had vanished again.

Aiden grinned at the thought of running into her again. For some reason she just intrigued him.

But as he just began to daydream, it was cut short from a jab in the back.

"Oi. Aiden." Theresa said. "Are you done spacing out?"

G-Gah!" Aiden turned to her. "I wasn't daydreaming at all!"

"Don't try to play dumb to me. You're bored out of your mind." Theresa grinned as she folded her arms. "Besides, I know you too well. You want out of here so we can get back home as soon as possible. Right?"

"...I..." Aiden sighed as he looked off. "It's more complicated than that." He whispered, his hands balling up into fists.

There was no need for words that had to be spoke between them to describe what was on his mind. Theresa knew. His hunched over shoulders, his tightened muscles, and clenched fists was all she needed to see. With no words, she gently placed an arm around him and pulled him into a reassuring hug.

"It's going to be okay." She whispered. "You are not alone. Just remember that. You'll get through this."

Aiden began to feel the stress within him begin to die down, slightly at her voice. A soft sigh escape his lips, followed by a serene smile. It was just like Theresa to speak kind words like that. Aiden had to guess they came from her past experience as a leader of an entire dragonic army.

He almost laughed to himself the more he thought about how good she was at being a leader. Never once, when he was growing up, did he ever imagine that the Theresa he knew from childhood was at one point in her life the absolute commander of a Dragon King's giant army. It was hard to picture her all dressed up in heavy metal armor giving orders in a war torn battlefield during the old days of the Kingdoms.

But despite finding that hard to believe, Aiden knew first hand that Theresa's leadership skills were second to none.

"Thanks, Thes."

"Any time, Aide."

The calm and relaxing moment of the last class of the first day of school was one that even those who dreaded the first day of school could not help but wish would last for awhile longer.

But life is cruel. And calm moments between friends end just as quickly as they began.

An ear piercing scream rang out from the hallway outside their classroom. Theresa and Aiden both turned their heads towards the door, it was slightly ajar. Had it been like that for the past few minutes? Someone must have gotten up to go to the bathroom before class ended, that was the only logical explanation. Regardless of why it was left slightly open, the entire class stood up and began to rush towards the doorway.

When they saw what it was that was the source of the terrified scream, most of them wished they had not left their chairs.

"Please take your seats!" The teacher called out, following her students. "The bell hasn't rung yet and...Oh my God!"

Aiden didn't blame his fellow classmates or the teacher for their reaction. A freshman girl was on her knees, hands over her mouth and tears falling down from sheer terror, stared at what was before her.

Laying there with his back to the wall, and head hunched over, was one of the security officers the school had hired. An older man to say the least, but his age was not what everyone was screaming about. Behind him, streaks of blood poured down the wall. And then Aiden saw where it had come from.

A large hole right in his chest, precisely where his heart would be, bled out onto the wall behind him and over his shirt. And right above the streaks of blood was a symbol. Aiden felt his blood turn cold the moment his eyes spotted it.

It was the sigil of the Dark Eye.

As each classroom in the hallway was emptied, more teenagers screamed in terror at the horrible sight. The teachers did their best to try and control the panic, but the shouts drowned out their attempts. Terror had already taken control of the students as they tried to make a dash towards the front of the hallway.

Their attempt was blocked off by a group of security guards. All younger than the one who was dead before the students.

"Everyone! Please return to your classrooms!" A security officer cried out. "Remain calm and return to your classes! Please, do not panic!"

Aiden shook his head at their attempts to get control of the situation. Don't panic? How could they seriously expect a bunch of teenagers who had never seen something like this to not panic? But at the same time, he couldn't blame his fellow students for their reactions at seeing someone dead before them.

He remembered the day he had seen Samael's work in the harpy den. The missing hikers that he had killed, just to prove a point to his sister, Lilith. It was a horrible sight that made Aiden realize the dangers of the world.

But not even Samael would have killed someone in this matter. At least, not in broad daylight. Nor would he have left a mark behind him to taunt his foes. Aiden clenched his fists tightly as the students tried to scurry their way back into their classrooms. As they did he found himself turning to Theresa. The white dragoness shared the same look of shock plastered over his face.

She turned back to him, nodding slowly as they went back to their class with the rest of their fellow students.

Once everyone was seated in their chairs, the teacher left the room momentarily to talk to the security guards about what they should do next. Aiden felt a vibration go off in his left pocket.

His cell phone.

He didn't waste any time. Aiden took his phone out and noticed that he had received a message from Theresa. Without even thinking he opened the message up and read it to himself.

It read "Text only. I don't want anyone to hear us."

Aiden nodded his head as he replied.

"Are you thinking what I'm thinking?'

"Yes. Somebody here is a member of the Dark Eye Clan."

"How the hell did they get past the security here? For that matter the cameras should have seen them attacking and killing the security guard."

"My guess, strong magic. Very, strong magic. Magic that can trick the eyes of humans into seeing something that's not there."

Aiden felt a shiver run down his spine at that. He knew only a few beings that were capable of using such magic. Dimitri and his student, Raven. But would either of them have gone out of their way to truly kill like this? To send a simple warning? He began to reply back to Theresa.

"You don't think it was Dimitri do you? Or Raven? I know they're powerful in the dark arts, but Dimitri wouldn't be THAT bold to attack in broad daylight, right?"

"No. I don't believe it was him." Theresa's response read back.

"Then who, Thes?"

"My guess is that this is someone else's work, but it's clear that whoever they are, they are in allegiance with Dimitri. That kind of hole wasn't made from a magical spell. Something stabbed him through his entire chest."

The back hair on Aiden's neck began to rise up. He could hardly imagine something being that terrifying existing. But then, realization came to his mind

"Do you think it's a Prime Demon?" He texted Theresa.

For a moment, there was silence from her. Then, a response.

"Yes. I do believe that it's possible that the killer was a Prime Demon."

Aiden swallowed a lump in his throat as he recalled the Teleranta from the mage academy. It certainly was one of the more terrifying things he had seen during that adventure. But he knew right away that they could rule out the fact that it was a Teleranta. They were too massive to fit into a school like this. The only kind of Prime Demons that could fit into the hallways were ones like Kali.

He gasped as he began to text Theresa again.

"Do you think it was a member of Kali's species?"

"No. Kali's kind, the Laminas, don't have the type of weapons or appendages to kill someone like that. But if there's anyone who knows about what kind of Prime Demon this is, it will be that snake."

Aiden had to agree that if anyone would know what kind of Prime Demon there was that could have killed the security guard in that fashion, Kali would be the one to know. As evil, and down right mythic bitch, as she could be, the lamina had proven that she was knowledgeable about demon species. She would be their best bet to knowing what kind of demon had killed the poor soul.

"Aiden. Listen." Theresa's next text responded. "When we get on the bus, keep any chat about what happened to text only. The moment you can, delete this entire conversation from our logs. I don't want our parents finding out about this."

"Thes, they're gonna hear the news anyway! This is gonna be over every news station in the county!"

"And that's exactly why I don't want them to see these logs. Could you even imagine your poor mother and father's reaction to seeing this chat log above this subject? They might think we're part of the Dark Eye."

Aiden frowned. Like it or not, Theresa had a point about this. This was the kind of situation that no one would want their family to find out about. Hell, Aiden had been hiding the fact that he had been training in secret behind his parents' back for two years now. What's one more secret to hide?

But this wasn't a little secret. This one was massive.

Part of him felt his stomach begin to tie up in a knot at the mere thought of it being discovered from his parents. They would certainly, without a doubt, stop him from talking to Theresa and his friends again, and take back Warfang from him. Hell, he could even imagine his father locking his entire house up to not let Aiden out ever again.

He didn't like it. But at the same time, what choice did he have?

"Understood." He texted back, a frown over his face. "I don't like the idea of doing this, but you're right about this Theresa. They can't know."

"Good. Now get ready, I'm going to form a group chat with the others."

Aiden nodded as he backed out of the chat with Theresa before opening the group chat that they had formed with the rest of their friends. Aiden swallowed a lump as Theresa's message appeared.

"We have a problem."

Liza's response was automatic.

"What the HELL is going on?!" It read. "Did I hear right that someone was killed?!"

"Yes." Theresa responded. "A security guard, looked to be in his late forties, early fifties."

"What the hell killed him?" Liza's text asked.

"We don't know." Aiden answered. "Theresa and I think that it was some kind of Prime Demon."

"A Prime Demon?!"

"Yes, we don't know what kind of Prime Demon it is, but I have a feeling that it's one on Kali's level." Theresa answered.

Then Seamus began to reply

"A Prime Demon? In your school? Rexkin this is very bad."

"It gets worse." Aiden added. "Above the security guard's body, drawn with his own blood, was the Sigil of the Dark Eye.

"Dammit. That makes things more complicated." Seamus responded.

"*Way more than just complicated, Seamus.*" Aiden thought, just as he was about to reply, he noticed that Kali had responded now.

"How was the victim killed?" She asked.

Aiden and Theresa looked at each other for a moment, then nodded as Aiden began his response.

"Through the chest. It looked like it pierced his heart and removed it from his body too."

"I see." Kali responded quietly.

"Out with it, snake." Theresa's next text came. "You know what kind of demon did this, didn't you?"

"Oh I do, little lizard." Kali responded. "Perhaps I will tell you, perhaps I will not. But I can tell you one thing, it is not for this clumsy way of communication that the humans have made."

"I'm scared..." Aello's text read.

"It'll be okay, Aelly." Liza responded quickly.

"Oh I don't think it'll be okay, at least not yet little bird." Kali replied. "All of you come to the apartment later when you are out of school. I may tell you what you want to know."

"Snake, this is NOT the time for you to be cryptic dammit!" Theresa replied. "Someone is dead! Dead!"

"And life will continue on. Where I am from, death is something one expects waking out. Now let's stop the conversation here, unless you want to make things more frustrating to figure out later~."

Aiden and Theresa felt like groaning. It was already impossible to even attempt to get along with her, but she had a point. If they were going to find out any kind of lead about the killer, they were going to have to cooperate with Kali and listen to what she had to say. Aiden turned his head back to Theresa, who was already texting back with a disgruntled look on her face.

"Fine. But you better tell us everything about what kind of Prime Demon could have done this, snake."

"You'll see." Kali responded. "For now, try not to get killed out there, darlings."

Aiden could hear Theresa mutter some kind of curse in draconic tongue that he did not understand. Not that he needed to understand what she was frustrated about though. He would even get frustrated himself about Kali's ways many times.

Despite everything though, Aiden felt his thoughts drifting back to Erienne.

Was she okay? Was she in a safe place in the school where she didn't see the body? And more importantly, would he see her again sometime soon? There was no way in hell that school was going to be open tomorrow after this. Aiden had a gut feeling that classes weren't going to be held for awhile due to this murder.

He clenched his hands at the thought of anyone in the school being killed by the Dark Eye. Innocent people who had nothing to do with the battle Aiden and his friends had fought against Dimitri and Raven.

Aiden turned towards the door of the classroom. The vivid image of the Dark Eye's sigil still burned in his mind's eye as he slowly began to realize the importance of that mark. If the Dark Eye was truly being led by Dimitri, which at this point was looking more likely than ever, then it had one very simple message. It wasn't just to terrify the student body, no. It was clear what it meant to Aiden and his friends.

War.

THE DARK EYE ATTACKS

*a*fter being held for at least an hour at their school, eventually students were allowed to go home. Aiden's class had to leave a different way to get to their buses, while other students were picked up by their parents or guardians. The entire ride back to their home was nothing but tension and nerves for every student. Who could blame them though? On the very first day of school there was a murder. One that had shaken every student down to the core, even Eric and his cronies didn't try to cause trouble out of sheer fear that they would be next.

Aiden and Theresa sat close together on the bus ride home, the latter holding Aiden's hand tightly, throughout the entire ride. Everyone in their group now had to be vigilant. The Dark Eye had proven that they were willing to kill to make their point. They all feared that it wouldn't be long until killings started to happen in broad daylight next.

The hairs on the back of Aiden's neck stood up the more he thought about the dead body of the security guard. The vivid image of his body, complete with a hole, still burnt into his mind. He knew that school killings had happened before in the past. When he was growing up he would hear on the news about another shooting at a school, and how he thanked whatever deity there was that it never happened to his schools.

But this was different from a school shooting. And the worst part was that Aiden felt like he had seen *worse*.

He clenched his teeth as he gave Theresa a tight squeeze on her her hand. The memories from what Ivan did still fresh in his mind. The latter returned the squeeze with her own before glancing back to him. Her emerald green eyes flaring with a mixture of different emotions.

Aiden had gotten use to seeing Theresa's eyes like this. So much so that he was able to tell at least three of the many emotions she was feeling right now. Fear. Anger. Concern. They were all but small parts of how the white dragoness felt at that moment. He knew better than to dare question how she was truly feeling.

The biggest problem came with how they were going to get to Aello's apartment after they got off the bus. No doubt their parents would be waiting for them at home to make certain that they were safe. Aiden had a brief image of seeing his mother and father lock up the entire house to prevent him from leaving until it was clear for the students to return back to class.

He even doubted that making magic clones to cover for their positions would work either. Every parent who had a child go to any high school in the local area would be on high alert right now. There was no way in the world there would be any sneak outs from any of the students that went to his high school tonight.

"Thes." He said finally, in a volume that was barely above a whisper. "How the hell are we going to meet up with the others tonight?"

There was a moment of silence between them for a moment, before his question was answered.

"Pay attention to your phone tonight." She responded, her voice calm and collected. Like she was still in control of the situation. "I'll work something out."

That was just like her. Even when things were at their worse for them, Theresa had some kind of plan being formed in her head. A strong trait of hers, it was no wonder that she was the leader of not only the Trinity, but their entire friend group.

It felt like an eternity, but they finally arrived at their bus stop. Both of them nodded to each other as they stood up, releasing their hands from one another as they stepped off. Sure enough, both of their parents were waiting for them at the bus stop.

"Theresa!" A slightly middle aged woman with long blonde hair cried out as she grabbed her tightly. It wasn't hard to guess that this was Theresa's mother. Or rather, her human mother. Sonya Goldwin. "Oh sweetie, are you okay?! They didn't hurt or upset you did they?!"

"N-No, mom. I'm fine." Theresa responded back to her as she returned the hug. "They didn't question anyone from our classroom, I promise."

"They damn better not have." A bruly shouldered man with a mustache and fading brown hair said. Aiden always swallowed a lump whenever he laid eyes upon Theresa's father. Edward Goldwin. His eyes, much like his hair, were starting to fade a bit, but they were every bit as green as his daughter's. "What kind of police force keeps our children at a school for longer than they should have? I outta have words with that damn police department about this."

"Daddy, please." Theresa said quietly. "They were just doing their job..."

"Your daughter is right, Edward." Aiden's father said. "Our two kids just went through a hell of an event today. Perhaps we shouldn't make them feel more tense they already are?"

Edward nearly let out a scoff of arrogance at his statement, but nodded his head regardless. The burly man turned back to face Aiden's father.

"You're right, Connor. I know that they're doing their job, but they wouldn't even allow us to come pick our children up ourselves. We have every right to take care of our children, especially in a moment like this."

"Daddy..." Theresa blushed at her father's overprotectiveness, "I promise, I can take care of myself."

"You can do MORE than just take care of yourself." Aiden thought to himself at his friend's statement. His thoughts were cut short though the moment he felt his mother pull him in close.

"Oh my boy!" Helena said quickly. "I'm so happy that you weren't hurt or attacked today! I mean, I hate to think what that poor man's family is feeling right now but if anything were to happen to you..."

"M-Mom." Aiden managed to breathe out. "Can't breathe."

That did little to stop Helena from squeezing her soon too tightly.

She pulled away for a moment before looking over his face with her hands.

"You didn't get hurt? You saw no one attack that man? Anything?"

"Mom, I promise, I'm okay..." He managed to say. Though he frowned. "I...I mean I'm as okay as you can be seeing a dead body like that..."

"Bah!" Edward scoffed. "If I was the head of security at that school, I would have made certain that no teen was exposed to that! Unprofessional I say!"

"Daaaaad...." Theresa groaned. "You're doing it again."

"Hmph. You'll understand one day girl." He said to her. "Now then, come on, back home!"

Aiden and Theresa both gave their parents short nods of acceptance as they began to separate from one another. As they went their different ways, Aiden looked over his shoulder to get a quick glance at her. Just like him, Theresa glanced over her shoulder back at him for a single moment. She gave him a short head nod before turning her attention back to her parents.

"Text me tonight. Please." He thought to himself as he and his parents made their way back to their house.

The evening that followed proved to be one of the most tense that the Russell household had ever felt. All over every news station was the story about what had happened today. Multiple interviews with different students were shown, as well as interviews with different security guards were shown as well.

It made Aiden furious at seeing how many of his fellow classmates were terrified out of their minds. Like they were going to be the next target of the Dark Eye cult. During dinner he got so mad that he nearly broke his drinking glass by squeezing it too hard.

He wasn't the only one on edge about what had happened. The entire night Aiden noticed that both of his parents kept their eyes on him. His mother would often bring him food, sometimes a bit more than was necessary, and his father would make attempts to start a normal conversation about his likes to get Aiden's mind off of the subject.

Aiden admitted, it was nice to have his parents try so hard to help him think about something else. But it did little to alleviate the horrifying image of the guard from his head. And the fact that whoever murdered him used his own blood to draw the cult's sigil on the wall. It was by far the one thing that made it almost as terrible as what he saw at the mage academy.

Still, it was nice to know that even though his parents had no idea as to what he was really doing in his spare time that they were there to help him feel a bit better. It did bring a twinge of joy to his heart to see his father ask what books he was reading, or what he found at the flea market that would have been to his fancy as well. Though he would be lying if he said that it didn't catch him off guard. Aiden's father had never really been one to show that much interest in fantasy stories. He must have been really concerned for his son if he went out of his way to attempt a conversation with him about it.

That at least confirmed one thing for Aiden. His father was by far better than Ivan.

As the evening passed on, Aiden would eventually take his leave from his mother and father's company back to his own room. There he plopped himself down into his computer chair and let out a massive sigh. The hours felt like they had been agonizingly slow as he pulled his cell phone out of his pocket to stare at the blank screen.

Still no new messages from anyone in the group. He gave himself a short nod as he opened up a small group chat with him, Liza, and Theresa in it. The messages from earlier having long been deleted, like Theresa told him to do so. It had been hours since they had all spoken last. If there was any chance to check up with his friends it would have been now.

"Are you two okay?" He texted them. "It's been hours, but mom and dad finally let me head off to my room for privacy."

Once his message was sent, a new message shortly followed after it. Liza. She was always the fastest typer out of them.

"Ugh. Finally." Her text read. "I thought my dad wouldn't leave me alone!"

"Sounds like you were in for it just as long as I was…"

"I am willing to bet I was going to be held in the living room for the rest of my life! Dad refused to even let me walk towards the bathroom by myself!"

"TMI, Liz…"

"Sorry. It's just, it's so frustrating! He kept asking if I saw the body and if I had anyone after me or if there was someone from the past that I made fun of that might be a member of the Dark Eye Cult. Ugh! Please tell me that we'll be leaving soon!"

"Hell if I know. I've been waiting for Thes to text us with some kind of instructions of when we head out to the apartment."

"How the hell are we going to meet up with everyone tonight? With what happened to that security guard, our parents won't let us out of their sights for weeks!"

"If Seamus was here? Use those magic clone things to trick our parents I bet."

"Oh like hell that'll work for us now!"

A new text came into the group chat now, Aiden felt a small smile come to his lips as he read it. Theresa.

"Both of you calm down." Her text started off. "I finally got a chance to get away from my parents as well."

"Sorry Thes, but this is so frustrating!" Liza replied. "I have a feeling that we're gonna be on TLM tonight!"

Aiden groaned at that short abbreviation that Liza had came up with. TLM, as he would come to learn from her, meant one thing. Total Lockdown Mode. As stupid as the abbreviation was, he knew that she was right about it.

"I know. My father wanted to make certain that everything is locked tonight. He even bothered to come into MY room to make certain I did so. But we can't complain about that now. We have bigger things to be concerned about."

"The Dark Eye Cult..." Aiden texted. "I can't believe they would do such a thing."

"Never underastimate a cult's will to do such terrible things, Aiden." Theresa responded. "We'll talk about them at the apartment, it'll be safer there."

"And just, HOW are we going to sneak out tonight leader girl?" Liza asked.

"Leave that to me. But I need both of you to do something. Make certain that all your lights are off tonight."

Aiden felt himself unconsciously nodding at her order. He had gotten so used to her saying things like that. A small laugh escaped his lips as he thought back to the first class of the day and how he managed to get the entire classroom to calm down.

"She would either be very proud of me for acting like a leader, or chastise me for doing it without her there." He said to himself with a short grin before noticing a new text from her.

"And remember, both of you, delete any conversation about this topic."

Just as Aiden was about to do that, a new message popped up in his notification area. This one was from Liza. A frown crept across his lips as he opened it.

"Don't think that I've forgotten about that girl, Aide."

Aiden sighed at the message as h began to type how it was just a misunderstanding, but stopped halfway as he thought more about it.

Erienne was without a doubt there. He knew she was real. Liza knew she was real. So how come she completely vanished when Theresa approached them? He wasn't naive enough to not believe that it was some kind of magic, clearly she was skilled with using magical arts. What did she have to hide from Aiden that she couldn't be seen by Theresa?

A terrifying thought came to his mind in that moment. Was she the one who killed the guard? Despite the unanswered questions about her personality, it was clear that Erienne was powerful in some regard. Aiden ran a hand over the cheek she gently touched when she saved him and Liza from death. How she was able to not only heal both of their wounds, slightly, but also drag them both out of a roaring river.

"Erienne…" Aiden quietly mumbled to himself as he closed his eyes. "Where the hell are you?"

He sighed before looking back to his phone. He stared at the screen for a brief moment, then quietly deleted the group chat messages.

Once that was done he glanced at the time on his phone's screen. 9 O'clock. If he had to guess, his parents would either turn in tonight early, or be up all night. No way he could blame them if they did the later. He waited a few seconds before he stood up from his chair, then turned off every light in his room, like Theresa had instructed him.

"Okay Aiden," He whispered. "Now we wait."

An hour passed by as he waited for Theresa to come. 10 O'clock. As the minutes passed by, the rest of the neighborhood lights began to die down as well. The waiting was incredibly boring to Aiden. He knew that he couldn't turn on any of his lights, or even pass time by looking online at his phone, as per Theresa's instructions. But that did little to alleviate the boredom he felt by waiting for her.

Another hour passed. 11 O'clock. If his parents hadn't already gone to bed before, they sure as hell had gone to bed now. Aiden thought about texting Theresa to ask where she was, but then there a tapping at his window.

For a moment the hair on the back of his neck stood up on end. He darted towards the window and mentally prepared to summon Warfang and PeaceGuard to his side should he need to have them. But shortly after the tapping came a familiar voice.

"Aiden!" Theresa quietly snapped. "Open the window and get out here!"

He wasted no time in obeying Theresa's orders as he stood up and rushed to the window. After gently prying it open, he slipped himself out of the room before closing the window behind him. Save for the dimly lit street lamps above them, it was pitch black outside. Aiden could barely make out where Theresa was due to the darkness that surrounded them.

"Theresa? You still there?" He asked out.

"Yes, dummy." She flicked his forehead. "I'm not about to leave you alone in the middle of the night like that.

"How did you get out?" He asks. "Did you make one of those magic clone things?"

"No. Not enough time for that. And I can promise you that if I even attempted to cast that spell, mom and dad would have noticed." She replied. "And I'm damn glad that you haven't tried to replicate that same spell. You're not even close to being ready to using that spell."

"So what do we do? We can't just WALK to Aello's apartment!"

"Sh!" She whispered to him. "We'll talk when we're not near the neighborhood, for now, take my hand and follow me."

Aiden wasted no time in doing as she said, quickly taking her hand as they rushed off into the darkness. Away from the street lamps.

Part of Aiden wanted to blurt out the obvious that he couldn't see, but he didn't. He trusted Theresa enough to guide him through the pitch blackness of the night. The only light that he could make out was part of the starry sky above their heads.

He didn't know where they were going, but Aiden got a pretty vague idea where it could have been by the sound of crunching tree branches beneath his feet. The forest. Theresa was dragging him into their old hang out area.

He had several guesses as to why Theresa was taking him to the forest. It was the furthest away from their houses for one thing. Unlike their small neighborhood too, there were no street lamps to expose them to the civilians. Smart move.

After what felt like it was forever, Theresa and Aiden stopped running as they found themselves at the sight of the first battle Aiden had ever been in his life. The old training grounds. The small goblins that Aiden had faced that day were like a small precursor to everything that had happened since that fateful year when Warfang became his blade.

He gave a small smile as he placed his hands on his hips, looking around at it with a sense of nostalgia.

"I know it's been only a few years since that day we killed those goblins, but this feels like a strange home coming, you know?"

"It does, yes. But we can reminisce later." Theresa said to him.

"Right. Sorry." He turned back to her. "How are we going to get to Aello's apartment? Do we warp like we did to get to the Academy?"

"Yes." Theresa simply said to him. "I would have done that to pick you AND Liza up at the same time, but it was too risky. The noise would have alerted both of your parents, and my own, immediately. And taking off in dragon form right now would be a suicidal move. The last thing this country needs to see is one of us in our true forms."

"So you wait for the cover of darkness." Aiden summarized for her.

"Yes." Theresa sighed. "I wish it didn't resort to doing this. But this can not wait until they feel safe enough to go out on our own. This is a matter that must be addressed tonight."

"It would have been easier if Garrett actually had a damn cell phone." Aiden grumbled.

"Not the time, Aide." Theresa said. "We gotta get to the others, and fast."

She held out her hand to him. Aiden wasted no time in taking it before the white haired dragoness turned to a spot before them. With a snap of her fingers, a portal began to open up in front of the duo. It took a few seconds, but soon it was completely opened and before them was Aello's apartment complex.

"I hate this part." Aiden admitted as the two of them took a step towards the portal. Theresa gave him a reassuring hand squeeze as they got closer.

"Just take a deep breath, and close your eyes."

There was some comfort in her words as Aiden took one deep breath and closed his eyes as they entered the portal together. Once they did, the portal closed behind them in that instant. After feeling like his body had been stretched out again by the portal's warp, Aiden and Theresa found themselves outside of Aello's apartment building. Aiden's cheeks had turned a little green from the speed, but he quickly regained his footing before shaking his head a couple of times.

"That. Sucks. So much."

"Save it for another time." Theresa told him as they glanced up to Aello's apartment. "We gotta get to the others."

They wasted no time in rushing up the stairs towards the apartment room. Theresa gave three short knocks at the door. For a moment there was silence. Then the door opened up ever so carefully as a pair of eyes peaked between the crack to see who was there.

It was Mia.

"You're here!" She gasped. "Oh thank the Gods, you managed to get here!"

"Quickly, open the door!" Theresa told her. "We don't know if the Dark Eye is here or not!"

Mia wasted no time in arguing as she opened the door, letting both Aiden and Theresa into the room without complaint. The sight before them made Aiden feel a bit unnerved.

Garrett was standing in one corner, back against the wall, with his arms folded. Aello sat on the couch, clutching a large pillow closely to her body. Gabriella trying her best to make her princess feel safe as she stroked her hair. Kali sat in one of the chairs, looking like she was quite serious for once.

"Where's Seamus?" Theresa asked, noticing that he was still absent.

"Right here, Rexkin."

The group turned their attention to front door. Seamus and Liza stood together, the latter looking like she was just about to go to bed before Seamus arrived to retrieve her. Aello leaped to her feet before literally jumping right at Liza with a tight hug.

"L-Liz!" She managed to get out. "I...I..."

"It's okay." Liza assured her, returning the harpy's embrace. "I'm fine."

"Understatement of the damn century." Kali spoke out, her tongue flicking out between her teeth for a moment. "You were all, VERY lucky today."

"You don't need to point the obvious out, bitch." Liza retorted as she pulled away from Aello. "We just had someone at our frigging school die!"

"And yet the human race continues on." Kali replied. "But that one man's death? It's the first of many. Especially knowing what demon is pulling the strings to your little cult."

The prime demon unfolded her arms as she leaned towards towards Theresa and Aiden. Her eyes seemed to flicker as the usual self lavishing snake began to take the situation seriously. The hairs on Aiden's arm felt like they were rising up just staring right into the lamia's eyes directly on.

"Tell me again." She said slowly. "How was the old man murdered?"

"A hole through the heart." Theresa responded. "We couldn't get close enough to inspect the blow, but from my guess, the killer was incredibly skilled with pinpoint strikes."

"And how large was the hole?" Kali asked.

"About the size of a hockey puck? Maybe a bit bigger?" Aiden added. "We couldn't really get close to the body after all."

"I see..." Kali mused quietly. There was a moment where no one spoke out, right before the prime demon let out a sigh, followed by an annoyed grin. "I'm quite familiar with our perpetrator."

"You ARE?" Liza asked.

"Much to my displeasure, little girl. The blow was precise, pristine, and powerful, something no lesser creature could hope to accomplish, let alone in broad daylight."

She placed her hands on her hips before grinning ever so slightly.

"Your little 'killer' is, quite similar to myself, a Prime Demon."

Aiden felt the color leave his lips. A Prime Demon. Possibly the highest class in the demon pantheon that Aiden had encountered. The memories of the Teleranta still fresh in his mind, the young teen shuddered for a moment before regaining his composure.

"So you're telling me there's another demon like you running around?" Liza asked.

"Another..?" Kali couldn't resist a single arrogant chuckle, "There is no other demon like me, I can assure you of that."

"Focus." Theresa ordered.

"Hn." Kali nodded as she continued on.

"This Prime Demon is nothing like myself. While I am the vision of grace, beauty, and power so perfect that others look upon me and despair that they can never compare, your murderer is a minion of Terror. A skittering menace that thrives on the fear of lesser creatures like yourselves."

The lamia gave a short dark chuckle as her eyes flashed.

"And it would appear that she succeeded in her goal: poisoning your school with fear and panic."

"Do you know specifically who she is?" Theresa asked. "We don't have the time for you to be cryptic!"

Just as Kali was about to speak out, a loud BANG went off down the street. The entire team froze in shock at the explosion, but they all rushed out the apartment and leaned out over the railings. Several other people had done the same thing, many of them screaming in shock at the source of the explosion.

Far off from the apartment building was a burning car. And surrounding that car were several cloaked beings.

The Dark Eye had begun an attack!

WAR BEGINS

"Son of a bitch!" Seamus shouted.

"The bastards are here?!" Liza asked in anger. "They already killed one person today!"

"Rule one about cults. They don't give a damn!" Theresa barked back.

As the apartment residents began to panic, many of them trying to rush away from their own apartment rooms, a loud PING went over the intercom.

"Everyone, please, go back into your apartments!" The building manager ordered. "Whatever you do, do not go outside! Wait for local authorities to handle this!"

"My ass the authorities will hand this!" One resident shouted.

Aiden clenched his hands tightly as he watched the raging fire ball reach up into the night sky. That one resident was right. There was no way in the world the police were going to be able to deal with the Dark Eye cult. Especially if they were capable of powerful magical spells that could explode a car in an instant. In that one moment, he knew that only he and his friends were capable of repelling the cultists away from the area.

He glanced to his right to look at Theresa. Her long white hair seemed to glow with intense power as he gritted her teeth.

"From the looks of where that car is, it was just driving down the street." She said quietly. "In other words, they picked a target and waited for the right moment to unleash their magic."

"Those monsters..." Aello managed to whimper out.

Aiden felt a twitch of anger begin to rise up within him. Aello was right. They were monsters. He clenched his fists tightly as he continued to watch the fire rise up into the night sky. Another innocent life taken away by the cult of the Dark Eye, this time so shamelessly as well. One thing was certain though, Aiden swore to himself that on this night he wouldn't stand by idly.

They would pay for this.

"Thes."

"I know. We can't let them get away with this." She turned back to the group. "While everyone here is freaking out, we make our way to the sight."

"What if the police arrive?" Liza asks.

"You better pray that we wrap this up before they arrive then." Theresa replied. "Let's go. There's no way that the local police could handle the Dark Eye."

The group nodded at Theresa's order. This was the perfect moment for taking advantage of the panicking residents of the apartment. They made their way down the stairs as fast as they could. But with each step they took, the giant fire from the car rose higher into the night sky above them. A harrowing sight to behold.

Aiden could feel his palms sweat as they ran together. He couldn't tell if it was nerves or the intense heat he felt from the fire. While he had fought against a human opponents before like Raven, he had never imagined he would have to face other humans like this. After all, humans weren't demons. They could be reasoned with.

Right?

That question lingered in his mind as the group arrived at the scene of the explosion. Standing around the exploded car were three cloaked beings. Each with a different build. The one to the left, a tall lanky looking young man with light brown hair. The one to the right, a short teenage girl with orange red hair with purple highlights. Standing in the middle of the trio was a husky young adult man with beady brown eyes and short black hair. Aiden guessed the one in the middle was the leader of this team, given how the other two were standing.

As Aiden's team approached them, the husky man turned towards back them. He sneered as he folded his arms.

"Well." He said. Aiden noticed his nasial pitch, "Look who decided to show up."

The girl seemed to take a step back for a moment, appearing intimidated.

"Don't fear them." The husky man told her. "They do not have the means to destroy us."

The girl reluctantly nodded her head, before getting back in line with the other cultists. Aiden compared to the other two, she looked like she was the most uncertain about what they had done. The leader of the trio grinned evilly as he took a few steps towards Aiden and his friends.

"Well, well, well." He said in a condescending tone. "Look at who decided to show up. The Toothless Reptiles and the damn fools who they managed to indoctrinate."

"So much for keeping our true identities hidden." Seamus muttered with an eye roll.

"Answer me this." Theresa ordered as she stared down the approaching cultist. "How do you know who we are?"

"Oh we know all about you." The trio leader replied. "The Master and his disciples have told us all about the worms that have somehow crawled their way out of extinction."

"That's a new one." Aiden scoffed. "Disciples? We know that Dimitri only has ONE student."

"You will not speak ill of our master, you cretin!" The lanky teenager spat out. "Master Dimitri has shown us a new world! One this putrid world will be replaced by!"

Liza groaned as she gave Aiden a look.

"You just HAD to say something."

"So we were right." Garrett spoke. "The mage has formed this cult."

The lanky teen began to open his mouth to speak, but the husky young adult put up one hand to silence him.

"Yes, dragon, our master did indeed found our cult. It was he, who showed us the true answer to everything. It was he, that many of us finally found a home with. It was he, he brought us together with one simple goal in mind." He held his hand up before him, then clenched it tightly. "To destroy this world that has been corrupted and spoiled by those who would deny us, and build a new empire for all who feel our pain!"

Kali let out a simple mocking laugh at the husky adult's declarations. Aiden noticed that her pupils started to become slit like as her human tongue began to morph into a forked one.

"Absurd." She replied. "You, your master, and all your cultist friends are being played by a greater power. One that you can't possibly begin to even fathom in your tiny human mind."

"You will be silent, traitorous demonic bitch." The lead cultist said. "It would be wise to not underestimate Master Dimitri's grand power. For he has found a way to give us all what we want!" His hand suddenly was covered in a dark flame with a sinister purple color. "You know nothing about what he seeks to accomplish."

Aiden got into a fighting stance as soon as the dark flame erupted around the leader's fist. The power that emanated from the leader's fist, he could sense it. Its malice, its strength, all of it. He and the others sensed that Dimitri had taught most of the cultists a good deal of magic, but he dared not dream that he had taught others how to harness that much power that quickly.

"You're a damn fool if you think following him is going to give you what you want." Theresa replied. "Because of you, two people died this day. Have you no shame?"

"Two?" The young girl asked. "There was only one person in the car though..."

The lead cultist thought for a moment on the matter. Then a cruel grin came to his lips as he laughed for a few seconds.

"Ah. I think I know who they are talking about." He said. "They are referring to the old man our Master's partner so mercilessly killed. Sad, that you would be upset over the loss of an old man who was part of this fallen world's illness."

"Damn you!" Liza shouted. "That man had a family, friends! People that loved him! People that will never get a chance to talk to him again because of your sick cult!"

"The ones who are sick are you and this world!" The lanky teenager said as he held his hands out, they too were covered in the same dark purple flames. "And it seems you will have to be taught the same lesson!"

"Rexkin." Seamus said. "We need to move this confrontation out of the street."

"What's wrong?" The leader asked. "Afraid of being exposed to the pitiful masses for what you are?"

"That's it!" Liza drew out her two daggers from behind her back. Oceanus and Gitanel glimmered in the night sky like beacons as she stared down the cultists. "You three, Dimitri, your whole damn cult is going to pay for this! I swear it!"

"Liza, wait!" Aiden shouted.

Too late. Liza began to charge towards the cultists, daggers flashing in the night. As she swung one of them at the leader, a large fox like demon, with sharp spines on its legs and tail, appeared in front of the leader, taking the blow for him. Liza gasped as she pulled her blades back, and jumped away to avoid being bitten by the new creature.

The leader laughed quietly as he stroked the top of his demon's head.

"It's nice to have something like demon summoning powers to deal with weaklings like you." He said. "This won't take long, little girl."

"Dammit, Liza get back!" Theresa ordered.

Liza jumped back, just in time, as the demon fox had swung its spiny tail right where she once stood. Aiden almost quivered in fear as he watched the demon's sharp spines pierce solid rock, as if it was nothing, and slowly lift its tail back. This did little to intimidate Liza though, who spun her daggers into a frontal hold position.

"Nasty little pet you have there." She said with a growl. "If I had been a second slower, that would have gone clean through my leg."

"And this, is just the first of many." The leader responded. "You wish to fight us? So be it. But know that you will not fight us alone."

He glanced at the teenage boy and girl once, giving them a short nod of confirmation.

The lanky boy grinned as he slammed the palms of his hands together then pulled them away from each other. A small portal opened up in front of him, which was soon followed by a large crocodilian looking beast that was covered in a silvery grey scale set and an armored shell like a tortoise rose up from it. What looked like pieces of decayed flesh was sticking out between its teeth. Aiden wondered if it was demon flesh or human flesh that it had in its mouth. Its' beady yellow eyes filled with malevolent intent, stared down the team before slamming its tail on the ground.

The girl was the more hesitant of the trio about summoning her demon, but she too placed her palms together. Aiden noticed that she strained pain as she gathered what magical power she had within her. Sweat falling off her brow as she did so. Finally she gave off an audible grunt as she pulled her hands apart from each other as her portal own opened up as well.

What walked out was not a beastial looking monster, but a more feminine looking version of Raven's most trusted demons, Zeratar and Zantul. The demon's frame was not as bulky or strong looking, her tail was far longer than either Zantul or Zeratar's, and her body was covered in what looked like obsidian made armor with pale golden highlights. At first glance this new demon did not look as powerful as Raven's, but Aiden had learned a long time ago to not underestimate appearances. Especially with demonic beings. This demon however was not covered in grey fire or chilling ice like her brethren, instead, her body crackled with flashes of white lightning.

"What the hell?" Liza asked. "That punk Raven isn't the only one with those ugly demons?!"

The lanky teen's eyes glinted dangerously as he pointed towards her.

"Don't you dare speak of the master's top disciple!"

The crocodilian like demon slammed its feet down on the ground hard, causing a circular ring to rocks to form around the cultists and Aiden's group. Aiden's eyes were as wide as saucer plates as each rock rose from the ground in a numeric fashion. If he had to guess about how tall they were, he would estimate that each rock had to have been at least two stories tall in height! As the last rock formed around them the cultist trio each took a battle stance as their demon partners stood in front of them.

"You are now trapped, fools!" The husky leader barked. "With your deaths at our hands, Master Dimitri will greatly reward us for taking care of the only ones who can truly get in the way of his plans!"

Aiden almost let out a laugh at the claim they were trapped. If

Garrett felt like it, he would have destroyed the one rock with a simple punch. But now wasn't the time for laughing as he held out his hand and summoned Warfang to his side. Beside him, his allies each summoned their own weapons into their hands.

"Aiden." Theresa spoke out. "Your shield."

"W-What about it?"

"Summon it." She simply told him.

"W-What?!" Aiden looked flabbergasted. "Thes, I haven't even-"

"Do it!"

His body did a weird combination of reactions to her shout. His left hand clenched itself, his head flinched, and his legs felt like they had been pushed back. Aiden wanted to argue with her that he wasn't ready to hold his shield properly yet, but there wasn't any time for that. With a defeated groan, he held his left hand out in front of him, palm open, as he spoke out loudly.

"*Hisdel!*"

At his order the dragon wing that formed his belt buckle flew out in front of him. In a brilliant flash of light the once tiny buckle morphed into its true form. PeaceGuard. The white shield floated momentarily in the air before him. Aiden's eyes narrowed in frustration as he slipped his arm into the straps of his new shield. The shield immediately struck his left arm with a dense weight.

"Gck..." Aiden grunted as he hefted the shield in front of his body. "How am I supposed to fight with this thing being so damn heavy?!"

"Stow it, welp." Garrett told him. "You are going to have to learn on the fly how to use it to block attacks for now!"

The husky cultist laughed loudly as he watched Aiden struggle to maintain the weight of his new shield on his left arm.

"What a truly sad sight!" He bellowed. "This boy is the foe that Master Dimitri's top student has trouble with?! What a farce!"

Aiden felt an audible growl rise up from his throat as he stared down the leader. The time for talking had come to an end as the leader pointed at Aiden's group.

"Rip them to shreds!"

The fox demon gave a scream like howl into the night sky, then galloped towards Aiden's group. Its spiked tail raising high into air as it leaped above them.

"Scatter!" Theresa ordered.

No time was wasted as the team jumped away from their previous spot just as the demon swung its spiked tail down where they once stood. The impact from the fox demon's tail attack was enough to crack the street beneath them. Aiden's imagination must have been playing tricks on him, as the demon fox seemed to have some kind of demented smile on its lips before it swing its tail out towards him at full speed suddenly.

There was no time to dodge, or even swing Warfang. There was only one option. Aiden used all the strength his left arm had in that moment to pull up his new shield up in front of him. He shut his eyes tightly as he held onto PeaceGuard as best he could.

The tail of the demon fox rammed into his shield, resulting in a loud CLANG that erupted from their collusion. Aiden flinched as he waited for the spikes of the demon's tail to pierce right into his arm, to reignite the sensation of a prickling pain.

To his surprise, PeaceGuard held off the spikes. In fact, the shield did more than hold off the spikes. The shield itself had not even been dented from the demon's attack! Aiden blinked in surprise at this before staring back at the fox. His eyes narrowed as he took Warfang swung it horizontally towards the demon, barely managing to cut across its leg as it pounced away from his attack.

"Damn." Liza managed to say. "That is one tough shield."

"Tch." The lead cultist scoffed. "You got lucky, boy! Don't think that's going to hold you over!"

The demon fox barked in an unworldly roar before pulling back one of its claws and slashing at Aiden. There was not time to think about what to do as he pulled Warfang up counter the attack. The sword's sharp metal met with the demon's flesh, cutting through it as the claw fell to the ground with a soft thud. The demon yelped in pain before jumping back, looking at the stump where its paw once was before glaring back to Aiden.

"You damn punk! How dare you mutilate my demon?!" The lead cultist started as he snapped his fingers.

The demon fox snarled as more spikes erupted from its back. It clearly wanted revenge for what had just happened to its body. With a great effort, it jumped into the air and shot forth hundreds of its spikes towards Aiden.

"Aiden pull back!" Theresa ordered.

Aiden jumped away from the demon fox's second attack in the nick of time. The sharp spines pierced the concrete where he once stood. He felt a wave of relief as he stared where he once stood. Even with Peace-Guard at his side, Aiden would have been pierced by the spines through the rest of his body.

"Alanza!" The lead cultist shouted to the teen girl beside him. "Don't stand there, order your demon to attack!"

Aiden's eyes glanced back to the teenager. Though she gave the lead cultist a nod of acknowledgement, he could see it. She flinched at the very idea of engaging in combat like this. If he had to guess, she was only a year younger than him. Maybe even two.

That didn't stop her from obeying her leader though as she turned to her demon. The demon glanced back to her for a brief moment as well, before nodding her head towards Alanza.

"Go, Zara." She ordered her.

Zara's eyes glinted as she stepped in front of Alanza, her long tail whip lashing for a second as she held her hands to her sides. Two large orbs of lighting gathered in the palms of her hands before she threw them at the group. Aiden had to keep himself from crying out, the two attacks were so strong they cut a straight line as they flew.

Seamus took his turn to counter the attacks, throwing out two large wind orbs to smack into Zara's blasts. When the four energy orbs rammed into each other, the result was a small explosion that sent debris below flying up over the two groups. Aiden quickly brought his shield up to cover his eyes from not only the bright explosion, but from any debris that could hit him.

The resulting blast did little to hinder Alanza's demon though. Zara already had prepared another attack to unleash against the group. With a glint in her eyes, the female demon unleashed a powerful streak of lightning into Seamus' body. The impact from the blow sent the mage dragon into one of the risen rocks behind them, pinning him there as the electricity rocked his body with incredible pain.

"Seamus!"

Along with Kali, Garrett rushed over to his friend, as the two did their best to try and aid the green dragon. His body jittered every few seconds, each time it did he coughed up some blood. Garrett gritted his teeth as he tried to hold his friend in place. He wasted no time in looking over to Kali with angered eyes.

"Pull your weight, serpent. Heal him!"

"Pushy pushy." She retorted before kneeling down. "Keep him still. I'll take care of this child's play magic."

Kali placed both of her hands over Seamus' chest, and the strange dark light of the healing spell that Aiden had grown used to came from her palms and settled over Seamus' body. The jittering began to die down, but the green dragon had not fully recovered from the impact of the attack from Zara.

Theresa's eyes narrowed in anger as she spun Snow and Fire in her hands. Zara glanced back to the leader of the dragons, her claws still covered with electricity. The white dragoness snarled once, her dragon teeth forming in her jaws before her twin swords were covered by the elements of fire and ice respectfully.

"Normally I would tell Aiden and Liza to calm themselves in the moment of a battle...but you'll pay for that!"

In what looked like only a second Theresa charged towards Zara, both of her swords raised high above her head as she slashed each of them at the lightning demon. Snow and Fire left energy streaks of fire and ice from each slash, which clashed with the lightning's energy streaks. It was a spectacle of three powerful elements doing battle with one another as sparks erupted from each hit. Some sparks flying right into the barrier that had kept the groups trapped. The heat from the clash began to melt some of the concrete below them!

As Theresa clashed with Zara, the lanky teenager grinned as he turned to his crocodilian demon.

"Go feast." He ordered it. "I know that you are hungry as hell. And these punks? They'll make a good appetizer before we destroy this entire damn down!"

The crocodile demon roared in what Aiden could only guess was a mixture of both joy and ravenous hunger. He felt the back of his neck shudder as the large beast fixated its glance on him, Liza, the Harpies, Garrett, and Kali. It's beady eyes looking between each of them before it galloped towards the harpy trio.

With Aello at the very front!

"AELLO!" Liza screamed.

The Harpy Princess stared down the charging crocodile demon, her legs shivering somewhat. It was if she wanted to move at the right moment to avoid being eaten alive but the fear she was feeling over-ruled her body's functions in that one critical moment! Just when it looked like the demon was about to have its' lunch, a loud scream came from its left.

"RAAAAGH!!!"

Liza had charged at the crocodile from the right, ramming her two daggers right into the neck of the beast. Gitanel and Oceanus made their mark, as black blood began to leak down the beast's neck. The large demon stopped its charge as it tried to shake Liza off its' neck.

The athletic girl would not be thrown off that easily though, as she flipped and jumped the demon to land on the back of its neck. With both Gitanel and Oceanus in hand, Liza began to rapidly stab the demon in the back of its neck. Each stab causing black blood to dampen the blades.

"You won't get her, bastard!" She shouted. "Not while I'm around!"

As Liza stabbed the crocodilian demon over and over with her daggers, Aello had snapped back to reality in that moment. With a flick of her wrist, her chain sword appeared in her hand. She waited for a moment, then when the beast let out a massive roar she swung her weapon towards the mouth of the demon.

The chain sword managed to wrap itself around the mouth of the crocodilian demon, pulling it down with a loud THUD. Aello grunted as she balanced, pulling with all her might to keep the demon's mouth shut.

"Gabriella! Mia!" She shouted. "Help Liza!!!"

The two Keepers wasted no time as they flew into the air above them. Both of them aimed towards the back of the crocodilian and dived with their massive talons open, stabbing right into its leathery hide. It did little to truly harm the demon, but they kept scratching and stabbing with their talons as best as they could.

The fox demon snarled as it noticed the joint effort to destroy its comrade. With a short howl it readied its tail and let loose a short burst of spikes towards Liza and the Harpy Keepers. However a quick

Flarnea blast from Aiden rammed into the spikes at the right moment and they burnt into nothing.

The demon snarled as it glared back at Aiden, who quickly pulled Warfang up from the ground after firing his spell at the beast.

"If you wanna fight someone, beast, focus on me!"

Aiden pulled Warfang back beside him and put PeaceGuard in front of him. The weight of his new shield made him grunt in frustration. Not having any kind of chance to train to get use to its weight was really putting a strain on his left arm. But he couldn't complain about that right now. Especially when it had managed to save his life from what would have been a deadly blow.

He gritted his teeth in frustration before running towards the fox demon. He held Warfang high above his head before swinging it right at his foe. The demon jumped back to avoid being slashed by the mighty blade before it began to snarl as it saw the reflection of its stumpy leg in Aiden's sword.

A smug smile came to Aiden's lips as he swung Warfang once more towards the fox demon, this time barely nicking its chest with the sword's edge. The demon skidded back a few paces from him, a glare of hatred forming in its eyes as Aiden spun his trusty sword in a circle.

"What's wrong, mutt?" He asked with a confident tone. "Too afraid that I'll take another paw off?!"

The fox let out an unholy roar before charging at Aiden, spikes still at the ready as the two clashed with one another.

Theresa's duel with Zara the white dragoness had managed to singe some of her opponent's skin with her mighty blows. However she too shared several spots where her clothes had been slashed or charred away by Zara's attacks. This didn't seem to bother the white dragoness though as she jumped into the air and did a dive bomb spinning slash towards the demon.

Zara jumped back, narrowly avoiding the fiery and icy aftermath that erupted when Snow and Fire met with the ground. Not to be undone, the electric demon jumped into the air above Theresa and fired out a stream of lightning at her opponent. Theresa's nostrils flared up before she reared her head up towards the incoming lighting blast. She wasted no time before she opened her mouth as a stream of white fire exploded from her lips towards Zara's attack.

Both attacks narrowly missed one another, each one making their mark on the opposing foe. Theresa grunted in pain from the electric blast, her white hair standing up on end from the shock her body was enduring. She dropped to one knee in pain as the lightning shocked her. Aiden knew it took a lot to truly hurt Theresa. The only ones he recalled being able to make her feel pain were Samael, the Teleranta, and the Overmind.

Despite the pain she was feeling she gave a short grin as she stared right back at Zara. Her attack made its mark as well on her opponent. The white fire she had spewed out had begun to burn at the demon's skin, forcing the humanoid reptile to land in pain. Zara gave off what sounded like audible cries of pain as she did her best to put the fire out on her body.

"Zara!" Alanza cried out from behind her demon.

The teeanager held one hand out, and spoke in a tongue that Aiden could not understand. A rain cloud quickly formed over Zara's body, as a torrent of rain fell down onto her. Theresa's flames soon died out as the demon glanced back to her summoner. Both of them shared a mutual head nod with one another before Zara turned her attention back to the white dragoness.

Theresa blinked in surprise at this, but glanced back to Alanza for a few seconds.

"You would save your demon?" She asked her. "Is she not your personal tool?"

"I..." Alanza started out, but the trio's leader placed an arm in front of her.

"Don't answer that, Alanza. Remember, they are the enemy." He told her, his tone icy cold. "Now finish the job."

Alanza whimpered at the tone of the husky cultist, but nodded in submission before staring at Zara.

"Zara, continue the battle." She told her. Theresa took notice of the quiver in her voice. "D...Don't let her survive."

Zara bowed her head towards her summoner before turning to face Theresa. Her eyes glinted with a dangerous power as she held her claws out in front of her. Lightning danced between her fingertips as she stared down the leader of the Trinity. Her long tail slammed against the ground a couple of times as she took a combative stance.

Theresa sighed as she shook her head sadly. Her white wings erupting from her back before she spun her swords in both hands.

"You and your summoner don't have to do this." She told Zara. "If I wanted to, I could transform into my full state and this battle could be over in an instant. The only reason I'm not doing that is because there's no space for my true form."

Theresa's eyes narrowed as she combined Snow and Fire into their double bladed state, Snowfyre, before taking her own combative stance.

"I'm warning you. This will not end well for you and your summoner."

Zara didn't respond, instead she charged at Theresa with both claws high above her head. Theresa sighed as she spun Snowfyre once before holding the weapon behind her back.

"So be it."

The two charged at one another again. Double bladed sword and demon claws clashed together in a horrific song of metal and flesh.

As they clashed, Liza's group had a hard time keeping the large crocodilian demon under control. Despite the repeated attacks from Liza's daggers and the talons of Gabriella and Mia, the beast had shown little signs of fatigue. Aello still struggled to keep her chain sword around the giant maw of the demon as well. Each time the demon pulled its head back in an attempt to break free, her talons drew across the concrete floor.

Tears began to form in her eyes she thought back to possibly calling out for her big sisters. She closed her eyes tightly as she thought about doing it. She should do it. They surely would have heard her cry out for help. Hell, Ocypete and Garrett alone would have been able to break the demon in half with their immense strength. But if Aello cried out for her big sisters to aide her, they would have also exposed them to anyone that was not within the arena!

"D-Dammit!" She thought. *"I'm so pathetic! I can't even keep this thing in place! Ozzy...Cilly I...I..."*

Aello's eyes snapped open as something began to dawn on her. Was she always so reliant on her big sisters? Ever since she was small, all she could remember was crying out for both of them to come save the day for her if it was too much. Every problem she had, they always took care of it. She never was able to stand up for herself.

"I can't...I can't rely on you forever!"

She gritted her teeth and tightened her muscles and dug her talons as deep as she could into the ground. The youngest princess pulled for all she was worth on her chain sword, forcefully bringing the demon's head down to the ground with a loud THUD. Aello gave off an audible grunt of strain as she pulled once more to keep the demon from opening its jaws.

"A-Aelly?!" Liza cried out from back of the demon's neck.

"Just keep attacking it!" Aello shouted through gritted teeth. "I don't know how long I can hold it down!"

Liza smiled as she spared no second in resuming her attack. Each alternate stab revealed that both Gitanel and Oceanu once clean blades were coated with the pitch black color of the crocodilian demon's blood. The same could be said with the talons of Mia and Gabriella with how quickly they were stabbing and slashing the demon's massive body as well.

Despite their consistent attacks on the hide of the crocodile, it did little to actually weaken the beast. A low growl escaped its vocal cords as it tried with all its might to break free once more, but Aello pulled even harder on her chain sword's hilt. It's beady eyes glanced around, spotting its summoner who looked a bit worried for his demon.

"What are you waiting for you fool?" The leader asked. "Grant it more power to crush these fools!"

"Wait, what?!" Aiden shouted as he kicked the fox away from him.

He prayed to whatever deity that was listening that he had just misheard the trio leader. That he did not just order the lanky teenager to increase the power of his demon with magic. His heart fell the moment he saw the sneer spreading across the lanky teen's lips.

"Hear me!" The lanky teen shouted. "I share my power with my demon! Increase in strength!!!"

A blast of grey light erupted from the palms of the lanky teen's hands, which rammed into the side of the crocodile demon. The moment that energy began to surge into his demon, was when Aiden's eyes shrunk. The large demon began to pull Aello slowly towards its' muzzle.

"Aello!" Aiden cried. "You gotta let go of the sword before it eats you!"

"If I do that, then it goes after Liz, Mia, and Gabby!" Aello cried back through a strained effort.

"Don't be an idiot! It'll kill you!"

Aello ignored his cries as she tried her best to reign the massive crocodile demon back in control, but her efforts had little, if any success in keeping the beast in place. Aiden watched in horror as the demon threw Liza, Gabriella, and Mia off its body before it pulled back with renewed energy. He clenched his fist tightly around Warfang's hilt as he watched, anger rising.

If he did nothing to stop this, Aello was going to die!

"Don't forget you're fighting my demon, brat!" The leader said. The fox demon leapt into the air with a loud howl. But Aiden paid no mind to the fox demon that tried to attack him from behind.

He knew what had to be done.

A bright red aura erupted around his body as he dropped Peace-Guard to the ground. Deftly stepping to the side to avoid the fox's spiked tail, Aiden rammed his blade into its side with a quick stab, then pulled his blade back, watching as the fox demon sputtered out blood from its mouth as it fell to the ground.

"I don't got time for you!" He shouted as he began to run towards the cultist trio.

"What are you-" The lead cultist sputtered at Aiden's charge.

As Aiden ran, he could heard the large crocodile demon break free from the bonds surrounding its maw. Now it was truly a race against the clock. He had to hurry!

"Please, let me go faster! Let me get to the demon's summoner in time!"

He didn't notice it, nor did anyone else, but the greaves that he had found at the flea market formed around his ankles. This time though, they didn't hinder Aiden's weight. In fact, he felt himself becoming faster with them attached to his feet! Now what looked like it was impossible seemed even more possible as he zoned in on the lanky teenager.

Aiden brought his left hand to Warfang's hilt, grasping it tightly as he reached his target. His eyes filled with a burning fire that seemed to grow more determined to stop the crocodile demon at any coast!

"Aiden wait!" Theresa shouted from afar.

Too late.

Warfang had met its mark as Aiden rammed the sword right through the lanky teenager's stomach.

The entire world came to a sudden halt in that one moment. As the burning fire in Aiden's eyes began to die down, he glanced down at his hands, still holding onto Warfang's hilt before he stared back into the eyes of the lanky teenager. As if in that same moment, the crocodile demon also came to a sudden halt.

"D...Damn...you..."

Was all he was able to sputter out as he pulled himself away from Aiden's blade, before he fell onto the ground, bleeding from the hole in his stomach. His eyes glazed over slowly, then his head tipped to the side before his eyelids closed forever.

AFTERMATH

"Jeremy!" Alanza screamed as she rushed over to her fallen cultist. "C-Come on, this isn't funny! It's just a stab! Wake up! Come on, wake up!!!"

Aiden felt himself stepping back slowly from the scene before him. A cold sensation ran down his spine, his entire body feel like it had just gone numb. Did that just happen? Did he really run the cultist, or rather Jeremy, through like he was some kind of pig? Did he just kill an actual human being?

He had killed enemies before, sure. But those? Those were demons. In his mind they were monsters, evil beings that did terrible things to humans. But never once had he ever killed a human. Not once. He dared not even think about raising his sword to kill another person!

"Jeremy!!!" Alanza cried out. "C-Come on! Wake up! Please!! Open your eyes!!!"

As Alanza pleaded for her fellow cultist to open his eyes, the large crocodilian let out a massive pained roar behind them. Aiden felt him looking away from the fallen teenager as his demon began to crack from the bottom up. Its beady little eyes pulsed violently in pain as the cracks reached its head. With one final pitiful cry of defiance, the massive crocodilian demon suddenly shattered into many pieces, exploding in a bright flash of light where it once was.

"Dammit all!" The lead cultist shouted. "You fools have no idea how hard it is to summon and control a demon associated with fear like that!"

"Your comrade is dead and you're only concerned about a demon?!" Liza snapped as she holstered her daggers up. "I was about to feel sorry for you and your friend losing someone, but now? I'll send you right to hell with him!"

"Liza!" Aello gasped.

Just as Liza was about to charge the two remaining cultists, Zara rushed between them. The athletic girl yelped as she jumped back to avoid a slash from the demon. The electric demon gave a short snort at her, before she turned her attention back to her young summoner. It was in that moment that Aiden had noticed that for a brief moment there was a tender look of concern in Zara's eyes.

"Jeremy! Please! Wake up! Wake up! You can't...y-you can't..."

The young redhead hung her head over his chest, eyes clenched tightly as she gripped his bloody shirt. Soft sobs could be heard from her as she tried to shake the fallen cultist back to life. Aiden felt his stomach shrivel up at the sight.

"Look at what you've done..." The lead cultist spat. "He was one of our finest summoners, Master Dimitri is going to be angry about this..."

The demon fox rushed over to its master side, its head brushing gently against his hand before the leader turned back to Aiden and his group.

"Do not think, that this is over." He managed to spit out. "You have only made our resolve to purge this putrid world even stronger. This death, it will not be ignored. On the honor of our lord and master, I swear that you will all face the wrath of the Dark Eye soon!"

"If you think you're going anywhere, you got another damn thing coming!" Liza shouted.

"Zara, blind them!" The leader ordered the electric demon.

Zara stood there, glancing back at the cultist before snorting in disgust at him. Her long tail slapping the concrete ground with an annoyed look in her eyes.

"Don't give me that!" The leader snapped back. "I am your summoner's leader, and therefore I can order you around as much as I want!"

Theresa charged at the arguing pair. Snowfyre spinning behind her back as she reached the grieving group of cultists. Just when it looked like the double-bladed sword was about to make contact with the electric demon, a voice cut through the argumentative voice of the leader.

"Zara. Let out a blinding light." Alanza ordered.

The demon's eyes glinted with a flash of blue white light before she turned on a dime to face Theresa. With a shout, an explosion of bright lightning exploded around the demon. Everyone was forced to close their eyes from the force, even Theresa had to drop her weapon to cover her eyes from the giant explosion of light.

As the group did their best to keep their sight protected from Zara's light explosion, Aiden could hear the voice of Alanza.

"You will pay for what you've done!" She shouted. "When Raven hears about this...there will be revenge! I-I promise you that!"

As Aiden's sight began to return, he saw it in that short moment. A dark portal behind Alanza. From what his vision was able to make out, it was obvious to tell that the cultist leader, who probably took Jeremy's body had already gone through the dark portal. The redhead stared at him dead on with heavy tears in her eyes.

"I won't forget this..." She spat out before she rushed into the portal with her demon.

"Dammit!" Theresa shouted as the portal closed. "They got away!"

"Did...did that really just happen?" Liza asked. "Did they seriously slip away from us like that?!"

"I..." Aiden stammered. "I..."

His hands began to tremble as he stared at his palms. They were covered in sweat. From the heat of battle? No. It came from the harsh cold reality that had just hit him in the face.

"I...k-killed someone..."

The world seemed to slow down to a slow crawl as what he had done slowly began to weigh down on him. The approaching police sirens, the destroyed street, the burning car, none of that mattered to him right now. The shock of what happened still all so fresh in his mind that none of that mattered.

"Aiden?" Liza asked as she notice his trembling hands.

"I...I...I..." Aiden stuttered out, the pupils in his eyes having shrunk down to the size of a small pea. "I...I killed h-him...I-"

SMACK!

His head reeled back into place from the sudden slap across his cheek. Aiden's eyes, once full with panic and shock, returned to normal as he stared at the person who had just slapped him. Theresa.

"Aiden!" She shouted at him. "Your shock will have to wait! We have to go, and we have to go now!"

Aiden gasped as the blaring sounds of the sirens erupted into his eardrums. Theresa was right. They couldn't stay here.

"Garrett!" Theresa shouted. "Is Seamus all right?!"

"I'm fine, Rexkin..." Seamus groaned as he walked up. "I've taken worse blows before..."

"No time to waste, Seamus!" Theresa snapped. "Get a portal to the apartment open and get it opened now!"

Seamus nodded his head as he clapped his palms together. As he pulled his hands apart from one another the blue colored magic appeared. He wasted no time speaking as he slammed his palms down on the ground. The blue portal opened up below all of them as they found themselves falling into it before the portal closed behind them.

Then in that short moment, the portal opened back up into the Harpy's apartment. Each person landed differently. Theresa, the harpies, and Kali all landed with grace. Seamus, Liza, and Aiden landed on their butts with a soft 'thud' on the carpet beneath them. Garrett had fallen face first into the couch, an act that annoyed the great dragon as he rose up from his spot.

"Not a word." He said specifically to Kali, who had a sly grin across her lips.

"Okay...everyone is safe back here." Theresa said as she took control. "I knew things were going to get bad. But this? The situation is a lot worse than I thought."

Seamus nodded his head.

"You're damn right, Rexkin. If Dimitri is teaching emotionally charged teenagers and adults how to summon demons as their means of attack, the world is going to get a rude wake up call."

"That was only three of them as well. From what I could tell based on their experience in combat, they were trained with the full intention of killing the people that they attack." Theresa frowned as she scratched her chin. "This is really bad. If his cult is as massive as he's making it sound like, then we have a problem..."

"You expect us to fight an army?" Liza asked. "With the snake demon here, there's only eight of us!"

"That's the main question then, isn't it?" Seamus retorted with his own question. "How do we counter a force of that size? There's several options to that. Each of them I don't think will bare any true fruit for now."

The conversation came to an abrupt end though as Aiden's voice cut through it like a hot knife through butter.

"I...I killed him."

The group turned their heads towards him. Each with their own look of concern as Aiden stared down at his hands. The young teen shook almost violently as Warfang and PeaceGuard laid beside him. The sword still covered with the blood of the slain Jeremy. Seamus snapped his fingers once as the blade floated into the air.

"Kiddo, you better learn to clean your sword. You wouldn't want the carpet to get stained, would you?"

"Shut up..." Aiden muttered. "I...I don't want the damn thing anymore."

"Eh?"

Aiden turned his eyes up towards Seamus, a fire filling them.

"I said I don't want it anymore!" He snapped out. "In case you haven't noticed, I took-"

"Yes yes, we heard you." Kali spoke in a mocking tone. "You make yourself sound like you're all so important with your claims of 'I killed him!'. You sound like a spoiled brat right now."

"Well I'm sorry!" Aiden argued back. "In case you haven't noticed, this was the first time that I...that I..."

Theresa frowned as she walked over to him slowly. Aiden stared at his hands, which were covered in sweat and trembling. Tears formed in his eyes the longer he stared at his open palms.

"I..I n-never w-wanted to kill a human..." He managed to say. "It...it all happened s-so fast. H-He...his demon w-was about to break f-free and kill the others and...and I-I had to do s-something before...I never..."

Aiden's stuttering came to a stop as Theresa gently pulled him into her arms. The familiar scent of her long white hair filled his nose as she held him. Her gentle hands stroking the back of his head like a dog that had been injured. He wouldn't lie. In that moment, it just felt safer to be there in Theresa's embrace.

"I know." She said. "I know that this is a shock to you. It's always a shock to everyone when they take their first sentient life..."

"T-Theresa?"

She pulled herself back a bit from him. A sad smile had replaced the worried frown that had been there.

"I know it's hard to remember this, Aiden, but me, Seamus, and Garrett have all been in battles like tonight. Where the situation was either that we died in battle, or that our enemy did." Theresa gently stroked his cheek. "All three of us went through that very first battle where we had killed a sentient being like a human being. And just like you, we all felt sick to our very stomachs."

"It's something all of us have to go through when we pick up our weapons to defend those who cannot defend themselves." Seamus spoke out. "It does weigh heavy on your mind at first, kiddo, believe me I know that. But you also have to consider what could have happened had you not done what you did."

"Like w-what?" Aiden barely managed to ask.

"For one thing, Liza, Aello, Gabriella, and Mia? They could have been lunch for that giant demon. If you hadn't attacked its summoner when you did, tonight could have played out very differently." Theresa said. "I know it's hard to imagine this, Aiden, and I know right now you feel that you never want to pick up a weapon again...but like it or not, this is what we are going to have to do."

"But..."

"Aiden." Theresa frowned. "We are literally the only ones who can stand in front of the Dark Eye's way. The harpy den won't care to help the outside world that much, and the Mage Academy is still recovering from what happened there. We are both the sword and the shield for the world right now. And if you don't fight, not only will you yourself be killed, but more innocent people are going to die as well."

She took one of his hands and squeezed it tightly in her own. The reassuring strength from Theresa's grip surged through his body in that moment.

"I understand how you feel. Better than you think I do. But you need to understand that if you hadn't did what you did, he would have killed our friends, you, and possibly many more people this night." She offered him a sad smile. "I promise, it's going to be okay..."

Aiden's eyes, still with tears, closed tightly before he leaned forward into her shoulder. The white dragoness gently stroked his back with both hands. Every now and then giving him short shushes and reassurances that it was all going to be okay.

While most people would not want to be seen in such a vulnerable state, Aiden was glad to have Theresa be there in that moment. The world was didn't exist in that moment. All that mattered was that he felt safe in that very short span of time.

"Whelp." Garrett's voice cut through the silence. "If you're done being coddled by Theresa, we have work to do."

Theresa and Aiden pulled apart from each other at that. The latter had a small smile on his lips.

"I still feel bad for what I did but...if we're the only ones that have a chance of stopping the Dark Eye Cult from breaking out across the country, or the world, then I'll...I'll continue to fight. If I can avoid killing them, I want to try that. But if I can't, then I w-won't hesitate."

"Atta boy, kiddo." Seamus said before tossing Warfang back to Aiden. The blade no longer covered by the crimson red blood from the cultist. "While you were having your moment, I took the liberty to clean the blade off for you. From now on, if you stab a human with it make certain you clean it off."

"Right..." Aiden said as he glanced back to Warfang.

The sword felt a bit heavier, mentally, to hold now. But despite the mentally added weight to it, it still felt right to hold the weapon in his hand.

"You also shouldn't EVER throw your shield to the ground." Theresa scolded him. "It took us awhile to make that thing you know! You could have left some ugly scratch on it from throwing it so carelessly to the ground!"

"S-Sorry!" Aiden yelped. "It was the heat of the moment!"

"Can we focus?" Garrett asked. "Rexkin, we need to find some kind of way to handle this."

"Right." Theresa nodded. "We can not afford to let the Dark Eye get away with what they want. Especially since tonight has taught us that they are not afraid of attacking and killing innocent people."

"But we can't be everywhere." Liza spoke out. "We're tied to this one part of Virginia of all states! And we can't just warp to each state to deal with what branch of their cult!"

"Then we need to take the heads off this snake as soon as we can." Theresa replied. "Dimitri and Raven are clearly the ones who lead the Dark Eye. If we take care of them as soon as we can, the rest of the cult will fall into disarray."

"You don't think they wouldn't have back up leaders?" Liza asked.

"Cults like the Dark Eye are run by figures who have the absolute power over all the others. If the leaders go down, the odds are the entire cult will fall apart." Theresa answered before folding her arms. "I don't think Dimitri would share all of his secrets with the members either. He strikes me as the kind of leader who would want to always have an ace up his sleeve."

"So what do we do now?" Aiden asked. A slight shake in his voice "We can't just go around attacking everyone who we think is part of the cult."

"We won't." Theresa said. "They're going to be bold in their attacks now. So instead, we'll wait for them to make a move, and then we'll take care of those that make themselves known to us."

She glanced at the clock on the wall. A frown over her lips.

"It's one o clock. We should get back to our houses and get back in bed. I doubt that our parents will let us go out on our own tomorrow, so everyone with phones text that way."

"And delete the conversation afterwards like we have been, right?" Liza asked.

"Yes. No one can know. No matter what."

The group all gave short nods. Aiden still felt terrible for what he had done to the teenager, Jeremy, but Theresa was right. They were the only ones who could truly stand up to the Dark Eye and prevent any more meaningless deaths across the state.

He just prayed that he would be able to get through this ordeal without losing who he had been all his life.

FATHER AND SON

*T*he rest of the night Aiden slept with an uneasy feeling in his stomach. Theresa's words of wisdom comforted him somewhat, but the image of him running Jeremy through played like it was on loop over and over. Every five minutes, Aiden felt himself waking up in a cold sweat before attempting to get some sleep. One time he swore to himself that he saw the slain teenager laying down on his floor, bleeding out like a stuck hog.

Sleep did come, but it wasn't easy. It was around three o'clock in the morning when he was finally able to put the events out of his mind. At least for the time being.

By the time Aiden woke up it was late in the morning. At first he worried he had missed the bus for school, but he later found out that school had indeed been cancelled for the next four days. The death of the security guard had raised some well justified questions and concerns for the parents of the high schoolers. Questions that Aiden could only imagine the school administration would have a hard time answering, if they were able to answer them at all.

How could anyone who had no idea what truly killed the guard even address that? Especially since none of the staff had ever seen anything of the magical kind. Aiden could scarcely even imagine answering those questions himself if the school had caught him using his weapons and magic abilities.

As Aiden sat there, watching the news carefully for reports about the Dark Eye, part of him felt lost and uncertain after the events that had preceded the day before. He wished things could have gone back to normal for him and Theresa. Before Dimitri's cult. Where they could have a regular high school life with each other, and deal with the mystical creatures and arts during their free time.

He still loved the magical aspect of the world they were in. He still loved being able to use magic on a whim, holding Warfang in his hands, and he loved the chance to vent some frustrations with combat training. But he still felt like something had ruined the image of what a fantasy world would have been like if it was real.

Never once did Aiden take into account that one day he might end up killing another human being. His battles with Raven were one thing, sure. But he never once entertained the thought of actually killing his hatred foe. Raven might have thought about killing HIM, sure, but how could one even remotely think about taking the life of another human being?

"Get your crap together, Aiden!" He thought to himself. *"You couldn't stop him any other way, right?? His demon was bound to break free from the chain sword!"*

He groaned as he rubbed his eyebrows with his fingers.

"It was the heat of the moment, that's what it was." He told himself. *"You got caught up in the middle of the combat, knew that he had to be stopped, and you didn't think it through all the way. There was no time to think! His demon could have eaten Liza and the harpies! But..."*

Aiden nearly jumped at the sound of his cell phone beeping once. He glanced over to it and saw that Theresa had just sent a text message to him and the entire group. His hand grabbed the cell phone and opened the group chat.

"School is closed for awhile. We'll have to talk." Theresa's text message read.

Aiden began typing back his reply.

"The problem is how are we gonna do that. My folks aren't gonna let me out of their sights for the new few days alone."

"Same here." Liza responded.

"Ya'll know that I can just make those magic clones whenever, right?" Seamus asked in his own text.

"That won't work forever." Theresa said. "What if they attack when some of us are out with our parents? That's a situation that will not work out well for any of us."

"That and I'm certain that some of our parents would recognize any differences between us and those duplicates." Aiden added.

"Fine fine. But we can't have you guys always held hostage by the fact that your parents want to keep you under lock and key."

"Honestly? I think it's because they're really spooked out right now." Liza typed back. "The death of the security guard is one thing, but have you heard the news about the area where we fought the cultists?"

"Heard about? It's been going on the news non frigging stop." Aiden replied. "I still can't believe they were able to bring down those giant rocks."

"Human machines did it, right? Cranes?" Aello asked.

"More like they had to somehow blow them up without harming the residence around the area." Theresa answered. "Listen, I don't know when this will come to a stop, but we need to begin plans for your new training sessions."

"Right, and at the moment that feels like its' a task that is on par with asking the world to come to a stop." Liza replied. "My parents keep checking up on me like I'm about to sneak out!"

Aiden felt himself peering over his shoulders every so often when she sent that message. A habit that he was sure to feel himself become more in tune with during the days ahead. Now the secret that he had been expected to hide for so long was at even more of a risk of being exposed if his parents began to suspect anything.

"It's totally like, BS! They keep looking over to me like I'm about to stand up and walk out without their permission. It's so frustrating!" Liza's next text message read out. "Dammit! Those stupid Dark Eye punks are gonna regret making moves like this!"

"Oh you poor insignificant little girl." A new message read out, Aiden had to bite his inner cheek to keep from groaning out. Even when they were away from her, Kali found SOME way to be insulting.

"Knock it off, Snake." Theresa replied, quickly adding. "You too, Liza. This is not the time for us to be at each other's throats."

"Thes is right." Aiden replied. "Like it or not, we are gonna have to find some kind of way to get training in while we can…"

"Yeah? And how long do you think we'll be watched over by the parent brigade?" Liza asked.

"The hell if I know, Liz. All I can really suggest for us to do now is to just endure it for the short term and not push things. If we start acting annoyed by their efforts to protect us then they'll start suspecting things. And you don't wanna have them actually catch onto everything that we have been doing, right?"

"I... Fine. You're right about that, Aide."

"Not bad kiddo!" Seamus' reply read. "If I didn't know any better, you sound like a leader there. It feels like you're rubbing off on him, Rexkin."

"Not now, Seamus." Theresa's response read quickly, like she was trying to avoid the subject. "So for now the plan is this everyone, we wait a bit longer before moving forward with the training. Seamus, I want you to get into contact with Ryan and make arrangements for us to train at the Academy from now on."

"I never thought we'd ever go back there..." Liza replied. "The horrors we saw in that place? I still wake up in the middle of the night thinking I'm still fighting those shadow demons."

"It may not be the ideal place, but it's the best place for us to train in private without being noticed." Theresa replied. "That'll be all for this talk everyone, delete this group chat so that your parents don't find it."

He knew that Theresa couldn't see it, but he gave a short nod to her order as he deleted the group chat.

As he did, another text message popped up. This time from Theresa. His heart almost fluttered at the mere thought of her sending a message. But his senses came back to him as he opened up the text message.

"How are you holding up?" It read.

Aiden thought for a moment about how he would reply to this message. Did he respond with how he honestly felt at that moment? Or did he make up a white lie to throw her off the track? On one hand, it he told her the truth she would have gone into a long lecture. But on the other hand, if he tried to lie to her about how he felt, she would have been able to sense that he was lying.

That was both the advantage and disadvantage for having a friend as long as his friendship with Theresa. Even if they weren't directly talking to each other face to face, she always seemed to know how he felt.

After considering his options in that small moment, he began to write out a reply back to Theresa.

"I'm still trying to wrap my head around it...It feels like some kind of sick dream that I'm trying to find a way to overcome and I just...I feel like I'm a monster." His reply read. After he sent it, a few seconds later Theresa's reply read out.

"I know. And I can tell you this, Aiden. You are not monster."

The image of Theresa giving him a tender smile came to his mind when he read those words. Aiden couldn't help but smile back at the message as he began to type back to her.

"What'd I do to deserve you, Thes?"

"I can name a few things...anyway, I better go silent for now. Mom and dad are freaking out about the news over here. Remember, we'll find time to train."

Aiden sighed as he closed the text message app on his phone before leaning back in the couch. The TV was still blaring the news report of their battle scene. Multiple citizens talking about how they were worried about the loud explosion that erupted from the car and how they were so panicked that they never noticed the rising rocks. His left hand covered his eyes as he tried to get his mind off of everything that had happened.

"Aiden."

"GAH!"

Aiden jumped at the sudden voice before looking over his shoulder to see who was speaking behind him. His heart felt a mixture of relief and uncertainty as he was greeted by his father's face.

"Crimminy dad! Don't do that!"

"Don't do what?" Connor asked, Aiden noticed his eyebrow had raised.

"Sneak up on me like that!"

"Last I checked this is my house boy. I can do whatever I want." Connor folded his arms. "Do you pay the bills?"

"Not what I meant dad..." Aiden replied with a groan.

"Watch your tone, son."

Aiden grumbled as quietly as he could before he looked over back to the TV. The report of the murder at his high school, and their battle sight from last night, still playing on loop. Connor frowned as he watched the news with him.

"Can't stop watching the news, eh? First it was small disturbances across the country, then the murder of the security guard, and now this." Connor frowns. "Seems like the whole world has gone to hell doesn't it?"

"You don't even know the half of it, dad." Aiden thought as he sighed.

"How do you think they brought up those stalagmites from the ground though?" Connor asked as he scratched his chin. "Explosives? No, that wouldn't make sense..."

Aiden grabbed his cargo pockets tightly as he let his father ramble on. If only his dad knew the truth about what happened. Part of him was half tempted to say that it was him and his friends that got into a fight with the Dark Eye cult members. Maybe as a joke to to get his dad to give out a short laugh.

Then Aiden remembered that his father was never one to like those stupid sarcastic jokes like that. He would have taken it too seriously, or worse, dragged the truth out of Aiden in order to learn everything Aiden had been hiding for the last three years from his parents.

Theresa would have killed him if he did that.

"Aiden."

Aiden felt himself jumping out of his skin again before glancing back to his father. The look in Connor's eyes was a bit more intense than before. Aiden felt the back of his hair rising up on his neck as he felt his father's stare. He knew that look all too well. As a child his father only used that kind of stare when he was deathly serious about a subject.

It tended to happen when Connor wanted the truth from Aiden if he was trying to fib, or whenever he got into some kind of trouble. Even now, his father's stare was more terrifying to him than any demon he had battled. In a way, that glare from Garrett was just as fear inducing as his father's.

"If you were a part of this cult, you would tell me, wouldn't you?"

"W-WHA?" Aiden managed to sputter out, a little louder than he intended. "Dad, why the HELL would I be apart of a cult that was crazy like this?!"

Connor sighed as he walked over and took a seat across from Aiden on the other side of the couch. Aiden could feel the tension rising up in the air between the two of them. What a stupid move for him to shout out his answer like that! If he wasn't suspicious before, his dad was clearly now suspicious about the truth!

"I don't want to think that you are apart of this lawless cult, Aiden." Connor said in a near hushed tone. "But every time I hear more about what kind of members this cult has, I worry. The news reports say that all of the the members are social outcasts. That they don't have any friends, family, or anywhere to go."

"And what does that have to do with me?" Aiden asked. Connor turned his head back to him, a somber frown on his lips.

"Before you started to go out with Theresa every other day, I worried Aiden. That you weren't getting the socialization you needed. You would never join a cult like this, would you?"

"Dad. Do I look like the type of stupid ass-"

"Language."

"Ugh...do I look like the type of person who would be dumb enough to join a cult that would openly kill people to make a point to the rest of the world? I would never even entertain the idea of joining a sick cult like this."

"I want to believe that, Aiden. I truthfully really do. It's just...other parents would say the same thing about their own children. That their kids would never join something like this. I used to think that as well. That you would come into your own and not become an outcast."

"Dad, I'm not an outcast." Aiden argued back. "I've been friends with Theresa for my entire life, and I actually have a group of friends. Why the hell would I throw all of that away for some cult that is clearly insane?"

"That's what I'm trying to figure out." Connor admitted. "I do trust you son, more than you think I do. But as a parent, you worry about your child no matter where they are. You'll understand one day when you're a father yourself that you want to do everything in your power to protect your child from the dangers of the world, but you can't predict everything."

"Dad..."

"I want to trust you entirely, son. But lately I've been wondering on things." Connor folded his arms. "Like your sudden interest of remaining in shape, or how you will be gone for hours on end outside of the house with your friends. How you don't always hide yourself in your room anymore, or how I don't ever see you playing your video games like you used to do."

Aiden felt his stomach beginning to tie up in a knot. It was true that he had been doing less of what he once loved to do. With the time he had to spend with training for combat and studies for his classes took away a past time that he truthfully enjoyed. But he never once thought that it would look suspicious to anyone that he was reading and playing fantasy games less.

Then again the only one that would have taken notice of that entirely would have been his father. He had grown up with Connor constantly watching him spend his days getting lost in a big fantasy story book, or go on virtual adventures in video games. As far as Aiden could even remember Connor had always been vocal about his favorite past times.

Connor sighed as he leaned forward and laced his fingers together. It felt like Aiden's heart was beating rapidly as he stared back into the seemingly all knowing eyes of his father.

"I'm sorry, son. I'm being judgmental on you at a time where you must have felt traumatized. I forgot for a moment that you saw the body of the security guard right in front of you. But you wouldn't hide anything from me, would you?"

A twinge of guilt hit Aiden in his heart when Connor asked that question. He knew that his father was only trying to make certain that he was staying out of trouble. What kind of answer could he give his father in that moment? Would he even believe any kind of white lie that Aide would be able to force out of his lips?

"I promise, dad." Aiden finally spoke out. Forcing himself to tell a fib. "If I was in any kind of trouble, or was part of anything that I shouldn't be in I would have come to you for advice a long time ago."

A brief moment of uneasy silence passed between the two of them. A long sigh came from Connor's lips before he nodded his head at Aiden's answer.

"I see. Thank you." He said before standing up. "While I do trust you, Aiden, I do not trust the members of this cult that are starting to grow bolder. From now on, you're not to stay out for too long. Not until the Dark Eye cult begins to die down."

"But-"

"No buts." Connor snapped. "Two people have already been murdered by this cult, and I'll be damned if your name is added to that list young man. Your mother and I would not be able to live if something terrible happened to you. Am I clear?"

Aiden felt the urge to argue back, especially since this would create a problem for him and his friends. The moment his eyes met with Connor's though, any will to argue was sapped by the hidden flame behind his father's eyes. A twitch of fear spread through his body at the very idea of arguing with him.

Better to just agree for now, and find a solution afterwards.

"Yes, sir." He said quietly.

"Thank you." Connor replied before giving him a short nod. "Go relax, Aiden. Try to get your mind off the cult and let the authorities deal with them."

No more words needed to be spoken between Aiden and his father in that moment as the former left the living room heading back to his room. As if the situation had to get more complicated, now his father had basically put a curfew on him. A curfew, of all things! And Theresa had just locked down hard on them getting more training.

There was no way he was not going to let everyone know about this though. Especially Theresa, she had to know. If anyone would know how to figure a way around this, it would be her and the dragons. There were certainly a number of solutions for them to take to get around this curfew thing.

Once Aiden arrived in his room, he quickly sat down in his chair before pulling his phone back out. He started another group chat with his friends before sending the first new text message to them.

"We have a problem…"

CONFRONTATION

*A*bout a week or two had passed after the murder at Aiden's high school. It honestly felt like it was a lot longer to the group. Time seemed to have no meaning in that moment of intense training that he and Liza went through at the mage academy, who had graciously let their doors be open to the team for the training. Just like the rest of the country, they too were aware of the Dark Eye Cult and their heinous acts.

Getting around Aiden's curfew proved easier than he thought it would be too. The plan they had come up with to get the training they needed for their battles against the Dark Eye was to warp Aiden and Liza to the Academy around the time that their parents had gone to bed. They were also going to use the magical clones to give the illusion that they were in bed if their parents came to check up on them during the night. All the while during that time, they would be training in a renovated room at the Academy.

The days felt like they were each a week, and the first week felt like an entire month of non stop working to improve themselves in combat.

Aiden's training was honestly harder than anything he had gone through before with the Trinity. While he was getting closer to being just as skilled as Theresa was with a sword, the shield was an entirely different beast for him to handle. Especially since he was right handed! And the shield felt like a ton of bricks had been strapped to the weaker of his two arms! More times than not, Aiden found himself falling onto the ground from the impactful blows from all three dragons.

Be it Theresa's twin swords, Seamus staff and magic, or Garrett's massive fists the young teenager fell flat on his back from each succeeding blow. Making things more difficult for Aiden when training with his new shield was trying to adjust his left arm to be used more in combat for actual physical battle rather than firing out Flarnea spells. Not an easy task when before he all he had to worry about was using his left arm for two handed slashes with Warfang, or using magic with it from a distance.

If there was one advantage of getting to train like this it was definitely being able to blow off steam. Ever since the security guard's murder, and their battle with the three cultists in the street, the Dark Eye cult had gone strangely quiet. Everyone had the main goal of taking down the cult for what they had done, and they all wanted to prevent any more unwarranted deaths at the hands of the Dark Eye.

The new head of the Academy, Ryan, also proved to be a good source of support for the group. After what they had done for his school during the Overmind incident, the remaining mages and their students were willing to help the team as much as they could. The only one they hadn't seen much of was Lewis.

That was something Aiden did not push the issue about. After all, he saw into Lewis' mind when he was the Overmind. The trauma that boy felt was something that no one could ever truly recover from. At least, not within the short amount of time since they last ran into the mages.

By the time the second week was coming to an end, Aiden's high school made the announcement that classes would soon resume on a regular scheduled basis, with far more security protocols to be enforced on the school grounds to prevent something from happening again. As if the situation wouldn't feel even more stressful to hormonally charged teenagers who were already stressed out from their social lives and classes.

While school would obviously happen during the day, what made it more frustrating and stressful for the group was the fact that after classes, those with homework would be busy for a good chunk of the late afternoon. By the time they would be done with their homework they would feel sluggish and tired which would affect the training time they had with one another. It was something that even Theresa down right hated the idea of.

The day came when the students would return back to school for the second time after the murder, and not a single one of them looked like they wanted to be there. Many were already on edge from just mere rumors about the Dark Eye, and now they couldn't feel safe for a moment at school. Even with the added security, the entire student body felt like they were walking on landmines waiting to explode at the first misstep.

Even Theresa would be on edge throughout the entire day!

That early morning there was one good thing that came from returning back to classes, Aiden running back into Erienne again after what felt like forever. He didn't know why, but part of his heart felt all flustered at the idea of finally having another chance to talk to her. He hoped that this time it would be without Liza getting in the way after class and causing another huge scene. Though he would never fully out right admit it to it.

When Erienne entered the class room, she still had the same clothes she had since the first day of school. Her strange amber orange eyes were once again filled with mystique and, Aiden swore at this, a strange playful deceitfulness. That mystique quickly disappeared though when she spotted him in class. A wide grin came to her lips as she plopped herself down in her chair, followed by her placing her head right onto his shoulder once more.

"Hi you!" She said in a hushed sing song tone. "I missed seeing your face~"

"Oi, knock it off." Aiden hastily said with a blush on his cheeks. Even if it was nice to see her again. "You're gonna give people the wrong idea again, and we don't want a situation where Liza is screaming her head off."

"Oh that girl?" Erienne tilted her head to the other side. "She's just jealous of me and you~"

"There is no-" Aiden started to argue as Erienne pulled herself onto his left arm, hugging it tightly. The mood seemed to switch from a comedic tone to a more serious tone as he felt Erienne's fingers dig themselves into his bicep.

"I thought...I thought you had gotten hurt, Ragnakin." She whispered. "When I heard that...that someone was murdered here I thought you...I thought you were the one who..."

Aiden frowned at Erienne's sudden tone shift. Even she seemed to have been taken aback by what happened. The orange eyed beauty quietly pressed her forehead into his arm once more, fighting back what looked like tears forming in her eyes.

"I couldn't s-stand the thought of you being killed. I t-thought you were taken from this world...taken from m-me." She said with a slight sob. "I thought I was g-going to be alone again..."

Erienne rubbed her face into his arm for a moment before she pulled away from him. Tears still in her eyes, but a small smile was on her lips as she looked up at him.

"But...but you were okay. You made it through and...I'm just really really glad to see you're okay!" She proclaimed before hugging him tightly.

Aiden gave a short yelp. Even after she had done this so many times, he was still not used to her suddenly lunging onto him and hugging him like she was about to lose him. It wasn't like he had not been hugged by a girl before in his life. Theresa and him had hugged several times before. Both growing up together and during their adventures together when the situation looked dire.

This though? This was different from Theresa's hugs. They felt like a sense of urgency. Or that there was something that Erienne was deathly afraid of that she couldn't tell him. Just like why she couldn't tell him why she referred to him as "Ragnakin" so affectionately like she did. As if Erienne wasn't already mysterious enough!

"Hey...hey come on, people are gonna stare." Aiden told her as he gently patted her back. "I swear, I'm going to be okay. Nothing bad is gonna happen, I promise."

Erienne pulled away from him ever so slowly before drying her eyes off from the tears she was crying. Despite his promise, a sad smile came to the girl's lips as she looked right back into his eyes.

"Sometimes, you can't always keep your promises, Ragnakin."

Aiden felt like the air in the room went a deathly cold at how direct that statement was. In that moment it felt like the happiness that Aiden had known from seeing this girl had just vanished like someone had snapped their fingers and it disappeared. It was that instant, and that foreboding.

A million questions erupted from his mind in that instant. What did she mean by that? Why would she say such a thing? Did she know something that he didn't? She was already mysterious enough already. But this? This just made it even more cryptic than it had been before.

Just as he was about to speak again, the teacher walked into the classroom, followed quickly by the sound of a ringing of the school bell. Class had officially started once more. Aiden sighed as he turned to face the teacher. In the back of his mind he prayed for the day to end quickly, or move as quickly as possible, so that he could finally bring this issue up to Theresa about Erienne.

Classes were dull and slow for the rest of the day, and barely anybody in the school dared to walk from one class to the next without looking over their shoulders. All day it was like this. Everyone on high alert, barely anyone trying to talk to one another, and if anybody bumped into each other they would try to accuse the other of being a member of the Dark Eye cult. Thankfully, none of those moments lead to physical blows between each other.

However whenever someone was accused of being a member, it all stemmed from one source. The bane of everyone who found themselves at the lower end of the crazed hierarchy system that was high school had one person who would harass other students each time they ran into him. Aiden's old arch nemesis.

Eric.

While the sophomore bully dared not try to attack the upperclassmen, especially the bigger and stronger bullies from the junior and senior classes, he was not above terrorizing those in his own grade and those who were a year below him. Each time he bumped into someone, he immediately would ram them against a locker and spew a hail of insults to them. How he was never stopped by a security guard Aiden had no clue. He did it after ever period, sometimes with the same person or a brand new victim.

It took all Aiden had to not charge towards what was once his biggest threat on his life. He knew that back when they were younger he could have never touched Eric in a million years. But that was then. Now? Now Aiden was far stronger than he once was. And he knew all that it would take for him to flatten Eric on his ass would be for the stupid bully to throw the first punch.

He sighed as he thought about what Theresa's immediate response would have been though if he got into a fight with Eric. She would have given him the longest lecture in his life. That, along with the fact that his intense training in combat that he would have smashed Eric into a wall, was all that kept him from starting a confrontation. And that was barely holding him back enough as it was. Each time he saw Eric, the more he wanted to teach the bully a lesson that had been **long** overdue.

For a good part of the school day, Aiden had kept himself under control. There were only a few hours left until the end of the day. If he could make it to the final hour of that day without something terrible happening, then the day would have been an accomplishment of some kind. So far? So good. All he had to do was to not focus on the annoying sound of Eric's ear grating voice.

On the way to his second to last class for the day, Aiden walked quickly past Eric towards the hallway he was suppose to be heading towards. He just had to keep his cool. Just do that, and everything would have been fine. All he had to do was not give Eric the attention the bully wanted from his victims.

But then he heard a voice he could NOT have ignored.

"Oh! I'm sorry!"

Aiden's heart felt like it had just stopped beating the moment Erienne's voice rang out. He wasted no time in spinning around to spot her, standing right by the locker that Eric had walked by. Books had fallen to the floor, Aiden had to guess that Erienne accidentally knocked them out of Eric's arms when they bumped into each other. Normally under a regular situation, this wouldn't have been too much of a problem. But everyone was on edge. A simple thing like this could set off even the calmest teenager.

The bully snarled his teeth as he glared right at her. Aiden swore he saw him putting his hands into his pant pockets to pull something out on her.

"Sorry? You knocked my books out of my arms!"

"Did I?" Erienne asked, tilting her head to the side. "Did you not have a strong enough grasp on them? I'm not that muscular as you can see-"

"Shut your trap." Eric barked at her. "You think it's some kind of joke just bumping into me and making a light JOKE about it?"

"Joke?" Erienne replied. "But I didn't make any joke. I'm just simply-"

The sound of a fist punching into a metal locker rang out in the hallways. Eric's fist had just rammed a sizable dent right into the locker door. Most people would have jumped at the impact from the punch. But Erienne didn't flinch from the sound. Instead she stared right at Eric's face, confusion still spread over her face as the bully clenched his left hand tightly.

"You are this close to making me throw a punch at you." He said in a low voice. "Hell, you look like you could be a part of that stupid Dark Eye Cult running around. So let's make this clear to you since you felt like messing with me. You better apologize, bitch, or I'll make you sorry."

That was it.

Aiden stormed over to the two of them. His reasoning disappeared within that moment as he shoved Eric away from Erienne with just enough strength to not make the bastard fall over. God did that feel good to do after so many years. Just to finally do something to put the tormentor of Aiden's youth in his place. But this wasn't the time to let himself get caught up in how cathartic it felt to push Eric.

The bully blinked in surprise before turning back to the person who shoved him away from his target. His mouth gaped open as he saw Aiden standing in front of Erienne protectively.

"Back off, Eric." Aiden spat out. "No one wants to deal with your BS today."

Eric gave a loud guffaw. He shook his head back and forth for a moment as he folded his arms.

"What's this? Aiden? YOU standing up for someone? When did you start acting like a tough guy eh?"

"When you decided to antagonize someone over a small mistake and resort to calling her a bitch, that's when." Aiden retorted. "Cut the crap already, you've been doing this all day to everyone."

A small crowd of onlookers began to notice the rising confrontation. Aiden didn't care. This was something that had been a long time coming ever since he could remember. His whole life Eric got away with bullying people and not paying for it. And if that required Aiden kicking his ass for threatening to hit a girl, he would GLADLY do it.

"You sure are sticking your neck out for this chick." Eric responded. "What? She your girlfriend? Or is she your fellow cultist-"

"Shut up!" Aiden shouted. "You've been accusing everyone who dares to glance at you as being a member of this stupid cult all day! Why? You're big and strong right? The cult shouldn't terrify you of all people, right?"

Aiden felt himself taking one small step forward towards Eric. The bully staggered backwards as his former victim walked towards him with confidence. A fire in his eyes as he stared down Eric without batting an eyelash.

"Or is the truth that you're just a giant yellow belly coward? You're afraid."

A loud audible gasp erupted from the students that had stopped to watch. Eric's ears turned a dark shade of purple at the accusation. Never in his life had he been that angry before at anyone. But Aiden didn't care about how angry the bully felt. Over the last two years he had stared down far more terrifying and more powerful beings than some slightly overweight asshole from his childhood.

"YOU!" Eric bellowed. "I'LL KICK YOUR ASS FOR THAT!"

One of Eric's fists came charging at Aiden's face with as much speed as the bully could throw. Aiden's eyes never wavered as he effortlessly held up his left hand and caught Eric's punch midway through it. There was no grunt, no struggle, nor any kind of fear from Aiden as he kept his fingers locked around Eric's fist.

The bully stared at him with the most confounded look. He tried to pull his hand away from Aiden's grip, but to no avail. Everyone around them started to wonder if there was going to be some kind of counter attack from Aiden as he effortlessly kept the punch in place.

"You know. I used to be scared to hell about what you would do to me." Aiden gave a short tight squeeze over Eric's balled up fist. The bully let out a shocked cry of pain as he fell to his knees. The first time that had ever happened in their lives! "But the simple fact of the matter is that you're nothing, Eric. Nothing but a giant coward who uses his size to intimidate others just to get your sick kicks out of tormenting people who did nothing to you, or are different from you."

"GRGH!" Eric grunted as he tried to pull his fist away from Aiden with all his might.

"All day you've been accusing people who just sneeze that they are members of this stupid ass cult. You know NOTHING about them, you just want a reason to punch someone. And I for one, am sick of you doing it to people who don't deserve it!"

Aiden effortlessly shoved Eric's fist away from him. The shove was enough for Eric to fall back onto his back.

"You're not even worth it." Aiden said coldly. "There's far bigger, and far more dangerous things than you, Eric."

The bully stared at Aiden in shock, confusion, and anger. Their entire lives, they had been enemies. But after all the crap he went through with Raven and Dimitri's heinous actions, he no longer feared Eric.

"That's quite enough." A female voice sternly spoke out from the crowd of gathered students.

Aiden's heart almost stopped. At first he thought Liza or, God help him, Theresa had spotted the moment. He, Erienne, and Eric turned their heads towards the source of the voice. Part of him felt relieved when he saw that it was neither Liza or Theresa that spoke out. Instead, it was someone Aiden had never seen before in his life.

The woman that had ordered the confrontation to cease stood behind the three students. She was an Asian woman, Aiden could only guess what her ethnicity was, dressed in a proper grey business suit with matching pants to go along with them. She also wore a narrow pair of red rectangle reading glasses. Her brown eyes stared directly at Erienne, a furrow forming in her eyebrows.

"You. Are late." She said to her.

"H-Hey wait a minute. Who are-" Aiden started to ask, but the woman ignored him as she approached Erienne.

"I told you that you need to be on time. Must you always be difficult?" She asked. Erienne shuffled her feet as she stared down.

"I wasn't trying to be difficult…"

"You not showing up on time is being difficult. How many times must you do this?"

"Hey!" Aiden interrupted them. "Just who are you to get on her back like that huh?"

The woman quirked an eyebrow at him. The look on her face was one of utter contempt for him. Aiden felt the hair on his forearms beginning to rise up. The look she gave him was one that shook him to his very core. But he stood his ground, he couldn't look like a coward after calling Eric out for his actions.

"I, am Erienne's private tutor." She spoke in an icy tone. "Haru Sirukku. She is late for her lesson."

"Private lesson- We're in school!"

"Yes, you stupid boy." Haru retorted. "And there are some things that this school cannot teach her. That is my job."

"But you can't just-"

"I can, and I am." Haru grabbed Erienne by her forearm. "Come. You have wasted enough time here with these nothings!"

"Yes ma'am..." Erienne said with a crushed tone.

"Erienne you can't..."

"Aiden." She looked up to him with a sad smile. "Thank you for standing up for me..."

With that, Erienne was pulled away from the crowd and him. Aiden watched in utter silence as Haru and her left the school. He couldn't quite place his fingers on it, but it felt like she knew that he could not have stopped Haru from taking her away. He rolled his hands into fists before letting out a frustrated groan escape his lips.

"You..." Eric said behind him, standing back up now. "I don't know how you got that strong, Aiden...but don't think for a moment that-"

"Oh shut the hell up." Aiden said. "You're nothing but a bully. And I've outgrown you."

Those words were so icy that even Garrett might have been shocked to hear Aiden speak them out loud. The crowd began to disperse, surprisingly the security had not rushed to the scene of the confrontation, as Aiden power walked towards his next class. Eric was old news now.

Haru Sirukku. Something was off about her. He just knew it.

* * *

"You could have seriously gotten into trouble you know." Theresa said on the bus ride home. Aiden flinched as she squeezed his left ear lobe tightly. "I understand getting frustrated with Eric being a jerk, but you did it for some random girl?"

"Ow ow ow. You can let go now!" Aiden said.

"I don't think I will." Theresa said. "This girl you defended, why did you do it?"

"You saw him, Thes! He was antagonizing people all day and accusing them of being cultists! It was just too much to let him just get away with it!"

"Did you ever stop to consider that the security would have jumped in at some point if he actively tried to hit someone?"

"Oh that's bull and you know it. There's no way that they would have stopped him." Aiden grumbled. Theresa sighed as she let go of his ear lobe, right before flicking it with one finger.

"Like I said, you got LUCKY you didn't get suspended. Hell, you're lucky that they didn't think to take you to the principal's office right then and there."

Theresa frowned as she folded her arms.

"And all this for some random girl you never met before in your life?"

Aiden sighed. While he did tell Theresa the truth about standing up to Eric, in that moment of telling the story to her he decided it was best to wait before telling her about Erienne. At least, when everyone was gathered together at Aello's apartment.

"Yeah I just...I can't stand him getting away with everything, Theresa. And I think I made my point to him not to do it again."

"You also could have broken his hand or arm if you used any real strength." Theresa scolded him....but a small smile came to her lips. "I kinda wish I saw it though."

Aiden chuckled at that before his cell phone buzzed. A text message from his dad. This made him curious to see why his dad had texted him. Aiden shrugged before opening the text message up. What he read made him feel a bit uneasy.

"When you get home, you and I are going out for a walk."

As if today couldn't feel any more intense than it already was. His dad wanted to go for a walk? With him? Why couldn't they just talk at home? Something felt wrong about this. And Aiden didn't like it.

After the bus ride was over, and Theresa went back to her own house, Aiden found his father waiting for him in the driveway. Connor was wearing more casual clothes than he usually had on today. This always took Aiden aback whenever he saw him in something that wasn't a suit and tie.

"Good to see you son." Connor said. "How was school?"

"It was...eventual, let's just say that."

"Is that right?" Connor nodded. "You'll have to tell me all about it sometime. But come on, go put your bag in the house and come to the car. We're going to find a nice place to have a walk, and we'll have a nice long chat as well."

CORNERED

*A*wkward silence filled the car as Aiden sat in the passenger seat. This was not how he thought the rest of the day would have played out. With Erienne being cryptic at the start of class today and the confrontation he had with Eric a few hours ago, Aiden just wanted to unwind somewhat for the rest of the day. Hell, even doing *homework* of all things sounded relaxing compared to what happened.

But here he was. Sitting in the seat of his father's blue sports jeep. Trying to think of some kind of subject to break the ice between him and Connor.

Aiden hated whenever this happened. The foreboding atmosphere. The thick air in the car. It was enough to drive anyone's blood pressure up. Not knowing who would be the first to speak up. Every time this kind of atmosphere brewed up it lead to either Connor making an accusation that was right on the nose or he would drag the truth out of his son.

"Why did it have to be today of all days?" Aiden thought. *"The first day back to school since the murder, and he wants to have a chat? Dammit dammit dammit!"*

As the unbearable car ride went on Aiden found himself staring out of the passenger window more often than attempting to start a conversation with his father. It was weird to put into words but he always enjoyed watching the trees pass by them like a green blur. It always felt like it brought a soothing ease to his nerves. It mostly helped whenever

147

there was a tense moment, like at the moment. A small smile came to his lips, right before the car turned down a different road.

"Where are we going?" Aiden asked. "I know you said you wanted to go for a walk dad, but do we have to drive to go for a walk?"

Connor didn't respond to him. This made Aiden turn back to him, perplexed at why he didn't answer his question.

"Dad? Did you hear me? Dad?"

Again there was no response. Connor just kept his eyes on the road as he drove the car. Aiden felt a shiver run down his spine as he slumped back into his car seat. Right then and there he knew why his father wanted to talk. His stomach began to tie itself up into knots right along with his heart rate beating faster.

His father still thought he had something to do with the Dark Eye Cult.

"Oh great. He looks pissed. Or suspicious. Or both. God dammit all. He seriously still thinks that I'm part of that stupid cult?" He rubbed his eyebrows with his right index finger and thumb.

"I mean, technically I have some kind of part to do with this stupid cult, but it's not like I'm an actual member! But...agh! Why me? What did I do this day to deserve this crap?"

Aiden sighed as he closed his eyes for a second. If there was anywhere he'd like to be right now, it would not be here.

After a few minutes the car came to a stop. Aiden glanced around their new surroundings for that moment. He realized where they were now. Cumberland State Forest. A national park within Virginia that was located in the piedmont of the state. The familiar smell of the forest was enough to bring back childhood memories of when his family and Theresa's would come out here. The memories of them picnicking, hiking, and even attempting to climb up the trees were enough to make anyone feel nostalgic.

Though Aiden knew that his dad didn't bring him out to reminisce on times that had passed. The stoic look that was in Connor's eyes was more than enough for Aiden to realize that this was going to be a lecture from him. That or it would be a bombardment of questions that Aiden would have to be on guard for.

"Come along now, son." Connor said as he got out of the car. "Let's take a stroll down the pathway here, recall some memories together."

"Right..." Aiden said as he left the car.

This was it. He knew that the moment he dreaded was coming. It would end up coming at the moment he probably didn't expect it. Do or die time.

The two of them walked down one of the two self guided trails. The longer of the two. Aiden felt himself fighting back an audible groan as they went down the longer path. This had to be on purpose. His father would never pick the shorter trail to talk.

The pathway had some wonderful trees, plants, and wildlife to look at in amazement though. Oak and hickory trees, stands of Loblolly Pine, and harvested areas that had attracted many different forms of wildlife. The most common being white-tailed deer, turkeys, and on occasion bobcats.

Aiden found himself smiling as they walked down the trail together. It was nice to find some quiet in the world. Or rather, his world. The Dark Eye Cult, the magic, the mythical creatures being real? It could end up becoming too much on someone's mind.

It was nice to see the world be so quiet outside of the chaos. It was tranquil. Something Aiden loved.

"Do you remember when you were five years old?" Connor asked. His voice had cut through the silence, but it was calm and gentle. "We took you and Theresa here when you two just finished kindergarten. You kept thinking that there was some kind of monster hiding between the trees, waiting to pounce out at us on this trail. Your mother found your imagination to be something to encourage, and was exuberant that you loved the unknown like that."

"I remember." Aiden admitted. "I carried around a small stick in my hand on this trail, pretending that it was some kind of sword. I would swing it around whenever I saw a tree branch like it was a giant monster claw trying to grab us all."

"Yes, you were so innocent back then." Connor smiled. "You were a happy boy, Aiden. And I always thought you would do some incredible things in your life as you grew up. Your mother always encouraged your love for the unknown and fantasy stories. I for one thought you could do so much more."

Aiden frowned as he looked over at Connor.

"You're smart, son. You may not believe it, but I believe that you are able to figure out any problem that is before you. I didn't want you to become consumed by one thing in your life. But I know that your interests are your own and I can't force you to change them. I guess I just don't want that to become the only thing in your life. At least, that's when I worried about you."

Connor stopped walking in that moment, right in the middle of the trail. Aiden stopped as well as he placed his hands in his pockets. He noticed that the smile on his father's lips had slowly vanished.

"Then came the day I gave you that Dragon figure. You loved it dearly, from what I remember. But after that day, you spent less time at home, and more time out of the house with Theresa. She's been your friend since you were small, I realize that. But you would be gone for hours on end."

Aiden felt his ears turning beat red, quickly interrupting his father as he knew exactly what he was going to say next.

"Oh my God, Dad, if you think me and Theresa are sneaking out for THAT-"

"That wasn't my FIRST guess." Connor admitted. "I know teenagers go through hormones and such and-"

"DAD!" Aiden blurted out. "I swear, that is NOT what what we were doing whenever we went to hang out!"

"All right all right. There's no reason for you to shout that out, Aiden."

"You brought it up first!"

Connor sighed as he turned to Aiden. His brow was far more serious now as he folded his arms across his chest.

"Then I started to notice that not only did your activities start to change. You started to get more muscular. You started to be more active than just sitting around all day playing video games or reading fantasy novels. And you started to get a larger group of friends with Theresa. And not once did I question it. Until what happened with the Dark Eye Cult."

"I thought we went over this already, dad." Aiden interrupted him. "I swore to you that I'm not a member of that insane group. Nor would I ever WANT to be a member."

"But yet there was a murder that happened at your high school. Right where you and your friends all go together." Connor said. "And what did I tell you about interrupting people, boy? It's incredibly rude and you know better."

"Sorry." Aiden apologized halfway. "It's just, I feel like you're trying to pull something out of me that's not there, dad."

"I wouldn't have to be trying to if you were being honest with me."

"And I told you I am being honest-"

"You're being honest with me about not being PART of the cult." Connor cut him off. "That doesn't mean that you're telling me the entire truth. You may not be part of the cult, that I believe, but I do believe you have something to do with that cult. And I want to know what that is."

Aiden's palms begin to sweat as his father pushed further for answers. He was nearly on the money about what was really the truth. He wasn't part of the Cult, but how could he tell his own father that he was actively fighting against the cult and was trained by a trio of dragons to use a sword, shield, and even magic to face off against these people? Any sane person would have called him crazy, even if he WAS his father.

"I want you to be honest with me, right here, right now." Connor said. "Tell me, Aiden. What are you doing every time you and your friends go out? Where do you go? And why is it that you always look dead tired when you return home?"

"I..." Aiden felt himself speaking out, but he stopped himself as he glanced down. "I'm not doing anything. All we're doing is just hanging out, doing teenager things."

There was an uncomfortable moment of silence that passed between the two of them in that moment. A small gust of wind blew the leaves on the trail blew past them. Aiden could feel his father's eyes gazing down right into his head in that moment. He knew that Connor would still be pressing for answers, even if he was being brutally honest with him.

Aiden's palms continued to sweat badly as he glanced back to Connor's eyes. They were rigid, and unconvinced. Part of him wished that he would have dropped the issue entirely and resume walking down the trail without bringing the subject back up. But he knew his dad too well. He knew that there would be a moment when the moment he let his guard down, the other would strike with the next question.

"Aiden Russell." Connor said slowly. "I want the truth."

"I already told you, dad." Aiden replied with a calmly. "I am not part of their cult, nor am I doing anything stupid with my friends."

Time felt like it had slowed down by several seconds as Aiden waited for his father to reply. The back of his mouth began to feel dry, as he watched his eyes intently. He could tell right away that his dad was trying to figure out if he was telling the truth or not. It was like he had been put on trial.

Just before Connor could make another word, a loud 'crack' sound went off behind them. A branch, most likely, was the culprit of the sound. Aiden and Connor turned together towards the source of the cracked branch. The color in Aiden's face turn into a ghostly white the moment his sight made contact with what he feared the most happened.

The Dark Eye Cult had found him.

There were four members, each with a different build than the trio that Aiden had faced just days ago. This time, all of them were at least the same height and weight. Their facial expressions hidden behind their hoods. One though, pointed his finger right at Aiden.

"We found you..." He spat out.

Not good. Aiden glanced to his dad, who looked absolutely flabbergasted to see four cultists before them.

"Who in the-" Connor started.

"Shut up, old man!" One cultist shouted in anger. "You have no idea what this sick bastard did!"

"Did?" Connor asked in confusion before glancing to Aiden. "What are they talking about?"

"I..." Aiden started.

"Shut your mouth!" The lead cultist barked as he slammed his hands together. "The master has given us our orders you know. To bring you back, alive, for what you've done."

"Aiden-"

A blast of lightning shot out from one cultist's finger tips, the blast landing right between Aiden and Connor.

"I said shut your mouth, old man!"

Dammit all! It had to be the moment when Aiden was that close to convincing his dad that he had nothing to do with the cult! It was the absolute worse scenario for Aiden to be in right now. He was by himself, with his father out in the middle of the damn woods, and no back up from Theresa or the others to help even the odds against the cultists! To make matters worse, they probably knew how to summon demons to make this situation even more of a nightmare!

"You'll pay for what you've done, you son of a bitch." The leader said as he pulled his hands away from each other. A ball made out of what appeared to be purple fire formed in between his palms. "We heard what you did to Jeremy...everyone wants your head for it. The Master wants you alive...but screw that! You'll pay for what you've done!"

He glanced towards Connor. Aiden felt his blood run cold the moment the head cultist pulled the fire ball back behind his head.

"Since you took one of ours, we'll take this old man away from you!" The cultist roared as he threw the dark fireball at full speed towards him.

While to the rest of the world, everything was moving at a normal pace. But to Aiden, in that one moment? It was all slow.

The worst thing had happened. His father was now, by association with Aiden, a target of the Dark Eye Cult. All because he stupidly killed one of their own in combat. And now, his own family was in incredible danger due to what he had done. As the fireball roared in the air, Aiden realized he would have no choice.

"*Theresa is gonna kill me...*" He told himself, right as a small fireball in his left hand began to form.

"Dad shield your-"

"Ultimato."

The entire world seemed to come to a complete stop as Aiden's father spoke out. His voice cut through the tense atmosphere like a small explosion. A flash of yellow white light erupted in front of Connor as the dark fireball was sent flying harmlessly into the air by the light. It was so bright that Aiden had to momentarily shield his own eyes from it.

As the light began to die down, Aiden's eyes shrunk and his jaw dropped at the sight before him.

What was now floating in front of Connor, was probably one of the most glorious looking magic staffs Aiden had ever laid eyes on. The head of the staff was a giant golden circle, with angel wings intertwined within it. At the center of the golden wings was a large dark blue sapphire that glowed with immense magical power. The shaft of the staff itself was three feet long with golden rims running down towards the golden pommel.

The staff was so vibrant and powerful looking that it even rivaled Seamus' staff!

Aiden couldn't find the right words as he tried to process what was happening before him. Not since Theresa's reveal that she was a dragon was he taken aback like this. Especially by his own father of all people!

"W-What the hell?!" One of the cultists said in shock. "Where did that come from?!"

Connor sighed as he reached out and took the staff into his left hand. He glanced over to Aiden for a brief moment.

"Let me handle this, son." He said. "Then we'll talk about you and your sword."

"How did-"

Aiden didn't get the chance to finish his question as his father held the staff, which he had to guess was named Ultimato, in front of him. A magical golden aura covered Connor as he stared down the four cultists.

"I am giving you this one chance. Leave now, or know what a true mage is, young ones."

"Are you stupid you old fart?" The leader retorted. "In case you haven't noticed, you're outnumbered and-"

Connor simply flicked Ultimato once at the head cultist. A large surge of wind blew towards the leader, smacking him straight in the stomach, as he was sent flying back a couple of feet away from his allies. The cultists turned back to their commander in shock, but then glanced back to Connor.

"That. Was a warning." He said. "I'll say this once more, young ones. You do not want to do this."

"To hell with you, old man!" The leading cultist barked as he stood back up. "Everyone, get him! Then we'll deal with his stupid son for what he did to Jeremy!"

The cultists all nodded as the each clapped their hands together. Minor demons based on several insectoid like animals formed behind each of them as they all stared down Connor. The lead cultist's demon let out some kind of low snarl at the Russell duo. Aiden nearly flinched at the smell of one, but his eyes were glued to his dad.

Connor sighed as he spun his staff once and took a battle stance. The normally calm eyes of his father turned into a determined gaze as he held his right hand up at the eight opponents.

"So be it."

Without wasting a minute, the four demons roared loudly before racing towards him. Despite being outnumbered by the four demons, Connor stood his ground. Aiden once again began to form a fireball into his hand, but he stopped when he saw his dad lift his right hand up in the air.

"Blades of Light."

With the snap of his fingers, four pure white energy swords appeared in front of Connor. Each one identical in length and beauty that they would shine through the darkest night skies. Aiden's jaw dropped in amazement at the beauty of the energy blades, but that did little to intimidate the demons from charging.

"Kill the old man!" The lead cultist ordered.

The four demons all leaped into the air together, each one poised to strike the moment they aimed right at Connor's body. Once more, Aiden's father snapped his fingers. At that command the energy swords aimed towards the demons and flew straight towards them. The impact was instant, as each energy sword rushed through the demons. Like a pair of scissors cutting straight through a piece of paper.

The demons all let out pained cries of anguish as black blood leaked out due to the impact holes left behind by the swords. Connor snapped his fingers again, the energy blades turning back towards their targets. Again, another snap. The energy blades charged once more at the midair demons before they sliced past them. Aiden's eyes shrunk as he watched the four demons begin to fall down towards the ground. He then realized that the intense heat from the blades was so hot that it dried any blood from the demons that would normally be spilling out around them.

As the four dead demons fell to the ground, Connor sighed as he tapped Ultimato's pommel on the ground.

"Cleanse."

A white holy circle formed around the four demons. With another snap of his fingers, the holy circle completely vaporized the demons' remains from the world. Once they were entirely gone, the circle itself vanished from existence as well.

"H-HOW?!" One cultist asked in fear. "No one should be able to do that!"

"It seems you're as young as you all sound." Connor said as he pulled Ultimato up beside him. "I'll give you this warning once more, young ones. Leave and survive. Perhaps your master will forgive you when you tell him that I know who he is."

"To hell with you, old man!" The leader spat back. "Like hell you know who our master i-"

"Dimitri Morozov." Connor abruptly said. "That is the name of the man you have sworn your allegiance too, is it not?"

"H-How did…" Aiden started to speak, but his father put one hand up to silence him.

"Tell your master this. I am aware of what he is trying to do now. Let him know that his old 'friend' will make certain that he is stopped once more."

The cultists all flinched at the threat from Connor, the leader gritted his teeth momentarily as he snapped his fingers once, opening a giant portal behind them. Aiden felt a wave of relief wash over him for that brief moment as one by one they rushed off.

The feeling was brief though, as in the very corner of his eye he spotted a new sight. Two new beings. He had to guess that they were watching the fight the entire time. One of them was a large spider like demon, with the body of a woman in place of the head by the large abdomen. Aiden couldn't make out her details exactly, but that wasn't the only being there. His eyes squinted momentarily as he was able to make out the second being.

It made his heart stop.

Erienne.

"E…Erienne?" He called out to her.

For a split second, Erienne starred back at him. The same kind smile on her lips from before still there. When her eyes closed though, that kind smile turned into a far more demented and crazed grin. Shivers ran down Aiden's spine at the sight.

Erienne turned around with the spider demon, a large portal opening up in front of them.

"Wait!" He cried out. "Erienne! What is going on?! What are you doing with them?! Erienne!!!"

There was no response, not even a glance, from her as the two of them walked through the portal together. Aiden reached out in futility towards the duo as the portal began to close around them. A small tear forming in his left eye as he called out her name once more. Again, Erienne gave no response as she and the spider demon vanished.

In that very moment, a part of Aiden's heart felt like it had just been ripped out of him. The girl that had rescued him during the summer camp trip, the girl who always seemed to have a smile on her lips...was working with the Dark Eye Cult?

"Aiden." Connor's voice called out to him. "Aiden!"

Aiden shook his head, coming back to reality in that moment. His left hand quickly shot up, drying his teary left eye in that moment before turning back to his dad.

"Son..." Connor frowned as he placed his right hand on his shoulder. "We need to get back home. There's a lot we need to talk about."

"Yeah..." Aiden quietly acknowledged. "I...guess there is a lot that we have to talk about, dad."

His mind told him that was the more important thing to address...but with the way his heart felt in that moment, how could anything else seem more important than the fact that Erienne was an enemy?

FAMILY HERITAGE

The car ride home was filled with a very tense and very awkward silence between Aiden and his dad. Neither one of them felt like speaking out in the open about what had just happened. Not that Aiden wanted to address it right now anyway. Try as hard as he might, his mind found itself drifting back to every single moment he had with Erienne.

It just didn't feel or sound right. Erienne. Of all the people he had met ever since becoming Warfang's new master, she was the very last person he expected to be part of the Dark Eye Cult. It didn't feel right. Hell, it felt like some kind of divine prank from whatever divine entities there were in the universe. The girl that had shown him immeasurable amounts of kindness, the girl that while a bit quirky, was just a joy to be around...was the enemy. The very thought of it made Aiden feel sick to his stomach.

Aiden's mind then began to look around for an excuse, any excuse, to come up with as to why Erienne was with the Dark Eye Cult. She had to have been forced into it! There was no way that the sweet girl that he had come to know would actively join a cult like that. Not on her own free will. That had to be it! Right?

Try as he might to make himself feel better, he could not deny the dark demented grin that Erienne had on her lips before she and the spider demon left. He always was a terrible liar.

He shook his head once and then shut his eyes tight before

rubbing his fingers over his eyebrows as he tried to force himself to come to facts about what happened. Erienne was with the cult. No lie or excuse that he could come up with could ever erase that fact.

That didn't mean that facing the truth didn't make that any easier to deal with though. In truth, Aiden was starting to really like the girl. Her quirkiness had a certain charm to it. The way she was always happy despite everything going around her, even when Eric was threatening to her, it had a strange allure to him. Even if the hugs she gave him were so forced and a bit awkward, he would be lying to himself if he didn't somewhat find those moments endearing.

Aiden gritted his teeth once again as he began to wonder if Erienne had simply been putting on a front before him. One to hide the truth about where her true loyalties lied. The very thought of it made his stomach turn in anger. Had she played him like a damn fiddle? Did she use him emotionally to help the Dark Eye Cult?

That is what his mind told him. Anyone logically would have reasoned her motives and actions there were all a front.

But that's not what his heart wanted to believe.

Dammit all! Things weren't supposed to go this way! She wasn't supposed to be part of the cult! She was a kind hearted teenaged girl who was just quirky! Erienne didn't have any kind of part to play in this secret war between him and the Dark Eye!

Again, he never was a very good liar.

Just as his mind was about to toil over it again with his heart, his father took the first step in starting a conversation between the two of them.

"Son. I know that what happened back there was unexpected...but I can tell by the look on your face that the girl you were staring at...you know her, don't you?"

"...I thought I did." Aiden replied, his tone more somber than it was before.

"Thought? Or do?" Connor asked.

"You heard me." Aiden turned back to his dad. "I thought I knew her. When in reality, she was playing me like a damn fool."

"Those are some harsh words from you, Aiden." Connor turned the car onto the exit they had to get on. "I for one never expected you to utter something like that."

"What would you have me call it then, dad? That she is brain-washed or something? I saw that look she gave me. She's not a good person." Aiden clenched his fists tightly as he glared out the passenger window. "Even if it hurts like hell to admit that..."

"Now why would you go and think that?"

"Why would I not?" Aiden sarcastically asked. "It was all an act. And I was a damn fool to not realize it until it was too damn late."

"You sound so certain about this."

"That's because I AM certain about it. She's not someone to trust, dad."

"Is that what you're telling yourself now, son? To make the pain you're feeling right now feel a bit easier to swallow?"

"You have no idea what I'm feeling-"

"I do." Connor cut him off. "I know I don't look it, Aiden, but I am far more experienced than you are in life, boy. Especially when it comes to the everlasting sting of betrayal."

The air in the car felt like it had just blasted down into the near freezing zone when Connor said that. The hair on the back of his neck stood up as he watched his father tighten his grip around the steering wheel. Aiden swore that ice was beginning to rise up around his finger tips.

"Dad, I-"

"We will speak about this more when we get home. There is much that we must talk about, Aiden. That includes your mother as well."

"W-Wait a minute. Don't bring mom into this! She doesn't have anything to do with what's going on right now at all!"

Connor let out a dry laugh at that before shaking his head.

"Oh my son. You have a lot to learn about your parents."

Great. That was just great. Even his mother had something hidden from him? This was practically the wrong time for his father decided to be cryptic with him.

He still couldn't believe it though. Did what he witness before his very eyes actually happen? His father, Connor Russell of all people, a **mage** of all things? He couldn't think of one word the describe what he saw better than ironic. It felt like the entire situation was like some kind of divine prank from whatever divine being was watching over the world right now.

After all those years of lectures from his father to not get addicted to the idea of the fantasy genre, to not fall in love with the idea of magic or magical creatures, only to be hiding what he truly was from him his entire life! It would have been funny had it not been his own father that was a mage.

Aiden glanced back to his father for a second as the familiar sight of their home town started to come into view.

"So...how much do you have to tell me?" He asked.

"A lot, Aiden." Connor's answer was brief. "Now quiet, we'll talk when we get inside our house."

"And why the hell can we NOT talk about it in the car?"

"Because you never know who is or might be listening." Connor spat. Aiden took notice of a much more stern tone from his voice. "Have you learned nothing about how some magics work, boy? There are some magics that spy on everyone. You have no idea what lengths I have gone to keep our family safe from the eyes of those who would follow Dimitri."

He turned his head back towards Aiden as they pulled into the driveway. His brow furrowed low as he turned the car off.

"Have you ever wondered why your enemies have never tracked you to this location? It was because of my efforts to keep our family safe, Aiden. Safe from maniacs like those that tried to attack us today."

Aiden flinched from the short lecture his father gave him. It was true that he often wondered why his enemies never seemed to bother to track him back to his house. He had always assumed that he had gotten lucky and that they were terrible in finding where he lived. It was a scenario he was very grateful for that he never had to worry about Raven finding him.

But this entire time it had been his father's own protective wards around their house that kept them out of the eyes of enemy mages? How had he not noticed? He had been practicing using magical spells for a few years now, and there was never a hint of magical energy around his home.

Not even Theresa seemed to notice the wards whenever she came over to visit!

That all lead to one very important question that Aiden had to ponder on. Just how powerful is his father?

"Come." Connor's voice brought him back to reality. "We need to get inside. Let me do the talking to your mother before you learn everything."

Aiden gave a short nod to his father's order before getting out of the car. The moment he took one step out, his cell phone began to vibrate. In that moment he cursed the moment. He glanced back to his father, who had been watching him carefully. There was no way in hell that he was going to be able to respond to whoever was calling or texting him.

He would have to ignore it for now. Whoever it was, and he the feeling that it was Theresa, would have to wait. For now he made his way to the front door as quickly as he could go. As he moved into the house, Connor snapped his fingers once. Aiden didn't flinch, but his eyes did catch glimpse of a magical shield going around their house.

"A protection spell?"

"A hiding spell." Connor corrected him. "It'll keep our enemies from finding this place, it's how we stayed out of Dimitri's sight for sometime. Until you apparently ended up on his radar."

"Honey? Aiden?" Helena's voice called out from the laundry room. "Is that you?"

"Yes, dear." Connor replied.

"Oh thank God." Helena made her way from the laundry room, carrying a large basket of clothes. "I thought for certain something happened to you two while you were out. The news report of this Dark Eye Cult have been making me uneasy as of late and-"

"Helena." Her husband cut her off. "He knows."

Aiden's mother blinked as a frown crossed her lips. She turned her gaze over to him, the latter trying to hide his eyes from her in an attempt to avoid being lectured, or questioned. Instead she gave a short sigh before closing her eyes. A single word escaped her lips.

"Leviatie."

Just like that, the laundry basket that she had been carrying in her hands floated away from her, and then flew towards one of the couches. Aiden watched in amazement as the basket landed with a soft 'thud' onto the cushions of the couch.

"Did you just..." Aiden started out, but his mother paid him no attention as she approached her husband.

"Did I hear you right?"

"You did."

"...Was he hurt?"

"Not at all."

Helena sighed once more before closing her eyes. Then she pulled Aiden into a very strong hug with both arms around his upper back.

"Oh my poor boy." Her tone changed from a happy one to a more saddened one. "I'm so sorry that you have to learn the truth this way..."

"M-Mom, please." Aiden gasped. "Squeezing too hard. Can't breathe."

At his request she released him from her arms. His mother was the biggest sweetheart that he knew, but sometimes she could have a killer grip.

"Everyone to the living room." Connor ordered. "Aiden, there's a lot that your mother and I need to tell you."

"Connor what about the wards?"

"Don't worry. I already re-strengthened them the moment we stepped into the house. Even Dimitri will have a hard time finding this place."

Helena gave her husband a reluctant nod of her head before literally pulling Aiden over to one of the couches. The teen had no time to make a complaint about being dragged by his mother before being plopped right down onto the smaller of the two couches. Once Aiden somehow managed to make himself comfortable, both of his parents took their own seats in front of him.

"This is...new." Aiden admitted. "Usually when you have me on this couch, it's to lecture me about something I did wrong."

"Not the time, son." Connor said. "As I told you in the car, there is a lot to tell you. So I suggest you let me explain."

Aiden felt his lips had a zipper pulled across them, he dare not retort his father. He would not do that now anyway after seeing what the man was capable of doing. Connor laced his fingers together in front of him as he tapped his foot a couple of times.

"Where to begin..." He mused. "There's so much to tell you, and so little time. I suppose I could tell you how I came to learn that I had magic powers, but I believe that doesn't truly interest you."

Connor let out a loud sigh before ultimately deciding on what he would tell Aiden.

"Aiden Russell, as you saw today when we were attacked by those cultists, I am not a typical person. Just like you, I have a connection to magic. Far more advanced than I'm sure of what you know, based on what you saw today, but that is not the point."

Connor unlaced his fingers from each other before bringing his right hand towards Helena's left. The married couple each gave the other's hand a tight squeeze as they looked for the right words to explain everything to Aiden.

"I'll spare you the story of how I came to the Academy, and yes I know you went there, for later. For now, you need to know something more important. And that is how your mother and I know about the leader of the Dark Eye Cult."

"Connor, don't tell me that it's..." Helena started, her husband gave her a grim nod.

"It is, my love. The leader of this cult is none other than our old classmate...Dimitri."

Helena brought her free hand to her mouth, at the revelation. For a split second, Aiden could have sworn that his mother's long hair had risen up into the air for just the briefest of moments, before falling back down.

"Then...is it what we feared?" She asked. "Is he doing what he sought out to do?"

"That, I don't know." Connor admitted. "But I know his teachings, all too damn well. The mages that attacked us today was the proof I needed."

"Mom, Dad." Aiden interjected. "Not to sound like a teenager who is always on the move, but I still need like, questions answered."

The two adults turned their attention back to him. Aiden fully expected one of them to scold him for interrupting a conversation, but instead they both gave sad smiles to him.

"You're right, son." Connor replied. "You do have questions, and you most certainly deserve those answers."

"Go on, honey." Helena added.

"Well...I guess the biggest elephant in the room is this. Mom...dad. How is it that you know the leader of the Cult?"

Connor leaned forward gently in his chair, closing his eyes. It was clear to anyone that it was a...painful subject to address. Aiden could tell that he was grimacing at the very idea of recalling his past.

"Dimitri and I were classmates together at the Academy. He was among one of the first that I got to know when my new studies began there. Him and another that I don't often talk about, Ivan."

"Tch, yeah, I know that jerkwad." Aiden grumbled.

"Aiden, don't interrupt your father."

"It's fine, Helena." Connor insisted before opening his eyes once more. "We'll talk about him later. As for Dimitri, I was a young lad when I began to learn that I had abilities that shouldn't seem possible. Setting things on fire when I didn't mean to, causing a bright flash of light to erupt from my hands whenever I simply waved at someone, or accidentally causing a power outage."

He let out a dry laugh.

"I thought I had been cursed by someone, or that I was some sort of freak. But that's when they came and brought me to the Academy. Told me everything that I needed to know about why I was able to do these things. As you can probably imagine, it was rough for me to adjust to a new life away from your grandparents. I felt alone there...at least for awhile."

A somber smile came to his lips.

"Dimitri was not always what you know him as today, son. Back when I was young, he was a kind hearted person. Talented, and a decent group leader when the moment called for it. Him, Ivan, and I got into many misadventures together during our youth."

"In fact that's how I met your father as well." Helena chimed in. "I had gotten caught up in one of their antics one day, that lead me almost getting in big trouble with the Grand Mage." She jabbed her husband with her elbow. "We could have been expelled because of you three deciding to go where your noses shouldn't have been!"

Aiden had to stifle a laugh from erupting from his lips. He could scarcely even believe the very idea of his own father being a trouble-maker. Connor also chuckled at his wife's jest before continuing his story.

"For years, the four of us lived at the Academy together. Honing our skills with magic, becoming stronger every single day with each training session we endured, and all the while learning more and more powerful spells." Connor clenched his fists together. "And all the while, I had no idea what Dimitri, my friend had been doing behind our backs."

Helena frowned, placing a soft hand on her husband's back ever so kindly. Aiden also felt sympathetic for his father in that moment. Despite everything that Dimitri had done since the very first encounter he and his friends had with him he could see that his father was pained.

"I'm sure you've seen them, the demons his cult now uses?" Connor asked. "When we were in school, were were taught to never seek out to use the dark arts, to never try to summon demons. It was forbidden. But the more we were lectured about why the arts weren't allowed to be learned, the more curious Dimitri became about them. I should have noticed it the first time he asked our instructor about how those who practiced the Dark Arts could have avoided being controlled...but I didn't see it as anything other than him wanting to theorize."

He let out a large sigh as he shook his head.

"I was a damned fool back then. But I wanted to believe so badly that my friend was not being tempted into learning the ways of the Dark Arts."

"I.." Aiden frowned. "Dad I, I didn't know..."

"No. How could you know?" Connor replied. "It was not something that I ever wanted you to learn about."

"But...what happened?" Aiden asked. "When we were there, Ivan admitted that he got this crazy idea to control demons from Dimitri himself-"

"He WHAT?" Connor asked in horror. "What did he do Aiden?"

"Dad-"

"What. Did. He. Do?"

Aiden felt himself slouching back in his seat for a moment, but swallowed a lump in his throat. It was only fair that they know the truth about what happened at the Academy. After all they were being truthful about their past right now.

He kept it brief, deciding not to go into the full on details for the time being, after all their story was far more important to him right now.

"I..." Connor's jaw hung open. "Ivan...did all of that?"

"He did..."

"Dammit...then Dimitri's words truly DID get to him..."

"W-What did he even say, dad?"

Connor rubbed his hand against his face. In his eyes Aiden could see a mixture of many emotions at what he had heard. Anger. Regret. Shame. Disappointment. All of them churned within the storm in his eyes.

"It was before you were born. Years ago, when your mother and I were just about to graduate from the Academy. We were young then, in our twenties. Ivan had already married, your mother and I had been going steady for sometime, but Dimitri continued to do..research." Connor explained. "One day, he called for Ivan and I to meet him in his quarters. Said that it was the discovery of a lifetime, that it would rearrange the world as we knew it."

Connor slammed his fist onto the armrest of the couch, rather hard.

"It still makes me furious to this day even thinking about it...but when we arrived at his dorm, the two of us were shocked to see that within a large cage, was part of a massive demon. A hand. It was obsidian like, with magma pouring out of its palm. But yet, it never melted the cage due to the strong magics that Dimitri had placed around it."

Aiden's pupils shrunk. He knew what hand his father was referring to. The same one that Dimitri had used back in the Harpy's Den. He dared not mention it now though. Not when there was much more to the story.

"You can imagine that we were taken aback by the very sight of the damn thing. When Dimitri came out from behind the curtains, we demanded answers. It didn't take a genius mage to realize that what he had within his possession was a very dangerous and very powerful demonic being. Dimitri tried to play it off as no big deal. That he had complete 'control' over the thing the entire time."

"How did the heads of the school not find out that he had this hand?" Aiden asked, flabbergasted somewhat.

"That's what we wanted to know. And his answer? He had been working on learning the Dark Arts in secret the entire time. That he had found a 'source' to practice those arts, to learn how to summon Demons and make them his personal servants. He even admitted that the entire time he had been studying with us, he would then study the

Dark Arts in his quarters when no one would bother him. And that the first demon part he ever summoned was the obsidian hand that was before us."

Connor gritted his teeth.

"I remember being so furious at him for it. I demanded he get rid of the damn thing. Get rid of it and the three of us would never mention it ever again. That we would go on with our lives. But he would not listen. He called me a coward for not seeing the 'potential' that he had just brought forth. Everything we were taught over the years? He claimed it to be a lie. That the demons were meant to serve mages instead. Ivan and I couldn't even begin to believe what we were hearing. Our life long friend looked like he had just lost his damn mind."

Helena placed her arms around her husband's neck. Her eyes beginning to swell with tears at her husband's story. Connor gave her arm a squeeze with his free hand before continuing.

"I told Dimitri that he was out of his damn mind. That what he had just done was against everything that we had ever learned. That we wanted no part in learning the Dark Magics due to what they could have brought forth. As the two of us argued about the morales of it all, Ivan began to...get curious." Aiden noticed small lighting bolts forming around Connor's finger tips. "He actually began to wonder if what Dimitri was saying was right. The argument had taken such a turn for the worse that I forced an ultimatum on Dimitri. Either he get rid of the damn hand...or I would tell the Grand Mage what he had done."

"...Did you?"

"He left me no choice." Connor said. "I thought for certain that if I brought the idea of the head of the Academy into the picture, Dimitri would back off. But he refused. In that moment he became furious with me and Ivan, who I had gone to great lengths in that argument to see that it was wrong, for 'abandoning' him when he was one the cusp of whatever he thought was 'greatness'. The argument got so intense that he actively pulled his staff out on the two of us and fired a blast of lighting. We were able to avoid the blast, but we returned fire back at him."

Connor's brow furrowed in anger.

"And that's when that damn hand broke free. During our scuffle we didn't notice it, but Dimitri had been chanting some unknown language to us, and it wasn't until the last moment that we realized that it was him gaining control of the demon hand he held captive. It blocked all of our attacks. Long enough for Dimitri to open a portal out of his quarters. That day, he swore revenge on the two of us, for not siding with him. With that hand in tow, they retreated...and in that moment both Ivan and I believed that we had truly seen the last of our friend."

"Dad..." Aiden managed to gasp out. "But...but what happened to you after he left? Did he attack the Academy?"

"No. If I had to guess, Dimitri knew that even with his new abilities to summon demons, he would not be able to fully take on the school." Connor admitted. "After the confrontation, the two of us reported to the Grand Mage and we told him everything that happened in that room. After the initial shock, he made it known to the entire school that Dimitri was to be considered a lost cause, and that should any of the students come across him to report back to the Academy immediately. That was at least 22 years ago."

He brought his head back up, staring Aiden right into his eyes.

"Ivan married his sweetheart and had their first child, Ryan, four years after that event. But I could tell that it had taken its effect on him as well. He and I barely spoke with each other after the events. And whenever we did speak, it was usually about if we were in the right or wrong. Those discussions started to turn into bitter arguments, arguments that I wish we never had. Eventually, I had enough of it. I had to leave the Academy. It was clear that nothing I said was getting through to him, and I had grown sick of being constrained within the school's walls."

"That's where you come in." Helena said with a tiny smile. "Around that time, your father and I had been married for at least a year after Ivan's son was born. A few months later, I found out that I was with you. "

"It was a moment of genuine happiness..." Connor admitted. "But I knew that I didn't want your life to be consumed by the ways of magic like it had consumed ours. I sought a way out and I took it. I would not have my wife and child constantly be exposed to what had happened between me and Ivan. So one night, we decided that it was time that we left. With what clothes we had, and what money we could conjure up with our magic, we left the only place we had called home and found ourselves here in Virginia. Hoping to live out a peaceful life here away from all of that."

Connor sighed as he shook his head.

"I suppose that's why as you were growing up that whenever I saw you get really addicted to a magical fantasy story, or get lost for hours in those video games you play about fantasy worlds that I got upset. I didn't want you to be exposed to what your mother and I had run away from. But I knew that eventually you would have found out somehow. It's in your blood, just like it's in ours."

"Dad I…" Aiden gaped. "I…I had no idea that the two of you were so closely tied to the school and to the ways of magic."

"And we wanted to keep it that way." Connor admitted. "We thought you deserved a normal life, son. But now? I can see now that you haven't had anything 'normal' happen to you as of late."

"Your father only wanted to protect you, Aiden." Helena added. "It was not out of resentment that we kept this truth from you for so long."

Aiden frowned. It was time that he took a turn.

"Guys it's…it's okay. I'm not upset with you two about this. I'm just flabbergasted that this all happened. And that you two are actual mages!" He let a grin escape his lips. "If anything it's awesome to learn that there's a reason to why I can use magic!"

Then a sudden realization came to him.

"Wait a minute though dad…how did you come across this?" Aiden held Warfang out in front of him.

"Ah. The Dragon King's blade." Connor mused.

"You know what this is?"

"Son, we were lectured by Seamus whenever he came to visit our school about the old Kingdoms and the weapon of the Dragon King. Of course I know what it is." Connor smiled.

"And as for why we have it…believe it or not, I came across it at the Flea Market one day. You couldn't sense it since you were so young, but I could. I knew right away that I could not run the risk of the sword being taken by someone who did not know what it was. I told myself that if I ever came across Seamus the Spellweaver again, I would pass it onto him. Though as the years went on, I began to accept that you did not have a spec of magic within your body, hence why I gave it to you as a present."

Aiden stared in awe at his father's confession, right before glancing at Warfang.

"Now then...I want you to tell me everything that's been happening with you, young man." Connor said sternly. "And I want every single detail about what's happening."

Aiden flinched.

"Dad I..."

"Don't feel bad, Aiden." Helena smiled. "We're not angry with you. On the contrary, we want to offer you any kind of support we can give you now."

"It's not something the two of us like to think about, but you are now caught up in this war with Dimitri. And it sounds like you and your friends need more help than you can know."

Aiden sighed. Everything seemed to be happening so fast. At once moment, his parents were normal human beings with no magical powers, and then in an instant they become incredibly powerful mages who want to help. He knew that there was going to be hell to pay with Theresa...but his parents had been honest with him about their past. Now it was time for him to be honest with them.

He only hoped that Theresa wouldn't kill him for what he was going to tell them...

THE SAD STORY OF ERIENNE

"*A*re you OUT OF YOUR MIND?!" Theresa shouted. Her index finger and thumb had an ironclad grip on Aiden's earlobe. "Unbelievable! You could have seriously gotten yourself hurt out there! I don't care if your father is some great and powerful mage, you shouldn't have gone alone without notifying me!"

It had been a day or so since the encounter between the cultists, Aiden, and his father. The hours following after their conversation, Aiden sent a group text chat to everyone to make plans to come to his house after school. Not just Theresa. Everyone in their group was invited to his house.

It wasn't something that he particularly looked forward to. But he knew that it would have to be done. He made a promise to both himself and to his parents that he would gather everyone together to talk.

"I didn't really have a choice!" Aiden yelped as she pulled his ear harder. "It wasn't like I could just tell dad that we had to run!"

Theresa snarled slightly as she tugged once more, a bit more ferociously this time.

"And what if your father didn't have magic powers?! What would have happened then?! You could have DIED you idiot!"

"N-Now now, Rexkin..." Seamus spoke out. "To be fair to the kid, it's not his fault they ambushed him-"

"And YOU!" Theresa glared at him. "You saw his parents at your

Academy years ago?! Don't you think that kind of information is important to share?!"

"I had no idea that he was the child of two former students!" Seamus retorted. "And even then, it's not like I remember every single face that I've seen in my years of wandering the world!"

"You still could have possibly mentioned that you MIGHT have known his parents from their youth!"

"Rexkin." Garrett spoke out. "While I can understand your frustration with both the whelp and Seamus for his foolishness, there is a time and place for that. The whelp's parents are in this room with us after all."

Theresa sighed as she released Aiden's earlobe. The throbbing pain he felt shift through his head raced like his pain sensors had been lit on fire.

"You're right, Garrett. There are more important things to address right now. The first and foremost though, is this."

She turned back to Connor and Helena. There was a brief moment of tension as the White Dragoness stared down Aiden's parents. But that moment soon passed. Theresa politely bowed her head towards them.

"Forgive me, Mr. and Mrs. Russell. We hid the truth from the two of you only because we wanted to keep you both safe."

"Theresa, dear, there's no need for you to apologize." Helena insisted. "We've known you since you were a little girl. We always suspected that you had something special within you. We could sense it the moment we first met you all those years ago. If anything, we should be apologizing to you and Aiden for hiding this from you for so long."

"And who are we to judge?" Connor added in, a soft frown across his lips. "We have hidden this truth from you kids for so long. We could have come forth at any time and reveal to you that we always knew once we learned the situation you had gotten yourself into. Everyone in this world has their secrets I suppose," He chuckled, a wry smile spreading across his lips, "That's one constant truth across all this world's clans."

"Then you know the situation we now face is dire." Garrett spoke out. "That the cult we face is the biggest threat to the world at this moment."

"Not yet they aren't." Connor corrected him. The fact he showed little fear in interrupting a great dragon like Garrett made Liza, Aiden, and the harpies all freeze up. "Dimitri is a great organizer, that can't be denied, but he has not spread the influence of his cult over the rest of the world yet. For now, the problem remains within the United States. But it could very well spill out to the rest of the world. And sooner than we think."

"Yes." Helena chimed in. "I've been paying attention to the news more often as of late. And what I've read and seen has disturbed me. Cities all over the country, not just this state, are starting to see more riots from members of the Dark Eye Cult. Many of them openly marching out against society, others starting fights with the local authorities, and some killing people in broad daylight."

Aiden's mother shook her head in disgust and shame as the very words came out of her lips.

"It makes me completely sad to see the world come to such a state like this. That everyone is on edge and seems to want to fight over every small little detail."

"Mom..."

"But. There is always hope." Helena gave a soft smile. "For now? Now we have the means to counteract them. All of you have been doing it for awhile, haven't you?"

"More like only a few days." Seamus muttered.

"And you walked away from that encounter victorious." Connor added. "Do not sell your selves short, Spellweaver. The fact that you all managed to fight off three powerful members of their cult is nothing short of amazing."

"But that still doesn't answer one question." Liza spoke out now. "Who was it that murdered the security guard?"

"If I had to guess? One of the top ranking demons within Dimitri's cult." Connor admitted. "If only I got to examine the hole itself, I could have possibly figure it out by now."

"Oh you poor humans. If only you knew indeed." Kali interjected. Everyone gave her a short glare, which she responded with a short grin. "It's clear as day. The demon that killed that sack of useless meat was a Prime Demon. But unlike me, a being of perfect shape, this Prime Demon is in the form of a hideous arachnid creature."

Aiden felt his blood ran cold. Without thinking about what he should say, he immediately stood up.

"Do you know what she looks like?" He asked.

"Maybe~"

"Don't play games with me, snake bitch!" Aiden snapped. "Tell me the truth! Do you know what she looks like or not?!"

"Aiden!" Theresa shouted at him.

"No, Thes, no!" He argued back. "This is too damn important to ignore! If it's who I think it is, then she...she..."

Aiden clenched his fists together as he hung his head. The memory of Erienne and the spider demon she was with still burned into his retinas. The cruel smile that she had given him before they left. The way she didn't even attempt to respond. It made his heart feel like it was cracking into several pieces.

"She was with one. A giant spider demon..."

"She?" Seamus blinked. "Kiddo, you okay?"

Liza frowned as she watched Aiden's hands tremble.

"It's that girl you had on your arm the first day of school, isn't it?" She asked. "That girl that vanished when Theresa showed up."

"Aiden..." Theresa frowned. "What is going on?"

Aiden took a deep breath. Now it was time for the second part of what he promised himself that he would reveal to the rest of the group. He turned back to his best friend, a small hint of tears in his eyes as he stared at her.

"Thes...there...there's been this girl that I've seen a couple of times now. She saved me and Liza after our fall when we were tracking down the den of the harpies two years ago and...and she's been showing up in the oddest of places for me this year."

"Aiden." Theresa spoke out. "I can tell in your eyes that this girl that she's...different, isn't she?"

"She is."

"I see...are you and her together?"

"N-No." Aiden responded quickly. "I mean, she keeps trying to insist that there's something between the two of us and I've told her before that there's nothing but...she's clingy for some reason."

"...What is her name?"

"Eh?"

"Her name, Aiden." Theresa repeated. "What is her name?"

Aiden took a deep breath. It was now or never.

"She calls herself Erienne. Erienne Ivy."

The moment her name escaped his lips, all three dragons stood up from where they were sitting. All three of them had the same look of shock and disbelief written over their faces. Theresa's emerald green eyes began to swell with hot tears as she took a step towards him.

"What did you say?" She asked. Her voice calmer than it had been throughout the entire afternoon.

"Erienne. That's her name." Aiden repeated.

"That...that's impossible." Seamus said. "There's no possible way that's her name."

"It is, Seamus!" Aiden barked, a bit louder than he intended. "She told me it herself!"

"Welp." Garrett's deep voice cut through the tension. "Look at Theresa, and say that you are lying to us right now."

Aiden blinked in confusion, but he did revert his gaze back to Theresa. The normally calm and collected eyes of the Dragon's leaders were no longer relaxed. Instead, they were filled with sorrow, regret, and...shame?

"What does she look like?"

"She...she has short black hair, it goes down to the middle of her neck, and orange amber like eyes..." Aiden told her. The white dragoness' eyes began to cry out several tears.

"Tell me you're lying." She begged. "Tell me that you did not say that name..."

"I..." Aiden frowned. "I'm sorry, Thes. But it's true...that's her name."

"Would someone please explain to me what the hell this is all about?" Liza asked.

Theresa took a few steps back away from Aiden, turning her back to him for a moment as she covered her mouth with both hands. Aiden flinched as he saw her shoulders shudder and legs tremble. Not out of fear, no, but out of what he could tell was a deep sadness.

"T-Thes?" He barely managed to get out.

"Theresa, honey. Please." Helena stepped in. "There is nothing to be ashamed of here. You are with all of us, your friends. You are more than welcome to feel comfortable to speak out."

There was a long pause in the room as Theresa kept her back to Aiden. He could hear a faint sob every now and then escape from her lips as each second seemed to pass by agonizingly. Aiden's heart felt like it had just been shattered by his best friend's soft whimpers as he waited what felt like an eternity for her to speak out once more. With a deep breath, she turned back to face him. Tears still in her eyes.

"That name..." She managed to speak out. "That was her name..."

"Her?"

"Do you remember the story I told you in the Academy, Aiden? The one about my family life back in the days of the Great Kingdoms?" She asked him. Aiden nodded his head once. "That name...Erienne...it...it is the name of my little sister."

The entire room felt like a cold blast of air had just rushed through it. If Aiden was holding a glass of water in his hand, he would have dropped it. Liza and the Harpies all gasped. Seamus and Garrett looked away, both looking ashamed to hear the name out loud.

"S-S-She's your sister?!" Aiden asked in disbelief.

"Erienne..." Garrett snarled. "If it's her, then you know what must be done, Rexkin. She must be..."

"Quiet, Garrett." Theresa ordered. Tears still falling from her eyes. "I will not hear you speak another word about what must happen."

"She must pay for what she has done, Rexkin!" Garrett argued back. "For the suffering she put our people through!"

"T-Time out!" Aiden managed to bark out. "Could everyone just calm the hell down for five minutes before you go saying something like that!"

"Why should we remain calm?" Garrett asked, his lip curling back into a snarl. "When it comes to that bitch, there is nothing to discuss."

"I will not have you speak that way about my sister, Garrett!" Theresa roared at him. "You will not call her that, not so long as I lead this group! Do you understand?!"

Garrett snorted once, puffs of black smoke escaping from his nostrils. He gave a short scoff sound to her, before slowly backing off the topic. Theresa brought one arm up to her eyes, drying them off as best as she could, as she took a deep breath.

"T-Theresa..." Aiden reached a hand out to her shoulder. "I..."

"It is something I hoped to never tell you, Aiden." She interrupted him. "The rest of the story of my baby sister. It is...not a pretty one."

Theresa beckoned him to take a seat. He hesitated at first, but eventually relented as he went to sit down. Once Aiden found himself in a comfortable spot, Theresa paced back and forth for a brief few seconds before taking a seat herself.

"As you know, my little sister was considered a runt among the dragons. The rest of our kind always wondered how such a dragon like her was born to a powerful family like ours. They often would try to openly mock her in our presence. Something that they learned not to do. But what they truly thought of her didn't matter to me, or my original mother and father. To us, she was a perfect little girl. One that we loved with all our hearts."

A brief wry smile came to her lips as she recalled memories from her past.

"I always told her when we were young that it did not matter the size of the dragon, what truly mattered was the size of their heart, and what they were willing to do for their homeland, and for their king. Those words always seemed to resonate well with her. As each time I spoke them, it brightened up her day just a tiny bit more."

"It sounds like you two were close." Liza mused, a small smile on her lips.

"We were as close as sisters could ever be," Theresa admitted. "I could tell her anything and she would swear to secrecy. As such, she could tell me anything and I would never reveal it to anyone. Not even to our parents or the Dragon King himself. That's how much we valued our bond together."

Theresa held her hands over her heart. Her eyes closing in that moment as she let the memories from her past flow back through her.

"I loved my sister. And she loved me. To me, Erienne was already perfect in every way that I could imagine. I could never picture a better sister. Not in this, or any life time. Those days, those happy innocent days, were the days I thought would never truly end."

Aiden couldn't help but blush at how content and happy Theresa looked in that moment. It wasn't often that she would speak out like this. Especially about her past in such a positive way. Every time they talked about her life from before, it was usually filled with gloom and doom. It was a nice change of pace to hear something happy come from her stories. Even if it was for just a short while.

But soon a frown replaced her smile. Tears beginning to fall down her cheeks once more as she found the strength to continue her story.

"But then, the Great War happened. All of you already know what caused it, and you already know that for the first few years of the war, the Dragons did not get involved with the battles. Something that my sister did not agree with."

Theresa opened her eyes. Though tears still flowed from them, Aiden could see that her emerald green eyes were now more steely than they were before.

"Being the King's second...it was the highest honor a dragon could ever dream. I was the right hand of the king himself. My parents couldn't have been happier, my ascension had made ours one of the most powerful families in all of Dragonic history. That position though...it came with heavy responsibilities. I was the highest ranking member of our army, second only to the king himself, which meant I was responsible for countless soldiers, including Garrett and Seamus. I oversaw many things in the Dragon King's stead, when he was busy playing politics with the dragon nobles or the other kingdoms. All those duties...I loved them, but they meant so many sleepless nights away from my family. I was sure they understood that I was doing what had to be done...but...on some level...I think I always knew that was a lie. Even if she understood why I had to be away, I don't think Erienne was ready to deal with me practically vanishing from her life overnight..."

For a moment, Theresa hesitated. Her gaze changed from one of nostalgia to momentary worry as her gaze flickered from Garrett to Seamus.

"Rexkin...is this about-" Before Seamus could continue, the air in the room seemed to become considerably hotter. For the briefest of moments, Aiden could have sworn he saw death in Theresa's eyes as they took on the unsettling intensity of her Dragon's Stare. As quickly as it came, the moment passed and Theresa's fury wilted, becoming grief.

"My sister had a gift...she could see glimpses of the future. Well...possible futures. When she was little, she'd see whimsical things like having my favorite food for dinner, or knowing about a meteor shower that even the wisest scholars were unaware was coming. They weren't always right, but they weren't always wrong either. But, as she got older...her visions got darker...and darker...until the day I left. That's when...that's when they became unbearable. All she could see when she closed her eyes was death and destruction."

Theresa's hands dropped to the bottom of her shorts. Aiden flinched momentarily as she gripped them so hard that if she pulled they would have been completely torn in that moment.

"What I didn't know, however, was that my little sister was getting herself into trouble when I was not around. At her school she would constantly get into shouting matches with the others students, fight with those who dared to mock her size in her draconic state, and those clashes nearly brought the school down a couple of times. As you could imagine, I was shocked to even hear the news that my sister would even dare do such things. Especially with the position our family was in."

"Sounds like your sister started to get really anxious about something..." Liza interjected. "Or at least was trying to live up to the expectations that were thrusted on her shoulders since you became the King's second."

"Believe me, Liza. I never wanted my sister to aim for anything that I accomplished. My original parents and I told her a million times that no matter what she would be able to accomplish, we would be proud of her." Theresa frowned. "But I guess that wasn't enough. As when I returned home for a visit, it was during one of her episodes with members of the school board. I was a bit upset with her attitude when I confronted her about why she was acting up. In fact, forget a bit upset, I was extremely upset with her. For I knew that she was better than how she was acting in that moment."

A long drawn out sigh escaped Theresa's lips.

"I pressed Erienne for answers. No matter what she was going through, I reminded her that I was her big sister. Her best friend in the whole world. There was nothing that she couldn't tell me that I would not understand. I told Erienne that she could trust me. And for what it was worth? I understood why she was feeling so frustrated. Many of her classmates were wondering why the King and I were remaining neutral in the Great War that was erupting between the rest of the kingdoms. Some said that I was too much of a 'coward' to send our forces out there. That in turn angered Erienne. As much as I loved my little sister, she was never one to keep her emotions in check when they truly mattered."

"Sounds like dragon puberty." Liza half jokingly said.

"You could call it that, yeah." Seamus admitted. "For dragons, being able to show that you can hold your own is a way of showing that you weren't to be messed with."

"And unfortunately for Rexkin's sister, she was considered a runt among her peers." Garrett added. "Which often made her an easy target."

"I can tell the rest of the story you two, thank you." Theresa cut them off. "Now...after I spoke with her, I truly felt like everything had been resolved. I had been able to make my sister feel at ease with herself, and that no matter what, we did not care what the other families thought of her." Her frown turned into one of great sorrow as she clenched her eyes tightly. "But then...that horrid day happened…"

"W...What happened?" Aiden asked.

"...Kiddo?" Seamus spoke out. "Remember that giant black hand that Dimitri summoned in the Harpies' Den? The one that took your attack like a champ?"

"Yeah? You said it was part of a demon, right?"

"Not just any demon. The Obsidian Demon. An incredibly powerful and monstrous beast that could have torn the entire world apart before the Dark One appeared." Seamus explained. "One day, it just appeared near the outer borders of our kingdom. No warnings, no messages, nothing. It erupted from the ground like some sick volcano, and began to attack everything that was around it."

Theresa nodded slowly as she gritted her teeth.

"When news broke out about the Obsidian Demon's rampage, I took as many soldiers as I could into battle. We believed at first that it was some sort of unprovoked attack from one of the other kingdoms, or rogues from the Mage Kingdom, they were upset with us for not taking a side in the war. But when we arrived on the scene, I was shocked to find not just the demon waiting for us...but Erienne at the edge of the town where it was summoned. And a summoning portal below her feet."

"S-She summoned it?!" Aello gasped.

"...I had a million questions running through my head in that moment. But we could not press her for answers. As the first thing the Obsidian Demon did when it saw our group was attack in full fury. The terror and horror that it exuded, a being such as that monster could have only been spawned by one of the Fallen Gods themselves. It was such a beast that the forces that we brought barely were even able to hold it back." Theresa shook her head. "I could have ended it there, I could have killed the damn demon in an instant if I wished... but I was too distracted."

Aiden frowned. The more Theresa continued to talk, the more he understood why it was such a sore subject for her.

"After what felt like hours of battling, the Dragon King himself stepped in to fight the giant demon. Even with his great power, he was barely able to win against the Obsidian Demon. It took everything he had to split the great demon into five different pieces. The head, the arms, and the legs. Each one would be sealed away, lost to memory, forever." Theresa continued. "Once the demon had been properly dealt with, I turned to where my sister once was. For a brief moment, she stood there, then she transformed and ran away before I could approach her."

She brought both of her hands to her face, covering her eyes in shame and sorrow.

"At that moment, when His Highness saw Erienne flying away, he made a decision based on what I, and the others, had told him. Based on what she had done, he declared her...he declared her a traitor to our people. And degreed that if she were to ever show her face to our Kingdom again, she would be put to death."

Aiden felt his blood ran cold as the usual strong voice of Theresa seemed like it was about to crack at the very mention of her sister being put to death. The back of his neck hair stood up as he glanced to Seamus and Garrett for confirmation. The two of them gave short sad looks at him before they each nodded.

"It's true." Seamus said. "Erienne became known as 'the Dangerous Traitor' to our people. Because she did something that she was never meant to do. She summoned a being as terrible as the Obsidian Demon to our world, and we could have all paid the price for such an action."

"After that day, we never saw the traitor again." Garrett added on. "For years we had assumed that she crawled into some kind of hole and died. For many of us, we all agreed that it was better off if she had died. She had already brought great shame on herself for daring to summon a demon of all things within our Kingdom."

"But now she's back." Theresa said, her eyes still full of tears. "I don't know how, or why, but my baby sister is among the living. And...and if what you're telling me is true she is a part of the Dark Eye Cult..."

"I'm sorry, Thes...." Aiden managed to say. "I'm s-so sorry..."

There was a short uncomfortable silence that filled the room between them all. It was only filled with the short sobs of Theresa every few seconds. Aiden stood up from his spot and approached her ever so carefully. He bent down to her level in her chair, then slowly pulled her into a warm embrace.

"It's gonna be okay..." He told her. "I...I don't know why she's with the enemy but...but if we can find out, we can get your sister back. I know that we can."

Theresa didn't say anything as she leaned into Aiden's hug. Her eyes still damp with hot tears as she placed her face into his shoulder. Aiden could feel her entire body tremble in his grasp. The pain and sorrow she had been holding onto this entire time. He could scarcely imagine the burden that she had carried for those thousands of years.

In the back of his mind though, Aiden still couldn't believe what he was just told. Erienne? She was a traitor to her people? To her family? To him? Theresa had just spilt her guts out to him about everything that happened in the past, and he still couldn't put it into his hear that she was a traitor.

"There's no getting Erienne back, welp." Garrett said. "She committed an act of treason against her people. How and why does not matter when the simple fact of the matter is this. She is a traitor, and she must answer for her crimes."

"I hate to say this, Kiddo, but the old lug head is right." Seamus admitted. "If you see Erienne, don't you try talking to her. At least not without us there."

"Seamus, come on!" Aiden argued. "There has to be some explanation for what happened! I know it sounds odd but-"

"There is not buts about it, welp." Garrett snapped at him. "I don't care what you think you know, if you ever see her again, you are to bring her to us so that we can do what MUST be done."

"To hell with that!" Aiden roared back at the large dragon. "You would deny your Rexkin the chance to talk to her little sister? To find out what happened? To learn why she would even do such a thing like summoning a great demon?! You just blindly decided that she has to die with no answers to her reasons?!"

"Stop it, Aiden." Theresa said in his shoulder. Aiden glanced down to her.

"T-Thes..."

"They're right. You are as well." She pulled back slowly. "She is with the enemy now...whatever reasoning there is, if we can find a way to bring it out of her, we will." Her eyes opened, a mixture of sorrow and fury raged within her emerald colored irises. "But if she refuses to talk...then she will have to answer for what she has caused..."

Aiden felt a shiver run down his spine. Could it be really true though? Did Erienne really betray them? Or was there another side to this story that the Trinity didn't know?

"Aiden?" Theresa tapped his shoulders. "I thank you for telling me about all of this. And I can understand how you truly feel about this but...if she's with the enemy."

"I know, Theresa. I know." Aiden frowned. "It bothers me but...if I have to fight her, I will. I just...don't feel comfortable about it at all."

"Neither do I." Theresa admitted before clearing her throat. "At any rate, the Dark Eye Cult is still a dangerous movement. No matter who is a part of it, be they classmates or family members, they have to be stopped."

"She's right." Connor said. "I don't know what will happen, but in the coming months, we will all have to be ready for whatever they try to pull. Be on guard. Always."

"Now would be a great time to say this. My Academy is still open for those training sessions." Seamus chimed in.

"Good. We can use their training rooms to hone everyone's skills." Connor said. "Theresa, can you help our son get better along with us?"

"Absolutely, Mr. Russell."

"Excellent. Then when we can, we shall return back to the Academy to train."

Liza let out a long dry sigh as she placed her hands behind her head.

"Something tells me that this is going to be one hell of a long personal war with this stupid cult, guys."

"Yeah...and I don't like it." Aiden said as hung his head.

In his head, he knew that what they had to do was the right thing. But his heart? His heart felt something was off. That there was far more to the story. But...what could that have possibly been?

Could Erienne really be that dangerous? Could she have really been a monster like they believed she was?

LIFE BECOMES AN INTERMISSION

*T*he following months felt like one long slog to Aiden. The combination of high school life and training days, thanks to the newly appointed Grand Mage Ryan, were spent at the Mage Academy. Both of them were beginning to become so interwoven with one another that it felt like there was barely any difference between them. During the slow hours of the early morning and mid afternoon, his mind would be numbed by the mundane learnings from high school. During long hours at the Mage Academy his body endured far more intense training than it had gone through before.

Aiden was amazed that they were able to train and go all out within the school walls though. Each time they came back to train there, the training room that they had used before was restored back to its former glory. Aiden and Liza often felt bad that they were doing so much damage to their training rooms, especially after the Hell the school had to endure, but Ryan insisted that it was no problem for them to repair each night.

It did take some time getting use to being trained by his father of all people in the forms of magical combat. While Seamus was already a tough teacher with how to use offensive and defensive spells, Aiden's father proved to be far more strict about how a spell should be used. If Aiden messed up one particular pronunciation of a spell, or if he wasn't in the right stance, he received a stern lecture.

One time during the long months of training, Aiden went and used a spell at full power to complete an exercise. Connor was less than pleased his son had spent such energy on a simple exercise. The words he spoke out to Aiden that day still rung in his head, even as the months dragged on.

"There is a time and place to utilize a spell at its' full power. What good does it do you to use all your power in one single attack, when a fight could last longer?" Connor's lecture would echo in his brain. "Think boy. What good is magic if you use it only to fight? Find a balance. Sometimes a life can be saved, without using magic to kill."

It made Aiden feel really confused inside whenever he tried to figure the meaning behind those words. He honestly didn't know what his father meant. What true balance? Against the enemy they were facing how can protecting something be just as important as winning a battle against a foe?

The answer seemed to elude him as he spent days trying to decipher the meaning. He even asked Seamus and the other dragons if they knew what it meant. They seemed to understand, but told him that it was an answert he would have to figure out for himself.

"Stupid secret hiding giant lizards." Aiden would think to himself.

He couldn't out right complain about the results of the training though. He was getting faster, stronger, and more agile than he ever had with the training in the forest. Thanks to the additional lessons from his father, Aiden was able to switch on the fly between using his sword and shield to casting spells with his hands simply by dismissing either of his weapons in an instance.

Despite all the new abilities he was gaining from training, none of them touched the power of his ultimate attack. The Draconic Firestorm. Warfang's most powerful attack had saved Aiden a few times in the past. The memory of its furious power still fresh in his mind, Aiden had a gut feeling that the attack alone would be enough to wipe out the Dark Eye Cult if it ever came to that point.

Sadly, for Aiden, he still wasn't able to fully call Draconic Firestorm from Warfang. No matter how often he tried during training sessions with the dragons, and with his father, the attack would not erupt from the blade. Aiden felt like the attack was like a temperamental child. Only coming out when it wanted to come out.

Theresa had theorized that the sword's most powerful attack only seemed to work in moments that were truly dire. Basically it would only activate in a moment when Aiden's life was on the line. This frustrated the young teenager. To have an attack come out only when the damn sword felt like was absolutely necessary? Not a very helpful move it the blade refused to release it in moments that could have turned the tide of a battle!

Regardless, Aiden couldn't complain about the sword's ultimate attack being temperamental. The training he went through with Liza produced new results for him, including with his own unique attacks with both the sword, and his Flanera abilities.

Sadly the only area where he was not yet truly good was the use of his shield, PeaceGuard. The shield often felt like a damper on what Aiden could truly accomplish. He abhorred training sessions requiring its use. For one thing, the shield was bulky. Making it very hard to use correctly in battle, and it made moving effectively hard to do.

It also made it very difficult for him to learn to use the sword with just one hand instead of two. While his right hand was the dominate hand, his left hand had always provided a sense of security for him if he felt like he was beginning to lose his grip on Warfang's hilt.

Training to use the blade with only one hand with PeaceGuard on the other arm just made that effort that much more difficult to master. If he had to be honest, Aiden would rather not learn how to use the shield. But every time he felt like complaining about the shield, he would stop and think about what it meant to Theresa and the others. They crafted the shield for *him*. They wanted to make certain that he was able to use it as a defense if they weren't around.

Aiden owed it to them to learn how to master it. Even if it was a giant pain in the ass to do it.

Despite spending every moment of their time training, when they weren't at high school of course, Aiden felt a terrible ache in his heart every single day. The absence of Erienne.

No matter how many times he tried to accept it, he couldn't. Erienne. The sweet, though at times a bit quirky, girl that saved both his and Liza's lives in the forest two years ago...how could he ever picture her as the enemy? Sure she was an oddball, but he couldn't even picture Erienne as not only being evil, but a traitor. To her own kind no less!

He knew that the way she was acting towards him might have been just a giant act, or that she never even truly cared for him. He knew that she was with the Dark Eye Cult, and that when they made eye contact on that day she gave him a twisted smile. But...It didn't feel right. Not in his heart.

Aiden knew that Theresa poured her heart out to him those months ago about what happened to her sister. But his heart didn't want to believe that Erienne would actively betray not just her sister, but her people like that. He wanted so much to believe that it was all some kind of giant misunderstanding. That Erienne was somehow forced into being a servant to Dimitri.

Wishful thinking. That's all he was doing to himself. Wishing for something to be true, when he knew that it wasn't the most likely case.

He didn't know why but it felt like there was more to the story. Something that even Theresa had not noticed about her sister. There was no proof to this theory, of course, but his heart wanted to believe it so badly that it nearly hurt him physically to even think about the black haired dragoness.

Such moments of weakness often got in the way of training. One time Theresa nearly smacked him for daring to think about Erienne. He learned that day to never casually mention her little sister. Not unless she brought it up herself. Even Seamus and Garrett seemed forbidden to mention Theresa's sister when she was in the same room.

Both of the other dragons had different opinions about Erienne however. When Theresa was not around them or Aiden, they would go into detail about what they thought of the young dragoness.

Seamus was far more merciful than Garrett was with his viewpoint. Like Aiden, he thought that Erienne might have been in the wrong place at the wrong time. He did however feel that if she truly had something against her sister, she should have come forth to her about it. Maybe the whole situation with the Obsidian Demon could have been avoided at that point. Did he view her as a traitor? Well, that would be based on what Erienne herself had to say about that terrible day.

Garrett felt no pity or remorse for Erienne. Instead, he was furious at the very idea that she not only was alive, but that Aiden had kept this information hidden from the dragons. At first Aiden believed it was because the three of them thought for the longest time that they were the very last. But the more Garrett talked about it, the more it became apparent that he was legitimately furious at her.

It was no secret that Garrett was fiercely loyal to what his people once stood for. And for one of his own kind to betray everything they stood for? It was too much to forgive in his eyes.

It still was a hard pill to swallow. But the fact was that Erienne was now an enemy that Aiden would have to face in battle. And he dreaded that day.

For the time being though, the rest of his days before that confrontation were mostly the same. Day in and day out. It almost felt like it was becoming too much of a regular routine before Winter Finals loomed their ugly head.

The less talk about them though, the better. For awhile, things continued the same way they normally did. Holidays came and went, the start of the second semester in January began, and the training sessions became even more intense as time went on.

Though at long last, the month of February arrived.

A month that would become home to the anniversary of one of the most eventful moments in his life. A day that would not only change his life again, but a day that would forever be burned into Aiden's memory. For while they had been busy training for encounters with the Dark Eye, their foes had remained busy as well.

This day was one where everything that happened changed the lives of Aiden and his friends. And it all began with a simple text message.

"News update. Ryan's spies have located the Dark Eye Cult. We need to go to Richmond. NOW."

BATTLE IN RICHMOND

"*R*ichmond? Of all the places in the world, RICHMOND?" Liza asked as she rode on Seamus' in dragon form, back. "Why would they be there?"

The date was February 14th. After months and hours of training and studying, it would all be put to the test. Ryan had ordered several spies out in the country to find the Dark Eye Cult's headquarters. If they could cut the head of the beast off, then this nightmare of rising riots and attacks would come to an end. It took some time, but they had finally located where the Dark Eye members were set to gather.

It was a race against time, a race they could not afford to lose. Not now. As soon as the text message to the group was given, the team immediately headed off towards Richmond. If they were to take down their enemy, it had to be done today. Each dragon carried a certain member of their squad. Theresa carried Aiden, Connor, and Helena on her back. Seamus carried Liza. And Garrett carried Kali.

Aello and her harpies were nowhere to be found at the moment. When pressed, the harpy princess responded with a text message that said "Family matters. I'll be there soon." Aiden wondered what she meant by that, but now was not the time to ponder.

"Remember, it is the capital of the state." Theresa said as they flew threw the skies. "If I had to guess, they want to make a huge statement in this state about their intentions."

"Which means a lot of innocent people could end up getting killed."

Seamus added as his mighty wings flapped. "As to why we're flying there instead of warping, the odds are they will be able to sense a magical portal opening. That's why we're flying, to have SOME kind of element of surprise."

"Like that'll be much of a surprise." Liza said with a coy smirk. "No offense, bu you three stick out like an eyesore in the sky above us. How are you gonna land with no one noticing you?"

"Leave that to me." Seamus replied. "My magic will make us look invisible to the naked eye of a regular human. Otherwise we wouldn't be flying there in dragon form. Basically how it works is that it tricks the eyes of a human."

"Is that why no one freaked out when Theresa and I went to Chicago to find Garrett?" Aiden asked.

"You could say that." Theresa said with a slight grin on her lips. "You didn't really think that we would openly fly above everyone in plain sight where we could be spotted so easily, did you?"

"If there's one thing you humans are known for, it's freaking out whenever you see something in the sky that you don't recognize." Garrett added from the side. "So in order to keep you all from freaking out, we have a perception change spell that we use when flying."

"Then how come you guys didn't fly us to California?" Liza asked.

"It would take too long to get there. Even with our flight speed, it would have been too late to stop the mess that was happening there." Seamus explains. "Think of it like this, a regular flight from Virginia to California is around five hours. For us it would be about two to three. Not enough time to get in there and stop the Shadow Demons from breaking out."

"Got it." Liza called back to him.

"So what do we know?" Connor asked. "Do we have the location where the Dark Eye Cult is located?"

"Ryan's spy told us that there's been activity all over the local area Hillside Court." Theresa answered. "Given that it is one of the worst parts of the city, it wouldn't surprise me that they use that as front."

"Figures they would use the ghettos." Aiden muttered.

"Either way, we will have to be careful. You don't know what will happen in that particular part of town. Be it from the Dark Eye Cult, or gangsters." Theresa replied. "Stay close together, at all times, and keep your eyes open for Ryan's spy."

"Do we even know who they are?"

"We do." A slight chuckle escaped her lips. "You'll see when we contact them."

Aiden shrugged at her answer before glancing over to look at the other two dragons. He knew that this was a mission that was high stakes. But he couldn't help but feel a bit giddy inside. Riding on the back of a dragon into a secret mission? It was something that he dreamt of when he was a kid. Had he been younger, this would have been the coolest thing to ever happen.

But he knew better now. This was not some level in a video game. It was real life. There were actual human lives on the line right now. Not just his, Liza, or his parents. But the innocents that lived in the Richmond area. Whatever plan the Dark Eye was brewing, it had to be stopped before it grew out of control.

But out of all the places for the cult to meet, why Hillside? Long before any of this, Aiden had always heard horror stories of the poor housing conditions in Hillside. Whenever there was a gang related activity, or crime in the Richmond area, it always seemed to stem from that particular county. What kind of advantage would the Dark Eye cult have by using that as base for their operations?

The only reasoning he could come up with is that it would be the least suspicious place. Even if it is one of the harshest places to live in Richmond. Dimitri probably gathered a lot of the recruits for the cult there. It brought a shiver down Aiden's spine to entertain the idea of how many youths the bastard corrupted.

Aiden felt Theresa's body slowly begin to descend towards the ground. Right into a small forest right in front of the James River. As the three dragons landed, as softly as they could, Aiden felt his stomach begin to turn into a knot as a sudden realization began to take hold as he, his parents, and friends climbed off the backs of the dragons.

This was truly it. This was where they would finally encounter the Dark Eye in their stronghold.

"Where's Ryan's spy?" Garrett asked as he transformed back into his human state.

"He had to go silent." Seamus answered him as he took his own human form. "Apparently the cult might have been catching onto him. All he could tell Ryan was that they have been coming to an old abandoned gravel company, and that they were planning something. A giant summoning of some kind."

"He didn't get to see what kind of demon it was?"

"Fraid not, Garrett. Seems like they wanna keep that secret from anyone that's considered 'fresh blood' in their ranks."

"Wait. The gravel company you mentioned. I know which place you're talking about." Liza said. "Old Gravel Crush Corporation, a giant rock quarry, right?"

"That's the one. According to the spy, the entire damn place has been abandoned. Looks like that the previous owners ran out of business. The place is practically a giant waste of land now."

"Makes you wonder why the city hasn't made any attempts to tear it down." Liza mumbled.

"Liza. Focus." Theresa ordered. Her long white hair blew a bit in the spring wind. "We don't have much time people. If what our mole said is true, then the Dark Eye Cult has begun to make their move. Whatever demon they're trying to summon, it has to be stopped."

"We shouldn't delay then." Connor said. "I've been to Richmond a couple of times on some business trips for my 'regular' job. I know the location of the site."

"Then we make our way towards the site. Mr. Russell, take the lead. Remember. Stay together."

The group gave a collective nod as they followed Aiden's father out of the forest. It wasn't the easiest trek. They had to get through Goode Creek. Which was filled with fallen dead trees, deep puddles of water, broken rocks, and sharp pieces of wood. It wasn't as rough as when Aiden trekked across half of the state to find Aello, but it was an annoying patch to travel through.

As they pulled away from the forest, Aiden could see far off in front of the group a small spec of a building. That could be their destination.

Old Gravel Crush Corporations' land. It was dusty, filled with gravel all over, and giant stones that were set to be destroyed by the machines. Aiden didn't really care for the history of the place, but he had to hand it to Dimitri and Raven. They had certainly picked a good spot to have as their headquarters. Abandoned, buildings crumbling apart, and not a single soul in sight.

A perfect place for a cult to gather.

"Up ahead, look! Get behind cover!" Theresa ordered.

The group quickly pulled together before rushing behind one large rock. As they crouched down, they could see them. Members of the Dark Eye Cult. All of them wearing long robes. Each one making small talk with one another as the sun slowly passed above. Aiden felt his hands get a bit sweaty as he stared at the gathered cult members.

"All of them are either my age or young adults..." He said. "Why would they be throwing their futures away for nothing but a lie?"

"They feel this world has abandoned them." Seamus answered. "I know it may sound wrong to you, kiddo, but the fact of the matter is that here they feel accepted."

"It's still wrong. They're committing heinous acts."

"On that I can agree."

Theresa put an arm up in front of the two of them. There were no words needed to be spoken by the white dragoness. Both of them knew that it was an order to shut up and stay low.

A good thing too, Aiden's ears picked up the faint sound of a familiar voice. It wasn't Erienne's.

"You don't know what Master Dimitri plans to do?" Alanza's voice asked as she walked with her two associates.

"Know idea. Apparently though it's some giant demon that the Master plans to use to spread the message of our family." One of them said, a young man probably in his mid twenties.

"You two didn't see it?" The other asked. This one was a bit higher pitched, but it was male as well. "The Master has gathered something that he referred to as 'the final piece.' I wish I knew what that meant though."

"The final piece of what?" Alanza asked.

"That's the thing. I don't know. Every time I try to ask someone if they know what it is that Master Dimitri, or Sir Raven, is planning to summon they always shrug their shoulders."

"You're so useless, dude." The first male voice said.

"Oh bite me! It's not like you're trying to find out anything!"

"How about both of you shut up?" Alanza demanded. Aiden felt himself nearly flinching at the harsh tone in her voice. She was not the same since they met months ago. "As long as it gets revenge on those stupid dragons and that boy who killed Jeremy."

"Still sore about that, eh Al?" The second male voice asked. "You know that he didn't swing-"

"Shut up!" Alanza snapped as her demon formed behind her. Zara's eyes crackled with electric power. It was enough to make Aiden squint his eyes at the brightness.

"I don't care if he didn't return any feelings of love for me or anyone! Jeremy brought me to this group! If this demon can bring about the death of those that took him from me...then that's enough."

"Eaaaaaasy there girl." The first voice said. "No reason for you to go and summon your pet. You know how Lady Joro is when using your magic recklessly like that."

"Tch. Lady Joro." The second voice scoffed. "I don't know why the master keeps her around. Even if she is some kind of great demon, you can't trust one that looks like her."

"Don't let the master hear you say that." The first replied. "Rumors are going around that it was thanks to Lady Joro that the Master was able to gather the pieces of whatever the master wants to summon."

Aiden's blood turned cold. His eyes drifted over to Theresa. Her own eyes were wide with shock, and a first for Aiden to see, fear.

"You two talk too much." Alanza said with a huff. "Come on, we should get going before we get into trouble for lounging around."

And just like that, Alanza walked off with her demon following closely behind her. Without much of an argument from her companions.

The three dragons all looked towards each other. Even Garrett, the most physically powerful of them all, looked stunned and worried with the situation they had found themselves in.

"He wouldn't dare..." Theresa breathed.

"Thes?" Aiden asked.

"Rexkin. This is worse than we thought. Way worse." Seamus said.

"Agreed." Theresa' eyes narrowed as she summoned her two swords to her hands. "Everyone. We do not have time to sneak around."

"H-Hold up. What are you talking about?" Liza asked.

"Do you remember the story about the Obsidian Demon? The giant hand that Dimitri summoned in the Harpy's Den?" Theresa reminded her. "What that girl and her companions said...they have them. They have all five pieces."

"Crap..."

"Rexkin. We can't waste anymore time." Garrett growled as his axe formed in his hands. "We need to move. Now."

"I agree." Theresa turned to Aiden, Liza and his family. "Listen well. Whatever feelings of worry you have about harming another human being, put them aside! We cannot allow Dimitri to complete the Obsidian Demon! If you have to stab or knock one of the cultists out with your weapon, do not hesitate!"

"What about your sister?" Helena asked.

"If we see her, leave her to me alone." Theresa said as she glanced back to her fellow dragons once more, then back to them. "Is everyone ready? We move on my mark."

Aiden felt a lump form in his throat. The very thought of maybe killing another human being still haunted him after what happened to Jeremy. But as soon as the odious thought entered his mind, he felt a soft hand gently hold his shoulder. His mother.

"I can feel it, Aiden. I can feel that you are afraid of repeating what you did to the person that girl mentioned, Jeremy. I can't begin to imagine how you feel, but I do have some advice for you. When you go to attack someone, don't aim for the chest area." She told him in a soft whisper. "Strike at their arms, sides, or legs. With a well placed cut, you can injure them to the point of being unable to fight back. But not enough to severe any major arteries."

"M-Mom? H-How do you know all that?"

"Your father isn't the only one who was taught how to fight in the Academy." Helena gave him a short smile. A long pink staff with a crescent moon formed in her free hand. "Remember, don't focus on one encounter too long."

The words of his mother's wisdom did bring a sense of soothing comfort. Sure she had always tried her best to calm her down during moments of stress when he was growing up, but the strength of her wisdom here felt different. He shouldn't have felt that taken back, but life continued to change and amaze him. Both his mother and his father were master mages. Just when Aiden thought he could not be surprised anymore.

"On my signal." Theresa ordered. "Rush forth, injure only, and don't stop moving."

"Why not use your dragon forms again?" Liza asked. Garrett growled at her answer before answering her.

"If that demon is summoned, we're going to need all the power we can manage! It's best to not waste such power on their small fry!"

"Garrett, Liza, save it for later!" Theresa ordered as she spun Snow and Fire behind her back. "On my mark."

Everyone nodded once as they prepared their weapons. Aiden tried to get away without summoning PeaceGuard, but the glare from Theresa convinced him otherwise to bring the shield up. The next three seconds felt as if they were the longest three seconds in the history of the world. Aiden was so nervous about the outcome that he could have sworn that his heartbeat was racing so fast he could have heard it in his head.

Then after what felt like an eternity, Theresa gave a short nod.

The first one to step out was Garrett, who swung his massive axe right into the ground with tremendous force. The shockwave from the slam was enough to make the earth violently tremble beneath the feet of the cult members.

Seamus followed after his fellow dragon by jumping up into the air. He he held out his staff in both hands before rapidly spinning it around. The cult members that had been knocked down from the shockwave from Garrett's attack were now blown away from the immense wind power emanating from Seamus.

"Now!" Theresa shouted to the rest of the group.

Not a second was spared as Aiden, Liza, Kali, and his parents ran after Theresa. All of them letting out their own war cries. The cultists were surprised by the sudden surprise attack!

"It's them!" One called out.

"Someone go find Master Dimitri!" Another replied.

Aiden pushed their voices out of his mind as he charged at one member. He brought his shield up in front of him to block a powerful fireball spell that was thrown at him. The impact from the blow felt like a sucker punch from Garrett, but he gritted his teeth and bore it.

His pulled right arm back, Warfang gleaming in the sunlight, before slashing the cultist right across his left arm.

Not enough to kill his foe, but enough to injure him, removing him from the fight. Just like his mother told him. Aiden felt his feet unconsciously begin to move again towards the next enemy charging towards him. There was no time to stop and think about whether he overdid it.

Once more he swung Warfang across the armor of his next foe, the result was the same from before. A surge of confidence began to bloom within his chest as he continued to move forward. If they could do this, stop the summoning of the Obsidian Demon, without actually having to kill someone, then it would make the victory sweeter in his eyes.

Not far off from him was Liza. From the corner of his eye Aiden could see that her two daggers had already been fast at work with how she parried enemy attacks. Unlike Aiden's sword, there was hardly any blood on their edges. Good. The less blood spilt, the better.

What surprised Aiden the most though was how feisty his mother was in combat. Her staff might look innocent, with the head piece shaped like a peaceful looking sun, but looks can be deceiving. Aiden's mom wasn't one to waste time unleashing quick and powerful attacks. They were so fast that Aiden had a hard time getting a read on them!

Any demon summoned by the cultists members were quick to fall from the fiery attacks of her staff.

It wasn't entirely easy though to get to the main building. As the group made their way down the quarry the stronger cultists members waited for them. Each one armed with unique and deadly demons that looked like a horrible amalgamation of many creatures. The details weren't the most important thing right now though. There was too much at risk to just stop and identify every single demon!

"Dammit! They just keep coming!" Aiden cried out, pushing back one tiger like demon away with PeaceGuard.

"Remember the goal!" Theresa shouted in return. "Keep pushing towards the building, don't focus on the minions too much!"

Aiden fought back an audible groan as he pulled Warfang back and slashed the next demon that charged him. The goal was just in sight. The main building was almost there! But every time he sliced a demon down, one would rise up from another cultist! If they were going to get anywhere, they had to somehow distract the cultists.

"Think dammit!" He shouted in his head. *"What can you do to get these folks off our backs! Ugh, come on! There has to be something that we can do..."*

He felt himself squinting as the sunlight bounced off his blade into his face. Aiden shook his head to regain his blurry vision. Damn sun. They just had to do this in daylight.

"Wait...sunlight. That's it! We have to momentarily blind them!"

Aiden quickly dismissed Warfang as he held up his now open palm above his head.

"Aiden! What are you doing?!" His father shouted.

"Trust me on this!"

A small fireball began to form in Aiden's palm. Slowly building more power up as each second ticked away. As each second passed, the small fireball grew larger and brighter. Aiden winced a bit as he felt his strength begin to decline from gathering so much magical energy. But he stood his ground as the fireball grew in size.

His action didn't go unnoticed though. More cultists charged towards the group with their demons in tow. Each one intent on bringing down their foes. Aiden felt a small spark of electricity smack his left arm momentarily. He grimaced in some pain before glaring off to where the blast came from.

Alanza. Her eyes were full of fury and hatred for him in that moment. Her demon, Zara, was already behind her as well.

"Come on already, Aiden!" Liza shouted. "We can't keep them off forever!"

"Working on it!"

Aiden turned his attention back to the fireball in his hand once more. He could feel it, the energy was just about ready to be used! He only need a few more seconds of precious time!

As the fireball grew in size, Alanza and her demon grew closer to the group. The redhead teen's eyes were cold, unfeeling, and full of revenge. She snapped her fingers once towards Aiden. Zara responded by unleashing a powerful lighting blast from her eyes. Her target? Aiden.

"Rashieldra!"

Aiden was nearly taken aback by the sudden magical shield that formed in front of his body. He glanced towards the source of the spell. His father.

"I've waited too long for this moment." Alanza looked as if she spat venom as she spoke. "You will not get away with what you did, Russell!"

"Funny that you know my last name..." Aiden responded as the fireball continued to grow. "Seems that you guys were spying on us since the day that security guard was murdered by this insane cult."

"Insane?! Don't you call this organization insane!"

Another blast of lighting was fired by Zara. This time the magical shield Connor formed began to buckle under the intense blast of energy.

"You have no idea what our lives were like before Master Dimitri found us! Before we found a cause! Before, we were the outcasts of society. People mocked for being 'different' from the rest of this putrid world! And you...you took the one who brought me here! You'll pay for what you did with your own blood!"

Aiden felt himself flinch at the reminder of what happened. How he stabbed and killed another human. But he shook his head slowly at Alanza as the fireball finished growing in size.

"Sorry, Alanza." He said once. "But today is not the day to settle that."

"What are you-"

Before she could finish her question, Aiden held up his hand above his head once more.

"Everyone, shield your eyes!" He shouted to his friends and parents. His voice began to have an echo around it as he felt the magic within his veins burn with intense power. And then, it happened.

"Light of the Sun!"

A flash of bright red light exploded from the fireball in his hand. The light was enough to hit the eyes of each low ranking cultist that surrounded them. Some of them fell to the ground and covering their eyes instantaneously while others tried to regain their vision. Alanza was the first among them to fall to her knees, howling in pain as she covered her eyes.

Aiden gritted his teeth as the magical energy from his body seeped into the ball of light. He had learned this spell during the training sessions within the academy from his mother. Light of the Sun. It would take a lot of energy for him to use, but in a tight bind the spell could be used to ward off many attackers to make a get away. A good move for a situation like this one, if he had to admit it.

It was hard to keep the spell going though. Due to the intense amount of concentration and energy that it required, it could only be used sparingly. Or else Aiden ran the risk of being drained of magical power for a few hours.

"Aiden, that's enough!" Theresa ordered. "You got everyone that's out here! We need to move, now!"

Aiden nodded once before dismissing the spell from his hand. Once more, Warfang came forth and returned to him. He glanced over to Alanza. A small frown on his lips.

"That spell won't blind you permanently, but it will leave you out of this for a few minutes at best. You stay here and stay out of our way while we stop your 'master' from making a mistake." Aiden turned his back to her. "And for what it's worth? I'm sorry that it had to be this way, Alanza. But we don't have time to mess with you."

"Shut up! I'll kill you for what you did! You took Jeremy away from me!" She spat out. Tears fell from her eyes as she tried to regain her sight.

"I can't take away what I did. But this is not the way to do it. Joining a cult? Killing innocent people? What good does that do you? All you'll do is confirm the fears of those who treat you differently."

He glared over his shoulder at her.

"Maybe you'll learn something from all of this. Maybe, just maybe, you'll stop and think about how absolutely stupid this entire cult is."

Aiden said no more as he and his crew rushed off towards the open building ahead of them. Even though his spell had been enough to blind the cultists that had been charging them, he knew that the entire thing was a distraction to their real mission.

And time was not on their side!

THE SUMMONING

"**What** are we going to do when they all get their vision back?!" Liza cried as they ran. "They won't stay blind forever, and we're still vastly outnumbered here!"

"We can worry about that later!" Theresa answered. "The most important thing right now is stopping Dimitri from summoning the Obsidian Demon!"

"Stupid teenagers!" Garrett bellowed. "They wasted too much of our time! If they already have the pieces of the Obsidian Demon, it's mere moments before it rises up!"

"Garrett's right! We need to stop this now!" Theresa pointed the tip of Snowfyre towards the building. "No matter what's in there, don't allow them a moment to complete the summoning!"

No words had to be spoke by any of them as they ran as fast as they could towards the building. Aiden felt a knot begin to form in his gut as the situation's dire nature began to dawn on him. With the threat of the Obsidian Demon rising, and with the possibility that the entire world would witnessing its horrors, they were racing against the clock.

And the clock is winning.

Still they ran into the building. A faint glimmer of hope was still in their hearts as they slowly found themselves looking around momentarily. Aiden and Liza looked confused in that moment as they took in the building's space. It was completely empty.

Or at least. That's how it appeared to be anyway.

"Where the hell are they?" Liza asked.

"You don't remember?" Seamus replied. "Magic girl. It can be used to hide anything from unsuspecting eyes. And if I'm right..."

The dragon of magic spun his staff behind his back once, then tapped the tip of it on the ground. Purple cracks in the ground soon spread away from his staff towards one of the walls ahead of them. The wall itself began to crack and fall apart before it revealed what was truly hidden from the normal human eye.

A mockery of what the Mage Academy looked like. Only this time it was completely crafted by the dark arts of magic itself. Much like its counterpart, it gave off an air of incredible magic around it. But that was about the only thing that it shared in common with the Academy. Instead of regal designs, everything was twisted, dark, and pitch black. Obsidian like even.

"What the hell?" Aiden managed to sputter out.

"I figured he would do something like this..." Seamus snarled. "That he would make some kind of 'school' to teach those who came to his cult the dark magic. Damn bastard."

"It mocks everything that you established, Spellweaver." Connor said. "But we do not have time to be disgusted by what he has done. We have more pressing matters at hand."

"Hmm, you could say that." Kali, in her true form, slithered up beside them. "But I wouldn't be rushing off too fast any time soon."

"And what's that supposed to mean you snake bitc-" Liza started, but the prime demon's hand slapped itself over her mouth.

"Be quiet, little one. Listen carefully. Do you not hear it?" Her tongue flicked out of her mouth at the last word. "That faint, skittering sound...oh I know what it is...but do you frail humans know?"

Aiden felt his muscles tighten as he lifted both Warfang and PeaceGuard up. Everyone else readied their weapons as well as they looked around. Kali was right. There was a faint sound of skittering. Aiden couldn't pinpoint where it was exactly. But he could hear it.

And it sent shivers down his spine.

"What is that?" Liza managed to squeak out. For a second it sounded like she was terrified.

"That? That...is another Prime Demon." Kali grinned. "Not as glorious or perfect as I, of course...but she is one of mine."

The snake demon slithered before the rest of the group now. Her eyes darting around quietly as a playful grin crept across her lips.

"You can stop pretending that you're hiding, you inferior spec of dust. I know you are out there."

No response. All Aiden could hear was the sound of skittering feet roaming around the room. Liza's whimpers began to become more noticeable now as she held Gitanel and Oceanus higher. Her arms began to tremble as she panic made her look around the room.

"Where is it?!" She asked, terror taking ahold of her. "Where is it?!"

"Liza, calm down!" Theresa said. "It's goal is to terrify you! Don't let it!"

"Oh but that's too late..." Kali spoke out in a sing song tone. She slowly turned her head towards the athletic girl. "You are already caught in her web."

Web? The sudden realization hit Aiden like a truck.

"Liza! Watch out!" He shouted

Too late. A large blast of webbing fired out from behind the group, grabbing Liza in one shot around her body. The blonde let out a terrified scream as she tried to break free from the webbing around her. Panic had spread through her as each of her attempts failed.

"Get it off! Get it off!" She cried. "I am terrified of spiders!"

"Aw, that's too bad." Kali frowned. "Looks like she picked that up on you, dearie."

Just before the others could make a move to break Liza free from the webbing, a pair of dark green eyes glimmered in the shadows behind her. Aiden felt like his entire soul had suddenly been pulled away from him as the demon walked into the light.

It felt like a monster from one of the tabletop game books that Aiden would read at the Griffon had just popped into reality. The Spider Prime demon's skin was a sickly pale green, with yellow eyes, and she had the palest of blue for her short low cut hair. Her body was that of a young woman, wearing what looked to be a warrior's tunic. The rest of her body had a massive dark grey spider body for legs and her abdomen was covered in what looked to be bits and pieces of bones from life forms. They looked to be both human and otherly.

But perhaps the most disturbing part of the spider demon was the gaping spider maw in the front of her lower abdomen. It looked like something that had come fresh from hell itself. Covered in broken pieces of bone and a dark green liquid that dripped with a toxic liquid.

"Joro!" Kali exclaimed, the surprise in her voice mingled with barely contained venom, "It's been so long...my how you've let yourself go...I suppose I shouldn't be shocked, you never were quite my...class."

"Kali..." the spider growled, making no effort to hide her contempt, "You would dare to mock me while you stand beside those brainless sacks of flesh?"

"Stand beside them?" Kali repeated, giggling softly before daintily covering her laughter with the back of her hand, "You insult me! I stand far....far above these insects...I'm merely along for my amusement." Her voice sharpened suddenly, and the disinterest in her gaze turned to unmasked murderous intent, "I soooo enjoy seeing filth like you suffer."

"What th...I mean..." Aiden stumbled over his words, taken aback by the intensity of such a short exchange, "Who is that?" He managed to finally ask.

Kali's gaze turned toward Aiden and, like it had never left, her composure returned.

"This is Joro, Aiden, dear." She explained, leaning back on her tail and gesturing toward Joro like she was regarding garbage, "A Prime Demon, much like...myself, "Kali couldn't help giggling again, hand rising to her lips. "Oh, but so quite unlike myself...so plain and disgusting. The poor thing has always loathed how miserable her station is when she gazes upon my radiance." Kali laughed again, but when she spoke once more, there was a certain edge to her voice.

"She's behind this plain little cult you've been on about. They reek with her stench..."

Joro scoffed at Kali's mocking tone before focusing her attention back to the captured Liza. The latter was so terrified that her trembling was causing the webbing to vibrate.

"So, young one." She taunted Liza, "Arachnophobia? How adorable...oh it's no wonder I could taste your fear the moment you stepped into this place."

Aiden's eyes widen. He was so taken aback by the appearance of the spider that he didn't realize it at first. But now he knew.

He knew that voice.

"YOU!" He roared at her, Warfang pointed in the direction of the spider's face. "You're that woman who took Erienne away from school!"

"Hm?" Joro tilted her head towards him. A cruel smile came to her lips. "Ah yes, I remember you now. You were that boy who tried to play the gallant hero. Ha. What sentimental nonsense."

"Shut up!"

Aiden put himself into an attack stance. An intense fire burned in his eyes as he stared down the giant spider demon.

"I don't give a damn about who you are! Erienne is a kind girl, and you turned her into something she's not! Where is she?!"

Joro blinked for a moment, then bursted out into laughter as she shook her head. A sickening grin exposed her yellow teeth.

"Oh? You think she's being controlled? My, aren't you creative." Joro chuckled, "It's always so interesting to see the lengths the human mind will go to in order to deny its own fear. You truly think you can play the savior for that poor little dragon and bring her back from the wicked demons? It would be sad if it weren't so amusing..." She laughed again, "Poor boy, thinking she was corrupted~."

She pulled on the webbing that had ensnared Liza, which pulled her down to the ground with a thud. Aiden clenched the hilt of Warfang so tight that the weapon could have broken. His eyes glanced over the Prime Demon, looking for an opening to strike at her. Then he spotted it. One of the tips of her spider leg was dyed in dark dried blood.

It all made sense now!

"It was you..." He said. "It was you that killed the security guard on the first day of school!"

"Hm?" She mused for a moment. "Ohhh, you mean that stupid old man? Yes, I remember him now. I had arrived in that moment to retrieve your precious Erienne for her next task. He spotted us and wanted to know how I got in without clearance. So, I did the logical thing. I killed him. It would have been too much hassle to make some kind of fabrication, so the best option was to take his life from this pitiful little world."

"You…" Aiden shook with fury. "You took an old man's life, just because he spotted you?!"

"Oh I took his life for more reasons than that…" The demon grinned once more. She pulled Liza up to her side and stroked her cheek with one finger ever so slowly. Tears were falling down Liza's cheeks at the mere focus on the demon. "I took his life because I wanted to see the fear in his eyes. Humans are afraid of so many things, it's almost a shame that they're so easy to prey on. Spiders, heights, germs, death, and yes, even snakes. It's almost comical."

"What's comical is that you believe that you're so powerful." Kali retorted, her tongue once again flicking out. "I am not the biggest fans of humans, but I believe that it would be in your best interest to release the girl, foolish spider. She is a source of amusement for me."

"Oh is that right?" Joro feigned surprise. "If I didn't know any better, I would say that you've grown to care for the humans, snake. Or do you hate the fact that I'm about to take away your precious little toy?"

"Enough!" Theresa shouted as her wings rose up behind her back. "Release Liza now, demon! Or face the power of Theresa! Leader of the Dragon King's Army!"

"Aw, how cute. You think you can order me around." Joro mockingly said, but stopped stroking Liza's cheek to stare down Theresa. "Your name…I believe I heard it somewhere before. Erienne said it a couple of times to me before."

"I warn you…"

"Oh that's right. Now I remember. You were her big sister in the old days weren't you? Aw, how sweet. The big sister returns, only to find out that her little sister is still what she fears. A traitor."

Joro pulled Liza up once more as one of her spider legs aimed right towards her heart. Fear and tears consumed Liza's face at the very sight of the spider leg before her chest. Aiden gritted his teeth as he took a battle ready stance.

"Drop your weapons. All of them. Or else this frail human dies for nothing."

"Do you truly think you can order ME to do such a thing?" Kali retorted, the tip of her long snake tail smacked into the ground. "You release the girl, Joro. Or you will be reminded of who is your superior."

There was a moment of brief silence in the air

That was shattered the moment Jorjo made a loud snarl sound as she pulled her leg back to stab Liza in the heart. Aiden took one step to try and rush the giant spider demon, but a crashing sound from above caught his and the other's attention. A smile of relief came to his lips as he saw a familiar face race down towards Joro.

It was Aello!

The harpy princess let out a screeching cry of anger as her sharp talons dug into the abdomen of Joro. The Prime Demon, taken by surprise, dropped Liza to the ground as she tried to throw Aello off her back. The youngest of the harpy princesses would not be thrown though, as her talons clung onto the abdomen with all her might as her chain linked lance formed in her hand.

"Keep your filthy demon hands off her!" She screeched, slashing at the back of Joro with fury. "You're never to wrap her up in that webbing of yours again!"

"Tch. Get off me you annoying BRAT!" Joro demanded, with a quick buck she dislodged Aello from her abdomen.

Aello reacted quickly though. With the flick of her wrist she made her lance turn into it's chain form before she whipped the tip right into the back of Joro. The cut it made wasn't deep, but it was enough to get the spider's focus away from the main group.

This gave Kali the moment she needed to strike her foe. The snake prime demon slammed the palms of her hands together as she formed a dark mass of purple fire between them. She wasted not a single second as she threw the fireball right at the spider demon's back. The force of the attack was enough to push Joro over, for the moment.

"Now, birdy!" She shouted to Aello. "Get your pretty friend away from her!"

Aello dove down to Liza, picking her up in her talons and carrying her away from Joro and back to the group. To say that there was a look of relief on Liza's face would have been an understatement. As soon as Aello's talons cut through the thick webbing, the athletic girl quickly pulled her savior into a bone gripping hug.

"Don't you ever be late again!"

"I won't. I promise."

That was all that needed to be said between the two, as they pulled apart from their hug before turning back to face Joro. The spider demon gave a series of unearthly grunts and snarls as she rose back up to her legs.

"You." Venom seemed to spit from her lips. "How dare you?"

An audible growl escaped from Garrett's lips as Joro rose up tall on all eight of her legs. A dark green fire spreading over the palms of her hands.

"We don't have time for this!" He roared. "The Obsidian Demon is our primary concern here!"

"White Dragon?" Kali glanced over her shoulder. "Why don't you and some of the others go on ahead?" The venom in her tone was beginning to rise up ever so slightly. "I believe that Joro won't let us all go without a fight."

Theresa's eyes narrowed a bit as she stared down Kali.

"And why should I trust a word you say?"

"Think about it, deary. If I wanted you all dead, I would have killed you all a long time ago." She flashed a grin, be it evil or playful Aiden couldn't tell. However she was not the only one to step up against the spider demon. Garrett stomped forward as well, his axe glistening in the pale lighting of the main hallway.

"I'll stay behind, Rexkin." He said with a low growl. "This spider has pissed me off enough to warrant my attention."

"Garret-"

"We don't have time!" He bellowed. "If the Obsidian Demon rises up, this entire city will pay the price!"

Joro let out an unearthly shriek as she slammed her hands into the ground. A flash of neon green bright light exploded from her palms as the earth's very crust seemed to mold beside her. Taking the form of several giant looking spiders. An audible whimper could be heard from Liza as she clutched onto Aello's arm.

"Great. More spiders." Seamus groaned as he took his staff out and spun it around. "Rexkin. Let me, Garrett, and the snake take care of Joro and her little cronies here."

"I can handle these spiders just fine, Seamus."

"Maybe big guy, but even you know that if you get too many on you, your great strength isn't gonna throw every single one of them off. Unless you want waste your true power in doing so."

"It matters not!" Joro shouted as her abdomen's maw began to spit out bile. "Two dragons and a snake, you will all feel the terror of death on your souls when I am through!"

Aiden turned back to Theresa as the trio in front of them charged Joro and her spider cronies.

"What do we do Thes?!"

Theresa gritted her teeth for a brief moment, but nodded her head once.

"They're right. We can't waste anymore time." She bitterly said before turning to Aello. "Liza needs to regather herself. Can you get her out of here?"

"N-No!" Liza managed to speak out. "I can still f-fight!"

"That's a lie, and you know it is." Theresa chastized her. "Your entire body is trembling from a traumatic experience. Get her out of here until she calms down, Aello. That's an order!"

Aello huffed at Theresa, but ultimately did not argue back against the white dragoness. She hovered over Liza's shoulders, grabbing them gently with her talons before flying into the air above them. She glanced over them one final time.

"Stop them before they bring the demon back!"

With that, the young harpy princess took off with Liza in her talons. Aiden felt bad having to watch one of their best fighters leave. But her mental state was clearly in no condition to go further right now. Not after experiencing a harrowing moment with Joro. Just one other thing on a pile of terrible deeds that he swore that the demon would pay for.

"Aiden, Mr and Mrs. Russell, let's move!" Theresa ordered.

The Russell family wasted no time in following her order. Aiden would only admit to himself that he felt bad that they were leaving the others behind to deal with a Prime Demon, especially when the previous encounters with Prime Demons prove challenging for even **three** dragons, but there was no time to fight a massive battle.

With Theresa leading the way down the pathway the four came across some of the cultists that had dorm room like areas. Each one of them tried to get in their way, only for the four of them to make quick work of them. Clearly unlike the cultists that were outside, they were the less experienced members. Aiden was glad that they were only newcomers as well. He didn't want to hurt another human being right now. Unless he had no choice in the matter.

"Up ahead!" Helena shouted as they made their way down the hall.

A large neon purple beam had caught their attention. It wasn't impossible to guess, but that beam had to be something that Dimitri or Raven had conjured up. The very glow of the light was enough to send shivers down Aiden's spine at the sight of it. Which meant only one thing.

The summoning of the Obsidian Demon was nearly done.

Aiden cursed under his breath as they got closer to room. If only they had known that entire time they were gathering the missing pieces of the beast!

The four found themselves at the end of the hallway in a massive room. Unlike the hallways before, there was barely anything in this room. Besides the giant purple beam that rose from the center of the room was Dimitri, who stood before the dark beam himself, arms wide open as he chanted. Beside him was Raven, who also was chanting right beside his master. But there were also four mages in dark purple robes standing on pentagram like shapes. Each one chanting a language that was not English or Draconic. Aiden could only guess that they were speaking a tongue that was used to summon forth demons. He had no time to muse on it for long as his father's voice shouted out.

"Quick! Attack the mages!"

Aiden snapped back to reality as he quickly dismissed his shield for a second, then throw a powerful Flarena attack at one of the mages. But just when it seemed that his attack would have an effect on the mage, it suddenly bounced off into the ceiling above them. A ripple effect was left behind from his attack though.

"Dammit! A force field!" Helena groaned.

Dimitri stopped chanting for a second as Aiden's mother threw her own attack right at the force field, attempting to break it apart.

"I know that voice..." He mused before turning around. A sick smile grew on his lips when he made eye contact with them all. "Connor. Helena. My, this is indeed a shock! It appears a reunion is in order!"

"Dimitri..." Connor lowly said. "I was hoping that you had abandoned this path..."

"Abandon? Me? Come now Connor, you of all people should know by now. I do not give up on my goals." His sick grin grew even more as he glanced over to Aiden's mother. "And Helena, my, you don't seem to have aged a single day. Time has been kind to you it seems."

"Spare me your false flattery, Dimitri." Helena retorted, Aiden could have sworn she had just hissed at him. "Just like it was in school. We both know that it was never your strong point."

"Ha, still a spitfire." Dimitri laughed as he clapped his hands together. "And it seems you have brought company with you. Theresa of the White Fire and Aiden. Your son. He must have had quite a shock to find out who the two of you truly are, hm?"

"Shut your mouth!" Aiden shouted. "So much has happened because of your idea to start messing with demonic magic, you bastard! The Harpies nearly were exposed, you formed this cult, and now you're trying to summon a demon from the past! And for what?!"

"Oh you think I'm trying to summon? No no no, dear boy. I'm undoing a wrong." Dimitri laughed. "I am simply bringing together the pieces of a grand being that a foolish king broke apart."

"Don't you DARE say that my King was foolish." Theresa snarled. "You weren't there thousands of years ago, you madman. The Obsidian Demon is a not like the demons that you and your cult control! Nor is it like any of the Prime Demons!"

"Ah yes, I am aware of this, Theresa of White Fire." Dimitri interlocked his fingers together. "Yes, the Obsidian Demon is not like any demon seen before on this world. A remarkable beast. They say that if it had not been stopped, the Obsidian Demon would have destroyed the old kingdoms before the rise of the Dark One."

Dimitri gave a short laugh before shaking his head momentarily.

"And to think, it all stemmed from the actions of your little sister. A traitor to her own kind I hear. Oh how that must infuriate you-"

"SHUT UP!"

Theresa's white wings exploded from her back as her true form's power briefly shined through.

"Touched a sore subject, did I?" Dimitri condescendingly asked. "Oh how could it not be though? Your sister was a stain on your family's name. Wasn't she?"

"You know nothing, about my little sister." Theresa growled.

"Oh on the contrary, White Dragon. I know more than you think." He glanced up above him. "Isn't that right, dear?"

Aiden felt his entire body go numb as the four of them looked up to where Dimitri was looking. Floating above them, flapping her own black wings, was Erienne. The crazed grin on her lips that Aiden remembered from the last time he encountered her was now a thing of the past. Instead, a more dismal expression covered her face. Her amber orange eyes gleamed like two gemstones in the dark of night.

Erienne floated her way down in front of the force field. Aiden noticed that while she still wore the same clothes that he had seen her in before, they were more ratty and ragged than previously. Her wings were the most striking change to her appearance. Black as the night sky. And unlike Seamus, Garrett, or her sister's own massive wings, the young dragoness's were much smaller, just shy of half the size of Theresa's.

"Erienne. You surely remember your big sister, do you not?" Dimitri asked. "Be a good dear, and keep them away from the forcefield until we are done, hm?"

Erienne gave no vocal response as she stared down Aiden, Theresa, and his parents. There was no one more shaken by the appearance of her than her own big sister. Theresa shook her head in disbelief before taking one small step ahead of them.

"Eri…" She managed to speak out, for a moment thought he heard the distinct sound of a sob in her throat. "Please…tell me that isn't you."

"…Long time no see, sister." Erienne responded. ""You look well…I suppose you should, considering your happy new life in this human world. What am I saying? You've never looked anything less than perfect, even back then."

"Don't do that, sister." Theresa frowned. "You know that I have always thought the world of you."

"Did you? Did you really think the world of me? If you thought anything of me at all, we wouldn't be here!" Erienne clenched her fists. "Why didn't you listen to me?"

"Eri-"

"No!" Erienne snapped. "Don't you dare call me that! Don't you dare act like you're happy to see me! Not after everything that's happened!"

Despite her shouting Theresa took another small step towards her sister. The smaller dragon held her hands in front of her and let out a thin dark firebeam. The blast narrowly sliced into Theresa's right cheek. Blood flowed down the cheek slowly, but Theresa didn't seem to notice or even care about the cut. Her emerald green eyes were locked right onto her sister's amber orange ones.

"That. Was a warning." Erienne hissed. "Don't you take another step towards me…"

The tension in the air began to rise up ever so slowly. Theresa gently took her left thumb, then wiped it across the cut on her cheek. All the while her eyes never left the sight of her little sister's gaze.

"Eri…what has he done to you?"

"Done to me?"

"Look at yourself, Eri." Theresa implored her. "Look at where you are. Does this look like a place for one of us?"

There was a moment of hesitation from the smaller dragon as her big sister took another step. What Theresa said, it must have rattled her somewhat. But Erienne kept her hands up in front of her, firing off another blast to the left side of her sister. The impact from the attack was enough to leave a small crater. It would have been enough to scare off any other person.

But Theresa was far from any other kind of person.

"This isn't you." She said in a soft tone. "I know that you wouldn't ever do this…"

"You know nothing about me!" Erienne screamed. "I thought that you did when we were young, but the truth is that you never understood me at all!"

"That's not true, and you know it." Theresa's voice was far more tranquil than Aiden had heard it before. "You and I both know that there was nothing the two of us couldn't talk about. Don't you remember? Who was it that was always by your side when you were a hatchling? Who was it that would stay up with all night until you fell asleep? You know that it was me. You know that I would never think terribly about you…"

Erienne gritted her teeth as her wings flapped once a couple of times. A gust of wind blew out from them. Her hands soon were covered by dark flames once more as she stared down her approaching sister.

"You shut up!" Her voice becoming noticeably distorted. "You act nice, Theresa, but you're just like all the others back then! Those that would mock me for my size, for my attitude! For not...for not being like you!"

"Like...me?"

"Do you have any idea what it's like to be in your shadow?!" Erienne bellowed. "Do you have any idea how it feels to constantly be outshined by you in every single facet?! Of course you don't! You were the perfect daughter! You were always so much better than I was, at everything! School, fighting, transforming, all of it!"

Erienne's eyes slightly were filled by angry tears. Theresa went quiet as she hung her head down.

"You said that you understood me. That you would always protect and believe me! But that was a lie, wasn't it! You never truly understood me! Not once!"

Before he knew what he was doing, Aiden took a step forward to stand beside Theresa.

"That's not true! Your big sister thinks the world of you, Erienne!"

Aiden ignored the death glare from Erienne. The black flames surrounding her hands did not intimidate him as he took another step forward.

"You say that she doesn't care, that she never cared? Well I'm sorry to say this, but that's a damn lie. A lie that Dimitri has forced into your head! Theresa thinks the world of you. She told me about how close the two of you were growing up. You meant so much to her, despite anyone else claiming that you were flawed compared to her!"

Erienne bared her fangs at Aiden, aiming both of her hands at him now. The dark fire formed around them grew larger in both size and rage. Aiden didn't let this intimidate him. He took another step despite the danger that was rising up from Erienne's flames.

"That should matter more than what everyone else would think of you, right? That the unrequited love from your big sister and your family is what truly matters? They're more important than the words of people who truly didn't know you!"

"And what do YOU know about me?" Erienne lashed out. "That's right, nothing!"

"You know that's not true either." Aiden retorted. "You're not some kind of monster like they are making you. You're a kind person!"

"Enough!"

Erienne roared loudly as she threw a powerful fire blast towards Aiden. The latter brought his shield up just in time to barely avoid being hit by the attack. But even PeaceGuard wasn't enough to stop the knock back from Erienne's attack. Aiden felt his feet flying off the ground in a second before flying backwards in the air. Theresa flew up after him, grabbing him from behind to avoid him falling down.

"You don't know anything about me, sweetie. Neither does my sister. After all, what am I to her and the other two surviving members of our race? Nothing. Nothing but a Dangerous Traitor who brought forth a terrible demon!" She turned her back to them. "And I'm about to see that demon be brought back once more. To finish what it started..."

"Eri!" Theresa exclaimed. "Think about this! You know what the Obsidian Demon is! Even the King himself had a hard time defeating it! You know that these mages don't have the power to control it!"

"HA." Dimitri laughed. "That's where you're wrong, dragoness. This demon will obey us. For it is WE that have reunited its pieces back together once more!"

"Dimitri, stop it now!" Connor shouted as he fired out a powerful magic blast into the forcefield. "You have no idea just what kind of power you're dealing with!"

"Silence!" Erienne bellowed before glaring at Dimitri. "Enough delays, mage! Bring forth the Obsidian Demon!"

Dimitri almost was taken aback by the order from the dragon girl. His brows furrowed as he stared her down. But Erienne did not flinch from the glare. Instead, she spoke out once more.

"NOW!" Her voice turned far more distorted, darker almost, than before. Enough to make the mages on the pentagrams flinch.

There was a moment of silence after Erienne's voice finished echoing across the room. Dimitri gave her a short grin before turning back to the beam in the center.

"Hear me, oh great demon of fear itself. We have brought forth the pieces of your body together once more. Let the crimes of the foolish Dragon King and his kind be undone! Let the pieces of your body be reunited, as one!" Dimitri held his arms above his head as a great force of magic spewed from his body.

"Rise once more! Oh Great and terrible being of old! Let the world know, of the fear and terror the legends have foretold! Rise now, Obsidian Demon!!!!"

The chanting from the mages grew louder and louder as Dimitri finished his incantation. The large beam began to stop shining, fading away in one moment. Right before a large black and jagged hand reached out from the hole the beam had made. The hand grabbed onto the ground and with all its might, its owner pulled its massive and shadowy body up from the ground.

It had been done. The Obsidian Demon, was complete once more.

TERROR UNLEASHED

*I*t was perhaps one of the most nightmarish monsters Aiden would ever see in his life. More terrifying than the Teleranta, the great beast seemed as though it were the embodiment of terror itself. As Aiden gazed upon the abomination, he felt his blood run cold and every instinct screaming at him to flee.

Its body was covered in jagged, broken obsidian armor that seemed to just barely stretch across its rippling muscles. Beneath the armor, Aiden could make out pulsing orange light. At first, he believed it may have been some kind of unholy power, but as it trickled from the gaping wound across the demon's shoulder, Aiden watched in horror as it collided with the ground and began to melt it away. It wasn't power, it was liquid magma, just barely contained beneath the beast's armor and charred flesh. But, most horrifying of all, was its face. A charred, human-like skull, eyes pulsing with the light of the magma coursing within it. Atop the skull, were massive curved horns that stretched out unevenly.

The Obsidian Demon was cloaked in a dense, suffocating black smog that poured from its burning flesh. Aiden felt his heart stop when he realized the smoke seemed to be alive, countless, writhing, screaming faces reaching out from the smog, as if the souls of those slain by the demon were forever trapped within some never ending nightmare.

Everyone in the room felt the sheet of terror that washed over their senses. The mages gathered around all stepped back. Aiden almost dropped Warfang. Theresa's wings flared up defensively. Connor and Helena held each other's free hands tightly. Even the bravest soul would feel an incredible urge to run away.

The only three who did not flinch were Dimitri, Raven, and Erienne. The elderly mage let out a dark laugh as he held his hands above his head.

"Behold, the Demon that shall plunge the world into a new era of terror! The mighty Obsidian Demon has arisen once more!" He proclaimed. "This world will bend to the knee of the Dark Eye, the pitiful rulers of this world will know what true terror is!!!"

Dimitri's sickening grin grew as he took his staff in hand, pointing out towards Aiden's group.

"Now, Obsidian Demon! Your first order from your master! Destroy these pests! Remove this irritable thorn from our side!"

The world felt like it had slowed to a crawl as the Obsidian Demon stood there. It didn't move, all it did was stare right at Dimitri. Who gazed right back into the lifeless eyes of the abomination. The room had gone so silent that Aiden could hear his own heartbeat exploding in his ear drums.

Then, in a few seconds, the Obsidian Demon let loose an unholy roar that made the entire building tremble. After the roar came to an end it swung its right arm once, shattering the force field that surrounded it with an invisible surge of power. It's free hand swung down onto the ground beneath it, emitting a shockwave that forced the mages around it to respond. The mages all let out terrified cries of terror as they each fell over. Only Dimitri and Raven seemed to not cry out in shock as the fallen mages began to scurry away from the enormous beast.

Aiden could feel the his nerve begin to fail as the Obsidian Demon observed the mages that had summoned it forth. It slowly brought its right hand into the air, a pulsing shadow ball formed right in its palm. As it gathered power what Aiden could only guess was a sickening grin appeared on its 'lips' before it crushed the ball with its fingers. A large gash of shadowy tendrils erupted from the ball as they began to search around the room.

"Don't let those things touch you!" Theresa shouted to everyone. Her twins swords cutting away the tendrils that dared to get close to her.

Aiden and his parents were quick to respond to her order as they fought back against the tendrils that tried to get near them. Even though he was putting up a good attempt to keep them away from his body, Aiden never had felt more scared of anything in his entire life. Each time one came near inches of hitting him, he thought his life would end within that moment.

The four mages that helped Dimitri and Raven summon the Obsidian Demon were not so lucky. Each of them was hit in the chest by the tendrils that lashed out. Aiden felt his breath vanish as he watched as a white energy flew from their bodies up the long tendrils back into the shadowy ball. As the bodies of the four mages fell over, Aiden knew what the Obsidian Demon had done.

It had eaten their very souls.

Dimitri and Raven jumped back to avoid the tendrils that were trying to aim for them. All the while, Dimitri was barking orders out to the Obsidian Demon in a vain attempt to gain control of it. Any orders he was shouting did not seem to make the demon acknowledge, or even really care, that it was because of him that it was once again complete. If it had the ability to laugh at someone's orders, it might have done just that to Dimitri.

"Thes!" Aiden shouted as he blocked one tendril with PeaceGuard. "We need to get out of here, and now!"

"Obsidian Demon! Hear me now!" Dimitri once more bellowed. "It is I who found your pieces, I who brought you back together! You will cease these actions at once and realize who is your master, you stupid beast!"

"Not a good idea to call it stupid when you are trying to control it!" Raven spat out to his master.

"Silence, Raven!"

However, the Obsidian Demon did stop its attack, and the shadowy tendrils returned back to the pulsing shadow orb it held within its hand. Its lifeless eyes gazed over every single one of them carefully. Aiden's entire face became damp with sweat and fear at the very sight of the demon. Every single part of his natural instincts made him want to start crying in despair as it considered every person in the room.

There was only one person it had any true focus on however. And she stared right back into its lifeless eyes. Seemingly unafraid at what had been released into the modern world once more.

Erienne.

The Obsidian Demon slowly pointed its left index finger right at the dragoness. As if he remembered exactly who and what she was. In that moment a dark bolt of lighting erupted from its fingertips right into her chest. Erienne let out a small cry of pain, but then began to float up into the air as the fist of the demon moved with her.

"ERI!"

Theresa flapped her mighty wings once as she flew up towards her little sister. But the moment she got close to Erienne, a blast of fire from the Obsidian Demon's left eye raced towards her. Theresa was forced to use her left wing as a shield of some sort to hold back the attack, but the very force of the demon's power was enough to slam her up against the wall behind her. As the fiery eye beam came to an end, Theresa unshielded herself in that moment. There were some burnt marks on her wing, but those would heal naturally over time.

"T-Thes!" Aiden rushed over to her, quickly helping her to her feet as best he could. "A-Are you okay?!"

"I'm FINE." She replied, a harsh growl was in her voice. "Dammit, Dimitri you fool. Look at what you've done now!"

"Be silent, worm!" Dimitri barked back. "I will gain control of this demon, and I will use it to destroy you!"

"You don't get it, dumbass!" She pushed herself away from Aiden as she took a step towards him. "The Obsidian Demon is a primordial being, more ancient than time itself! It's not something that even the greatest Dark Mages of old could control! It's so powerful that even the great Dragon King could not kill it! What makes you think that YOU of all people could harness its power and control it?!"

She spat some blood out of her mouth as her eyes turned a bit more fiery.

"The truth of the matter is that you can't! What you have done is possibly doom this entire world to a monster!"

Raven nearly flinched as the reality of Theresa's words began to seep into him. Dimitri blinked for a few seconds, before glancing over to the Obsidian Demon. Then, a small slick smile grew over his lips.

"It's...marvelous..."

"It's. WHAT?!" Connor shouted. "Marvelous?!? Dimitri, do you know what you have just done?! You possibly have brought about the end of the damn world because of this! You know full well that this modern era is not equipped to destroy such a beast!"

"And that, is where I shall take pride in this, Connor." Dimitri responded, his eyes glimmering with glee. "It's true that this world does not have a single weapon that is capable of bringing the Obsidian Demon down...but, it will do what we wanted all this time. To make this pathetic world burn. To bring it to its very knees, so that those who should truly rule will take the place of the liars and the sycophants! So that **we**, the rightful leaders, can steer this world into a new direction!"

"You're a sick bastard!" Aiden roared. "You don't have any means of controlling this monster!"

"Not yet I don't...I will admit to that fool, but, soon, we will learn how to harness its power. And with it, the Dark Eye will make this pitiful world rue the day that they forsake their truths!"

Dimitri threw his head back and began to laugh loudly. All the while Erienne continued to float in front of the Obsidian Demon. Aiden gritted his teeth at the sound of Dimitri's laugher. Why would he do this? What did he have to gain from the world possibly being destroyed by this monstrosity that he had unleashed? Was he truly mad to believe that such a demon could really be under his control?

Something in the back of his mind began to try to put the pieces of the puzzle together. It was almost as if Dimitri had expected the Obsidian Demon to resist his orders. But why would he knowingly summon a demon so powerful that it wouldn't heed his command? Why would he take such glee in the idea of unleashing it upon the world? It didn't feel right.

Unless...

"...You didn't do this alone, did you?" He asked.

Dimitri stopped laughing in that second as he stared back over to Aiden. He tilted his head in curiosity at what Aiden had just asked.

"If you truly expected to be able to control this Demon, it would be attacking us right now. But it's not...you knew that it probably would have ignored your commands. You knew that it more than likely would have begun to kill anything it wanted. But why? Why would you summon such a beast?"

Aiden's eye brows narrowed as he pointed Warfang's very tip at Dimitri.

"You wouldn't dare unleash a power like this unto the world without some kind of back up plan. Unless...unless you had someone tell you how to assemble it and how you could destroy it after its purpose was done." Aiden's grip on Warfang became tighter as he leered right into the eyes of Dimitri. "I'm right. Aren't I?!"

Dimitri gave no response to him.

Not that he would have been allowed to answer Aiden's question in full, as there was an ear piercing screech that erupted from above them all.

Erienne was the one screaming as the dark lighting bolt began to turn into a smothering black fire that completely covered her entire body.

"ERI!!!" Theresa cried out, white flames began to spark up from her mouth. "YOU BASTARDS! YOU DID THIS! YOU DID THIS TO MY LITTLE SISTER!!"

A flash of intense white flames spewed out from her jaws that roared its way to towards the two mages. Raven was quick to block Theresa's white flames with a shield spell, before glancing back over to his master.

"We must retreat, Master!" He plead. "We must take every one that is part of our order away before The Obsidian Demon notices them all!"

"Tch. Retreat? And why would we do that now and not witness the end for these pitiful fools?"

"If we stay, we won't be able to reap the benefits." Raven argued. "What good will reshaping the world in our image be if we're killed by the very thing we seek to gain control over?!"

Dimitri scoffed at the truth in Raven's argument, but relented before snapping his fingers once. A large portal formed behind the two of them. Before they left though, he stared right at Theresa.

"Know this, White Dragoness, this is not the only place where we have set up a base. The Dark Eye will not fall this day. No. We will wait and see the results from the Obsidian Demon's rampage, then we will take our place as masters of this world while the rest of this rotten planet suffocates on the terror it exudes!"

"DIMITRI!"

Connor yelled out as he fired a powerful blast of magic towards his former friend. Before the attack could make contract with him or Raven though, they portal had completely taken them away.

"DAMN YOU!" Theresa roared out. "DAMN YOU, DIMITRI!"

"Theresa!" Aiden grabbed her shoulder. "Now's not the time to focus on them! Look!"

Despite her anger towards the escaping duo, Theresa did return her focus back to the primary problem they had right now. The Obsidian Demon. It's malicious eyes still pulsed with power as the smothering fire had all but covered Erienne. Aiden felt his gut tie into a knot at the very thought of Erienne being burnt alive by the demon's powers.

But that was not what the fire was doing to the younger sister of Theresa. Oh no. It was doing something far worse.

Just as soon as the fire had spread over her body, it came to an end. Erienne hung her head over as the Obsidian Demon held out its left hand towards her ever so gently.

The tension in the air had risen to a boiling point as Theresa waited no longer.

With a loud roar she took her dragon form. Her emerald green eyes flashed with pure anger and hatred for her foe that she let loose another roar before a stream of hot white fire flew towards the demon's head. Just as the flames approached their target, Erienne's body suddenly moved on its own, racing towards the stream of fire herself. Just as it was about to hit her, the younger sister of Theresa held her left hand out and a stream of black fire erupted from her palm. The flames from her palm were enough to not only block Theresa's attack, but with the flick of her head, Erienne's attack knocked away the white flames.

This took Aiden by complete surprise. He had seen many things become burnt, or badly damaged, from Theresa's flames. There were times that he thought that her fire breath couldn't even be deflected due to how hot it was. And Erienne had just tossed it aside with her own flames as if they were nothing!

Theresa stopped her attack as she stared right at her younger sister. The latter returned the gaze for a few moments before both of her eyes turned blood red. The Obsidian Demon let out some kind of gurgling sound as Erienne floated over to its right shoulder. Once she was by its side, the massive beast punched a hole in the wall. The very punch incinerating everything it had made contact with.

Aiden winced for a moment as the bright daylight sun entered the room. But he soon realized the horrible reality of the Obsidian Demon punching the wall down like that. It was free to roam into Richmond itself.

With Erienne by its side, this violation from the past began to take large steps towards Richmond. Theresa let out another stream of fire towards the Obsidian Demon, but again Erienne blocked her sister's attack. But this didn't stop Theresa from letting loose another stream of fire in a futile attempt to do damage to the Obsidian Demon. Each time, the white dragoness let out an anguish cry.

"ERI!!!!!!" She lamented. "ERI! NOT AGAIN! DAMMIT ALL! NOT AGAIN!"

As Theresa wailed out in sorrow Garrett, Seamus, and Kali approached them. The largest of the dragons had a frown on his lips at the sight of his leader's grief. Seamus gave no witty remark of the situation. Even Kali seemed somewhat sorry for the pain that Theresa was experiencing right now.

Connor and Helena looked down. Both of them at a loss for words at what Theresa was experiencing in that moment. The dead weight of silence filled the room. They had failed to stop the summoning of the Obsidian Demon. The world itself could be destroyed by the sheer amount of terror that it would bring across the lands. The Dark Eye Cult had won…

…At least. That's what most people would have said in that moment.

"Theresa." Aiden said in a soft, but firm, tone. "Theresa Goldwin. Do not let this be the end for you or this world."

Everyone blinked in confusion at Aiden's sudden tone change. Even Garrett was perplexed by the very mature voice that was coming from the teenager. Theresa's eyes opened slowly as she stared right at Aiden.

"Aiden...you don't have to pretend to be brave." She said with a sorrowful smile. "This? This is the end of the world...not even the Dragon King-"

"Could kill it. I know." Aiden cut her off. "But I don't give a damn about what happened in the past. Not anymore."

"You what?"

"You heard me." Aiden said, quickly dismissing Warfang before he reached out towards her face, gently stroking her reptilian snout with one hand. "What happened in the past, it's in the past. I know that back then you couldn't kill the Obsidian Demon. It had to be broken into parts and sealed away. Right? Well, that's just what we're going to have to do."

"What are you talking about, whelp?" Garrett demanded. "You do not know of what you speak."

"I hate to admit it, kiddo. But the big guy's right. You don't even know what it took to completely separate the Obsidian Demon in the past." Seamus grimaced. "You don't have to put on a brave show for us. It's clear as the day itself that you're terrified right now."

"You're right." Aiden admitted. "I am terrified. But you know who will even be more terrified? The millions and millions of innocent people that will have no idea what that thing is the moment they spot it. We can't just stay here and wallow in the fact that we couldn't stop it from returning to this world. We have to stop it."

"Aiden..." Theresa started, but he put his hand up in front of her to stop her from speaking out.

"Listen to me, everyone." Aiden slowly stepped into view for them all. "What we are facing now is quite possibly the greatest threat to the modern world. I know that this is not the Dark One itself, but you all know that the Obsidian Demon is so powerful that the people in its path won't even have a chance to defend themselves from its oncoming wrath. All three of you who lived in in the past know what it's capable of. You all know that if we don't stop it now, nothing will. That's when the Dark Eye Cult will truly have won."

He pointed towards the Obsidian Demon, who was quickly approaching the city limits of one of Richmond's smaller districts.

"I don't know why Erienne has been taken by that bastard. And I don't know why she would say such things that weren't true about you,

Thes. But I do know this. She is the key to why the Obsidian Demon is walking about right now. You saw how it reacted when she made eye contact with it. It knew that she was the reason it was summoned all those years ago, and it knows that she is important now."

"Because she's a damn traitor." Garrett interrupted.

"Garrett? With all due respect to your position and power as a great dragon? Shut the hell up." Aiden ordered.

Garrett nearly blew fire at him, but Aiden continued to speak.

"You three weren't here when it happened, but for a split second I could tell that there was more to the story of Erienne's actions. Her eyes painted a sad picture of hatred for her sister, but her words? They did not sound words she truly believed. But we can cross that bridge when we come to it. Right now what's truly important is that we're the only ones that can stop the Obsidian Demon from rampaging. If you look at the situation you know I'm right. The Harpies wouldn't dare leave their dens for the sake of the human race, and the Mages at your Academy aren't ready to battle a beast like the Obsidian Demon, Seamus."

Warfang reappeared in Aiden's hand once more as he held it high above his head.

"I know that we do not have the army that you had in the past. Or that we don't have the great and all mighty Dragon King to help us. But to hell with that. If we wallow in our sorrow about how we don't have those that helped put an end to this demon's terror before, then all hope is truly lost. I don't know about the rest of you. But I will not, no, I refuse to give up here and now. We're the only ones that can defeat that bastard. And you all know it. Sure I'm terrified of that thing...but I will not let it harm innocents, or let it use Erienne like some kind of sick puppet."

Theresa blinked for a moment as Aiden stared right back at her. The gold and silver blade of Warfang shimmered in the sun light as he gave her a soft smile.

"But I can't do it without you. All of you. So please...please, help me stop the Obsidian Demon before it brings the world an era of absolute fear."

The trio of dragons all glanced at one another for a moment. There was no words needed between them as they each gave another a short approving nod. Seamus let out a long sigh before putting his hands behind his head.

"Ah what the hell? It's not like anyone else is able to do anything against a being like that bastard. Might as well be all of us." He gave Aiden a lively grin. "Ya know, kiddo, you're not bad at words."

"You're too kind on the boy, Seamus. His praises can be sung another time." Garrett interrupted him. "But you are right about one thing, whelp, the Obsidian Demon must be stopped. No matter the cost."

Theresa rolled her eyes at Garrett's dismissal of Aiden's speech before she gently nuzzled his chest with her snout.

"Don't listen to Garrett, the words you spoke out have truth in them, Aiden. And had you not spoken them, I would still be wallowing in sorrow over the loss of my little sister."

"She's not gone, Thes." Aiden corrected her, gently stroking the left side of her snout. "Not yet."

The white dragoness snorted before rearing her head back. She glanced back to her fellow dragons and Kali. The three of them nodded once before Seamus and Garrett assumed their true states. Theresa snorted once, white embers escaping her nostrils before her large wings opened up.

"Aiden is right. We cannot let our fear or sorrows stop us from doing what must be done. You all know the objective, stop the Obsidian Demon. It cannot be allowed to roam freely."

Seamus and Garrett both gave short snorts of acknowledgement as they turned their attention to the giant hole in the wall left by the Obsidian Demon. Each step the monstrous demon took made the very earth vibrate beneath a mere mortal's feet. Aiden glanced back to Theresa, watching her eyes become determined as she lowered her neck down for him to climb onto.

"You know...that was very impressive." She admitted to him as Aiden sat on the back of her neck. "You could have some fine leadership skills within you, Aiden."

"Ha. Me? Lead? No way, Thes. Bad things tend to happen whenever I lead." Aiden jokingly said to her.

Theresa didn't laugh as she glanced back towards him. Then back to the field in front of them. Aiden blinked in confusion before tapping her shoulder with the pommel of his sword.

"Thes? You okay?"

"I'm fine it's just...that sounded familiar is all."

Before he could ask her another question she began to move out of the building. Aiden turned quickly back to his parents before they were out of sight.

"Mom! Dad! See if you can convince people in the city to evacuate! Use magic to get there before us or something!"

Both of them opened their mouths to begin an argument with him, but once Theresa and the three dragons were outside they took off into the air. Any argument the two of them could have possibly had with him was moot at this point. The Obsidian Demon was their primary focus. With the very fate of the world possibly in the balance, Aiden was willing to get scolded later if they managed to win against the demon.

As they flew in the air above Richmond, positioning themselves just above the Obsidian Demon, Aiden could already see that the beast had set many houses, buildings, streets, and fields ablaze within the Richmond area. He felt his soul cringe at the cries of the innocent civilians exposed to the madness emanating from the beast. He couldn't even imagine how scared they all felt in that moment.

Suddenly a realization came to him as they hovered over the Obsidian Demon.

"How are we supposed to fight this thing and not be exposed?!" He cried out. "I know you guys can cast a spell that tricks people into not seeing us, but this could be a problem! No doubt the innocent people down there can see that damn monster!"

"Not exactly!" Seamus replied. "The Obsidian Demon is so ancient and powerful that the mortal eyes of this time can't exactly see it like you and I can."

"What?!"

"Think of it like this! Right now it can only be seen by those who are in tune with magical energies! Not a lot of humans in this world are tuned into magic anymore! It only makes sense that what they're seeing right now is some kind of storm mixing together a tornado and earthquakes!"

"Lessons later!" Theresa ordered. "Garrett, Seamus! Form the triangle formation! On my signal we dive down at the Demon and attack it with our flame breathes! Aiden, you try to slash away any attacks that it throws at you if you can! Kali!"

""Yeeeeees?" Although she spoke in a teasing manner, there was a noticeable hint of disgust in the snake's voice.

Theresa slowly turned her attention back to the snake demon, who was coiled right around Garrett's neck.

"Can we trust you?" She asked, bile nearly escaping her throat.

The Prime Demon scowled, her eyes flashing a poisonous shade of green.

"What kind of demon do you take me for? Why would I ever associate with such violent garbage? Everything about this beast offends me, I want to see this filth wiped from your miserable planet!"

Theresa groaned before returning her attention back to the Obsidian Demon below them. Her eyebrows furrowed in anger at the sight of the beast holding her sister in some kind of trance.

"Listen up! On my signal, unleash your flame breathes at its back! Try to do whatever damage you can to its body! But don't aim for Erienne! I want her pulled away from the bastard if we can!"

"And if we can't?" Garrett asked.

"You will let me deal with it. My way." Theresa ordered before rearing her head back. "On my mark!"

The trio of dragons hovered in midair momentarily as Theresa waited for the right moment. As the Obsidian Demon swung its left arm into one building, the white dragoness' eyes shimmered with a desire for revenge.

"Now!" She ordered.

Seamus and Garrett roared before they dive bombed towards the Obsidian Demon with Theresa. Aiden held onto Theresa's neck for dear life as the speed of the diving dragon began to test the amount of strength he still had within his body. His eyes leaked some tears the faster Theresa dove. But he refused to let go of her neck. They had a job to do.

The Obsidian Demon barely paid any mind to the approaching dragons. Only shrugging once Theresa let out a challenging roar. It's right hand rammed itself into a small coffee shop, causing it to explode from its sheer power. The cries of fear erupted from within the shop, several people even catching fire momentarily from the impact.

Theresa snarled as she and her fellow dragons landed on the ground. With the perspective spell in place, they could not fight freely without being noticed by the thousands of human eyes that were no doubt witnessing the destruction of Richmond. Once more she let out a challenging roar towards the Obsidian Demon. Once more its answer was its back to her face.

The white dragoness glance over towards her fellow dragons, gave a short nod, before taking a deep breath. Power formed within her throat as she reared her neck back. With a loud growl the leader of the Trinity expelled a torrent of white hot flames towards her enemy. Beside her, Garrett and Seamus followed suit with their regular color flames. The damage from their combined flame breath was no doubt devastating. The very heat from their combined attacks was enough to make several metal poles begin to melt in certain sections.

Just like before in the false Academy, Erienne flew in defense of the Obsidian Demon. Her black flames rising up from the ground to act as a shield of sorts for the fiend. Though there was an audible grunt from her lips as she felt the combined powers of the Trinity's flames push against her protective shield.

Sparks flew off in many directions from the clashing flames. Some of them flew into cars, causing them to explode on impact. Others collided with buildings, setting them ablaze in mere moments. One particular building caught fire so fast that it suddenly crumbled to the very ground itself!

Aiden winced as he witnessed the building collapse. He could only pray that there weren't any innocent people within it at that moment. But his attention turned back to the clash of flames. Sweat began to run down his brow as he watched the multi colored breath attacks push against Erienne's shield. If this kept up, they wouldn't be able to get even close to the Obsidian Demon.

"Theresa!" He shouted. "We can't focus on one spot! We gotta create an opening! If she ends up throwing your attacks away, scatter apart!"

Theresa's emerald green eyes glanced back at Aiden for a few seconds, then back to Erienne's shield. She gave a short approving nod.

That was more than enough for Aiden to realize that she approved of his suggestion. Not like she could vocally accept it right now of course.

Just as he predicted though, Erienne did manage to throw aside the three flame breaths aside with her black fire. Each one spread out across the streets of Richmond. Causing the ground itself to split apart from their intense heat before dying down away from the battle. Erienne floated there, her eyes still pulsing red as she glared down the trio of dragons. Aiden gripped tightly onto Warfang's hilt as he readied himself.

Erienne let out her own battle cry, which sounded like a mixture of a teenage girl screaming and a full dragon roaring before countering with large black fireballs towards them.

"Scatter!" Theresa ordered.

The dragons quickly took off into several different directions from one another. Garret to the left, Semaus to the right, and Theresa took off into the sky. Aiden once more hung onto her neck for dear life before dismissing PeaceGuard from his side for a moment. His eyes glistened with magical power as he formed a spell in his left hand.

"Flarnea!"

The fire beam erupted from his palm towards the head of the Obsidian Demon. Once more, Erienne was there to block the attack. This time actively catching the blast with both of her hands before tossing it into the air harmlessly. A sneer crossed her lips as she stared right at Aiden and Theresa, a small hint of tears forming in the corner of her eyes.

"Just hang on, Erienne." Aiden whispered. "We're coming for you."

Aiden could see Garrett charging towards the Obsidian Demon. This was the first time he had ever seen the strongest of the trinity run on all four legs. To put it mildly, he was far faster than Aiden expected him to be in his true form. Each step he took caused the ground to shake as well, sending several cars flying up into the air.

The Obsidian Demon glanced over to the charging dragon and gave a dismissive snort. As Garrett approached, the foul fiend turned and readied both of its massive hands to catch him in mid charge, grabbing Garrett by his shoulders. Though the demon had caught him by his shoulders the impact from Garrett's charge was felt as several glass windows shattered from the shockwave. A low growl escaped both of their mouths as the largest dragon pushed with all his might against the Obsidian Demon's grip. Each step he took caused the ground to crack, and small craters formed away from their battle.

Despite how massive Garrett was, the Obsidian Demon had at least two more feet over the massive dragon. But this didn't stop him from using every bit of strength he had in his body. With a mighty roar, Garrett bit down on one of the exposed parts of the Obsidian Demon's body. The bite only annoyed the creature, but it did give Garrett an opportunity to begin pushing it into a large building behind it.

Once the demon realized what Garrett was doing, it was too late for it to counter attack. The four story building began to crumble down onto the Obsidian Demon. Shards of glass and chunks of rocks landing everywhere in the gaping holes of its armor. They in turn melted away from the immense beat that spewed from the demon's magma like blood.

"Garrett poo, do me a favor and get back!" Kali ordered him.

Though he did not like to be addressed as such by the snake demon, Garret did pull away from the Obsidian Demon. Once he did, Kali slithered her way up his neck towards the top of his head. Her hair seemed to float wildly in the wind as she took a deep breath. Her two hands soon were covered by a pale bluish tint of magical power. As her foe began to pull itself back up from the collapsing building, the magic she gathered reached full power.

"Glacial Flare!"

At her command a blast of bone chilling ice magic spewed from her hands. The attack was enough to catch both the demon and Erienne off guard momentarily as it managed to land a direct hit right into the chest of the abomination. The Obsidian Demon didn't let out a grunt of pain from the impact, but it did find itself being pushed backwards by Kali's impressive attack. It was even forced through several buildings behind it!

Kali gritted her teeth as she kept adding more power to the ice beam. As she did so the Obsidian Demon kept being rammed through several buildings.

"Kali that's enough!" Theresa ordered. "You'll end up destroying more of the damn city then helping it if you keep pushing the bastard through more buildings!"

The snake Prime Demon laughed at the order, but she did relent. As she ended her attack steam rose up around her hands. She looked over both of her hands ever so carefully. She frowned as she took in the after effect of using such a powerful attack.

"Oh dear. It appears that I broke a nail! How dare that, THING, force me, ME, a being of perfection to put that much effort into an attack? It's downright disgusting!"

"How did you even do that?" Aiden called out from above. "I thought you were more of the mystical and poisonous kind of demon!"

"Just because that is my preferred way of attacking, does not mean that I can not use other spells, little boy." Kali snorted. Her attention was fully on her hands. "But look at my poor nails! Ruined by the very spell I used! Ugh, that bastard better hope I don't get a chance to shock the life out of him!"

"Now is NOT the time for you to be worried about your damn nails, snake." Garrett responded, his voice deeply annoyed by her focusing on that of all things. "If you haven't noticed, it's not dead."

True to Garrett's word, the Obsidian Demon began to rise up from the ground. Despite the damage caused by it plowing through the buildings like a bulldozer, it hardly seemed damaged. Aiden felt his blood run cold as it brushed its shoulders off of any debris that littered them.

"It took that and barely got a scratch?!" He proclaimed.

"Focus, Aiden!" Theresa ordered. "Remember the main objective is to get Erienne away from it!"

Right as Theresa finished speaking the Obsidian Demon let loose a massive roar. The roar itself causing everything around it to either fall apart or tremble at the force of the volume. Its full attention now focused on the group.

With a great burst of speed the abomination ran back towards Garrett and Kali. It moved so fast that it took even the great dragon of strength by surprised as he braced himself for impact. The demon's hands grabbing hold of Garrett's left top horn and right shoulder. This time Garrett found himself being pushed back by the sheer force of the evil creature, ramming through several buildings himself.

All the while the innocent humans that could not see the battle screamed out in terror at what was happening around them. Some of them barely escaping the broken debris sent flying their way. As far as they could tell, a superstorm was happening just outside of their windows. All the while their fear was empowering the Obsidian Demon.

"Gary!" Kali shouted to him. "Don't just let it push you around! Push back!"

"You're not helping!" He spat back.

"Hmph. Must I do everything for you?"

The Prime Demon placed her fingertips gently over his temples. A small faint light went off as her magic began to empower the great dragon of strength with new energy. Garrett's eyes flashed a bright green before his muscles seemed to bulge out. As the new strength from Kali's enhancement magic the Obsidian Demon reared its left fist back to throw a powerful punch right at them.

Garrett quickly reacted with a quickly 180 turn, his massive tail tip clashing with the punch. The moment the two forces collided a powerful shockwave exploded from the impact. Enough to force the two fierce beings away from each other momentarily. As if sensing that Garrett had increased in physical power, the demon stomped on the ground once. Pillars of lava erupted from the ground around the dragon, trapping him and Kali from making another attack.

"Garrett! Kali!" Seamus roared before taking a shot at the Obsidian Demon.

"No Seamus!"

Too late, the Obsidian Demon was not be taken by surprise by the dragon of magic. The moment he tried to approach the abomination it grabbed him by his throat, and hurled him right into several buildings that were to its left. Seamus rolled like a ball into the buildings, each one falling apart from the sheer force of the impact.

Aiden stared in shock as the debris began to clear out, revealing Seamus, possibly dead, on the ground.His pupils shrank, his mouth went dry, and every single muscle in his body felt like they were screaming. In that moment, the anger and hatred for the Obsidian Demon that Aiden held for what it had done to Erienne snapped.

"You bastard!!!!!"

Theresa let out a massive roar of her own as she flapped her wings, dive bombing right at the Obsidian Demon. Both her and Aiden determined to take revenge on the Obsidian Demon for everything it had caused in this fight. The countless innocents harmed or killed by its rampage. Using Erienne like some kind of puppet. Forcing the two sisters to be driven apart in the old times?

It would end this day. Aiden swore it to himself that the demon would pay!

THE TRAITOR'S TRUTH

*A*iden's eyes glistened with hatred for the Obsidian Demon. Hatred for what it had done to Theresa and Erienne in the past. Hatred for killing countless innocent civilians. And, most importantly, hatred for using Erienne as some kind of sick shield in its battle with them. He didn't care what it took. He would do what the Dragon King could not. He would see the Obsidian Demon defeated this day!

Theresa also intended to avenge her comrades and regain her lost sister. The moment she landed she charged directly into the chest of the Obsidian Demon with her shoulder. At first the vile fiend didn't budge, but then Theresa flapped her mighty wings rapidly. The power from her wings provided the strength to begin pushing the Obsidian Demon back.

At the same time Aiden threw Flarneas right at the face of the Obsidian Demon. As fast as Erienne was, she could not block every single attack Aiden was throwing! Each time she stopped at least three Flareneas, another one of them managed to get past her, barely scraping the ripped flesh in the broken pieces of the foul monster's armor.

Theresa gritted her teeth before bringing up her front claws. With all her might she rammed them through the holes in the Obsidian Demon's armor. She ignored the burning blood from the beast as her wings flapped harder and harder. Each time she flapped her wings the feet of the Obsidian Demon began to rise up from the ground itself.

"AIDEN! HOLD ON!"

Aiden wrapped both his arms around Theresa's neck at her order. Not wasting a moment of their sudden advantage, the white dragoness let loose an earth shattering roar. The force she produced was enough to lift the demon off the ground. In fact, it did more than lift the damn monster off the ground. She was taking it away from the section of the city they were in!

Theresa's sudden burst of strength, combined with her wings' powerful flaps, were enough to move the two giant creatures in an entirely new direction. Aiden closed his eyes as he felt the speed pick up.

Much like the battles with the other two dragons, Theresa was literally pushing the Obsidian Demon through any building that was in the way, even a bridge at one point, towards a new section of Richmond. Aiden swore at one point that they had flown right past the Governor's mansion! But that didn't make him or Theresa falter. They would win this battle today. They had to!

Soon, the two giant beings found themselves in an unexpected place - an airport. Not just any airport though. The Richmond International Airport. Aiden shuddered as he realized just how close they would come to the building if their battle went that far. The people that would end up becoming hurt from their clash.

They had to make certain no one else suffered because of the Obsidian Demon!

Their clash with the vile being might have been invisible to human eyes, but Aiden noticed they were in the middle of a runway. He glanced over to his left, noticing an approaching plane that was preparing to take off.

"Thes!"

Theresa snorted once as she dislodged herself from the Obsidian Demon. A stream of white fire spewed from her maw right into its chest at full force. This time, it was too fast for Erienne to counter attack! The impact from her attack looked like a sudden bolt of lighting to the humans inside the airport. The plane racing down the runway came to a screeching halt at the sight of the bolt of lighting.

Aiden would have felt bad for the people on board the plane, but right now their focus was on the Obsidian Demon and his captive.

While the attack from Theresa was surely enough to take it off guard, there was hardly any damage to its body from her flames. The horrendous monster's throat roared as it looked around its surroundings. Its eyes found a small plane. Thankfully no passengers were onboard as it picked it up by its tail.

Aiden gasped in shock as the demon lifted it with ease. Soon it held onto the plane like it was a sort of crude club. It slammed its new weapon on the ground a couple of times before growling at Aiden and Theresa.

The latter snarled in anger before flapping her wings. A powerful gust of wind slammed right into the demon, who merely looked annoyed at this attempt to knock it over. Showing the same amount of speed as before, the Obsidian Demon rushed towards the duo.

With the airplane in its right hand, it swung its new weapon towards Theresa's head. The impact caused Theresa's head to recoil from the hit. The force was so hard that it completely shattered the plane. Pieces of its debris flew everywhere, some flying right through the windows of the center of the airport. With Theresa's blood splashing the ground near one plane.

"THES!" Aiden screamed in horror.

Theresa shook her head slowly from the impact, but there wasn't enough time for her to recover as the Obsidian Demon suddenly grabbed her by her tail. Slowly it began to spin in a circle. The tactic was enough to take Theresa off guard as she tried to break free from its grip. Aiden clung to her neck for life as each spin became progressively faster and faster. If he had a weak stomach he might have thrown up right there and then.

Just when it felt like it wouldn't stop spinning Theresa, the Obsidian Demon let go of her tail. Sending the white dragoness and Aiden right towards one of the hangar bays for the planes. Theresa quickly grabbed Aiden with one of her claws and pulled him to her chest. Bracing herself to take the impact. As her body rammed right into the hangar, a set of explosions went off from the unmanned aircraft within. Fire spread out around them as planes blew up one after another.

Though Theresa had taken much of the blow for them both, Aiden felt an aftershock from it. Every single bone in his body felt like it had just been hit with a giant truck at full force. How he wasn't broken apart, or even dead, he had no idea. All he cared for was that he and Theresa were alive.

That is to say that he wasn't completely unscratched. He had two large cuts over his eyebrows, his arms were scrapped and there were holes in his jeans right over his knees. They too were bleeding.

Theresa sustained the most damage from the fight. Parts of her neck were bleeding. As were her legs and underbelly from taking the impact of the throw. Despite the pain that ran through her dragon form, she was determined to stand up. Some blood poured out onto the ground, but that didn't seem to bother her.

"Hold...hold still." Aiden said as he rose up from the ground as well. "I have to h-heal what I can."

Theresa reluctantly nodded her head in response to his request. After placing his weapons on the ground Aiden gently placed both of his hands on Theresa's body. He quietly whispered the healing spell as the soothing light washed over her body slowly.

"Hell of a fight we're in right now, huh?" He asked with a dry laugh. "I'm almost starting to miss the Overmind."

"We got through that, we can get through this." Theresa replied, hissing in pain from her injuries. "At least, I hope we can..."

The two of them stared back to the Obsidian Demon, who was just standing there in the runway. Waiting for the two of them to make the next move. Aiden felt a shiver run down his spine since it didn't make any kind of gloating response after what it had done. The broken pieces of the airplane that was its temporary club littered the ground.

"That thing took my flame breath at point blank range, and it didn't even flinch. Just like in the past. I'm starting to wonder if the bastard's invincible."

Aiden shook his head as he stood back up after healing what he could of Theresa's wounds. He hated to admit it, but she might have been right about that. Everything that was thrown at the Obsidian Demon didn't seem to even phase it. Not even Garrett's seemingly unrivaled strength seemed to directly damage the beast.

Was it truly invincible? Could such a being even exist?

There was no way it could be real. Not after everything Aiden had been through with his friends. Nothing was invulnerable. Not even the mighty dragons that he admired so much. If they had weaknesses as well, then the Obsidian Demon had to have one too. He knew it had to have one!

"Think dammit." He told himself. *"What is it about this thing that is similar to anything you read in the past! There has to be something! Come on, think!"*

Try as hard as he could, nothing came to mind about the demon's seemingly invulnerability. None of the stories he had ever read before ever mentioned a being like the Obsidian Demon being this kind of powerful. It was like something out of a video game, completely over-powered in a way that would force the player to approach the enemy in a different way.

"Wait. Just like a video game?"

Aiden gasped as sudden realization came to him. He had played a great amount of video games in the past. It was just like this. There was almost always a boss with this kind of set up. Invulnerable in most areas, but it had one spot that it couldn't afford to lose at any cost. Aiden stared at the entranced Erienne, who floated beside the vile soulless beast.

That was it.

"Thes, I got it!"

His declaration wasn't unnoticed by the Obsidian Demon. With a unholy roar it let loose a stream of magma from its left hand. Theresa wasted no time in grabbing Aiden with her front left claw before dodging the stream of magma. Aiden felt himself being plopped down onto the back of her neck as she took off into the sky. The two of them keeping a close eye on their target.

The Obsidian Demon didn't stop attacking. Its left hand continued to let loose short blasts of magma fireballs at the duo. Each time Theresa tried to get close to the foul monster to counter attack it would shoot another blast that would force her to dodge. Every time she dodged one though the magma would burn and even melt away the ground where they fell.

"I'm still waiting for you to bring me your revelation, Aiden!" Theresa shouted as she dodged another magma ball, which smacked into the bottom of the control tower of the airport. "I'd prefer it now rather than to let innocent people die from this thing's attacks!"

"Right, sorry!" Aiden responded. "Listen, it IS invulnerable. We know that. But it has to have something that is allowing it to not be damaged! Think of it like a video game boss!"

"Aide, now is really not the time to compare-"

"Just trust me!" Aiden interrupted her. "Think on it, remember those games where no matter what we tried they wouldn't take damage?! They always had something that was giving them that invincibility! This guy's just like them! And I think I know whose repairing damage it takes!"

The two of them, almost as if in unison, turned their attention to their true target. The one person that had been giving the monster its protection throughout the entire battle.

"Erienne." They said together.

"If it's her, then the Obsidian Demon will do whatever it takes to protect her. You know that, right?"

"I'm aware." He said. "But we don't really have a choice, Thes. We have to get Erienne away from the bastard long enough for us to actually harm him. Hell, we might be able to save her!"

Theresa hesitated for a moment as she floated in midair above them. Dodging the magma the Obsidian Demon would hurl at her.

"And what if you're wrong? What if we can't save her from it?"

"I don't know...but we'll never know if we don't try. Theresa..." His left hand gently stroked the side of her neck. "I'm asking you to trust me..."

Theresa let out a sigh before nodding her head once.

"All right, Aiden. I'll try to distract it while you grab her. Don't mess up!"

With that she let out a loud roar towards her enemy. The cruel demon responded in kind with its own loud roar. Together the roar sounded like an explosion of thunder went off above the airport. Theresa pulled her large white wings back and flapped up a powerful gust storm right into the Obsidian Demon, nearly knocking it over. It was in that moment that Theresa took her chance to strike.

She dive bombed right towards her hated foe, fangs and claws wide open, as she rammed herself into its body as she slammed it to the ground. Before the Obsidian Demon could react to the sudden tackle, Theresa opened her mouth wide and bit down around the neck of the fiend. Her front and back claws finding spots on both the ground to keep its body in place. Aiden winced as she struggled to keep the demon pinned. If he was going to do this he had to do it fast.

Erienne floated above Theresa's head. Her lifeless like eyes examined her sister carefully for a few moments before aiming her right hand at her head. Aiden knew that it was now or never! He dismissed Warfang and PeaceGuard as fast as he could before running straight up Theresa's neck to Erienne. With all the energy he could muster in that moment, Aiden leaped up and grabbed one of Erienne's legs!

"Erienne!" He shouted. "You're not doing this!"

Erienne's lips turned into a scowl as she glared down at Aiden. She tried to kick him off of her legs, in a vain attempt to shake him off. But Aiden refused to let go. Not after Theresa had done such a daring dive into the Obsidian Demon to give them this chance. With every bit of strength he could muster in his body, Aiden wrapped his other arm around her other leg.

"Wake up, dammit! Wake up!" He plead. "You know this isn't you! You know that you're not some damn puppet to a crazed demonic bastard! You're more than that! I know that! Your sister knows that! You know that!"

Erienne's scowl turned into a loud snarl as she closed her eyes and brought her hands up to her head, holding it tightly. So tight that what looked like black blood began to pour down her head onto her arms. Audible grunts and groans escaped her throat as she thrashed her upper body around. Whatever was happening in her mind, Aiden knew that it wasn't going to be that easy to break her free.

"Erienne, listen to my voice! Whatever's going on between you and this bastard, you have to fight it! You're not its slave! You're Theresa's precious little sister! You're stronger than this! I know you are!"

"E...E..." Erienne's lips quivered in fury and rage. Aiden couldn't tell if it was her, or the 'voice' of the Obsidian Demon trying to speak out in that moment. "E...E...ENOUGH!!"

The Obsidian Demon began pushing back against Theresa's grip with its impressive strength. Aiden could tell that Theresa was losing her grip on the mighty demon. He was running out of time and they needed to do something. What could he do though? He tried everything he could think of. Everything except the one thing he didn't want to do.

"...I'm sorry." He said quietly as his left hand glowed with a fiery orange light. "Erienne...wake UP!"

The heat from the fire on his left hand spread across Erienne's body. The intense heat from it caused Erienne's eyes to snap wide open from the sudden pain to her body. What came out of her mouth was probably the most disturbing sound of pain and horror that ever erupted from somebody's lips. It made even Theresa wince in pain from the sheer force of its volume.

Aiden refused to let go though. He absolutely hated that he had to use a fire spell to try to wake the dragoness up from her entranced state, hated it! But as much as he hated to do it, he hated the Obsidian Demon even more for turning Erienne against her own people. For making her become a traitor!

Below him, Theresa released her jaw from the Obsidian Demon's mouth for a few moments before screaming out.

"ERI!!!!!"

Erienne's roar became so loud that a large ball of white energy suddenly exploded from her body, covering herself, Aiden, Theresa, and the Obsidian Demon within it. In that one very moment, it felt as if everything had suddenly come to a complete stop in the world. Aiden felt himself losing slight consciousness as his eyelids fell over his eyes.

Had they failed?

* * *

"AIDEN….AIDEN...AIDEN WAKE UP!"

Theresa's voice was loud as usual. She always had that effect on him to bring him out of any deep slumber as kids. And it seemed to ring true now. Aiden groaned as he placed his hand over his head. Pain rocketed through his body as he tried to lean up from the ground. His eyes were still closed as he felt for any broken bones within his body. His vision slowly came back to him as he spotted the vague shape of Theresa, now in her human form.

"Ow...what...what's going on?" He asked. "Wait...Thes!"

His eyes slowly opened as he tried to force himself to stand up. They had a battle to finish with the Obsidian Demon!

"Where's Erienne?! Where's the demon?! Where's...where's...." As his vision came back to him, Aiden couldn't believe what he was seeing. "Where...are...we?"

Before him and Theresa was not the airport. It wasn't even the modern times. They were on a cobblestone street. Surrounded by a row of two story houses that stretched down all the way down the street. At the end of that street was a bazaar, with open aired shops for food, weapons, clothes, and a water fountain in the middle of a circular center. This in turn lead to more streets with taller buildings in each direction that it faced. The direction that pointed north, however, was reserved for another section. A large castle.

Aiden would have been taken aback by amazement at what his eyes were showing him. Hell, he should have been amazed at what he was seeing. But it wasn't awe that filled his eyes. It was shock. Not because the city wasn't a wondrous thing to look at. No. In fact, it was the opposite.

The city, was destroyed.

"What...what the hell is this place?" He barely managed to speak out, his shock overtaking him. Theresa gritted her teeth as she stared down at the ground beneath her feet.

"This....this was the crown city of the Ancient Kingdoms of the past..." She said. "This was once the seat of power throughout the known world. This was the home of so many people, civilians and soldiers."

Tears came to her eyes as her voice began to tremble at the mere thought of saying its very name. Aiden could feel his heart shatter when she spoke out again.

"This...was my birth place. As was it for Garrett, Seamus, Erienne and many other dragons. This...was Dragonera. The mightiest city in the old worlds."

"W...Wait...Dragonera?" Aiden somehow sputtered out. "This...this was the crown city of your world?"

"Yes...this was my home..."

"But...but I thought all the old kingdoms' cities were destroyed?"

"They were...." Theresa clenched her hands. "I saw it with my own eyes as the city fell to ruin. Buildings destroyed, in an instant. Lives snuffled out. Nothing was left. Not even the castle."

She stared up at the sky above them. Which was a dark red color with black clouds. Above them, a dark mass of energy that took no true form swirled around them. Aiden thought he had felt sheer terror and power before, but now? Now he knew what it truly felt like. Every single bit of his body quaked in fear at the entity that flew above him and Theresa. Its very power was enough to make buildings topple over by just being under them.

"Is...is that what I think it is?" He asked Theresa. "The...The..."

"The Dark One." Theresa finished. "...I see now." She gave off a short dry laugh. "This isn't real. We're in a vision."

"We...we what?"

"Somehow, that energy field that Erienne expelled from her body is letting us see into her visions. Or her mind, so to speak. It's not a normal kind of magic, I don't even think it's possible for people to see into the minds of others like this."

"Wait...you said that this was her vision right?" Aiden asked. "How can that be? I thought she disappeared?"

"She did." Theresa admitted. "Look up to the fountain ahead."

Aiden wasted in no time in looking at the fountain. Right there, kneeling on both knees, was a somewhat taller looking Erienne. At least, that's who Aiden had to guess she was. Both he and Theresa gave each other short nods as they walked down the street towards the fountain.

The experience was haunting, to say the least. All around them dragon bodies were littered. Not just humanoid bodies, no. Full dragon bodies had fallen to the ground. Some bleeding from where they had fallen. Others with what looked like savage slash marks across their chests and necks. Aiden felt himself flinching when he saw what he hoped he wouldn't end up seeing as they approached the fountain.

The dead bodies of the Trinity lay near one another. He took a step back for a second as he spotted what was the lifeless body of his best friend in dragon form laid sprawled out on the ground. He couldn't even imagine that she would have ever died like this. Tears formed up in his eyes at the very idea that Theresa had suddenly died right before him. Just when it felt like it had become too much for him, he felt Theresa grab tightly.

"Aiden. Breathe." She told him. "This isn't real. This is...this is what my sister possibly saw as our fate..."

He took a few deep breaths as Theresa kept her grip on him. She was right. This wasn't a real thing. Even though it wasn't real, it felt like it had just been somehow narrowly avoided by the dragons.

"Thank God this isn't real..." He said. "If...if you were dead I..."

Theresa gently slipped her hand into his own and squeezed it tightly. A faint sad smile came to her lips.

"I'm right here." She softly said. "I'm right here..."

The two of them had silent moment for a few seconds, then turned their attention back to the kneeling Erienne. She had her face in her hands. Loud sobs could be heard from her as the two of them approached her ever so slowly.

"Erienne-" Aiden started to say. But Theresa placed one wing in front of him

"Don't. This isn't the real Erienne. Much like how those dead bodies of me and my friends aren't real." She frowned. "This is a vision, Aiden. Or if I have to be more accurate, a nightmare."

Theresa looked over to her sister's visionary self slowly.

"One that my poor baby sister saw, and tried to warn us about..."

Aiden felt his heart shatter at the sadness in his best friend's face. He realized in that moment that to her, Theresa felt like that all of this was somehow her fault. He wanted to say something to make her realize that it wasn't her fault. But before the words could even escape his lips Erienne spoke out.

"Gods...Gods no..." She sobbed. "This...this can't be real. This can't be r-r-real..."

Her short black wings hunched themselves onto the ground piti-fully as she trembled. There was a rough hoarseness to her voice as she tried to come to terms with what she was seeing before her. Erienne reared her head back, Aiden noticed that her facial features were almost murky in this timeline as she screamed out to the sky.

"Why does this have to happen?! Why can't I get her to listen to me?! Is this our fate?! Is this truly what is meant to happen to not just

Dragonera, but the world itself?! To be destroyed by that...that THING above us?!"

She slammed her fists down into the ground, tiny craters formed under them when she did so. Her loud sobs could still be heard.

"This...this can't happen." She managed to sputter. "It c-c-can't happen..."

Aiden frowned as the young dragoness sobbed her eyes out. The knowledge she had gained from this vision. It would drive anyone to do anything to save their people and kingdom. How she never went insane with this intense vision he would never know.

"...She tried to tell me that this was going to happen..." Theresa said to Aiden as the image began to fade away slowly in front of them. "That the end of the Kingdoms was coming. She tried so hard to tell me..."

Both Aiden and Theresa felt a twinge of guilt flow through their bodies as they watched Erienne cry to herself in sorrow. The latter felt more guilty about what was happening before her. In her deep emerald eyes, she could tell that she was wrong to doubt her little sister's visions.

"And she was right...the Dark One did come for us. It destroyed all the Old Kingdoms, and nearly ended all life on Earth as it was at the time..."

"But that still doesn't explain why she summoned a demon." Aiden pointed out. "If she knew that the literal end of the era was coming, why would she resort to summoning something as powerful as the Obsidian Demon?"

"...I think we're about to find out." Theresa admitted as the scenery began to change.

Aiden watched in amazement as the once destroyed city of Dragonera began to mold and change as the very image of the destruction flew away like a blur before them. The city pieces that had fallen to the ground rose up once more, placing themselves back into place like a jigsaw puzzle. The dead bodies that had littered the streets vanished away into nothingness. And the sky above them turned back to its proper shade of blue.

Soon new illusions of the citizens of Dragonera sprung to life. There were so many different vendors that were succeeding in their trade. The dragons were laughing in joy, talking about their daily events to one another. There were even small street shows from some dragons that had taken their true forms to entertain the young drag- onlings that squealed in joy as fire breath clashed in the air.

It truly was a fantastic sight to see. To witness the home city of Dragonera itself, the very birthplace of Theresa, be so vibrant and alive. You would have thought that it would have never fallen. It was a far more welcome sight to Aiden than what he had just seen moments ago with Theresa.

"Is...this what it was truly like?" He asked.

"Yes." Theresa gave a sorrowful smile. "Some say that every capital city has days like this. But to us? Dragonera was not just some capital. It was the safest place in the entire world. Where everyone could be happy. I just wish that you could somehow have seen it in person."

The two of them watched the busy and happy streets of Dragonera go on with their daily lives for a few seconds, right before they spotted who they were trying to save. Erienne. This time, Theresa's young sister was sitting in front of the fountain, head in her hands, breathing heavily. The dragons coming and going around her seemed oblivious to the dragoness, even as she grew more and more panicked.

"What the..." Aiden started to ask, until he felt someone brush against his shoulder. His eyes went wide, his words freezing in his lips as a wave of complete and utter terror washed over him. He turned to the side and noticed, much to his surprise, a similar look of panic on Theresa's face. Without thinking, he reached out and took her hand. Without hesitation, she held on tight, her eyes glued to the figure that had passed through them.

He was tall, taller than should have been possible, but somehow went unnoticed by the other dragons. Though it was the middle of the day, with the sun high in the sky overhead, he was cloaked in shadows, his features utterly imperceptible by either of the teens. He paused for a moment in front of the fountain, before taking a seat beside Erienne.

Aiden felt Theresa's grip on his hand tighten and could have sworn he heard a whispered "No," escape her lips. He turned back to the mysterious figure, straining his eyes to try to make out his face. It was as though the light refused to touch him.

"Poor child," He spoke, his deep voice echoing around him. Though he spoke just above a whisper, his voice drowned out the sound of the bazaar. "No one believes you...do they?"

Aiden realized that the bazaar was empty.

"Why...why can't I make her understand? Wh-why won't she believe me?" Erienne cried, tears rolling down her cheeks. She shivered when the man reached out, brushing away one of her tears.

"They will never believe you...their eyes cannot see what yours can, and they will never believe what they cannot see." He explained, tracing his finger along the side of her cheek. When it reached her chin, he tilted her face up to look at him. He was smiling, though there was no joy in his expression, "But I do."

Erienne trembled, trying to look away, but her body refused to move.

"Y-you do?" she whispered. There was no relief on her face when the man nodded. If anything, she seemed to panic even more, "Wh-what can I do?"

The sun turned black in the sky. A frigid wind blew through the bazaar, chilling the pair as they watched the memory unfold. The man's smile became a grin, his eyes grew wide as he continued to caress Erienne's face.

"Let me inside, and together, we will save this world."

"D-don't...pl-please don't..." Theresa murmured, tears rolling down her cheeks. She covered her mouth to muffle a sob as she saw her sister slowly nod.

"Oh...okay, I will...wh-what do I have to do?" Erienne asked, still unable to tear her eyes away from the man. Her eyes grew wide and her mouth fell open as the man suddenly leaned in closer, until his lips touched her ear. The entire bazaar fell deathly silent, the wind no longer blowing. The man's voice changed in and instant, becoming some incomprehensible snarl, like a beast claiming its prey.

"Whatever I ask of you." His words echoed through the bazaar as his body became a swirling miasma of darkness that engulfed the young dragoness, flowing into her ears, her eyes, and mouth. When the darkness faded, Erienne was doubled over, face buried in her hands. When she looked up, her amber eyes had taken on a deadly gleam, a wicked smile spreading across her lips.

Aiden felt like the worst nightmare in the world had just

happened before his and Theresa's very own eyes. Whatever that man...or *thing* was, it was so terrifying that even the Obsidian Demon itself paled in comparison to the sheer amount of fear running through his body right now. He glanced over to his best friend. The same look was painted over her face as well.

"W-What was that?" He somehow managed to get out.

"I...I'm n-not sure. I...I think that was a...a god..." Theresa replied. "That...that means this entire time my sister was-"

"Used like a puppet."

The new voice caught both Aiden and Theresa off guard. The once double over Erienne was now standing up right. Looking far more prideful of herself than she did in the visions. The evil grin she gave them both was unsettling, right before she glanced over at her right hand. Wiggling her fingers ever so slightly.

"Quite the amazing story, isn't it?" She asked. "All this time, you had no idea of what truly happened to your poor sweet sister."

"You!" Theresa summoned her courage as she clenched Aiden's hand tightly. "What are you?! Why did you use my sister to do this?!"

"Hm? Why did I do this?" She replied before laughing. "Well, dear sister. Allow me to tell you something. I wanted this to happen to me. After all, look where it's landed me now~."

"You lie..." Theresa glared daggers at Erienne. "You're not my sister..."

"Does it matter?" Erienne asked as she flicked her index finger a couple of times, shattering the peaceful image of Dragonera around them. "Truly, I don't think it does. Possessed, not possessed? The truth is that poor sweet Erienne knew what was coming, and she was trying to do anything she could to stop it. And you? You wouldn't't heed her warnings. The great and 'perfect' Theresa of White Fire was too prideful to ever think that such an attack could happen!"

"Shut up..." Theresa growled. "I know that I wasn't there for her when she needed someone to believe her. I know that I pushed her concerns away. Hell, I will always carry those mistakes with me for the rest of my life. I don't need you reminding me of them."

"The truth hurts, doesn't it Theresa of White Fire?" Erienne asked, floating above them in the air ever so slightly now. "To know that your little sister had been telling the truth this entire time, and you made her feel like she was worthless. That you didn't believe her visions anymore. A shame really. You claimed to love her. But what kind of sister doesn't believe the truth from their very own flesh and blood?"

"Y-You shut up!" Aiden snapped. He was still terrified about what they had just saw. But he wasn't going to let his fear hold him back from defending Theresa. "You don't even know the half of why Theresa was skeptical about her visions!"

"Oh is that a fact?" Erienne asked. "Well, allow me to tell you something about your dear sister, Theresa. And you too, young Aiden. The Erienne you know? She has since passed on from this world. No, instead, I am in her place." She gave a dark laugh, which vibrated the illusionary ground around them. "You see, the man you saw there appeared before me in a nightmare. And I invited him into my heart. He took control of me and made me what I am today. An Aspect of Terror itself. It was then that I went on to summon the Obsidian Demon from the bowels of hell. But after I summoned the beast, and that insufferable KING split the Obsidian Demon apart, my nightmares continued to grow worsen. I became dependent on him and the dark side of myself became far more powerful."

She hissed somewhat.

"But then came the day that cursed Dark One attacked. I was killed by the bastard. Much like any other dragon that wasn't as lucky as you were, dear sweet sister. But, because my soul has been, shall we say, blessed, by that man, I was not allowed to go onto any after life. Instead, I was put into a state of limbo by my lord. To recover until the moment was right."

She clapped her hands together with great force, a violet crescent like circle exploded from around her body as it raced right towards Aiden and Theresa. The two of them surely would have been vaporized by the attack if they hadn't jumped away in time. The illusionary buildings however were not so lucky. The moment the crescent wave touched the very bottom of the houses, they disintegrated into nothingness. Both Aiden and Theresa landed together, still holding onto each other's hands as they stared up to the possessed Erienne.

"As you can see, Aiden Russell. The Erienne you thought she knew? She was nothing but a facade. A ruse I used to get close to you. And you fell for it like the pitiful fool that you are." She laughed once more. "Humans. So predictably GULLIBLE that it's sad."

As Erienne's distorted laughter echoed across the area, Aiden went silent. Everything that had happened between him and Erienne in the past. It was all a ruse? Every single moment? He wanted to believe that it wasn't true. That whatever it was that was using Erienne like some sick puppet was lying. But...his despair began to take over him as he realized just how feeble their situation had become.

Every moment...was it always a lie?

"What's wrong?" Erienne asked. "Heart broken, little human? Don't tell me you actually thought I 'cared' for you. How sickeningly human of you."

"...You're lying."

"Hm?"

Aiden's brow furrowed as he stared right back into Erienne's pure dark eyes. His heart was racing so fast he could hear it beating in his own skull. His tongue began to turn dry from the terror she was exuding around her, but he didn't stop.

"I said. You're lying." He pointed his right index finger at her. "Do you want to know why? If you said Erienne didn't truly care about me, she wouldn't have gone out of her way to help me when I was in dire need."

"What are you talking about, foolish boy?" Erienne asked, an amused smile on her lips. "Just what part of me do you think actually cares for trash like you?"

"Not you. No." He grinned, trying to put on a brave face. "But the real Erienne does."

"Are you stupid?" She scoffed. "I am the real Eriennn-"

"Bull crap." He cut her off. "You're just using her like some kind of shell right now. You have control over her now, sure. But the real Erienne? She wouldn't do this. If she was purely corrupted like you suggest she is, why did she drag me and Liza out of the river when we fell into it? Why did she heal our wounds when we would have surely died from them?"

He took one step forward, his step illuminating the dark ground around him. Theresa followed him quietly. Keeping her eyes trained on Erienne at all times.

"Why would she do that if she was truly corrupt? In fact, why would we be here in her mind if she wasn't trying to break free from your grip right now?" Aiden asked. "The truth is this. Erienne IS fighting you. You know it. I know it. And you can't keep her from breaking free. Not when me and Theresa are here to break her out of this hell that you put her through, demon!"

Erienne, or whoever was using her as a guise, gave another distorted laugh before pulling up out a large dark orb of shadows. Aiden's eyebrows narrowed before summoning PeaceGuard in front of him.

"I am far more than just a 'demon', you specs of dust." She said, Aiden noticed that a more masculine tone began to take over. "Learn your place!"

With a simple swish of her index finger, the shadow ball flew right at Aiden and Theresa. The former didn't flinch though as he brought his shield up and dug his heels into the ground. The impact from the attack was still enough to cause Aiden to strain, even push him back a few feet, but he and Theresa refused to give up. With a mighty yell Aiden managed to direct the attack into the air above them, causing it to harmlessly explode.

The Entity that was using Erienne, looking amused, grinned as it beckoned them to give chase to it as it flew backwards towards the castle.

"Don't let it escape!" Theresa cried out.

The two of them ran, or in Theresa's case flew, after the Entity that had taken control of Erienne's body. Both determined to get the true Erienne back from it. Even if that meant risking their lives to bring back an innocent soul that been forced to bear a terrible moniker over her once good name!

As they gave chase after the Entity, they could see it flash around them. Bits and pieces of Erienne's life in the dragon kingdom, and her life when she was reborn into the modern world. Her life in the dragon kingdom played first in front of them. Aiden and Theresa saw it all, what she had to endure. Mocked for her small size. How she got into trouble with her elders when she shouldn't have. The self loathing she would have for herself in her moments of weakness when no one was there to offer support. The possession from the Entity.

Then the life she had gained when she was reborn into the human world. At first, she had no clue who she truly was. That for awhile, she had a happy family with a loving mother and father. Like any normal human child in the world today. But, just like her previous life, she became the target of bullies. It was like the exact scene from her dragon childhood was on repeat. But each time she was mocked as a human, something stirred within her.

She fought back against her aggressors, becoming angry whenever they mocked her. She ended up hurting a lot of bullies. She got into trouble with the teachers of her schools, her human parents tried to figure out was was going on with their daughter. But no matter what she or they tried, it seemed to only get worse.

Aiden couldn't help but pity the poor girl. To endure so much and only snap in those critical moments. He thought he had it bad with Eric growing up, but this? This wasn't bullying. It was straight up abuse. But each time she fought back, each time she hurt one who dared harassed her, the dark piece of the Entity grew stronger.

Another scene played out, where Joro appeared before Erienne in her own home. Blood on her front two spider legs. Aiden didn't dare to wonder what had happened to her human parents. The memories then show her becoming a member of the Dark Eye Cult, and how the ever kind Erienne had seemingly faded away into nothingness.

"Erienne…" Aiden quietly said in sorrow.

"Hang on, little sister." Theresa begged. "We're not letting you go."

Soon the duo found themselves in front of the castle's gates. The Entity floated there, waiting for them with its arms crossed over its chest. Aiden felt sick at the mere sight of such a perverse force controlling an innocent soul's body like that.

"As you can see, the life of Erienne the Black and the life of Erienne Ivy are quite similar. Both mocked, both hated, and both pushed to such extremes." It said with a dark laugh. "It would be funny if it wasn't so pathetic."

"Extremes that YOU forced!" Theresa bellowed out, white sparks of fire escaped her nostrils. "Enough of your games, release my little sister, NOW!"

"Or else what, dragoness?" The Entity asked. "What power do you

and this frail human think you have over me? I who knows what absolute true fear is."

"I'll tell you what we have." Theresa snarled as she looked over to
her right side. Aiden took a step as Warfang gleamed in the darkness
that surrounded them. "We have each other. We have our friends that
are waiting for us. And we both have the same wish to see Erienne, the
REAL Erienne, freed from your grasp!"

The Entity tilted its head to the left curiously, then grinned as it
held up both hands above its head. A much larger shadow orb, about
the size of a jumbo airplane, formed right over it. Aiden sensed the
impending danger and quickly took Warfang in both hands. The
golden and silver blade burst into crimson red flames as its most
powerful attack. He had no earthly clue if the attack would be enough
to counter what was about to come. But he had to try!

Beside him, Theresa took on her full dragon form as she inhaled a
deep breath into her lungs. The fires within her throat just waiting to
be released in unison with Aiden's most powerful attack in this critical
moment.

"Then prepare to become just like her. Drowning in your own
nightmares...FOR ETERNITY!"

With that the Entity threw forth the orb of shadows right towards
Aiden and Theresa. Both of them braced themselves before unleashing
their counter attacks towards the orb. As Theresa's white hot fire
mixed together with the Draconic Firestorm's crimson red, the two
attacks began to ever so slightly push back against the orb. An otherworldly glow pulsed from the clashing attacks, the shockwaves alone
were enough to crumble the remaining houses of the dream world
around them.

Aiden's muscles screamed in agony at holding onto the Draconic
Firestorm for this amount of time. Usually whenever he released the
true power of his sword, the crimson flames were enough to take care
of any foe with a single hit. But not this time. The orb's power was
holding its own against the combination of his and Theresa's white hot
flames. Any other two attacks would have been consumed by the Entity's blast at this point.

"Submit to your fears!" The Entity demanded. "Join your pathetic
Erienne in eternal nightmares!!!"

Aiden gritted his teeth as he felt his heels ever so slightly being pushed back from the orb. They had come so close. So close! It couldn't end like this. He couldn't let it end like this! Not after everything that they had just learned about Erienne! Not after everything that he, his friends, his family, and Theresa had gone through together! Not when Erienne was trapped against her own will!

"I refuse to let this happen! I won't let this happen! It can't be allowed to happen dammit! Power!" He screamed in his head. *"I need, more, POWER! Give me more, POWER!"*

While he and Theresa's attacks clashed with the orb, the two of them didn't notice the pieces of armor that Aiden had found slowly form around him. When they did, a new surge of strength welled up from within his body. With an inhuman roar Aiden put the new source of energy that the armor had given him into the Draconic Firestorm. It was enough to boost the power of Warfang's ultimate attack to the point that both it and Theresa's white flames were overcoming the Entity's attack!

"I don't know what the HELL you are!" Aiden roared over the burning flames. "But this nightmare ends! RIGHT HERE! RIGHT NOW!"

The Entity, looking somewhat surprised at the sudden surge of power, leaned back some as its own attack began to crack from the sheer force of the two flame streams. A sly grin came to its lips.

"Do you truly think that this will work? That you can kill me in this realm?"

"We don't need to kill you…" Theresa replied. "We just need you to release Erienne's body!"

The orb continued to crack and crumble. Just as it was about to shatter, Theresa's voice screamed out from her own white flames.

"ERIENNE!!!!!!!!!"

As soon as the orb exploded into nothingness a flash of bright white light covered all of them. What happened next seemed to play out in slow motion for Aiden, Theresa, the Entity, and Erienne's soul. The Entity, as if pushed back from the pure love for Theresa's sister, found itself releasing its hold over the young girl. Once its shapeless form left her body, it merely moved out of the way of the two rising flames while Erienne's body began to fall towards the ground.

Theresa stopped her attack the moment she saw Erienne falling, reverting back to her human form as she rushed to catch her little sister. The armor pieces that had formed around Aiden vanished as well. As Erienne fell down into Theresa's arms, the Entity watched momentarily, giving a short chuckle as the elder sister wrapped the unconcious girl into her arms."

"I see…" The Entity intoned. "How very…interesting…"

With that, it faded away from Erienne's dream world ever so slowly. As the dream world itself began to fade away, Erienne's eyelids stirred for a few seconds, before opening up. Her amber eyes met with Theresa's emerald green for the first time in what felt like a lifetime for the white dragoness. A soft smile grew on her face in that moment. The last thing spoken in that dream state before it vanished was a simple question.

"ThesThes?"

THE BREAK OF DAWN

*A*iden felt like a freight train had just run right over his body. His eyes opened ever so slowly. The pain spread through his veins like a wildfire. Even though they had just fought in the dream world, his body let him know there were consequences for using such power. He would make a mental note to note not to use so much power if anything like that happened again.

His eyes quickly glanced over his shoulders and legs for see if any parts of the crimson armor were still worn. To his disappointment it were not there. He groaned as he slowly forced his body to rise up from the hard ground of the runway. Aiden rubbed the side of his head with one hand as he tried to handle the pain his body was feeling.

"Son of a bitch…" He said, his voice now hoarse. "What happened…Theresa…Theresa!"

"Sh." Theresa's voice came from his left. "Don't scream so loud."

Aiden followed the sound of her voice right behind him. He gave a tiny smile as he spotted her there. She was no longer in her dragon state, but was most important was the being she was cradling in her arms in that moment. Erienne, who was starting to wake up ever so slowly. The younger dragoness gave out a sort of discomforted groan as she tried to cover he eyes with one hand.

"Too…bright." She murmured. Aiden noticed that her voice was far softer than it was before. "Five more minutes…"

"Eri…" Theresa's eyes welled up with happy tears as she moved her sister's hand away from her face. "It's me."

Erienne blinked a couple of times before realizing where she was. She gasped before throwing herself in a tight hug around her big sister.

"ThesThes!" She cried out, tears falling down her cheeks. "You're here! Y-You're really here!"

"Shh. Don't cry now…" Theresa said as she stroked the back of her sister's head. "It's okay…it's okay…"

Aiden's smile widened when he saw the two sisters hold each other in a happy reunion. In that moment all the pain, all the sadness, and all the sins of the past seemed to be washed away. It was a scene Aiden was certain that even Garrett himself would have been touched to see. Heck, maybe even Kali would have been moved by it.

But that happiness quickly vanished as he realized that there was a tall shadow standing over the three of them. They might have won in the dream state. But they were back in the real world now. Right where the Obsidian Demon was waiting.

He turned his head back to the demon, fully expecting it to be in a post attack movement. To his surprise though, the Obsidian Demon wasn't in any kind of attack stance. Instead, the once lava filled eyes of the vile creature had dimmed to a pale color as its entire body convulsed violently. Aiden nearly yelped out in surprise as one of its fingers fell down to the ground with a loud 'thud' that shook the area.

That wasn't the only part of the Obsidian Demon that fell off though. No, the rest of its body had suddenly hardened and fell apart as well. Becoming clouds of ash that blew in the wind after they broke apart. The final part, the head, released one final pitiful roar that haunted the runway of the airport. A forever reminder to the passengers of the damage the storm it brought had done to Richmond.

"W-What the hell?" He asked. "Why did the bastard just fall apart?"

"My…my link to it…" Erienne weakly said in Theresa's arms. "The Obsidian Demon it…it was connected to me through my connection to that…that…"

"Sh." Theresa shushed her sister. "Don't speak anymore about it, Eri…it's over now."

"T-ThesThes…I…I…"

Erienne's eyelids began to drop down slowly as she passed out within her big sister's arms. Aiden felt himself sighing in relief before wiping his brow. For a few seconds he was afraid the younger sister had passed on to the next life. Once he saw that Theresa had checked her pulse, his fear was quickly erased.

"Aiden." Theresa spoke out. "We need to get out of here. And fast."

Aiden felt a shiver run down his spine at those words. She was right. The battle with the Obsidian Demon might have ended, but there was no doubt that the people who were in the airport were about to come out to investigate what had just happened. How would it look to them when they found three teenagers that had been outside the entire time?

"Crap! You're right!" He pushed himself up, a move he regretted immediately as his muscles roared with extreme pain. "Owowow! Bad idea, bad idea!"

Theresa groaned as she used what energy she had left to open up a portal back to the apartment room.

"Let's go. We can't afford to linger here any longer."

"W-What about the others?"

"You know they'll catch up. Now's not the time to ask stupid questions, get in the portal before security gets down here!"

Aiden didn't argue back before limping into the portal. Behind him, Theresa stood up with Erienne in her arms. The two of them smiled at each other before glancing down at the rescued dragoness. For the first time in what was probably a long time, Erienne looked peaceful.

And this time, no bad dreams were haunting her.

* * *

A FEW WEEKS had passed since the epic battle in Richmond. A lot had happened since that fateful day. Almost too much for Aiden to keep track of after what they had just gone through. News reports all over the country had covered the damage that had been done to Richmond. Everyone who survived the storm, which in actuality was just the group's clash with the Obsidian Demon, claimed that it was the most dangerous storm that any of them had ever seen.

Aiden knew it was because regular human eyes were not used to seeing giant demons like the Obsidian walk around, and that the loud cracks of thunder that the humans heard were the force of the attacks used against its body, but he couldn't help but wonder if any of them wondered what really caused it.

Their battle with Obsidian Demon did more than just trick the human mind into thinking it was some kind of freak storm though. It left a giant scar within the city itself. Houses, towers, streets, and the runway for the international airport had been completely destroyed by the clash. People remarked how at times they swore that it felt like they were about to be crushed by some overbearing weight, or crushed by debris from broken buildings.

The news, and weather experts, had labeled the event as 'The Day Richmond Burned.' An event in the city's long history that would probably go down as the worst natural disaster to ever happen within its borders. Aiden laughed the first time he heard them say that. If only they knew it wasn't just the city itself that could have been lost.

As for him and his friends? Life had somewhat began to return to some kind of normal. Well, as normal as it could get with the mystical things that kept popping up around them. Aiden found out that after Aello took Liza away from the battle, the two of them were actually waiting back in the apartment, debating about going out to the Harpy's Den to get the help of Queen Lilith, Aello's mother, herself.

As for why Aello wasn't part of the initial attack when they rushed the Dark Eye's base? The young harpy wouldn't exactly say why. All she would hint at is that it involved 'family.' A subject that Liza convinced Aiden not to push too much about for the time being.

Garrett and Kali told him and Theresa how they were able to get back to the apartment after the battle ended. Once the Obsidian Demon passed on from this world, or more like its essence returned to wherever it was summoned from, the lava cage that had trapped Garrett and Kali vanished, giving them time to grab Seamus before getting away from the destroyed city.

Of course they had some injuries, but it wasn't anything that they wouldn't be able to truly recover from. Garrett even remarked that he had had worse injuries from the FIRST fight with Obsidian Demon. What those injuries were, Aiden would only have to guess as the large dragon refused to talk any further about the subject.

Though there was one subject that had become a source of friction between him and Theresa. Erienne.

After the long battle with the Obsidian Demon, everyone was shocked to see that Erienne had been brought back the Harpy's apartment. Garrett nearly broke down a wall the moment his eyes got a glimpse of the 'traitor' still being alive. Even Seamus was skeptical about allowing Erienne to live after what had happened in the past.

It was a long drawn out conversation between the three dragons and everyone else. Aiden and Theresa told them everything they had learned in the young dragoness' mind. It caught the group off guard, especially the idea that something out there existed that was more terrifying than the Obsidian Demon itself, but it did open the hearts of certain members of the group to the plight that had befallen the young dragon girl.

After long hours of debate it was decided that Erienne would be given a proper chance to live. To be free from the nightmares she had experienced since she was reborn into this world. A morale victory for Aiden, but a more important one for Theresa. She had finally gained her little sister back. Someone who was part of her family in the old kingdoms.

There was still the one obstacle about how Theresa would introduce her sister from her former life to her human parents. It wasn't like they were going to believe her story about being a dragon from days before recorded history. There would have to be an alternative story to get them to go along with the idea of having another person living in the house with them.

Aiden later found out that Theresa had passed off her little sister as someone that had been taken from a terrible home. She would claim that Erienne was like a sister to her at school that had grown up with some rough parents and that she needed a place to stay and no one else was willing to let her come into their home so her parents could be punished. Amazingly, Theresa's parents bought it.

Amazingly, Theresa's parents were more than open to the idea of letting her stay with them. Aiden was both delighted, and shocked. Theresa was hopeful that this would eventually lead to them formally adopting Erienne. Oh little did they realize that the two girls were related by actual blood.

Though when it came to Erienne, she was far different than she was whenever Aiden had run into her in the past. The overly flirty, clingy, and playful Erienne was nothing but a facade that, thanks to Theresa assuming it, the Entity had used to further the agenda of summoning forth the Obsidian Demon.

The real Erienne though? There was only one real word to describe who she truly was.

Skittish.

Any loud sound that came from a nearby room, or whenever Garrett spoke, caused the young dragoness to flinch or hide behind Theresa. A far cry from the false persona she was forced to wear when a part of the Dark Eye cult. It was gonna take awhile to get used to a personality shift like this. Despite this change Aiden had to admit that it was easier to be around this Erienne than it was when she was overly playful and flirty with him.

No one dared bring up her time with the Dark Eye cult. Even as the weeks passed, and she started to become a bit more open with the others, it was still too much of a sensitive topic to address. The first time it was mentioned by Kali, the younger dragoness broke down into tears and incoherent babbling among a string of apologies.

Despite everything that was now different for the group, it was back to a somewhat regular life. A couple of months had passed since the Battle at Richmond, with barely any activity from the Dark Eye in the state of Virginia, and regular training lessons returned during that time. Though Aiden and his friends were keeping an eye out for any other activity that could erupt.

Aiden found himself reading his old fantasy books during his spare time. He would often find himself laughing at his life though whenever he would read his old books. It was a nice escape from the reality that he found himself in, but ironic that he was now living one of the fantastic lives he always dreamed about having.

One day at the Academy, Aiden was approached by Erienne during a small break. The first time she had come up to him alone since the day he brought Eric down a level.

"Hey." She said, her voice softer than it was before. "Aren't you supposed to be training? You know that ThesThes will be upset if she sees you relaxing."

"I think she'll let me have a minor break." He replied with a short chuckle. "Especially after what we all went through together."

"Then you are lucky." She pursed her lips before sitting by him. "Back in our time, ThesThes would smack a dragon for goofing off when they weren't supposed to."

"Makes me glad that she doesn't do that anymore then." Aiden said with a grin. The two of them laughed for a bit before Erienne sighed.

"...Are you mad at me?" She asked him.

"Eh?"

"Are you mad at me?" Erienne asked once more. "For what happened a couple of months ago?"

"Erienne..." Aiden frowned.

"I know that you are going to say you aren't. But I just...I just can't figure out why you aren't mad." She admitted, glancing down to her feet as she squeezed her dress. "I tried to kill my own sister, was willing to attack you of all people, and brought back the Obsidian Demon I summoned before. Anyone else would have been mad at me..."

"If by anyone else, you mean Garrett." Aiden reminded her. "You know no one has ever said they aren't happy with you-"

"Not to my face." Erienne cut him off. "I know they might be silently judging me. That they're upset I have been allowed a chance to be here after what happened. Even if I was being used against my own will to do it, I still allowed it to happen again...because I'm weak." e

Tears formed in her eyes as she thought back to what happened with the Obsidian Demon. The very thought of her telling her sister such terrible things still haunted her mind as she tried to stifle a cry.

"That...thing made me spew out things I would have never truly thought about saying to my sister's face. Never in a hundred years! And...and I said them anyway. My dark thoughts about her, about how I 'hated' how she was perfect, while I wasn't. How she was always favored while I was not." She brought her head up look directly at him. "Do I even deserve this new chance after what I've done? After being so foolish to allow some Demonic...THING into my heart?!"

"Erienne..." Aiden gently closed his book, then placed both hands on her shoulder. "What happened at Richmond, that wasn't the real you. You know that, don't you?"

"How can you be so certain?" She asked, her voice cracking some-what. "I was so terrible when I first saw her that-"

"Because." Aiden interrupted her. "Because I know that the real you, the part of you that loves your sister more than anything in the world, was the girl that saved me and Liza when we fell."

"Eh?"

"Heh, don't you remember?" Aiden grinned. "At summer camp. Liza and I had fallen down into a river from high ground. We would have been dead if you hadn't pulled us out of the ground and healed our wounds as best as you could."

"You...you still remember that?"

"Of course I do. It was the first time I was actually able to get a good look at your face." Aiden gently took her right hand into his left hand. "What you did that day wasn't malicious, or ill intended. You saved our lives, and if it wasn't for you healing us, the Harpies might have been fully discovered by humans once again."

He gently gave her hand a squeeze.

"Besides, you also warned me not to attack the Harpy Queen either. And for good reason. The power she had was so immense it's no wonder that Dimitri and Raven wanted her to work with them."

"Aiden..." Erienne blushed at his kind words. "You...you really think that of me?"

"Of course I do." Aiden admitted. "Erienne, you're not the monster Entity made you into. You're better than that. You may not believe it right now...but I think out of everyone that I've known in my life, besides Theresa, you have the best intentions. And this time? This time you're not going to be alone."

Erienne shuffled her feet for a few seconds at Aiden's kind words. Her amber eyes shimmered in the room's light as she tried to glance away. It was almost too cute for words to see a dragon, no less Theresa's SISTER of all people, be bashful or embarrassed by such kind words.

"So believe in yourself more often." Aiden told her. "And know that no matter what happens now, you have your sister again. And you have me and my other friends. I mean, yeah, Garrett will probably take some work getting to accept you, but this time you're not alone."

A nice peaceful moment passed between the two of them. Erienne grinned to herself before turning back to face Aiden. In that moment Aiden felt a warm kiss against his left cheek from her before she pulled back. Aiden's entire face turned beet red from the kiss as the younger sister of Theresa giggled.

"That. Was for being so kind." She said with a playful giggle. Not noticing a rising figure from behind her.

"Eri...." Theresa said with a low growl. Her emerald eyes glistening in the shadow she cast over her and Aiden. "Just what. Was. That?"

"Oh, Hi ThesThes!" Erienne beamed up at her big sister. "That was me giving Aiden a nice thank you for being so kind to me."

"You. KISSED HIS CHEEK." Theresa said with a slight annoyed smile. "Just what is going on here, **hm**?!"

"T-Thes! I swear! Nothing's going on!" Aiden put his hands back up. "She was just feeling down and all I did was offer her what advice I could about feeling accepted here is all!"

"Oh that better be it..." She said with pursed lips. "Honestly, the fact you kissed him on the cheek Eri, why would you do that?"

"Aw, what's wrong ThesThes?" Eri giggled. "You're not, jealous are you?"

"JEALOUS?!" Aiden and Theresa spat out together. The latter now blushing herself as her little sister giggled like crazy.

"Ah! You're totally jealous, ThesThes!" She said in a sing song tone. "Jealous of me and Aiden~"

"T-There's nothing to be jealous of at all!" Theresa spat back, her face dark red in a blush. "You know what?! You are evil! You totally are the most evil little sister in the entire world!"

"That's not what Ragnakin thinks~"

"ERI!" Theresa pounced at her little sister, who had rushed off to avoid being tackled by her big sister.

Aiden couldn't help but laugh as the two sisters ran around in circles in the training room. He was happy to see the both of them being so happy together. Especially Theresa. Who had endured the nightmare of possibly having to kill her own sister, only to be rewarded with getting her back. It felt like it some sort of story book ending for them.

But as he watched the two of them playfully chase one another, Aiden felt a twitch of curiosity. That word Erienne used. She had used it several times before. And this time, she used it right in front of her big sister like it was no big deal. But, Theresa didn't react to it.

What was that word?

What did it truly mean?

What, or who, was Ragnakin?

* * *

"You know I heard you say that word, right?" Theresa asked as Aiden went back to training with Seamus. "You never were good at whispering the old languages."

Can't you blame a girl for trying, big sister?" Erienne asked with a tiny giggle. "I thought I was going to be sneaky this time around and make sure you wouldn't pick up on it."

"Please, you've never been able to hide a whisper from me. Not even when we were young back in the old days." Theresa grinned back at her sister. "Then again, you never were one to even try to hide a secret. Weren't you little sister?"

"Ha. Guilty as charged."

The two sisters quietly watched Aiden's training as he threw attack spells at Seamus. As the sparks from his attacks clashed against Seamus's staff, Theresa's smile turned into a more serious look.

"It's quite bold of you to say that word like that though, dear sister. It's a word that I dared not even speak of when I spoke in the old tongue with Seamus and Garrett when we first reunited in this modern era."

"...I apologize, sister." Erienne closed her eyes. "I know the weight of that word is not one to be thrown around lightly like it was some childish title."

"Then why did you say it to him?" Theresa asked. "To say that word, you must have more than just a cute reason of 'flirting' with him."

"Who said anything about flirting?" Erienne gave a playful grin.

"Oh please, you were like a teenage dragonling in heat with that kiss you gave him." Theresa shoved her shoulder with a playful nudge.

"I was not!" Erienne puffed her cheeks up. "And just for the record, you're in a teenaged human body yourself too, ThesThes!"

"That doesn't change my point though." Theresa gave a know it all grin to Erienne, who glanced away from her sister with a loud 'hmph' escaping her throat.

"...Eri. Be truthful with me right now." Theresa implored her. "Why did you refer to Aiden Russell, my best friend in this world, by the title of Ragnakin?"

Erienne went quiet for a few seconds. Trying to piece together her answer as best as she could. She let out a long drawn out sigh before giving her big sister a sliver of a tiny smile.

"Because...because I can see a lot of **him** in Aiden." Erienne admitted. "Come on, ThesThes...you have to admit that he is very much like him. Don't you think so?"

Theresa blinked at this statement. She knew what her sister was talking about, but she never once thought about the similarities to whom she was referring to.

She glanced back over to Aiden, who was still in the middle of training with Seamus. The white dragoness stared for a few moments at her best friend, right before giving her sister a slight smile of her own.

"I...I guess he is kinda like he was." She admitted.

To Be Continued in
"The Dragon's Bane"

DRAGONIC LANGUAGE APPENDIX

*E*nglish Dragonic Pronunciation

AFRAID KITHOR (KIT-HOR)
    After Foful (fo-ful)
    Again Bentia (bent-e-a)
    All Span (span)
    Allow Spenzer (spen-zer)
    Although Spafiveenarre (spa-five-en-air)
    Always Spaveteran (spa-ve-ter-an)
    Am Ka (car)
    An Ki (key)
    And Tim (tim)
    Any Kif (keyf)
    Air Floia (flow-e-a)
    Abandon Fiekona (fee-kon-a)
    Are Guo (goo-o)
    As Guto (gu-to)
    Be Lo (lo)
    Because Lokhan (lo-kan)
    Been Lowen (low-en)
    Before Bealom (bear-lom)

Being Lowing (low-ing)
Believe Demanda (de-man-da)
Bird Beasttee (be-st-tee)
Born Feiry (fair-e)
Brother Stragna (stragna)
Bugger Liaron (lair-on)
But Xou (zoo)
By Heel (heal)
Bye Heel (heal)
Can Toa (toe-a)
Calm Queet (queat)
Care Hito (hi-to)
Careful Hitokan (hi-to-kan)
Carry Titoa (ti-toa)
Chosen Denengar (de-nen-gar)
Claim Nevi (ner-vi)
Crap Xot (zot)
Currant Cresion (crez-e-on)
Current Cresion (crez-e-on)
Cyclone Featheroo (fef-e-roo)
Day Veek (v-k)
Dark Rappra (rap-pra)
Decide Hoaliea (hol-e-a)
Dictionary Diarra (die-a-ra)
Discussion Iletian (il-et-ian)
Did Highroal (high-rol)
Die Pearoo (pair-roo)
Differ Haven (hay-ven)
Dispose Depoa (dep-po-a)
Do Jey (j)
Down Tuggr (tug-gr)
Dragon Drakon (Dra-kan)
Earth Gitanel (Gi-ta-nel)
Eight Ipoy (i-poi)
Eighth Ipoyo (i-poi-o)
Eighty Ipoyven (i-poi-ven)
Eleven Difer (dif-er)

Ember Em (m)
Enough Aimabel (aim-a-bell)
Eve Dect (det)
Even Dectven (det-ven)
Female Jilbecken (jil-bec-ken)
Fifth Hityo (hi-ti-o)
Fifty Hityoven (hit-ti-o-ven)
Fire Beut (be-oot)
First Guyger (guy-ger)
Five Hity (hit-ti)
Flow Spatter (spat-ter)
Friend Jid (jid)
Foe Laco (la-co)
For Uranni (you -rain-ne)
Forest Teena (teen-na)
Forth Uranio (you-rain-ne-o)
Forty Uraniven (you-rain-ne-ven)
Four/For Uranni (you -rain-ne)
Fourth Urannio (you-rain-ne-o)
Garden Jeadit (gee-dit)
Get Gag (gag)
Give Kilo (kil-lo)
Glad Sient (si-ent)
Go Sie (sigh)
Good Singl (sing-l)
Guardian Familiu (fam-a-lee-u)
Guess Deed (deed)
Had Tid (tid)
Happen Foulger (foul-ger)
Have Tieg (tieg)
Heal Emalla (e-mal-la)
He Gan (gan)
Hell Hilk (hilk)
Hello Kaby (kar-be)
Help Ihan (ir-harn)
Her Gar (gar)
His Gos (gos)

Him Go (go)
Hold Petir (p-tear)
Hope Jetoo (jet-oo)
Home Dunu (dun-oo)
How Tyan (tie-an)
Huh Rye (rie)
Hundred Weloect (we-lo-et)
I O (o)
Idea Kipit (kip-it)
Idiot Kalen (kal-en)
If Of (of)
In On (on)
Is Os (os)
It Ot (ot)
Just Golt (golt)
Know Xorea (zor-e-ar)
Land Piane (p-ain)
Langue Opilain (of-fil-e-an)
Let Heardl (hear-dl)
Leader Rexkin (rex-kin)
Life Doll (dol)
Lighting Ragnatorm (rag-na-torm)
Like Cuay (q-ray)
Live Dollvie (dol-v)
Lives Dollvies (dol-ves)
Long Whyt (white)
Luck Valo (val-o)
Male Becken (bec-ken)
Mana Kotura (ko-tu-ra)
Many Zane (zain)
Master Kinsaur (kin-saur)
Memory Lockieo (loc-key-o)
Might Tenara (te-na-ra)
My Min (min)
Name Cert (kert)
Never Sandra (san-dra)
Next Gon (gone)

Nice Fasy (fa-c)
Nine Leo (lee-o)
Ninety Leoven (lee-o-ven)
Ninth Leoo (lee-oo)
No Yed (yed)
None Rikie (ric-key)
Not Reo (ree-o)
Now Rew (ru)
Of Ewra (oo-ra)
Off Ewrana (oo-ra-na)
Oh Gad (gad)
Okay Pomain (po-main)
One Zon (zon)
Our Zo (zo)
Or Li (lee)
Other Keddit (ked-dit)
Over Zitter (zit-ter)
Past Beta (bay-ta)
Peace Avena (A-ve-na)
Petition Gemala (ge- ma-la)
Piss Vaoo (var-oo)
Planet Soaku (so-ku)
Poor Fraw (fraw)
Prevent Joarhand (Jo-ar-hand)
Previous Joarietin (jo-ar-e-tin)
Pronounce Joyerition (joy-er-i-tion)
Prop Dryan (dry-an)
Really Funnel (fun-nel)
Release Joinne (join-ne)
Relax Elgane (el-ga-ne)
Remember Canoain (can-o-ain)
Right Ritted (rit-ted)
Rope Ohnalga (oh-nal-ga)
Sake Litin (li-tin)
Sad Ditin (di-tin)
Scary Zanatone (zan-ar-tone)
Second Poite (poi-te)

See Lon (l-on)
Separate Tineat (ti-n-eat)
Serenity Sinotu (sin-o-to)
Serious Silowin (sil-o-win)
Seven Youao (u-a-o)
Seventh Youaoo (u-a-oo)
Seventy Youaoven (u-a-o-ven)
Shelter Wyen (y-en)
Should Shumbel (Shum-bell)
Six Dren (dren)
Sixth Dreno (dren-o)
Sixty Drenven (drenven)
So Ceo (c-o)
Some Merm (merm)
Sorry Forfit (for-fit)
Speech Stutak (stu-tak)
Spirit Shimera (shim-er-ra)
Stand Keya (key-a)
Still Tair (tear)
Stop Nomaran (no-ma-ran)
Sword Ladbe (lad-be)
Take Yakki (yak-ki)
Tantrum Onergall (o-ner-gall)
Tell Kidon (ki-don)
Ten Wari (wa-re)
That Hubo (hub-o)
The Aba (a-ba)
Them Abam (a-bam)
There Abaren (a-ba-ren)
These Abasen (a-ba-sen)
They Abat (a-bat)
Thing Ittye (it-tie)
Third Itin (it-tin)
Thirty Itinven (it-tin-ven)
This Bah (bah)
Though Fiveenarre (five-en-air)
Thousand Veinatim (vein-a-tim)

Three Itoa (it-toe-a
Through Ficenarre (thick-en-air)
To Ter (ter)
Together Tergaggar (ter-gag-gar)
Tomorrow Teragain (ter-a-gen)
Too Ter (ter)
Torture Deertom (deer-tom)
Turn Goar (go-r)
Twelve wave (twa-ve)
Twenty Twaven (twa-ven)
Two Ter (ter)
Under Quake (quake)
Understand Quakekeya (quake-key-a)
Up Vuat (voo-at)
Was Ghan (gr-han)
Water boakuo (bo-koo-o)
Way Vun (voon)
Warrior Eltraga (El-tra-ga)
We Tolua (to-lu-a)
What Bouk (book)
When Bein (bee-in
Where Beian (be-arn)
Why Quic (quick)
Will Dagal (dag-gal)
With Sammoo (sam-moo)
Would Umbel (um-bell)
Wow Fair (fare)
Yeah Sear (see-er)
Year Quiv (quiv)
Yes Seah (see)
You Yokee (yo-key)
Your Yokeer (yo-keer)
(an) Before
(ed) After
(er) After
(ex) Before
(im) Before

(ing) After
(less) After
(ly) After
(r) After
(s) After
(teen) After
(un) Before
(y) After

The Dangerous Traitor

ISBN: 978-1-7335318-2-5

Publisher: Broken Tower Press

United States

6261 14th Avenue South

Suite 201

Gulfport, Florida 33707

Phone: 813-924-4717

Copyright Broken Tower Press, April 2019

All Rights Reserved

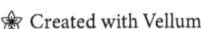 Created with Vellum

ABOUT THE AUTHOR

Living with the stories in his head from the time he could talk, Charlie Rose describes himself as a writer, first, last, and always. In his spare time he can be found on the internet or playing one of his many different gaming systems. He loves animals,Tolkien, and stories - in all their forms. He also loves to hear from his fans. If you want to talk you can reach him by email at chroseiv@hotmail.com.

He looks forward to hearing from you soon!

Books by Charlie Rose